THE CATALYST TRILOGY: BOOK 2

SOMETIMES MISTAKES REQUIRE A PRICE BEFORE FREEDOM

THE PENANCE

A NOVEL

SELIN SENOL-AKIN

COPYRIGHT © 2022   SELIN SENOL-AKIN

ISBN: 978-1-7346563-8-1

PRINTED IN THE UNITED STATES OF AMERICA

Edited by: Kirsten McNeill

Dedicated to my daughter, Dalya, for being the salvation after any penance…and to everyone in search of authentic-living, acceptance, and freedom.

"...And I (Allah) created the jinns and humans so that they should worship Me (alone)..."

(SURAH 51/56, HOLY QURAN)

"Chaos is the penance for leisure."

AMY TAN

CHAPTER 1

THE PENITENTIARY

C-318

C AN EVIL PERSIST ENCOMPASSED BY PURITY? The question had been lingering in the back of the prisoner's mind for what felt like an eternity. Looking at the newspaper article in front of him, he couldn't help but drown in his inquisitive thoughts once again.

Is innocence powerful enough to trump over a disturbed soul? He shook his head while releasing a long-held breath. Stuffing the ripped page back into the rusty white metal drawer that had accompanied him since the beginning of his sentence, the prisoner plopped down on his creaking bed.

It must be true what they say about the senses, he thought, eyes still shut though his mind was opened wide now to nostalgia. He sniffed the enclosed air. *My sense of smell is coming alive again, connected to my memory- more now that my eyes are closed.*

Strawberries. That was it! The last couple of times he could have sworn it may also have been green apple or grape instead. *Those were also her favorites*, he had recalled.

But the prisoner was now as sure as day it had been the smell of strawberries he smelled on her breath the last time he'd seen her. And not only because it tended to be her most frequent gum flavor of choice either. She'd adored the perfume of strawberries on everything in her bedroom, her clothes, her shampoo.

Her soft hair, he thought with a smile. *Did I pick enough strawberries with her? Was I able to be there for her? Was I enough?*

The prisoner licked the salty liquid that had befallen his cheek once again, sensing the scruff on his face along with it. The past somehow always had a way of creeping into the present at the strangest of times.

Maybe it's for the best her life went on without a man like me, he reasoned solemnly. *Maybe she now has a chance for happiness. True happiness. In a way that I could never provide.*

Sometimes sacrifices were necessary for true love.

CHAPTER 2

Sandnes

B IRDS CHIRPING AMONGST LUSH GREENERY HAD replaced her grand oceanic view, yet Kaitlin Maverick was not disheartened in the slightest. Inching closer to the kitchen window to inhale one big gulp of floral air, before delving into what she knew would soon transform into an aroma of greasy cooking, a grin formed on the corners of her lips.

Who knew a change of address could feel this refreshing?

Tucking a strand of loose, thick auburn hair behind her ear, Kaitlin smirked as she caught a glimpse of her disheveled-bun reflection on the glass.

She hadn't exactly been welcoming to change when she'd first moved to Norway to accompany her computer specialist husband, Paul, who worked in Statoil in the port city of Stavanger. Kaitlin had missed the relatively fast-paced life in her native Toronto terribly. Yet now after two years in Norway, with motherhood and adaptation to a larger apartment in a smaller neighboring city: Kaitlin found herself embracing the newfound peace amidst the solitude. She was also grateful for the lesser amount of secrets and confusion when compared to all the events that had transpired back in Stavanger- with *him.*

Back to food, she repressed the past, stifling a yawn. *I have got to listen to Sibel and try to get some rest too when the baby sleeps, but these chores never end!*

Peeling the skin off of the potatoes she'd prepared to make some traditional Canadian poutine- from scratch, no longer from pre-sliced frozen potatoes- Kaitlin felt the hairs on the back of her neck stand up. A ringing in her ear unnerved her as she dropped the peeler into the sink.

"Hello?"

Finn.

She hadn't seen him in over a year now, but his name inexplicably popped into her head. Looking around the kitchen for any glimmer or spark she could once again associate with him, Kaitlin could sense that her body had calmed down.

"I need to snap out of it," she boomed audibly to herself. "He wouldn't. He promised, and he's kept it. Why would he now? He wouldn't..."

Turning on the radio to keep her company, Kaitlin glided the potatoes on a slicer. *I think I actually want Paul home early today,* she thought, examining the lock screen of her mobile phone; no notifications showed.

"You say 'for cowards, there's no reward'. Feel the heat..."

The Norwegian entry for the 2013 Eurovision Song Contest had been on her tongue lately. She loved it whenever it occasionally still came on the radio. It reminded her of watching it live together with Paul during that particularly lovely spring day the previous year. With his hand on her growing belly. *Maybe our little boy or girl will be able to sing just as beautifully,* he'd said. *Lord knows I don't have such talents. I always wish I did.*

"Take my hand, I trust your word..." Kaitlin sang louder, heating the sliced potatoes on the skillet. She thanked her lucky stars that Malin could nap through any sound.

"Bring the fire, I don't care that it hurts..." Kaitlin did a little dance to the beat and looked up from the stove. A shadow of something moving behind the cloudy glass separating the kitchen from the living room jolted her toward the counter.

She turned the stove off with a yelp. Her heart started beating faster than the song's choral beats. Shutting the radio off, Kaitlin turned first in the direction of her daughter's room, and then back to face the living room.

Nothing.

"Finn?" she called out with a whisper this time, walking toward Malin's room. She inched the door open, sighing with relief upon seeing her daughter's chest move up and down.

Kaitlin smiled and gently closed the door, heading back toward the kitchen. The hairs at the back of her neck stood rigid and upright once again.

"I'm here alone. You can just say hi, you know…" Kaitlin called out, eyeing the kitchen knives. Her parched tongue clung to the roof of her mouth- transfixed in anxiety.

"Please. Don't do this. Not like this."

A sudden burst of crying by her daughter had Kaitlin running back toward Malin's room. She pushed the door open with her entire body, nearly bruising her clenched fist.

"Baby?" Kaitlin sighed with relief to see Malin's smiling almond eyes lock with hers. Giggling now and no longer crying. She was sitting up in her crib.

"Momma…" Malin smiled.

"Oh, my girl," Kaitlin picked her up and cuddled her close to her chest. She sniffed her fuzzy head. *Heaven.* "What happened, *mon ange*? Why did you wake up so soon? Are you okay?"

Holding on to her tightly, Kaitlin looked all around the nursery. Nothing seemed out of place. Not even the stuffed elephant that continued to lie next to Malin's baby pillow, in the same exact position Kaitlin had left it. Paul insisted the pillows still posed a suffocation risk, but Kaitlin would assure him not to worry since Malin could now sit up straight on her own.

No. Nothing looked out of the ordinary. Except the heaviness that catapulted into Kaitlin's heart. The standing hairs on her neck now almost burning her skin.

§

Stavanger

THE FATHER WAS ASTOUNDED. The Norwegian spruce trees were not only both taller and leaner than any he'd previously encountered back in Quebec, but they looked sturdier too.

"Ouch..." he snapped from his thoughts, as a graying branch managed to hit him across the forehead whilst he was continuing his walk. "I wish the coordinates were a little clearer than this."

John Walker had been walking non-stop for what felt like an hour now, following his arrival at Stavanger's Sola Airport and the subsequent shuttle bus to town. "Maybe I should have first slept off the jet lag tonight," he mumbled under his breath, his head pounding.

I can't give up now, he subsequently decided. *Sleep can wait. That scoundrel better be here, and he better have some answers.*

Holding on to the large-sized 7/11 cup of joe in one hand, John continued on his search for the 'reddish cabin with the bright red-door', described as such by the old roommate of the young man he was searching for.

"Tan is trying to convince me to live with him," Linette had written in one of her last e-mails, "...but I don't want to leave *mamma* alone in her house again. Besides, he's been acting kind of weird lately..."

"He wasn't treating you very well here in Canada from what I recall, *habibi*," he'd written back, smiling since he knew his daughter would be rolling her eyes at the Arabic term of endearment he often liked to use with her. Back during their conversations over lunch. *I don't want her to ignore a quarter of her heritage like I know I've tried to do for so long to half of mine*, he'd often think before losing contact with Linette. *It's never too late to at least try to make some things right.*

Too late.

John tried his best to hold back his drops, preventively wiping his eyes with his lower arms. There was no time for such thoughts. He was on a mission. He'd wanted to at first directly visit his ex-girlfriend, Annika, in Trondheim to relish in their daughter's belongings. To be able to experience the furniture and everything else Linette had used before she was taken away from this earth too soon.

"I donated a lot of her old clothes and some of her furniture. But there are some things I still can't let go of," she'd told him through her heavy sobs on the phone. "It's all my fault. I should have reported her missing to the authorities earlier. I am such an idiot. I just assumed she didn't want to hear from me, knowing I didn't approve of that Tan character…"

As much as he'd wanted to avoid seeing his old flame, John knew he had to pay her a visit after the cabin. Not just to obtain a keepsake from Linette, but also because he knew they were the only two people who would understand. They'd be able to provide some solace to each other over the loss of their secret daughter.

The man inched closer to the cabin that finally entered his line of sight, right after he'd passed two particularly tall spruces; one at each side of the cabin, almost as if framing it. The melancholy chirping of crickets accompanied him, matching the tone of his mood. He was keen on getting some answers, and, from what he'd been able to gather from his daughter's last correspondences with him before her disappearance- he still couldn't bring himself to even think of the word 'death'- she'd indeed still been seeing that Tan Kuvvet guy, despite her mother's warnings. Even if he hadn't been the one who'd killed her (and John simply didn't believe Linette would commit suicide), Tan would know something. He was sure of it.

"What the, bloody…?" he gasped as a dark shadow passed the lower corner of his vision. The man then chuckled with relief, as he saw that it had been a black cat purring at him. With piercing green eyes following him intensely until he took a couple of steps away from the cabin.

"Here, kitty, kitty," he called out with a reassured smile. He hadn't seen any cats roaming the center of town and thought it strange to see one in the middle of the woods. *Must belong to whoever lives here.*

His mind suddenly went to the streets of Dubai, full of stray cats on every street corner. *That was one crazy summer,* he thought. *And would you look at that- fate has brought me to Norway too, now. This is where he last told me that he was, too*, he thought with a smirk. *What a funny twist of fate.*

For all he knew, his summer fling in Dubai- his first forbidden one with someone from his own gender- was probably having a grand ole time somewhere here. Perhaps even legally married to some Norwegian man. *Lar, after all, was ever the romantic.*

His intensity was also precisely the same reason why he could never bring himself to mail Lar a response to the letters he'd sent to his home address back in Montreal. How fast his heart had been beating as he rushed to open that first letter, before his curious and suspicious mother could do so.

"Something has changed in your behavior, young man, since you returned from that internship. And I don't like it one bit!" His mother had had both her eyes and running mouth focused on him like a hawk. "Oh, I knew Allah would be punishing me for having a child with a non-Muslim man. Your no-good father…"

12

Luckily, John had read the letter in time, all right, and managed to avoid another one of his mother's tirades. And it had surely been beautiful, and made his eyes teary. But, no, he did not respond. He was sure Lar would move heaven and hell to get to him in Canada upon any glimmer of hope he would possibly conceive from anything he'd have written. And John couldn't risk losing his family's support.

For what? Some fling? A drunken mistake which had only awakened a curiosity in his younger self one night in his youth? *Oh, alright,* he thought with a sigh, staring at the cabin's crimson door. So, it had lasted for several more occasions in addition to that night- right up until the moment when Lar had accompanied him to the airport and they'd both been crying.

I was just young...so young. Jaan was still a fully straight man as far as the world- and his wife and family- were concerned, and he intended to keep it that way.

"John," he spoke out aloud, clearing his throat.

This was no time to get nostalgic.

He would be starting everything over, renewed. He would no longer be called by the name 'Abdul' or 'Abe', as Lar had called him, alongside of his mother too, of course.

'Abdul Jaan Vaziri' was now 'John Walker'- he'd adopted his biological father's last name on his Canadian passport once he could so. And he was now hell bent on moving heaven and earth to avenge what he instinctively knew was his daughter's murder.

CHAPTER 3

Stavanger

FINN DU FEU WAS PERPLEXED. He knew that random passersby were an anomaly for their cloistered cabin, yet the man at the door wasn't familiar.

Using the rear entrance to enter back in and hop onto the window sill, he sized up the well-dressed stranger. This was a tall, middle-aged but ruggedly handsome man in glasses. He tried to decipher any detail in the man's thoughts that could pinpoint his intent, but to no avail. The man's energy felt too distant for Finn to tap into- even presently in his relatively most comfortable, feline form.

Whenever he had to manifest most visibly in the human realm, transforming his fire energy into anthropoid flesh had exhausted his vigor. Both in professional pursuits, and, most recently, in his pursuit of *her*.

The image of Kaitlin's shy smile forming on her ivory face crossed his mind just then, and Finn knew not to dwell there a moment longer. He stretched his ebony-fur covered limbs as far from one another as he could on the carpeted tiles.

"Meredith, manifest yourself already and answer the door," he called out upstairs, where he knew she had herself lost in some book again. The stranger had begun to edge closer and closer, hesitantly reaching for the doorbell only to subsequently retract his hand and eye his surroundings. "Some refined type. Dressed well, though not a client. I'd recognize him."

Where is Anja when you really need her? Finn thought with a sigh. *She's the only human we've got left here for occasions like this. And much more dutiful.*

"I'm coming," Meredith called out, rushing downstairs in exasperation. She flipped her long brown hair over her shoulder. "Don't you think I've been observing the man too, Finn? You never give me enough credit. I've got this. Stand back…"

"He's been lurking about, but looks harmless enough so I don't think we have to call Lar." Finn continued, halting his circular gait around the corridor right by Meredith's ankles. She'd put on reindeer-designed home slippers, rounding out a cozy outfit of a fitted turtleneck paired with faded jeans.

"Ahem," Finn cleared his throat, staring up at her approval-expectant expression with a sneer. "Cute. Cabin casual. It should cut it. But, umm, your pants, Mer…"

"What about them?" Meredith asked nonchalantly, only to almost simultaneously feel a breeze between her thighs. "My zipper!" she yelped through flushed cheeks, glancing down her legs as she inched closer to the living room mirror. Transforming had always felt the most awkward when she was called to do so in a hurry.

"How's this?" she straightened her already straight locks further around her face, hands placed in her jean pockets. "Natural?"

"It'll do," Finn replied with a sigh. "I'm staying put like this. If you need help, you know I'll intervene."

"Sounds like a plan," Meredith reached down to pat him on the black heap of fur on his head. "Don't worry. I'm sure he'll just ask for directions. Like that sweet old lady the other month who also happened to be able to see us, remember?"

"Yes, I remember," Finn smirked. "Maybe we'll luck out this time and this one won't be able to see us."

The sanctity of The Group, Inc. had partly been able to survive for as long as it had since not all humans could visibly discern the jinns inhabiting their various locales- even when they'd manifested in human forms to put those who could see them at ease. Lar would make sure to balance out human and jinn members of their chosen family. A cabin, house or apartment could never risk being seen as empty. Lar feared it'd likely prompt intrigue from passersby, which could in turn lead to a legal search, their documents and bank dealings would be discovered, and so on and so forth.

Finn's parents had always preached their dogma; telling him to stay inside 'the lines' as 'intended by God'. To lead a traditional life with them in the local woods, keeping to their own realm and not getting into the separate one God had intended for humans. They could never understand that- for Finn- love had known no boundaries. He'd once truly loved his beloved - and his family had shunned him for loving a human. Lar had understood, and The Group had long become his new family.

"He looks around Master's age, doesn't he?" Meredith further examined the man from the window, her arms folded in anticipation. Finn let out a soft purr. Lar Iktar was on a plane where he had become open to his kind- championing a brilliant fusion of both humanly and jinn skills and resources to maximize profits across their Norway branches. Despite also providing various private boat tours and other touristic services, The Group Inc. had found the most success through resourcing paper production services- working with the major pulp and paper factory, Norske Skog, in Oslo. Convincing both tourists- as well as paper manufactures and other paper-interested clients- in a myriad of attractive ways had proved to be an asset that had only grown to thrive when the jinns and open-minded humans were able to work together. Not simply accepting and assimilating into a world order that had only had them alienating one another, despite both being creations of God.

Finn was- nonetheless- a realist. He never imagined he'd exactly be able to frequent human bars and manifest into human flesh and – *bam* -before he knew it, some local babe would give him the googly eyes. No. He knew it took a certain level of mental and spiritual space in particular humans in order for jinns to be perceived. He'd risked as much with Kaitlin on that fateful day in the forest, and was delighted beyond his wildest dreams that she'd indeed turned out to be one of those to whom his kind would be fully perceptible.

"And what if he can't see me?" Meredith asked as soon as the man had finally rung the doorbell.

"Well, then, he'll simply see it as an empty cabin and hopefully leave us alone," Finn scratched himself with his paw. "Or, come back on a day when hopefully Anja will also be here. Whatever, Mer. I just want to see why this man is here. Open the door, already."

§

JOHN WAS NOT A MAN ACCLIMATED TO GOING TO stranger's homes, but somehow the smiling brunette that had opened the crimson door helped to ease his nerves. "May we help you?"

"Oh, hello there, young lady," John stammered, scratching the back of his ears. "I'm really sorry. I don't mean to bother you. I wasn't sure if anyone had been in here. I'm glad there is. How are you doing today?"

"We, umm, I'm doing fine, thank you," the woman answered, crossing her arms around her waif frame. "Are you alright? Are you lost?"

"Oh, sorry, young lady," John flinched, placing a palm on his forehead. *I hope I don't scare her.* "Where are my manners? The name is John… John Walker."

"John Walker…" the woman repeated with a pause, averting her eyes to the side.

Had she heard of his name before? Her hesitance to shake his outreached hand or respond with her own name took John by surprise. *If I'm in the right place, that lowlife Tan may have mentioned me.*

"I'm Meredith Olsen," she finally responded, extending her hand back feebly. "Is everything alright?"

"I hope it will be," John started, shaking his head with a heavy sigh. "I mean, yes, I'm alright, I suppose. Sorry again for the disturbance. You see, I was just looking for someone. I was given an estimate of the coordinates here in these parts, and I haven't seen any other cabin so far."

"Who were you looking for?" Meredith asked, eyeing him from head to toe.

Isn't she going to let me in? John thought. But then again, her hesitance was normal, he supposed. Women especially had to be careful allowing strangers into their cabins, didn't they? *How would she know I don't mean any trouble?*

"You can come in, if you'd like," the woman stepped aside just then, causing a black cat to brush against her calves with a hiss. She picked up the cat- the same one John had seen outdoors. "It's okay, kitty."

"Thank you, thank you," John replied, awing at the exquisitely decorated living space just beyond the corridor. Creamy cocoa walls with white trimming lacked any hanging frames or decorations. Two velvety armchairs surrounding an antiquated, gold-mantel fireplace looked uncomfortable; yet his tired legs would take anything to sit on in that moment. Aside from a glass table situated before a black leather sofa, all the surrounding bare drawers and desks were various shades of dark red-crowding the living room space, as far as John was concerned. *Doesn't quite feel like Scandinavian minimalism,* he thought with a smirk.

The place had certainly had a look of being lived in by an older person or couple, rather than a young woman like this Meredith in front of him. Had she perhaps been staying with her family living upstairs?

18

The simple wooden set of stairs lacked carpeting- the only 'cabin-like' norm so far, as far as John was able to observe. *What exactly had I been expecting?* An image of his wife back in Montreal popped up in his head. *Helen would have thrown plaid blankets and flowered-vases all over this place.*

"I won't be long. This is a lovely place you've got here," John particularly couldn't take his eyes off the inviting hearth inside. It reminded him of how cold he'd felt standing aside.

"Shoes, please, sir," Meredith smiled as she gestured him to the living room. "Right this way."

"Oh," John chuckled, taking off his brown loafers. *I hope my socks don't smell after the long flight.* He cursed himself for not recalling the hygienic Norwegian habit Annika would employ on him all the time, once upon an extramarital affair ago.

"I'm sorry about that," he started, taking a seat on one of the armchairs Meredith had led him to. "I'm still feeling disoriented, I suppose. I just arrived here this morning from Quebec. It was a long…"

"Quebec? You're from Canada?" the woman asked, glancing at the cat that had followed her to the three-person couch, where it had now taken a seat next to her.

"Yes, yes, I am," John stammered, inexplicably unable to take his eyes off of the cat's emerald gaze. "From the city of Montreal, actually. Why do you ask?"

"That's a long flight," Meredith took a deep breath and flipped her hair back with sudden exuberance. "You came all the way here to search for someone, was it?"

She's making an effort to appear more certain of herself than she actually feels, John sensed. It was then that he noticed her eyes. Her dark optics almost appeared to be crying, hidden behind the neutrality of her current expression. *Not just her eyes and timidity. Her hair, her rather pointy chin….*A loud *meow* from the cat brought him back from his reverie.

"Mr. Walker?" Meredith asked sternly.

"I'm so terribly sorry," John did his best to shake off his thoughts. "The jet lag. And, well, I'm also sorry for staring. The resemblance…you remind me of my daughter. She has… Well, she had, almost the same facial features as you."

"Your daughter?" Meredith jolted in her seat. "You're looking for your daughter?"

Distraught, John couldn't hold back his tears any longer. *I should have. Much, much sooner.*

"I'm looking for a young man possibly in connection to her disappearance, actually," he tried his best to speak through his state, wiping a tear with the back of his hand. "A young man by the name of Tan. Tan Kuvvet. Is he here?"

§

THE SOUND OF HER EX-LOVER'S NAME COMING OUT OF the man's mouth rendered Meredith senseless. *The diary*, Meredith jolted in her seat, staring straight into Finn's eyes. *Linette's diary. I remember. Tan's ex. The dead girl. This is her father. No wonder he can see me. He's involved! Finn! Help!*

A reassuring purring sound from him allowed her to take a deep breath. *"It's okay, Meredith,"* she heard Finn whisper in her mind. *"I recognized the name. Paul's ex-boss. Tan talked about this man he'd been jealous of for nothing. He'd shown me Linette's diary entry talking about her secret father even before you found out about it, remember?"*

"Oh," Meredith responded in her mind. *"Once again, somehow, it's all about that Linette girl again, isn't it?"* How the young woman had managed to cause such earthquakes in Meredith's emotional world- albeit even now, and from beyond the grave at that- still shocked her

20

beyond belief.

"It's natural he's looking for answers, Mer," Finn insisted mentally. *"But he doesn't have any proof yet. Look at him. He's so unsure."*

"Young lady?" John Walker asked. "Are you alright? Does that name ring any bells? Tan?"

"But who gave him our coordinates, then, Finn?" Meredith's thoughts implored as she locked eyes with Finn once again. *"Maybe someone knows we hid a killer? We'll all be exposed. Lar will ruin us…"*

"Lar has his own tricks he's got to keep hidden, don't fret Meredith," he reassured her. Ever since spotting Tan and Lar during a happy-looking stroll on one of his trips to Oslo, Finn had begun to have his doubts about so many things. *"Keep calm and answer the man with the truth. Lying will induce more suspicion. Tell him you broke up."*

"We broke up," Meredith blurted.

"I'm sorry? You were dating Tan Kuvvet?" John's straightening back inched his body closer to the edge of the couch.

"Yes, but it's been a while, now," Meredith stammered, cursing her impulsivity as she caught the disapproval in Finn's reactive purr. "It's over. Long story. He's gone. He doesn't live here anymore."

"So, it's really true," a certain tone of hope was becoming more and more audible in John's voice. "He really did live here after leaving Trondheim? Oh, my dear. Please tell me. Where is he now? I have to find him. Please help me. Help us- her mother and I…"

"It…was a bad break up, and I'm afraid I wouldn't know where he is these days," Meredith said, caressing Finn's back as she inched his face closer to hers. *"How do we get him out of the house, Finn?"* she directed her ponderings toward him once again. *"I'm too nervous. You know this isn't easy for me to talk about."*

"It's all right. Just relax. You're doing great," Finn assured her, his whiskers tickling her palm.

21

"A phone number, perhaps?" John insisted. "His old roommate back in town said he must have since changed it and he couldn't reach him. But maybe you have a more updated number?"

"He's desperate, the poor man," Meredith shared.

"Okay, so it looks like the old roommate gave him the coordinates, Mer," Finn shot back. *"Don't lose focus. Didn't you hear? We'll have to pay that guy a little visit, it seems."*

"Fake number, it is?" Meredith pressed telepathically. *"Quick, Finn!"*

"Fake number, it is," Finn affirmed.

"I'll give you the last number I had saved, sir," Meredith put Finn down and stood up to reach a cellular phone that had been on the glass table. "I don't know if he still uses it, though. You can imagine, I haven't used it since we were through. I never wanted to hear his voice again since, well, yeah; it was a bad break up."

"So you've said, yes," John said with curiosity. "I'm sorry to hear that, young lady."

Shoot. Meredith had to distract him. "Why are you looking for him, anyway, sir? Did your daughter know him?"

"Let it go, Mer," Finn's thoughts were angry now. *"We're almost rid of him, and, of course, you have to know more. Stop! You know why!"*

"She did, yes, unfortunately," John began to tear up. "I'm sorry. She was just taken from us so soon. Too soon…"

"This is the number…" Meredith handed the man a piece of paper with seven digits she'd concocted on the spot. "I hope you can reach him and get the answers you seek."

"Thank you…" John was downright balling now. Meredith grabbed a box of tissues to hold out for him. "Thank you. Oh my God, look at me, crying like a little boy."

"The loss of a loved one couldn't have been easy, sir," Meredith answered reassuringly, looking toward the door. "It's alright. Like I said, I hope you can find the solace you need." *Come on, poor man, please leave already.*

"I should go," John stood up and headed toward the furnace. "Where was the door again? Oh my, this fireplace is truly magnificent. Is this antique?"

"Yes, it is," Meredith said politely. "Right this way, sir. I'll show you out."

"Can you please let me know if you can think of anything about Tan's current whereabouts, young lady?" John asked by the door, reaching deep into his pocket for the leather wallet his fingers sought. "Here's my card with my information on it…"

"Thank you for the card, sir. Of course. I'll call you if I remember or hear anything…" Meredith rushed, twiddling with the gray-hued card in her hands.

"By the way, I never asked what happened with you guys…," John's solemness was palpable. "I know you may feel it's none of my business, young lady. But I really need to find out what happened to my daughter. I don't believe I've caught your name…Maybe I forgot, I apologize. My mind isn't exactly…"

"Meredith," she answered, after a nod of affirmation from Finn encouraged her to repeat the truth. "Meredith Olsen."

"Oh, right, right. So you've said. Nice to officially meet you, Meredith,"

"Likewise, sir. I just wish I could have been of bigger help. I mean, as you can imagine, I don't really like to talk about him…"

"Oh, but you have," John said. "Seeing you has brought her face back in my line of sight once again. My Linette…"

"Linette…" Meredith spoke out loud, the name still tinging her with a curious combination of jealousy, admiration as well as sadness. "Lovely name."

"Dear Meredith, please at least answer me this, before I go…" John found himself whispering, though he was sure the two of them had been alone. "Linette occasionally confided that she was afraid of him. Tan. Was he ever violent with you?"

"No, sir. It was nothing like that with us," Meredith answered dreamily. "In our case…well, let's just say it was…infidelity."

"Oh. I see. Loyalty is hard to come by these days, *eh* young lady?"

"It sure is," Meredith nodded behind the closing door, peering at Finn grazing her ankles. "Take care, Mr. Walker. Good luck!"

Loyalty truly is hard to come by.

CHAPTER 4

Sandnes

MALIN MAVERICK WAS WATCHED. Kaitlin now felt almost certain of it. She could have sworn she'd caught her daughter staring off into the empty space around their spacious, three-bedroom apartment complex on several occasions now. Today, however, there was no question remaining in her mind about it. Malin's sudden wake from her nap- with a grin in place of the usual wails of an 11-month-old before being cuddled- was all the proof Kaitlin needed to affirm her suspicions.

The adorable toothy grin she'd give to whatever she was seeing- often on walls and near the windows- but not yet able to verbalize had been the most bittersweet. Kaitlin attempted to ignore it for as long as she could in her and Paul's new beginning as a family of three now. Yet she was also more confused than ever precisely because she was witnessing that ever mysterious smile on her daughter's face each time she'd stare off into the distance.

Malin wasn't being scared or seemingly threatened, as far as Kaitlin could tell. *If it is indeed Finn appearing before her, though, wouldn't she technically be scared upon seeing a stranger?* How would her daughter's crying when awakened manage to turn to reverie so quickly?

"Here…walk here honey," Kaitlin encouraged her daughter from her beige recliner. Malin was still hanging on to the cabinet handles on the television wall unit. *I hope she doesn't break those glass figurines from our Euro-travels memorabilia collection,* she thought through gritted teeth. "Come on. You can do it. You can walk to momma. You just have to take that first step, my angel…"

"Momma," Malin cooed now with her mischievous smile as of late each time she would attempt to take her first steps.

"That's right my brave girl," Kaitlin beamed, catching the teasing look in her daughter's deeply-set, hooded eyes. *She's definitely got Paul's gaze. I really don't see why people are saying she resembles me more lately.* "Momma will hold your hand, my brave girl…"

Their brave girl. Of course, she was. Whatever the reason was for their daughter's uncharacteristically-high level of baby-bravery when faced with the unknown, the alternative burning at the back of Kaitlin's mind could not have been it. *Weren't Finn's eyes a bit hooded also?*

"Get a hold of yourself, Kaitlin," Kaitlin shook her head as she gently caressed her daughter's arms. Her grown-out hair tickled Malin's cheek. *She's just brave. She isn't sensing some innate sense of affinity with whatever or whomever she may be seeing or anything. No. Our daughter is simply brave.*

"Your daddy will come home soon. Maybe we can surprise him with your first steps…"

"Ooh," Malin cooed as the doorbell rang.

"Ooh, look at that my angel," Kaitlin welcomed the signal that her husband had arrived. She'd already breastfed Malin but remembered she needed to stir something up for the two of them whilst Paul played with her. "Speak of the…. daddy," Kaitlin stopped herself from completing the devilish idiom, only partially because she didn't want Malin to hear such language yet. *No negativity in this house.*

Not walking into wooded areas- distant from dense human populations- was yet one of the several ways in which she'd long decided she'd tried to avoid attracting jinns or any other potential beings toward her and her family. She'd Googled it all.

Paul had already done what he'd persuaded both of them to have been his 'part' in protecting their unity now as a family of three. Moving to a bigger place to raise a child. A place that would still be close to his office, yet far enough from the Stavanger woods- where he'd been convinced his wife would continue being targeted.

Kaitlin heaved a deep sigh. She'd never confided to Paul the exact nature of The Group's heterogenous members- consisting both of humans and powerful *jinns*. She'd discovered much of what she now knew through the help of her new, Turkish friend in Norway- Sibel Pak- back in Stavanger. She couldn't even take a stab as to what her husband's reaction would have been. Additional fear? Ridicule? Disbelief? Suspicion?

Astrologically a Libra, Kaitlin was no Leo like Sibel, yet motherhood had sure made her one protective lioness already. Keeping certain information to herself in regards to her whereabouts back in Stavanger had been one thing, but Kaitlin had decided that white lies now to ensure Malin's well-being- accomplishing coparenting as a peaceful unit for as much as possible- would always take precedence.

Peace.

They'd mostly kept to themselves in Sandnes, looking out at mostly neighboring small apartments in the green hills from their corner on the top floor of the dual-story, four-family living quarters. Paul had even uncharacteristically declined her offer to invite their three neighbors for coffee- and hadn't even invited his office mates over. In fact, they'd only paid them one visit- quick and united- bearing 'gifts for the baby' and 'not staying for long' as to not 'bother' them- and that had been it. Paul was no king of any jungle, but Kaitlin had to admit he'd perhaps been better than her at protecting their little pride. She often oscillated between finding her husband to be going overboard and feeling that she herself was perhaps not taking the otherworldly dangers they'd all faced as seriously as she should.

"Hello, my lovely girls," Paul quipped as soon as Kaitlin opened the door, kissing the tip of her nose right before delving into a big sniff of Malin's head, resting now in her mother's arms.

She appreciated how he'd still been keeping up with his affectionate ways despite the baby. *Or perhaps because of the baby*, Kaitlin admittedly couldn't also help but think from time to time.

"Welcome home, his daddy- highness," Kaitlin said with smiling closed eyes.

"Mmm, I can never get enough of hearing that," Paul whispered, exciting Kaitlin.

"*Oh, la la.* You mean, his daddy-highness?" she raised her eyebrows up and down suggestively.

"No, silly goose," Paul chuckled, picking Malin up to give her two quick jumps in the air and causing her to have a high-pitched giggle fit with her stomach being nuzzled.

"*Daddy*. I'm this princess' daddy. Right my birdie?"

"Oh," Kaitlin smirked, heading toward the kitchen with slumped shoulders. *Get a grip, Kaitlin. Not everything has to be sexual to prove your marriage isn't on the rocks. Does it?*

She took in a deep breath and exhaled through pursed lips, adding a smile over her shoulder. "I love seeing you two like this."

"Oh, here are those pears you asked for, babe," Paul quipped, gently placing Malin in her baby chair and reaching for the plastic bag on the floor. He proceeded to then take out and hand Kaitlin two sheets of grocery ads. "Check these out, too. Lots of fruits were cheaper in the bulk at Coop Prix this week. Here are the ads for my lady…"

"Great…," Kaitlin rolled her eyes as she picked up the neatly-folded, miraculously-uncrumpled sheets and gave them a quick glance-positioning her body in a way where Paul could witness her fake interest.

"Some baby items are at reduced price as you'll see," Paul went on to Kaitlin as if he'd just discovered a fun new theme park or restaurant. "We have to watch out spending, darling, don't you agree? We kind of went all out on the house and Malin's room. Of course, my princess deserves the best, but surely, she can go without designer bibs, can't she?"

Why, of course she doesn't need brand-name bibs, Paul, Kaitlin wanted to retort. *Why, when there are starving children around the world? I mean, I don't know- perhaps because they also happen to be organically-made with safer chemicals for our baby's skin? But, what does your spoiled wife know, right?*

How she just wanted to scream her thoughts out. Her now New Yorker friend from her university years in Canada, Sandy Burns, would surely tell her 'Go girl,' if she could. Yet marriage was something Sibel was more experienced in, and she'd been trying her best to control her temper and heed her advice over the past year. "Sometimes you've got to choose your battles carefully, and let some comments go without a response", Sibel would often advise Kaitlin.

"I'll check the sale out tomorrow, babe," she chose in response, tossing the ad on the couch. "Malin could use some fresh air on a walk with her mommy tomorrow if the weather cooperates. We just may add Coop Prix to our route."

"So, what did you girls do today? How's the writing going?" Paul asked nonchalantly, plonking down on the couch.

"Argh, don't remind me on a day like today, Paulie," Kaitlin kneeled down on the playmat spread across adjacent to their leather couch, gently placing her daughter next to one of her favorite bunny rattles. *How could I forget?* "Not exactly a happy camper with my professionalism as of late."

Happiness was measured differently in Norway: nature walks, outdoorsy lifestyle, weekend beer with mates. Professional success was the least of many of its inhabitants worries. They often wanted to simply feel joy- at least enough joy not to fall victim to depression in the longer hours of darkness, Kaitlin would often hypothesize. As visually-breathtaking as the southwestern part of the country she'd become accustomed to was- with longer hours of daylight in comparison to the darker parts affected further by the concept of the 'midnight sun', life could still become very dull- and fast- without tasks and activities.

The side gigs for 'keeping busy and entertained'- as Paul had coined them- that Kaitlin had picked up during her pregnancy had certainly slowed down in productivity ever since attending to her newborn took precedence. Somewhere along her second trimester, Kaitlin had created a blog entitled, *'Enthusiastic Musings of a Reluctant Housewife'*. Providing book and product reviews with tongue-in-cheek commentary on the new lifestyle she had to adjust to in Norway had gradually begun to gain her quite a following. The last post she'd posted on her daughter's half-birthday celebration had, in fact, gotten her nearly a thousand new subscribers- with numerous comments on how other mothers could also relate to her difficulties.

"Uh oh, babe. Spill. Like oil. What's going on?" Paul's eyes were miraculously still glued to the three-page ad from the market.

"Well, umm, don't get me wrong. I mean, it's…going," Kaitlin started, stifling a giggle in response to Paul's cheesy joke. "…And, just, going, and going, and going. I've been progressing slower than that bunny in that battery commercial I suppose, eh?"

"Ba-ba," Malin cooed, shaking her rattle ferociously with a mischievous smile.

"That's right sweet pea. Bun-ny," Kaitlin enunciated. She had also provided her online marketing services for the Statoil website- arranged by Paul, of course, who never seemed to miss a chance to redirect her attention to her new 'hobbies' secondary to Malin. It'd felt nowhere nearly as exciting as her days in charge of closing two major marketing deals for two different promotional projects- one of which had even made it as a story in a local newspaper in Toronto. But, feeling of *some* use- in a field *somewhat* close to what she'd had a background in- would have to do, Kaitlin had decided.

Her husband, bless his soul, always longed to take control of situations- in his own mind, anyway. *Too bad for him: I'm not one of his office tasks.* How Kaitlin longed, too. To simply just leave the house every morning to go be of some importance in an office somewhere. Her only concern being the possible wrinkling of her button-up blouse or the delay caused by traffic, cursing drivers holding it up.

Increasingly annoyed tickles coming from her daughter halted Kaitlin's thoughtful reverie. "Alright, I think that's enough, his tickle-monster highness," she quipped, kneeling down to caress Malin's soft mane. *I guess I'm needed more at home now. By someone more important than some boss, at that.*

Something good to have come out of everything that had come to pass over the past year in their lives, in Kaitlin's opinion, was Paul's relatively lesser emphasis on a 'well-kept' home, at least. He'd luckily acknowledged- for the most part- that she'd now had a more prominent role to focus on while he was at work.

"Hey, not fair that I have to be away from you girls during all those hours at work while you're here bonding without me," Paul quipped, exaggerating a pout before continuing in a more serious tone. "What did you mean by what you said earlier, by the way? You said 'on a day like today'. Anything else I should know?"

Oh, shoot! Of course, he caught that. Paul had made her promise to immediately go to him at the first sign that it had been happening again. Any form of communication with anyone from The Group. Phone calls. E-mails. *Random appearances and disappearances.* Kaitlin hadn't exactly shared that latter one with her husband- there was no need to irk him any further with her jinn experience.

She'd only felt comfortable telling him about the part that he'd already found out on his own, after going through her phone. As far as

Paul needed to know- *The Group, Inc.* was a paper-producing/rustic organization that had targeted her in order to help one of their members, Tan, avenge the loss of his girlfriend, Linette. They'd blamed Paul's admittedly machoistic yet ultimately wrongful suggestions to Tan- when he stormed their office building back in Quebec- that Linette may indeed have been having an affair with her boss.

Kaitlin remembered having first seen the dead woman's photograph on the evening news- her curiosity piqued by the beautiful and young vision of silky ebony hair and contrasting fair skin on the screen, especially in response to Paul's elevated interest. She could also never forget the vow she'd made to herself to track the man down somehow; to lead him on to find Tan's culpability. Ideally, without any traces back to her as that particular catalyst.

"Oh, well, you know. Malin woke up early from her nap today, and I couldn't update my blog as planned, nor even glimpse at that most recent page layout suggestion for you guys," Kaitlin added the pout which she knew still had the ability to disarm her husband.

"Not to mention prepare any dinner for us," Paul interjected with a wink.

"Oh! That's right! I was thinking the leftovers were enough to fill you, while I'll be just fine with a salad," Kaitlin rolled her eyes, getting up toward the kitchen after gently placing Malin on her play mat. *People never really change too much, do they?* "I'll make a little avocado salad for myself. I need to lose these last several kilos of the baby weight anyway."

"I'll tell you what, *ma chérie*," Paul chimed, reaching across the table to hold Kaitlin's hand. "I've got the dishes tonight. Try to put Malin to bed early and work a little bit on your...laptop stuff. I know it...relaxes your mind."

My laptop stuff. Kaitlin nodded with a half-hearted smile, though this was not the first time Paul had been nudging her toward professional

32

work with the reasoning of it 'relaxing her mind'. *He must think I'm on the edge of crazy after everything.* She didn't dare verbalize it, however. Kaitlin hated proverbially waking up any sleeping bears, and knowing her husband's temper- she preferred him in hibernation. *What if he senses I haven't been able to shake off Finn- whether he's been visiting our home or not- and then goes off into those woods to find and confront him somehow?*

"Did you hear that, my sweet?" she nudged closer to her daughter, whose head was turning right and left in her high chair as she eyed her parents in conversation. "Your daddy still thinks there's some magical button I can press to get you to sleep whenever we want..."

Feeling simultaneously like a bad mother and bad friend for avoiding Sibel's amiable but obsessive tirades to try the 'Ferber Method', Kaitlin was beginning to lose hope she could ever manage to get her nearly one year-old to fall asleep before 10 pm. She'd tried everything she could Google-search, including spreading some of her breastmilk on Malin's blankies, to regulate her daughter's sleep. But try as she might, her conscience got the better of her and she couldn't allow her daughter to 'cry it out', often fondling her back to sleep with minimal breastfeeding through the night.

"She's been better this week, though, hasn't she?" Paul insisted. "Even fifteen-minute intervals of slowly pulling up her bed time can be helpful. We can't give up. We have to set a strict routine..."

"What does it matter since you fall asleep and wake up early to go off to save the oil business, Paul, while I'm home dealing with everything?!" Kaitlin was immediately sure her voice had sounded angrier than she intended. Pressing the 'bake' button to heat their chicken dish from the previous night, she didn't like the palpable silence that matched her from Paul, rather than the usual retort. "Sorry, Paulie. It's just that, you know, I've been trying..."

"You're feeling frustrated right now," Paul rested his chin on his hand, studying her with a stoic expression.

"Umm, yes, well...I suppose I am. I mean, can you blame me? My mom hasn't been able to fly out yet to help me out, and Sibel's closer enough back in Stavanger, but feels miles away now and...and..."

"Look, I've been reading up on something called 'post-partum depression', darling, and..." Paul interrupted her.

"No way!" Kaitlin interrupted back, grabbing her hair by the scalp. "I don't know what website you've looked up or magazine you've read in the waiting room at your physical check-up last week, Paul, but I'm *not* depressed!"

"Momma?" Malin cooed, causing Kaitlin to crumple her body on the floor next to her, squeezing a curious sound from one of the plastic toys she'd sat on. Malin's eruption into giggles became Kaitlin's cue to tearfully let out a laugh as well. "You make mommy tired, baby, but what would this crazy mommy do without you?" She nuzzled her nose against her daughter's, darting a look at her husband form the corner of her eyes.

Watching them, Paul was smiling. *Thank God.*

"Look, remember when Engin invited me to catch the game after I'd dropped him off the other day?" he asked softly, kneeling next to them on the mat. "You know. When his car was at the shop?"

"Hmm," Kaitlin nodded with a subdued smile. How could she forget? Even she hadn't had the opportunity to hang out with her friend since their congratulatory- and only- house visit. *Our husbands discovered their mutual love of Norwegian hockey and now they're apparently hanging out. Joy.* "I'm a tad bit jealous, Paulie. Just have to get that out there," Kaitlin threw in chuckle. "You boys have socialized more than Sibel and I have been able to lately. I mean, I don't want my truth to brew inside me and grow into something later..."

"Wait...I was just about to surprise you with something, my impatient one," Paul grinned. "Sibel made me sit down with them for a little bit over some tea she'd just prepared, and offered to watch Malin tomorrow! For you to have your much-needed alone time since the baby, finally! So, you know, that Coop Prix walk may have to wait another day actually."

"Oh. She suggested alone time…" Kaitlin nodded in the direction of Malin's room. *What was I expecting? Some crazy night out on the down, dancing with the least-likely friend to do such a thing?*

"Exactly, babe. I think it's a swell idea," Paul's eyes were sparkling. "Your friend's experienced with children, and you've begun pumping milk now. Remember how Aylin and Hakan absolutely adored fawning over her on their baby visit? Remember that Turkish-style evil-eye safety pin they gifted Malin with?"

"Oh, yes. They call that evil-eye '*nazar*', I think," Kaitlin nodded. *The only visit.* Kaitlin thought again with a heavy sigh. She was relieved yet taken aback at the same time. As supportive as Sibel had been over the phone throughout her pregnancy, Kaitlin found herself missing their cathartic coffee and gym dates in between bi-monthly women's club benefits- where they'd met through their commonality of being spouses of professional businessmen in Stavanger.

It amused Kaitlin that she now noted those days of 'fun time' nostalgically- whereas the title had previously belonged to the post-work networking events in Toronto. *This is what getting older must be like*, she thought, smiling as she peered at Paul's full-cheeks chewing his food like a squirrel. As she neared 30, Kaitlin missed having coffee with girlfriends more than she missed the days of wearing miniskirts and knee-high boots to discuss 'world affairs' around circular bar tables. Surrounded by whisky and worldly appetizers equally-pretentious as the crowd. Where everyone really would have preferred to be kicking their legs up with some beers and fried snacks.

During what had to have been the uncanniest winter and experience in Kaitlin's life- meeting handsome Finn Du Feu- Kaitlin would always be thankful for having met Sibel's acquaintance around the same time, as well. Like a lifeline- to confide in when she certainly couldn't do so neither to Paul nor to any of the superficial half-friendships she'd forced herself to attempt with the wives of his professional circle.

"Will it work, Paulie?" Kaitlin was genuinely not sure. She hadn't been away from Malin for longer than twenty minutes so far- and even that had been for a 'quick walk around the block' when her parents-in-law had visited then during Malin's seventh month. "I've been pumping- yes- but you know Malin's still not gotten around to preferring the bottle over me. Can I really risk leaving her for two-three hours?"

As Paul shrugged and muttered something about it being worth a try, Kaitlin had another thought. *Why couldn't Sibel have offered this to me, directly?* Had her friend decided in time that Kaitlin was nuts for having a jinn experience? Or was she not as genuine as Kaitlin had imagined? Maybe she'd been one-sidedly building up their friendship in her head out of need, rather than actuality. *How well can we really know someone we've recently met, anyway?*

After dinner was gobbled up rather quicky and lacking any further discussion of the matter, Kaitlin dreaded the next step she knew she needed Paul's help to tackle if she was to be serious about setting a routine for Malin. *Bath time.*

"Kaitlin, this water is too hot for a baby," her husband's complaining soon after dinner had become as reliable as the sun rising each dawn. When she vented about it to Sandy on the phone, her friend would try to assure her it was actually 'sweet of Paul to worry so much', and for Kaitlin to 'ease up on the poor fella'.

Paul placed the finger he'd put in the baby's bathtub on Kaitlin's cheek for emphasis. "Did you even use that water thermometer this time!?"

"Paul, if I can put my finger in it without feeling burning heat, Malin can surely…" Kaitlin retorted with a heavy sigh.

"Your skin's heat tolerance is not the same as our baby daughter's, Kaitlin!" Paul's nostrils were wide now like the bulls they'd seen on their trip out to Spain while Kaitlin had been three months pregnant.

Malin erupted into a wail in her mother's arms just then, causing Paul to mouth, 'oh great'.

"Well, our daughter must certainly be cold *now*!" Kaitlin managed through gritted teeth, simultaneously rocking her body side to side to appease her daughter. "Wrapped up only in this towel, while you're here belittling me about something you have no experience in yourself!"

"I know right from wrong, Kaitlin," Paul insisted sternly, changing his expression 180 degrees as he tried to hush Malin through forced smiles. "It doesn't take a genius to know you have to use all the tools available to ensure that a baby is able to…"

"Okay, see- it's cooled down a bit while we've been arguing over here," Kaitlin knew she had to lay down the artillery if her daughter was to be washed quickly and back into her warm onesie-pajamas soon. She placed both her pinky finger- as well as that of Malin's- in the water playfully. "See? All good, his highness. Our finger thermometers have saved the day," her smiles turned genuine as Malin appeared joyful now, being comforted. Enough to stop crying, anyway.

"A finger to test the water isn't the same thing as her entire body being drenched in an untested temperature which…" Kaitlin had already drowned her husband out while she sat Malin up in the bathtub, distracting her with a rubber duck toy while applying baby shampoo on her head.

There it was. *She's saving us from ourselves once again,* Kaitlin thought. Malin cooed and giggled, smiling back and forth at the two of them whilst showing them the toy in her hand.

Growing up under her overbearing mother's auspices, Kaitlin had

had numerous concerns about becoming a mother, and had certainly been delaying getting pregnant since the beginning of her marriage. Sleepless nights and a decrease in a social life had gradually not seemed to be such sacrifices when she'd been facing the consequences of both. With her boredom and rampant thoughts for the past two years in her new domesticated life, anyway: even before motherhood.

"Make sure it doesn't get in her eyes...." Paul's voice was indeed calmer. "She doesn't like that..."

At least he's gotten over the damned thermometer, Kaitlin thought, rolling her eyes and taking in a deep breath while she applied more of the shampoo on Malin's back with a pink washcloth.

Suddenly, taking Sibel up on her babysitting offer in order to take a breather downtown for a couple of hours wasn't sounding as needless to her.

Paul isn't exactly going to give me a medal of sacrifice. Kaitlin would take whatever she could get.

CHAPTER 5

WITH THE NORTH SEA SPARKLING BESIDE HER, Kaitlin halted her casual stroll in Stavanger harbor to take in the moment. Behind the outdoor tables of bundled-up locals dining near heaters in the autumn cold were identifiably-Norwegian, triangle-roofed sets of house-like, commercial buildings.

A couple of local fishermen giving her physique a look-over made her blush further after the memory of *him* had already done so. She continued her gaze at the bronze statue of Alexander Kielland in a top-hat before her. She'd once waited for Finn at that same spot, for him to walk with her to the semi-professional cabin in the woods. The forest had inexplicably proved to be vaster than it'd appeared to be from the city- even now, as she peered toward the direction of the lake to gaze at the area beyond it. Indeed- all the marvels she'd seen there, from waterfalls to high mountains, had still felt like a dream of another realm rather than an actual memory.

Kaitlin felt her stomach growl. Would she have enough time to grab a quick lunch before heading to Sandnes? She smiled at the familiar Romanesque-style, historic church at the end of the uphill stairs behind the statue. *Do they still have Burger King here?* Sure enough, the corner of the coastal street had her once favorite fast-food chain still in business, Kaitlin noted. Or, should she grab a tuna fish sandwich instead, from the 7/11 she'd also glimpsed along the cobblestone path that led to other shops? Would she dare think it? Could it be possible that she'd actually missed Stavanger?

Kaitlin smiled, tightening the belt of her beige trench-coat, seeking further coziness around her torso to fight the windchill. *I should spend most of my time today in Sandnes harbor, as promised*, she decided with a sigh. She closed her eyes as seagulls hawked in the near-distance. His image, sure enough, crossed her daydreaming- her little self-indulgence. She visualized him there- with his black leather jacket and blond curls. Pointing toward the distance with his green, mischievous gaze. "Right this way."

"*Ops, beklager*," a fair-headed local smiled with an apology for bumping into her, forcing Kaitlin to pay attention to her present moment once again.

"It's okay," she responded in English, taking out her phone. *Is it too soon to check in on Malin?* She'd just left her daughter with Sibel, and reminded herself that she had to catch the next bus to head back to Sandnes, or her little 'day-trip to herself' would turn into a pointless disaster. *Maybe I'll check in once I'm actually in downtown Sandnes.*

Talking on the phone in public had always made Kaitlin self-conscious, and even a bit paranoid that everyone would be listening in on details from her personal life- especially with video. But she knew she had to get over it. She was surprised to see that she'd begun to miss her daughter already.

"Will you relax? Everything is just fine. See for yourself, Kaitlin," Sibel assured her an hour later when Kaitlin had sat herself down by the harbor. Luckily the green, *Kolumbus* bus had arrived on time and taken her to downtown Sandnes in less than half an hour. It was for the best- not only for her outing to begin already, but she'd realized she hadn't been prepared for any further memories of the last year to haunt her. Including the temptation to walk again in those woods, as she'd looked out from the bus window.

"I know it'll be a hassle," Paul had insisted, dropping her and Malin off at Sibel's before hurrying to work that morning. "But I just wouldn't feel comfortable with you strolling around our old spots by yourself, Kaitlin. He…they…might spot you, and, well, you can understand."

It had felt like a hassle indeed to take an extra bus trip- not to mention be farther from Malin should any emergency have occurred. Kaitlin had agreed she'd enjoy the bus rides which she had 'missed', and that she'd ride one back to Stavanger after her little outing, heading 'directly' to Sibel's house on Hundvag island to get picked up along with their daughter. "The additional walk would also be exercise, Paulie, it's all good."

This is all ridiculous, Kaitlin was now thinking, holding on to the thick, wide-brimmed crimson hat she'd decided to put on to make her little wardrobe feel 'autumn-chic'. It had taken all of Kaitlin's strength not to blurt out: "Finn- that Brad Pitt version of Paul Bunyan, as you'd deemed him- is a friggin' *jinn*, who can travel anywhere at the speed of light! Keeping me away from downtown Stavanger isn't going to be able to keep him or The Group away from me, as your mind seems to think, Paul!"

But she kept her mouth shut; as she'd gotten used to doing so over the past year in order to maintain a peaceful pregnancy as much as she could. Kaitlin liked to think she'd known her husband long enough- having been his friend before they'd gotten married. He would not only have questioned her unorthodox explanation, but also believed her to be unhinged.

Sibel positioned the lens to face the carpet in her daughter Aylin's room. Her new bob-hairstyle moved vivaciously as she pointed the phone's camera to capture Malin sitting straight up with her trusty bunny rattle, as well as the soft blanky Kaitlin had smothered in her breast milk for the 'comfort' the smell was supposed to provide for babies. According to the countless magazines she devoured each time she'd needed 'alone-time' in the bathroom at home, anyway.

"Is that a Barbie doll I see her picking up now?" Kaitlin asked into the camera. "Baby? Mal? It's mommy, sweetie pie."

"You need this, Kaitlin," the ever-warmth in Sibel's vibrant smile was palpable even through the phone screen. "Don't worry about us. We're having a grand 'ole time. Go get some shopping done- heck, your nails too when you're at it. I saw them today. I'm going to check when you return to pick her up…"

"Lady, these nails haven't seen polish…nor much of filing…for the longest time," Kaitlin snickered.

Sibel chuckled as she bent down closer to Malin on the carpet. "Aylin, hold the phone sweety, and film mommy and Malin for Aunty Kaitlin. Say hi! *Hadi kızım*…"

"Hi," a five-year old brunette with almond-shaped brown eyes spoke directly into the phone screen.

"Hi, *canım*…" Kaitlin waved at her, using the term of endearment in Turkish she'd picked up from Sibel. She felt nostalgia of her life back in Toronto, once again. As would interestingly be the effect each time she'd be in proximity to witnessing families from the myriad of cultures in the petroleum city of Stavanger, anyway- and even in Sandnes.

She didn't get along too well with her domineering mother in-person, but in that moment, she missed her terribly. Her mother- Linda Ramsay- had finally managed to buy the plane ticket to visit her granddaughter, and Kaitlin had to admit her arrival that following week would be a welcomed change from routine.

"Thank you for helping your mommy babysit, Aylin. I promise: Kaitlin *teyze* will take you to *Kongeparken* as promised, okay?" The little girl nodded excitedly in response, causing a look of curiosity in Malin.

"She's braver at those amusement parks than her father, her Aunty dear," Sibel chuckled. "Kaitlin, thank you. Please just enjoy yourself. Everything will be fine. I'm keeping that bottle you sent warm. I'll feed her soon and we'll rock her to sleep for her nap. I cleaned

Aylin's old baby rocker twice already- no need to worry…"

"Oh, you didn't have to, Sibel, thank you," Kaitlin smiled with affection. In all honesty, Paul had been more paranoid about germs than she was. But confessing that to a seeming domestic goddess like Sibel had felt somewhat embarrassing for Kaitlin.

"Nonsense, only the best for the little princess," Sibel went on. "I'll call you in case of any emergency. But don't even think about that now. Just focus on getting some fresh air and alone time, Kaitlin. You need this."

"Thank you, lady," Kaitlin replied. "It'll be good to sit with you a bit longer when I come back to pick her up. It's been ages."

"Oh, I know, you're right, you're right," Sibel shook her head side to side. "We said we wouldn't let that happen when you moved. But life happens sometimes, doesn't it? And I can understand that, with the baby…"

"Yes, yes," Kaitlin didn't want to spend any further time on a phone call and take away from her 'me-time'. "I'll see you guys in two hours or so. And, please. Don't bother to prepare anything…"

"Oh, hush," Sibel smiled. "I'm already defrosting the *börek* I keep in the freezer for last-minute guests. You're going to take the bus back here? Are you sure you don't want Engin to pick you up? I think he gets out early today…"

"No, the bus has been perfectly fine, don't sweat it. And I am serious about the no-food part, lady." Though she adored Sibel's cheese-filled pastries, she didn't want to bother her friend with food preparation. She didn't intend to stay long, yes, but admittedly also due to Sibel being the only adult in a house with three children now. She was sure her friend- having more experience- may possibly have been better with multitasking than Kaitlin herself. And seeing her daughter's content distraction on camera, playing with the other children surrounding her, helped soothe Kaitlin's fears of Malin possibly wailing non-stop as soon

43

as she'd stepped outside of Sibel's door. Regardless, she still wanted the babysitter *du jour's* attention on Malin- as much as possible.

No need to turn my first day of alone-time into an 'uh-oh' time. "I'll see you girls, soon. Thanks a million, Sibel!" Clicking off the video call, Kaitlin inhaled the crispy fall air into her lungs and closed her eyes. She reopened them without haste, staring out into the rapid waves sparkling before her. A subtle wind almost brushed the hat she'd placed on her auburn locks- cascading now across her bosom that had grown fuller since motherhood and breastfeeding. Stretching her arms in front of her, she held on tighter to the suspense novel she'd picked up at the local *bokhandel*, enjoying the intoxicating print.

Despite the stirring wind, mere clouds had managed to be scattered across the zenith. Gazing directly into the sparkling sun for a moment without squinting- Kaitlin reveled at its majestic star quality. *Beautiful,* she thought. Motherhood had pleasantly disproved Kaitlin' fears of no longer feeling attractive in her femininity.

Still holding on with one hand to the trendy hat she'd been gifted with by Paul recently on her October birthday, Kaitlin also caught a whiff of her signature, floral perfume she'd sprayed onto her wrists before leaving home. *I need to take myself out on dates like this more often*, she chuckled behind unparted lips that were barely holding onto remnants of matte mauve lipstick for dear life.

With the exception of a couple of statuesque Norwegian women sashaying by in trendy outwear and knee-high boots, most people around her had been dressed rather casually on a weekday, she observed. Kaitlin didn't mind standing out- she'd missed dressing up, and she was going to indulge herself if this day were to count for something more than simply testing Malin with babysitting. She fastened one more button around the chest of her designer coat to protect against the breeze.

Kaitlin's eyes squinted as the sun began to lower in the sky, and she blinked rapidly back into the moment. *Forget websites and reviews.*

I could probably write an entire book or even movie script about the things I've gone through. She chuckled, caressing the ends of her hair as she peered back at her book. It was still opened to page 18. She hadn't been able to read further, and surely, she couldn't do so at home with Malin needing her attention.

The image of her daughter's heavenly smile- which could already manage to make every sleepless night and breastfeeding frustration worth it- crossed her mind just then. *What time is it?* She checked her phone. 15:30. She'd been seated leaning against the corner of the pier by Sandnes harbor- less crowded than Stavanger, but certainly no less picturesque. The smaller neighboring town had felt a tad bit more modernized than her old address to Kaitlin, lined with more residential buildings of rectangular-shaped glass windows on each floor. Even the curvy concrete sculpture her eyes traveled to just then as she was gazing at her surroundings- which Paul had told her was named *Eurytmi*- looked more modern than the numerous historical-figure statues back in Stavanger.

I hope the meager milk I was able to pump is holding up well, she thought. She'd been thanking her lucky stars that breastfeeding hadn't proved to be as difficult for her as her mother had apparently found it to be when Kaitlin herself was a baby. *Probably the first of many subsequent ways in which I would then go on to disappoint my mother.* She sighed.

Sibel had suggested eating a handful of black poppy seeds with every meal. A tradition she'd apparently picked up back in Turkey, she swore it worked wonders with her two children. Luckily her taste in international cuisine had expanded her tastebuds over the years, and Kaitlin had actually begun to crave the seeds' bitter taste.

She felt her left breast begin to throb whilst she sipped the now-cold cappuccino she'd gotten in a takeaway cup from her favorite small coffeeshop on the main *Gågaten* street. *I have to return home before they become fully engorged*, she whined to herself, closing her eyes in frustration. It'd been a wonder her and Paul hadn't walked around their new town much, as they'd once used to do in Stavanger. Parenting and slowly setting up a new home had taken up most of their time. *If all goes well today, maybe Sibel could watch Malin again, and Paul and I can have a drink out here sometime.*

Deciding to at least finish the second chapter she'd begun reading, Kaitlin focused on the novel in front of her. 'Exquisite Captive'. She'd spotted it straight away on the top shelf, after inquiring the salesclerk about the section with books written in English. It was the only copy and had been positioned face-up, while the surrounding books had been placed with only their spines visible. *This is meant for me.*

She was drawn to it, there was no question. And when she read the blurb and saw that it was about a woman jinni- she'd dashed to the cashier right away, secretly hoping it wasn't one of their registered books on file. Kaitlin felt certain in her heart that this had been no coincidence. But this time she had to admit she wanted more. Something special meant just for her to find. Placed there by a certain seducer that she continued to feel simultaneous anger and fire for.

But, alas. It hadn't been the case. *218 NOK.* It was a registered book the store was indeed selling. The young woman with a high baby-blonde ponytail had rung it up.

"Takk". After paying, Kaitlin had almost run to the coffeeshop to pick up some caffeine before heading to the seaside. Frankly more eager to devour the book than the drink this time.

Pushing aside a strand of the auburn mane that had been grazing her flushed cheeks, Kaitlin focused back to the pages placed on her thighs. She'd seated herself on one of the steps leading to the harbor basin before the newly-opened and wide, modern town hall building. She straightened a crease on her black pants and hoped they wouldn't become wrinkled any further. She couldn't bring herself to have the enthusiasm of her day be dampened with the uniform of her new, quotidian routine: her 'mom sweats', as she called her most favored navy-blue sweatsuit.

The Ifrit jinni pursuing her evanesces just outside the square of pale moonlight that shines into the center of the courtyard. Red smoke billows out around his massive body, filling the air with the scent of sulfur.

"Oww," Kaitlin jolted and stopped reading, sudden pain rigidifying the hairs on her neck. "What the…?"

A herd of seagulls dashed rapidly toward the left of her and past between two majestic private boats with tall and lean masts. Kaitlin put the book down on her lap to follow the commotion.

Nothing.

She smiled. *Maybe I shouldn't exactly be reading about his kind while alone.* Another sip of the frothy coffee eased her nerves. *It's been a year. Everything is all good. It's alright.*

Picking the book back up, Kaitlin tried to return her attention back to the words.

She couldn't.

She was staring at the page, and it had begun to somehow feel like it was staring back at her. She shivered, despite the rising intensity of the subtle burning she began to feel on her right cheek. Her thoughts traveled to the kitchen, where she'd last had the same sensation before Malin was awakened.

"Hello?" she whispered, comforted in the lack of any density of people near the docks who'd surely look at her like she was mad for talking to herself. As the brazen wind suddenly palpable across the entire right side of her body intensified whilst it blew, Kaitlin took a deep breath and closed her eyes.

She put the book down once again, and opened her eyes to face the undeniable truth now that had now materialized beside her. Upon seeing Finn sitting with his chin resting on his knees- clear as day in flesh-form, as if he'd been accompanying her the entire afternoon, Kaitlin's lack of fear threw her in for a loop. She wasn't shook, or feeling anything she could pinpoint just then, in fact.

Neutral.

Her lack of reaction was stranger to her than his appearance. His hair looked shorter than she'd remembered. The several strands of curly blond hairs, which she recalled had boyishly framed his face, were no longer there. *Do jinns get haircuts?* His piercing emerald eyes had become more subdued, and less ambitious somehow. He was wearing mostly black, just as he had that fateful day in Stavanger. She stared at his crisp, dark jeans and shoes.

"Hello, beautiful stranger," he finally spoke softly. His drawn-out, commanding yet slick smile could still be counted on to induce shivers across her spine. Any neutrality Kaitlin had initially sensed diminished the minute his evergreen eyes locked on hers, and his unique tone of voice delighted her entire being.

"Mr. Du Feu," she mirrored his smile.

§

Oslo

THE CHIPPER FEMALE VOICE AT THE OTHER END OF THE LINE SOUNDED vaguely familiar. Yet in his new life, Tan knew he had to be cautious. "Tan? You there?"

"May I ask who's calling?" he inquired.

"Oh, but it is I, your old lady from the old country," the voice answered in an exaggerated accent, followed immediately by a snort. "My *kebab*, I'm offended you haven't saved my number."

Anja could never keep serious for longer than a few seconds, Tan

48

remembered as he burst into feigned laughter. *And still manages to deride non-Norwegians.*

"Anja! Oh, my goodness, I'm so sorry. I didn't expect to hear from you. You know I've been paranoid about being found ever since you-know-who practically kicked me out all the way to here. Let me finally save it. So sorry, once again. I don't even talk on the phone much out here, to be honest. My dear friend. It's only three of us and Master, here. We mostly text when we have to, and, well, yeah. Sorry. How are you?"

"Are you finished?" Anja quipped after allowing a brief silence. "You still love to ramble on and on, I see, my dear Tan. Look. I'm telling you. I don't know about the ladies or jinnis out there in Oslo, but us women in general like calm and collected men. Come on! Relax!"

Genuinely laughing along with her now, Tan realized how much he'd missed the way things were back in the Stavanger cabin. He was thankful the only other human of the cabin had become a true enough friend to ask him how he was doing, once he'd been shunned and forced to seek refuge with Lar Iktar in Oslo. He'd never made any real friends in Trondheim, where he'd first flown to after Canada, to be closer to her. *Linette.* Tan shut his eyes as he inhaled. He was glad the lease had finally ended on his old flat and he could be rid of any ties to the memory-bomb that'd been the university town where he'd mostly continued dating her in this new country. Right up until releasing her soul from her aimless life.

Bjorn and Finn were initially not to know about his whereabouts, per Lar's instructions. And certainly not Meredith- his exporter, and ex-lover. But Nora- director of The Group's Oslo branch- was Anja's cousin, and had spilled the beans to her in exchange for a promise of discretion.

"Oh, my beauty," Tan went on with a soft chuckle. "No. No ladies. No jinnis. I've mainly been helping Master out with his research now more than recruiting. I told you the last time, too. I've got to be laying low for a while longer. I'm all work these days. You know? But enough digressing. How have you been? I've missed you!"

"Same old, same as you left it," Anja said with a sigh. "Finn's moody as always. Bjorn seems tired of me still. We haven't had someone extra to spice the energy up in the house since you left, I'm telling you..."

"Oh, you flatter me," Tan played it off as if he didn't thrive on such words. A part of him had often wondered why he and Anja couldn't have given it a go. As a real, romantic couple. Two humans. It could have made things so much simpler. Yet, homogenous couples weren't exactly welcomed by Lar. The reasoning continued to mystify him, though Lar would often brush it off as 'dangerously romanticized and ordinary' and 'unsuitable' for The Group's mission of a human and jinn community to form a chosen family. The possibility of members having children and straying from The Group to start their own core families terrified Lar, and he would become very irritable whenever any of them even casually questioned it.

Besides, Anja had always been drawn to Bjorn, and he to Meredith. *Linette.* He shooed away the forbidden name off of his mind as soon as it crossed it again. *I'm lucky*, Tan thought. Without The Group, where would he be? *What other friend- especially a woman-would treat me so kindly after knowing all the details?*

Murdering an ungrateful love- the woman he'd introduced to Lar Iktar during their on-again moments in Stavanger when she'd sometimes visit him. Master had looked into her eyes and through her soul. "She's not worthy," he'd whispered into Tan's ear, and the rest was history. Tan had listened to his directions word for word.

"How's *she*?" Tan cleared his throat. He instinctively felt the need to inquire about Meredith, though her betrayal still managed to quake his Adam's apple. *She can play the victim and the 'jaded lover'*

50

all she wants, his thoughts caused the smart phone to quiver in his hand. *But she seduced me, and then proceeded to backstab and ostracize me from the only real family I've ever known.*

Except him. Tan still said a little prayer of gratitude for Lar Iktar whenever he recalled the distraught state in which his sweaty palms had phoned him after his plane had landed in his native Istanbul. "I will not let you regress your elevation there among a family that won't understand you, lad," Lar had told him. "Wait in the lounge area for the new E-Ticket I'm about to e-mail you." *If Master hadn't saved me after Mer's betrayal, I don't know what would have become of me, had I not been able to remain in Norway.* Tan had long overstayed his student visa, and had only had an inside connection of Lar's to thank for it being extended. *He understood. Once again in my life, he didn't judge. Lar doesn't judge.*

"She's- you know- just being Meredith," Anja gabbled. "Same old bore. Spending more time on those books than concentrating on her tasks. Look, I'll get to the chase, Tan..."

Anja sounded more serious than he could ever remember her being in recent memory. "I just wanted to give you a heads up. A man came asking for you."

Tan pulled himself upright on the soft lounge chair. *Ah, siktir,* he cursed in his mind. *The murder.* "A man?" he stammered, making sure to lower his voice as he peeked a glance toward the door. He didn't want Lar or Nora to overhear; no one in the suite had exactly been too comfortable with the topic. He knew their fourth suitemate- his athletic roommate, Stig- to have luckily been out on a run. "A cop? A detective?"

"No. I don't think so," Anja went on. "I mean, none of us said anything, not to worry. He said he is, well, *was* Linette's father. Didn't cause any trouble. Just inquired if Meredith knew anything. I just thought you should know. We've got to watch out for each other amongst them, you know. In case...I don't know..."

51

John Walker. "Does he have something solid?" Tan panicked. "Does he know where I am? How did he even know about the cabin?"

"Not sure, my kebab," Anja's voice sounded relaxed with the removal of the news as weight on her shoulders. "I think Mer said something about him mentioning your old roommate before The Group. That other Turkish guy…What was his name?"

Damn it! "I knew I should have been tougher on that Serdar when I told him to leave me alone after my initiation!" Tan mustered all the strength he could not to smash the smartphone against the wall.

"Tan!" Anja tried on the other end. "Tan? Are you there? Calm down! Please. What does it matter? I don't think he meant anything bad by it. Did your old roommate even know what played out between you and Linette?"

"I hope not. I mean, I don't think he did," Tan placed the phone back onto his ear. He had told everyone he knew from his old life not to contact him anymore. That he'd wanted to start fresh, living in the woods after things had 'soured for good' with Linette.

"You see?" Anja asked in a sing-song voice. "He probably thought your information was needed as a *witness* in your ex-girlfriend's case- not as a suspect."

The cyanide. Tan knew he'd left his old place messy in his haste. He'd left behind the extra tubes of the material he'd obtained from Lar to use in injecting the needle into Linette's neck. Along with a framed photograph of him and his sister as kids in Turkey, from what else he could recall.

Tan had contemplated going back to retrieve his remaining things, but ultimately couldn't bring himself to revisit where he'd last watched Linette collapse into his arms, eyes wide open in shock. *She was actually kind to me while it lasted,* he recalled. The treatment of his father had become intolerable before he'd gone off to Canada. Yet his mother's silent acceptance would somehow always pain him more. *Linette actually loved me. Until her rich-girl transformation, at least.*

Tan had gone straight to the cabin for refuge upon his return to Stavanger once he'd buried his girlfriend. Later cursing himself for forgetting to pack any incriminating evidence in his old room, along with the most essential items that had already been loaded into his oversized backpack. Lar had assured him not to worry about it. Serdar had been out of town that night from what he knew- but could his old roommate have kept his old things to give to the police?

The night of his last dinner with Linette painted a slew of colors across the jumbled canvas that had become his mind since the incident. Tan had later told Serdar that he'd found solace in the woods, and instructed him to 'throw out everything' in his old room. Had he done so?

"Hello?" Anja's impatient voice brought him back from his rumination. "Earth to Tan…."

"Sorry," Tan shook his head. "I'm thinking. What if Serdar had secret cameras installed in our place, Anja? Or returned early, and watched the whole thing. I'm not an idiot. Her body left no traces of blood or anything. The needle was perfect. The truck has since been rid of. But maybe he secretly took pictures of us as she collapsed in my arms…"

"My kebab!" Anja's laughter surprised him. "You've watched too many movies, I'm afraid. If Serdar indeed had any, he would have given such evidence to the police a long time ago, wouldn't he?"

"My life is like a movie already," Tan attempted a snicker despite still trembling. "Romantic adventure overseas, turned thriller. You never know, Anja. You never know."

CHAPTER 6

Sandnes

KAITLIN WAS STILL STUNNED BY THE RELATIVE ease of seeing him again. Like an old friend from school she'd just run into downtown. Where the events that had taken place the previous winter were all merely but a dream. Since she'd become a mother, things had been feeling subdued and safer somehow. Kaitlin had even begun to aspire to filling-up more holes in her life by taking on additional roles on top of the one of 'wife': not only as a mom, but with freelance gigs as well.

Translating documents for some paper business, my ass, she would often sneer when alone with her thoughts of Finn. *The world is growing greener by the minute- soon enough, no one's even going to use their environmentally-wasteful business anymore. And then what will Finn do? What excuse will he contrive to lure women then- logging wood to create animal shelters?*

She'd promised herself long ago to forgive herself and accept everything she was feeling. Like the butterflies she'd had each time her mind wandered to such random thoughts of *him* over the past year- even while criticizing The Group's professional values in her head. That fluttering grew only more rampant in her entire being now that they were finally face-to-face.

"Long time no see," Kaitlin said coyly. "Well, visually anyway…"

"Dreams don't count?" Finn retorted with a wink, causing Kaitlin to chuckle softly through crimsoning cheeks. Despite the passage of months, Kaitlin still couldn't distinguish whether her skin flushed due to her shyness or if he'd been able to heat it with desire. *Maybe it's simply that fire energy his kind is created from,* she reasoned in her mind.

"I don't know about dreams," Kaitlin continued, fiddling with the book in her hands. "But I guess new home visits are open to interpretation. You could have dropped off a housewarming gift, you know. A box of chocolates perhaps?"

"Home visits?" Finn's puzzled look surpassed a similar one given by a nearby seagull, eyeing them hungrily for any leftovers.

"Or better yet, you could at least have sent your warm wishes on a post-it note, since I believe that seemed to be more your style..." Kaitlin was on a roll, crossing her arms across her chest. "Speaking of post-it explained animal abductions- where's Bo?"

"Miss Kaitlin; even after all this time, you are assuming things," Finn closed his eyes and shook his head side to side. "Bo is at the cabin- playful as ever. Taking him was merely insurance, not a threat to his life. You know, it's a pity. I would have thought the smaller-condo lifestyle in Sandnes would have relieved your anxiety condition somehow..."

"No food here, birdie. Sorry," Kaitlin forced her attention to the gray-streaked white beauty waddling on webbed feet before her on the promenade. "Just coffee."

"Nonsense," Finn retorted, as a pair of poofy buns- goldened, as if oven-fresh- were displayed on his outstretched palm toward the bird. The seagull fearlessly grabbed one before abruptly taking flight. "We must always nourish the animal world where we can. Animals are always sensitive to my kind. And, unlike many humans, we respect them tremendously."

"Wow, Finn, you're its hero," Kaitlin chortled. Extra loud to disguise the rumbling of her stomach just then. Cardamom buns were one of the few local treats she'd grown to love over the past two years.

A second seagull who'd noticed the handouts soon became accompanied by a third and fourth one, as they all gawked at one another competitively, still circling Finn's palm.

"Look at that, Ms. Kaitlin," Finn smiled at her. "It's in all our natures to fight for what we want- with success particularly achieved if we also *need* it."

Kaitlin had grown accustomed to such philosophical quotes on life from Finn. *Is he still trying to initiate me or something?* She'd read up, after all, not only on jinns. but various fraternities and organizations she'd found to have some features in common with The Group. She returned Finn's emerald-gaze with a smile, despite her trepidations.

"I didn't know jinns could materialize *hveteboller* out of thin air."

"Oh, is that what that book you're reading claims about us, now?" It was Finn's turn to snicker, reaching toward the book now on Kaitlin's lap. "Let me take a look at this thing. May I?"

"Not so fast," Kaitlin teased, hiding the book behind her. "No more secrets. First, explain the buns to me. Now!" Finn's raised brow couldn't be ignored. "*Vær så snill? S'il te plaît?* Please?" she added, throwing in a toothy smile for good measure. Which language was Finn most confident speaking, anyway?

"First of all, *mon Dieu*! It seems you've mastered some things since I saw you last, Ms. Kaitlin! Your simultaneous usage of Norsk, French and English is impressive!" Finn chuckled excitedly. "I've always told you how your brightness enhances your beauty."

"Thank you," Kaitlin replied, holding the ends of her trench coat with a fake courtesy. *Oh, God, this must look so cheesy sitting down.* "You know, I'm, uh, even increasing a little Turkish on the side from my friend back in Stavanger. I actually read this article on globalization and the translingual movement…"

The silence that ensued Kaitlin divulging a random fact about her life began to feel more awkward than the seagull that was still encircling them, hopeful for more snacks.

"Okay, lady polyglot, that's very cool," Finn finally spoke, his slick smile hadn't left its place. "Lean closer. I'm going to tell you our little secret to food manifestations. Now, are you ready?" Finn whispered excitedly. "Maybe you'd even like to share this secret with the author of whatever book this is. They may use it in a sequel or something. So, listen now…"

Kaitlin rolled her eyes, but obliged with titillation. *No surprise.* She inched close enough to notice his scruff had also diminished along with his longer hair, making him appear handsome in a completely different way. *Do jinns shave?*

"Here it is…our secret," Finn started, the warmth of his breath lingered in foggy form on the corners of his plump lips as he spoke. "I was hungry on the way here, and had a couple of buns from home wrapped in a napkin in my pocket…"

He unwrapped two more buns from a white napkin in his right pocket whilst laughing in his distinct, gargantuan way. Kaitlin felt the cool sea breeze enter into her mouth through her dropped jaw.

"Oh, you think this is funny, do you?" Kaitlin asked in a stern way she couldn't prolong for longer than ten seconds before chuckling herself. "Okay, okay, you got me. Yes, I remember. You eat. But you don't always materialize in flesh as you have now, do you? And it's interesting the seagulls see you and your provisional hand. I recall a certain ball a little over a year ago, where you'd made a surprise appearance, and I'd been the only one really to see you in your tuxedo. Oh, and, just how do you nourish yourself in your natural form?"

"Animals can see what many humans cannot, Ms. Kaitlin," Finn explained. He looked to Kaitlin as if he were enjoying himself with her questions. "I was blessed that you were one of those who could see us. Oh, and, what was that last one? Nourishment? We're not picky- we can fulfill our natural forms with pretty much anything from nature."

"Alright," Kaitlin nodded slowly, biting her lip. "I'll accept that. For now. Where did you even get these buns?"

"Oh, but don't you know, Miss Kaitlin?" Finn opened his arms wide after taking a bite. "I'm a creature of outlaw. I must have shoplifted, mustn't I?"

Kaitlin froze in silence. For what felt like an entire minute or so before Finn erupted in laughter once again.

"Miss Kaitlin, you continue to amuse me," he smiled warmly now. "I told you, I brought them from home. We like to bake, if you recall. We live as you humans- in every way- only on a different dimension that most people don't see. That's all. You really think I'm some terrible being? After everything? And especially after I've kept my promise?"

"No, Finn, "Kaitlin pulled all her hair on one side down her shoulder after a sudden burst of wind had dashed all the strands around her face. "I'm sorry. It's not that. I know. I'm just still so curious, as you know. I mean, even this book...I thought it may somehow shed a light. I felt I may have even seen it in the store because of something other than pure coincidence. I even thought that maybe you...you know..."

"Yes?" Finn encouraged. "Have a bun, will you? I promise it's good. Look at the seagulls- have you seen any drop dead back down to the sea yet? It's safe. Here...you poor, hungry thing."

"Thank you," Kaitlin didn't know whether it was trust or her extreme sudden hunger overcoming any trepidation, but she gobbled the bun in Finn's outstretched palm up after just two bites. "This is delicious. Did you make it?"

"Mer..." Finn started blankly off into the distance, his visage facing the sea.

"Oh, of course," Kaitlin nodded. "She liked baking; I remember. You know, she congratulated me right after Malin was born. But I haven't really talked to her since. How has she been?"

"Everyone's fine, Ms. Kaitlin," Finn's voice shifted. "I think I preferred your curiosity about our hair-trimming habits…"

His added wink wasn't a surprise. His capture of the question in her mind upon seeing him shouldn't have been either. Kaitlin ogled her wedge-heeled suede boots. *Wait a minute,* she thought just then.

"Cat got your tongue?" Finn intensified his liquid green optics on her hazel ones. "What is it?"

Cat. Cat. For some reason, his cat reference was reminding Kaitlin of something she couldn't then quite place her finger on. At the moment, something he'd mentioned about the book she was reading took precedence over the rest of her questions.

"How did you know I was reading a book about your kind?" Kaitlin asked softly, tilting her head to the side. Her eyes began to squint upon gazing at Finn's face. She couldn't tell whether it was the setting sun- or the brightness around his face- that had been affecting her eyes more.

"Oh, let's just say I've been sitting next to you for a tad bit longer than from the time you finally sensed me," Finn highlighted his short-length reference by uniting his thumb and index finger. *Adorable, only second to his youthful smile*, Kaitlin thought.

"Red is definitely your color, by the way, Ms. Kaitlin. Distinct. I remember your coat when we first met near the cabin. Your hat today almost matches that same shade…"

"Thank you," Kaitlin blushed before attempting a quirky retort. "I'm *red* with your flattery."

"Not just any red," Finn's intense gaze maintained its hold. "This shade in particular becomes you. Cardinal. Like the Sin…"

Kaitlin was taken aback by the sincerity she could construe on his face. Staring into his eyes a good moment longer than intended, she was swimming in his forest-green pool once more. *And your eyes are comforting, inviting.*

"Now, go on, please, with your book store experience," Finn said, smiling right as Kaitlin completed her thought. Had he read her mind again? He didn't clarify.

"You were saying, Miss Kaitlin? You thought it wasn't coincidence that you saw the book?"

"Oh, well, yes," Kaitlin cleared her throat. "I felt like you may have placed it on the shelf, with its cover facing me- just to entice me, or something. You know. So I could go to it and see it was about the jinn realm. So that I may buy it and...and..."

"...Let me see this thing," Finn interrupted in a monotone voice. From his tone, Kaitlin couldn't pinpoint any answers that could possibly answer the millions of questions still burning inside of her. "Hmm. The title doesn't exactly say 'All about my jinn lover' or anything," Finn smirked suggestively, moving his eyebrows up and down. "How would I have somehow 'made' you- as you imply- drawn to it?"

"Are you serious?" Kaitlin shook her head with an eyeroll. "Oh, I'm sorry. But, didn't someone tell me once that there was 'no such thing as coincidence'?" She tried her best to impersonate his voice.

"You remember well, Miss Kaitlin," Finn smiled once again, plopping the book on the wooden space between their legs, their bodies separated only by centimeters. "I don't believe it was a coincidence, either. For certain. It just wasn't planned by me, this time. I'm serious."

"No? So, you haven't somehow been following me again after all this time, and didn't just happen to appear next to me right as I'd begun reading a novel about your kind?" Kaitlin raised an eyebrow at him, tucking in a strand of fallen hair on her face underneath her hat. "Who would have planned it, then?"

"God," Finn responded matter-of-factly. "He's created all of us. He must have wanted this additional connection to bind us together."

"Finn...please," Kaitlin closed her eyes, suddenly urged to eye her surroundings once again. Surely enough, an elderly man with a cane was seated on a bench near her corner of the dock, eyeing her curiously. *He wouldn't call the cops on me, would he? What harm could a woman seemingly talking to herself cause?* Kaitlin smiled at him sheepishly with a nod, anyway, just in case.

"Hey, more people talk to themselves than you'd think," Finn softly nudged her shoulder with his own. "And they're not all what society calls 'crazy', nor do they all necessarily have a jinn lover…"

I seriously need to control my thoughts around him. "Friend, Finn," Kaitlin turned her attention back onto his emerald gaze, clearing her throat as she emphasized the word. "Special friend, maybe. But, nonetheless-friends. We are not lovers…"

"Ok, Ms. Kaitlin. Calm down," Finn started, throwing back his head. "You're still a ball of fire, I see…"

"Can you blame me?" Kaitlin said, attempting to sound as confident as she could muster. "I mean, it's kind of funny. I often remember last year- when you told me that our meeting was no 'coincidence'. Little did I know at the time- of course- that it indeed was ordained. But more because of The Group's attempt to seek some twisted, indirect vengeance for Linette's murder. I'm still disgusted, by the way. I'm simply appalled, Finn, at the idea that Tan is still out there and…."

"Ms. Kaitlin, please," Finn started. "Let's not talk about all the baggage from last year, now. You don't know as much as you think you do. Keep drinking your coffee. Okay? I'm not here to discuss all that."

He turned his frame back out toward the sea, just as a strong breeze pushed him toward the bench again. "I should have obliged your curiosity about my hair and facial scruff when I had the chance, before this conversation took this unnecessary turn."

"Why are you here, then?" Kaitlin slumped her shoulders with a vehement sigh, wrapping her arms around her body. *That night, Finn. Are we ever going to get to the night Paul came in through the door, right after I thought it'd been him who had already come in and made love to me? Am I mad? Was it really all a nightmare? Or fantasy?*

"Hey, this wind cuts strong and it's not even winter yet," Kaitlin went on upon noticing Finn's silence- as well as the rest of his body. His dark jeans were only a shade or two different from his black wool coat. "You're not even wearing a scarf- aren't you cold? Isn't your human body cold, at least?" Kaitlin found herself asking.

"I only grow cold off of forcibly-frozen statements, Miss Kaitlin," Finn winked. "I know you're warmer than this guard that you've still got up. Oh, by the way- Bjorn is good at hair-trims. In case you were still curious. We tend to help each other out with services for our own. Don't really feel the need to waste energy to manifest our body forms for barbershops and the such. Depending on our forms, we…"

"Finn" Kaitlin responded, stern-voiced. "I appreciate the jinn lecture- because, you're right, I'm admittedly still very curious. But- too late! My mind is already on 'the baggage of last year', as you've put it. I'm sure you can tell. So, what happened? What really happened, Finn?"

"The beautiful night you're thinking of was not exactly the baggage I was referring to, Miss Kaitlin," Finn cusped her chin with his searing fingers, allowing a tear that had formed in the duct close to Kaitlin's eye corner to finally set itself free across her cheekbone. "And you know it was real, by the way. You don't even need to question yourself…"

Was that a tone of sadness she'd picked up in his voice? "Finn, I'm sorry. But I still can't process so many things. And I can't ignore them anymore either, now that I have you here in front of me. I really need to get this off my chest. I haven't been able to talk to anybody about this. Can't you see? It's been eating me up inside."

"I know. I know, my darling." Finn muttered, releasing his grip from her face.

No, Kaitlin thought as she closed her eyes. *Please don't call me that. That's Paul's word. Allow him that. That's only his.* "I have to ask. Why *now*? You always discussed nature and how it somehow empowers you. We're by the sea now, which of course, yes, is nature as well, and you've got me alone out here. But how are you so comfortably materializing before me? There are people around…"

"Are there…?" Finn winked. Kaitlin surveyed the harbor to momentarily see absolutely no one. Once again, like that day in the woods, she felt as if she were in a time warp.

"Umm, right…," Kaitlin looked around them to notice that suddenly it truly seemed as if the two of them were the only ones sitting on the wooden stairs. Had an event begun at the hall? Where had the decent-sized crowd suddenly disappeared off to?

"Mankind becomes especially limited in the five senses the further they are from nature," Finn lectured in a serious tone. "Humans cannot reach their full potential without allowing nature to seep through every cell of their being and expand their capacities."

"Right," Kaitlin nodded blankly. "Finn, look, I've been trying so much to be strong for Malin, as you can imagine. And I've still got to many lingering questions that I'm not even sure, to be honest, I could handle it right now, were they to be answered. And…"

"Shh," Finn caressed her hair softly, and Kaitlin was butter. "I know baby, I know. It's okay. It's okay…"

"That's another thing," Kaitlin dismissed, allowing her better judgement to trump over her affected soul. "Please don't call me these things. Especially not out here- in public- like this." Kaitlin eyed her surroundings once again. If she were melting- she'd just have to solidify, and fast.

A couple of teenagers passed by just then, allowing Kaitlin to let out a sigh of relief. They didn't appear to be paying much attention to them, or even to her, at least. The old man- however- was suddenly in sight once again. Still staring at her. *If it's just him thinking I'm talking to myself- whatever. He'll just have to do.*

"No one can see me, remember?" Finn shook his head, gauging the area himself. "Maybe a few can, but it's rare. No one around here much today, anyway. It's actually why I wanted to see you. I never want to bother you with the husband, as promised. And it is certainly never my intention to scare you with Malin. But, my goodness, Miss Kaitlin. You've been a hard woman to catch alone lately!"

"How about during my pregnancy..." Kaitlin asked assuredly, recalling a strange dream she'd had which she'd mostly chosen to maintain buried inside her subconscious. "Sibel's told me that..."

"Oh, no, there goes that whistleblower's name, again," Finn sneered. "What did she tell you about us this time?"

Part of Kaitlin had wanted nothing more than interview him for the longest time. Like a teenager excited to ask a whole slew of questions to the star quarterback for the high school newspaper. "Do jinns really like to-umm, well- frequent pregnant women when they're alone?"

"It depends," Finn responded comfortably. "Procreation is of immense importance for our kind. Humans have made it rather difficult for us to thrive on this planet as our ancestors were once able to do. Our population isn't what it once used to be. So, when a woman is pregnant, and especially in the later stages of her pregnancy, we're lit up. It's easier for us to observe the miracle of life without distractions around the mother. So, yes, some of us have indeed taken a fascination with studying the beautiful embryos great God has helped form in the uterus. The process of childbearing is different among us, so we're particularly intrigued. It's truly nothing short of a miracle: the miracle of life."

Kaitlin was befuddled, nodding as Finn spoke. Somehow, she'd have thought it would be a sensitive subject for him. *Malin.*

"That is a beautiful way you've coined it," Kaitlin smiled. She checked her watch. "And speaking of miracles, Malin is with Sibel and

I need to breastfeed rather soon. This is embarrassing, but I'm engorged and…"

"I think I get the hint," he chuckled. "But, hey, I'm glad you've enjoyed my discourse, Miss Kaitlin. You've evolved into a better student."

"Finn, come on, you were no teacher," Kaitlin rolled her eyes, despite being unable to repress the smile inherently forming at the corners of her mouth.

"Wasn't I?" he winked.

"You were my *friend*. Someone I met in the woods; I would hardly call our discussions 'lessons'. I never joined The Group. Those- uh, discussions- weren't really my thing."

"Ouch! There you go again with that word. 'Friend'. You're breaking my heart, Miss Kaitlin."

"Well, I'm sorry," Kaitlin exclaimed. "But *lover* certainly isn't an appropriate word, either, Mr. Du Feu! Especially since I am…And I never knowingly, or willingly, you know…Anyway."

"We both kept our promises," Finn drilled his gaze into her. "You didn't foolishly go to the cops. We all left you alone. Though, of course, doing that last part apparently has been the hardest for me…"

"Well, leaving someone 'alone' is also a relative term, I suppose," Kaitlin remarked more calmly now, taking a sip of her now unpleasantly-cold drink. She felt flabbergasted at how they'd seemingly been able to make chit chat about everything over the past 10 minutes or so, except the elephant in the room. An adorable little baby one named 'Malin', to be exact.

"Malin…." Finn interrupted dreamily. "You've given her a beautiful name, by the way. A beautiful name befitting a beautiful daughter, from her beautiful mother. You've been doing an amazing job…"

Damn it, Kaitlin cursed herself. *My thoughts.* "I mean- thank you, for leaving Paul and I alone in terms of, showing yourself or anything like that but…Finn…what *about her*? I can feel you; you know? I sense that energy, and I see her smiling."

"She's got the most disarming smile," Finn was gazing into the sea.

"At first, I told myself- she's a baby. She could literally be amused by the littlest things," Kaitin went on. "A glimmer of light reflecting on the wall, a flower or the shadow of the branches outside of our window. But gradually it all became too much…too consistent."

"She loves it when I make these rapidly-changing funny faces…" Finn chimed in. "This one's her favorite."

"Finn…" Kaitlin whimpered, feeling tears forming right at the edge of her eyeballs. She couldn't help but smile at Finn's tongue sticking out, his eyes opened like saucers.

"A promise is a promise. I told you. Until you call out to me, I do not appear. But, once or twice, I admit I couldn't help but sneak a peek. At the miracle."

"Ok, I don't think I can handle any more of this," Kaitlin waved her hand dismissively. "I thought I was maybe ready to discuss some things, like *that night*, but…"

"I told you. That night was the most beautiful night of my life, Ms. Kaitlin," Finn said with a smile, extending his hand near her chin, then softly dropping it back onto his lap.

"I felt…well, not in that moment, but when I realized what had happened…Finn, I felt violated!" Kaitlin asserted in a near-whisper.

"Whoa! Slow down there, Miss Canada. What are you talking about?" Finn shook his head as he waved her to stop with outstretched palms. "Violated?"

"Yes!" Kaitlin's screamed in a whisper. "What do you call it? I mean, there I am. In bed. I think my husband has come and…and…naturally I allow him to be with me…and… we fall asleep.

66

And…and…I wake up to see him come through the door, as he says, for the first time that night, and, and…"

"Kaitlin!" Finn grabbed her shoulders, inching his imploring expression closer to her face. "Please, don't deceive yourself! I simply manifested in flesh form for you when you were alone that evening. I couldn't take it anymore. To leave you alone, after our connection, without a proper goodbye to do this love justice. And you had already welcomed me prior to that for me to even be able to do so. But I didn't pretend to be Paul or anything…. we have no such magic tricks. Just like your assumptions about those buns today. You likely saw whatever you wanted to see. You knew perfectly well it was me, as far as I was concerned…"

"Finn, stop," Kaitlin begged. She looked around to see a young woman shoot her a creeped out look as she jogged on by. The old man was no longer sitting on the bench. *Just what does he mean? I 'welcomed' him?*

"When good old Mr. Maverick devised his oh-so-genius plan of relocating to somehow improve your lives…Away from the cabin. Away from us. Did he really think distance could make me forget about you? Make me not show myself after your soul calls out to me?"

His mocking tone was nothing compared to the spew of anger blazing in his eyes. Kaitlin had to admit she was beginning to feel fear.

"Do you think it would have pleased me to see the woman I …to see you in privacy with your damn husband?" Finn turned his eyes away from her and out toward the sea again.

"I wouldn't know. I mean, you guys- ahem- frequent other couples during your cabin activities, don't you?" Kaitlin shot back, standing up to face him.

Finn didn't respond. Yet his silence was thunder loud in heaviness. *Oh, shoot, I don't even have metal on me.*

"You've already offended me, and now you're back to offending

The Group once again, I see." Finn bit his lip and sat back down on the dock. "I'm not going to hurt you. I would have thought you would have realized that, by now. You don't need a damned flashlight or knife or whatever else you think. Those things just irk us- not scare or harm us. You still don't trust me? Forget it. I don't even know why I bother…"

"Finn, please…" *Wait a minute.* Had Finn almost just said that he loved her? *Did he just nearly refer to me as 'the woman he loves'? Of course, I had to ruin the moment with my rebuttals.* Kaitlin knew she'd always had a way of letting her mouth get the best of her. Before consulting even momentarily with her heart or even her logical mind.

"All I meant was: I was seeking hints. Crumbs. Any indication I could that you felt it too. Our connection. That this wasn't one-sided on my part. And that it wasn't just a fleeting dash of naïve, extra-marital excitement on yours. That you may have wanted to move to Sandnes- where I told you I was from- because it was close enough to Stavanger. That you'd wanted to be somewhere where our paths would cross…That you feel these things, as well…."

"Finn…this is deluging. I can't even hear myself think…."

"Then perhaps, don't think, Miss Kaitlin," Finn stared intensely into her childlike expression. "I've always told you. Overthinking separates us from the animals, and allows us to experience less joy in the moment. Look, the other day… when you called out to me…"

"I…. did…what!?"

"You spoke my name," Finn continued. "At your place. You called for me. I wasn't following you like some stalker you must watch in the movies. I merely sensed it, Miss Kaitlin. And that was my permission, by nature. My sign. But, it's okay. Forget it. I'm not going to be a fool again…"

"Is that why I get burning goosebumps when you're near…I flush around my chest, and my neck feels…"

Finn shrugged. "Your earthly being feels as such, I suppose. It's funny. I don't feel anything different when I'm around my kind in my human-manifested form. But, it doesn't matter now. You ask me about that night- but I could ask you the same thing. You allowed it. But I see now I was just a being to add a little spice to your marriage, apparently."

The heartbroken disappointment discernable on Finn's visage felt genuine to Kaitlin. "I thought you were Paul!"

Finn raised an eyebrow and smiled confidently. "Okay."

"I absolutely thought it was Paul!" Kaitlin insisted louder. *Who am I trying to convince?* "And no- you weren't some extra marital excitement, or whatever," she continued with a stammer. "But what do you want from me? I'm not a woman who is built to have some sort of affair! This isn't right. On *so* many levels. Look at me. I'm in downtown Sandnes, talking to myself."

"Everyone talks to themselves sometimes, Ms. Kaitlin," Finn opined.

"If my new neighbors see me, forget making new friends."

"It's alright," Finn added. "You've got me, as your 'friend', right? A friend you can call on to appear before you whenever you're bored, I guess."

"Finn…I didn't mean…"

"Keep reading your book, Ms. Kaitlin. Or, better yet, just go! Malin needs her mom," Finn's gaze at the ocean rather than on Kaitlin's pleading eyes pained the very pit of her stomach. "Go feed her. I'm serious. She's more important than this fight…"

"Finn..." Kaitlin uttered through a single falling tear, smearing her mascara. The rollercoaster of emotions ranging from anger and disgust to infatuation and affinity were stirred up instantly in her-following the retraction of his pursuit. She cursed the frailty of the borders around her heart. Regardless, she blurted out the unrehearsed and unfiltered scream from somewhere in the depth of her very core.

"I feel it, too!"

CHAPTER 7

Oslo

WITH THE GLARE FROM THE CITY LIGHTS STILL reflecting on his sunglasses, Tan Kuvvet was grateful for their superpower of hiding his tears well into dusk. He inhaled the aroma of *kaffee* filling the busy streets downtown, eyeing the second of the only two tall buildings in the otherwise historic city. *Posthuset.* He couldn't yet muster up the strength to enter the commercial building where Lar Iktar had bought two large suites next to each other: one for personal use and the other for his writing and meetings.

I'm weak, he thought. *It's a miracle I haven't yet been banished from The Group.* If his father back in Turkey could see him now, crying like a little girl since the sin. Since he'd taken Linette's life, and cursed his own. He'd likely hand him to the police with his own bare hands. "Maybe prison can man you up," he'd say. Tan was sure of it.

Lar Iktar had already witnessed his teary state far too many times, as far as Tan was concerned. He'd gotten the feeling of no longer being Master's favorite recruiter- his once favorite disciple.

He's not even sending me out to recruit the ladies as Stig has been doing, Tan thought with melancholy, his roommate's muscular arms and slicked-back dark mane crossing his mind. Walking circles around a small fountain where locals and tourists had thrown in wishful coins, Tan gazed at the sky. He knew he couldn't keep being a personal assistant and doing paperwork forever. Lar already had Nora for most of that.

Master had enough on his plate: keeping a full-pledged business running, aside from publishing his philosophical bestsellers and organizing the recruitment of disciples. He was undoubtedly going to be annoyed that many of the close calls that could potentially jeopardize The Group's existence were seemingly stemming from Tan as of late.

Soon enough he'll realize he's got no use for me here. If I can't be utilized to entice new members like Stig, and of course- like Bjorn and Finn back in Stavanger. He'd already helped Tan keep up the rent on his first studio in Norway back in Trondheim through the end of his lease. It had certainly come in handy on the night of Linette's murder. Tan had indeed hidden out there to rest for the entire day after burying her. Lar had supported him every step of the way to his enlightenment. Tan was sure his Master's sympathy must have been running thin.

And now this. As if it weren't enough that whatever strength he'd had left, he'd managed to muster it to move on after Linette in Stavanger- and Meredith had pulled it from him like a rug from underneath his feet.

Linette's secret father-dear had now apparently come to Norway looking for answers. *Okay, so Linette wasn't having an affair. But she did betray me. I was never enough, and was never going to be enough. Even if I didn't send her off with the angels like I did. If it hadn't been John, it would surely have been one rich man or another soon enough.*

Tan could never let down his defenses. Even with Meredith. *It wasn't supposed to be anything serious with her. Yet look how she betrayed me too? How can I trust her to not join Walker and turn me in to the authorities?*

"Lad, aren't you going to come into the building?" Lar's deep and comforting voice awoke Tan from his self-pity. When had he come outside? He strolled over and took a seat at the edge of the fountain, apparently unconcerned that his black blazer and matching pants would get wet in doing so.

"Master, good evening! Let's go in. I'm sorry, I was distracted," Tan sat next to him. He straightened out his own blue suit- casually unbuttoned, and revealing a white shirt unfastened near his neck to reveal a golden chain. Tan knew Lar appreciated it whenever he put on his latest birthday present from him. *He's so good to me. Why couldn't my father have been like him?*

"Relax, lad," Lar chuckled. "You know? I never really got into those substances some of our family in The Group enjoy at the gatherings, but maybe it would calm you to snort some…"

"No, Master, no," Tan shook his head with a chortle. "I've been trouble enough. I don't want to add potential addictions that would jeopardize our missions, and your patience, any further…"

"Tan? Look at me. Look at me, lad!" Lar grabbed Tan by the chin, placing the Ray Ban shades off of his face and onto his own lap. He tilted his face to gaze straight into his eyes. "Get a hold of yourself."

"I'm a murderer! I'm a murderer, Master!" Tan groaned in a whisper. "And they're coming for me. Like I knew they would! They're coming for me!"

"I told you I was never to hear that word again!" He lifted his forefinger and held it in front of Tan's face. "Who? Who's coming for you?"

"Linette's father, Master. He knows," Tan noticed a little boy eating ice cream, eyeing him inquisitively as he walked past them with an elderly lady holding his hand. He was hoping they were of the rarer Oslo citizens who didn't also understand too much English. "He must. Why else would he be in Norway now asking about me? He must have found something. Or her mom. Or the police. He knows. They know. They're going to take me away, Master! I knew I couldn't run from punishment for too long! I don't want to go to jail!"

"Hey, look at me!" Lar's pitch-dark eyes were lost in Tan's tearful brown ones. "No one here is going to jail! Not on my watch, you hear me?" he continued softly, caressing his cheek as he wiped away a falling teardrop. "I promised you I wouldn't let anything bad happen to you. You are so close. So close to reaching your full awareness. Your even bigger purpose. You are safe here. Now, come on. Let's go inside."

§

TWO MEN HOLDING HANDS DARTED SMILES AT THEM IN conversation, right before showing their IDs to enter the building; it had been yet another sign, Lar Iktar knew. *All couples can recognize true love when they spot it- fellow romantics like us, destined for one another.*

It pained him to his very core every time he had to caress Tan's cheek or playfully rub his shoulder to ease his nerves, when all Lar wanted to do was look him in the eye, confess his feelings and kiss him passionately. *Not the time,* Lar thought as they all rode the elevator. *Not yet. He hasn't recognized his grand purpose. He's not ready. I must hold back.*

"After you…" Lar ushered Tan into their suite after unlocking the digital security system with the card in his hand.

Who the hell was this father looking for Tan? Lar mentally noted to check the camera he'd had set up at the Cabin; he hadn't been keeping up as much as he should have lately.

"Nora, did you check the footage of that cabin visitor?" Lar called out. Nora unlocked herself from an embrace with Stig as the two had been sitting side by side by the shiny, oval table. "In Stavanger?"

"Welcome, Master," she stammered, smoothing out her skirt as she stood up. "Umm, not yet. Anja's told Tan. Linette's father. Goes by the name: John Walker. I just assumed he'd be some regular older man…"

"I'll be the judge of that, Nora!" Lar barked, pounding his first on the table.

"Yes, Master," Nora gulped.

"I say we just get rid of the old goon, too," Stig muttered with a smirk, biting off half of his banana. "I don't even think it's worth us contemplating so much over."

"Cut it out, Stig!" Nora punched his arm softly, flipping back a strand of her coiffed, white-blond hair with purple acrylic nails. "We are not hitmen. Murder isn't up to humans or jinns. Life is given by God and hence can only be taken by Him. You very well know that…"

Stig cleared his throat with a glance in Tan's direction, and Nora halted her citing of one of Lar's 50 maxims he'd outlined in his debut book, 'Atlas for the Meaningful Life'. "Tan is not a murderer, Stig," she shrugged.

"It's okay, Nora," Tan began munching on crackers and cheese, staring at the table with slumped shoulders. "Stig's right to think what he's implying. I did murder my ex-girlfriend. No other way around it. I'll be paying for it. I know it. I just do. No matter how much I try to repent through aiding Master's mission…."

"You're both ignoring the latter part of the 32nd maxim, guys!" Nora was adamant. "Removal of life to ease suffering is justified by…"

"That's enough!" Lar pounded his fist on the iron table twice in a row this time, causing a vase with fresh peonies to quiver. "This is not the time to talk about the difficulties Tan has had to face while inching closer to his mission. Or even about what had to happen to that young woman. Because of her own foolishness. Her own inability to be satisfied in life…"

"Yes, Master. I apologize," Stig glared down at the oriental carpeting.

"Besides," Lar continued. "We have more important business to take care of. Namely, Linette Peterson's father. My sweet Nora here is right about one thing. Murdering the man is out of the question."

Nora beamed proudly as she returned Lar's head tilting in her direction.

"Do not forget that all living things deserve a chance," Lar went on. "A chance to prove themselves worthy, even after they've wronged someone on *the path*. Linette, sadly, could not do so. But we do not know her father personally. Perhaps he can be redeemed. All we know about him so far is he is some businessman from Canada who's simply looking for closure after his daughter's death- correct? We are not savages. We can empathize. Can we not?"

"Yes, Master," Tan nodded rapidly.

"I asked- *can we not*?" Lar repeated louder.

"Yes, Master," Nora and Stig chimed in unison.

"Killing is never ideal," Lar continued softly once again. He took a puff of the Cuban cigar he'd picked up to light from the tray that had been placed on his usual edge of the long table. "It is also not a creative and clever enough solution for advanced followers of *the path*, like we are. It is merely a quick one. An easy path. And we cannot reach ultimate salvation without the arduous, true path to enlightenment."

"Master, forgive me, but I have to ask," Nora bit her bottom lip, focusing on Lar's eyes. She could feel Tan eyeing her intensely, but she didn't want to look at him just yet. "We all know it's a matter of time. Tan was Linette's ex-boyfriend, after all. We all know ex-lovers are often among the first to be questioned…"

"Well, let's not forget this is still not an official homicide case, Nora," Stig muttered, stiff-lipped as he popped open a can of Hoegaarden beer.

"She's right about that, Stig," Tan stared blankly on the marble floor tiles. "Since the discovery of our note made to look like her own handwriting- they have been considering the possibility of a 'suicide', yes. But the investigation is still a cold case. It's still an open one due to- what did they call it- 'insufficient evidence', remember? My mother always said it when I was a young boy: the truth always eventually comes to light…"

"I think I have a better idea," Stig exclaimed, placing his beer

75

glass on the table with an audible *cling*. "Something to throw the investigators off of any tracks that may lead your way. May I, Master?"

"Let's hear it, Stig," Lar said with a smirk, rubbing his scruffy chin. "Let's pick that brain underneath that strong body."

"You're too kind, Master," Stig ran a hand through his wavy hair as Nora sat on his lap with her arms around his neck. "I don't think the old goon, whoever he is, would have anything tangible, honestly, that could point to Tan. But we can never be too careful. If the police are seeking substantial evidence to lead to a murderer, then that's just what they can get. I can- untraceably, of course- plant some…"

"Umm- sorry to interrupt, Stig. Master?" Tan asked with his voice shaky. "Can I talk to you privately for a moment?"

"Tan, you know we're family here," Nora started. "There's nothing you can have to say that we will judge you for…"

"We'll be right back," Lar stood up and nudged Tan closer to the window on the opposite far end of the dining area.

"I just thought we were not to have any secrets that we couldn't share with our sisters and brothers…" Nora's head was shaking rapidly in confusion.

"That's enough, Nora," Lar turned to raise a bushy black eyebrow, staring straight into her turquoise eyes. "Tan's in an especially vulnerable position here. He's an exception. Now excuse us for a moment…"

§

"I KNOW THIS ISN'T EASY FOR YOU, LAD," Lar spoke softly, his hand squeezing Tan's shoulder. *My exception.* Lar would never have gone to the trouble of securing cyanide for anyone other than Tan. *I was almost caught*, he remembered. The black market in Norway wasn't as easy to navigate as it'd been for him in the Middle East.

"Master, I don't think I could handle it once more," Tan spoke softly. He was pacing back and forth in front of the window overlooking the entire city, rubbing his face in all directions.

"I just wanted you to know that. The pressure and the burden of knowing I'll have been- directly or indirectly- responsible. Again. If something were to happen to Linette's father, too. That is, if that is indeed what Stig meant by…"

"Your body is becoming stronger too, by the way," Lar interrupted impulsively. "I hope you don't think I was favoring Stig back there. He's got muscles galore- more than us as the other men in this house- sure. Before Stig, we're mere mortals. But your own vessel on this earth- you've been taking care of it. It's been strengthening by the day through your workout regimen, lad. I don't want you think it's gone unnoticed."

"I appreciate that, Master," Tan let out a laugh, more to ease his nerves than flattery. "I have also been taking in more protein. Regardless- I know you're trying to make me feel better. You're always very kind. But, Master, how can I relax? Stig is already talking about planting evidence. I have a feeling he's going to try to frame John, if not straight out murder him."

"Not necessarily, lad," Lar dismissed nonchalantly. "You're all in your head again."

"I mean I never liked the chauvinistic bastard- even if he is Linette's father," Tan continued. "I remember when we met. He was bragging about his damn company putting Canada's software prowess on the map. But Linette has been haunting me enough already. If we somehow incriminate her father…"

"You know, this is starting to offend me," Lar cut in. "Your tendency to assume without facts is making me think you don't trust me, even after everything…"

"Master, no, no, no," Tan got down on one knee. "I just panic. I still remember what I've done. I am so sorry if I offend you. I know Linette was…the out one…the…."

"The *outlier*," Lar finished with a blank expression transforming into a smile with Tan's language confusion. If only Tan could realize how adorable he sounded to him.

"The outlier, yes, that's right," Tan continued. "The exception, not the norm. Right? Murder is not natural. Unless it's for survival. And for the land of the human and jinn, that survival includes the prolongation of mental stability. That…"

"Oh, my boy," Lar chuckled, patting him on the back. "Stand up. You've forgotten, it seems, the fifth chapter. It's alright. You can review tonight before dinner. Reading will remind you of your life's mission."

"I will read, Master, I promise," Tan stood up with a heavy sigh. "I love revisiting it. You have my word. Your book changed my life."

And you just may have changed mine, Lar thought, eyes glued on Tan's increasingly commanding frame walking toward the door. *My exception. My own outlier here in this new land. You've brought me back to life.*

CHAPTER 8

Sandnes

FINN WAS TAKEN ABACK BY THE TEARS CARESSING his human skin once more. Had Kaitlin finally spoken her feelings? How he'd fantasized about her looking straight at him and actually verbalizing the words that her dark hazel eyes- and entire quivering body- had already been communicating. He could not recall a single night over the past year where he had not been fighting the urge to ring her phone or show himself to her again.

"Kaitlin, I feel you *more*."

He could never be sure of what Kaitlin must have felt each time she was near him, genuinely astounded by her references to heat and tingling sensations. He couldn't fathom how a human would feel around him. *Freya never talked about these things.* He shook his head to get the name of his first human beloved off his mind, touching another tear on his cheek. Freya's name had a sneaky way of popping up in his mind each time he was near Kaitlin, and the pain she'd caused his soul would usually accompany the nostalgia as well.

At least her face is no longer crossing my mind, Finn thought, gleaming. He'd silently said a little 'goodbye' to her in his mind on his last visit to New York City- where she'd run off to long ago- as a matter of fact. Spotting Kaitlin's friend Sandy in the same midtown Manhattan area, he had decided to amuse himself at the coffee shop as an afterthought. *After all- no such thing as coincidence*, he knew. He'd recognized Sandy's dark curls and dimpled face from the pictures he'd hacked into back when he'd begun studying Kaitlin's phone and pretty much everything else about her. *My only joy now stems from visualizing the face of this woman before me. Kaitlin's beauty hasn't faded a bit since motherhood.*

"For so long, I've never felt a being's thoughts and emotions this much when physically so far from them," he spoke right into her eyes, noticing just then that her thin lips had begun to quiver. "You don't have to be a jinn like me for that to happen. You have a spirit in that humanly-beautiful, imperfectly-perfect body of yours…"

"You can't do this," Kaitlin protested softly, arms opening wide around her frame, revealing to Finn that the top buttons on her trench-coat had opened loose.

"Button up, Miss Kaitlin," he inched closer to her, fastening them back together. "You're going to catch a cold. Autumn in Norway can be tricky. An entire roller coaster of temperatures all in the same day."

"I think I'm used to roller coasters," Kaitlin managed a feeble smile, allowing his hands to button all the way up to the top of her neck. "Finn, you know I have to focus on my life with my husband and daughter. I have to…wait a minute. Just what did you mean by-'imperfectly perfect'? Oh, so my body isn't exactly your type, Monsieur Du Feu? Is that it?"

Finn couldn't help but let out a laugh at her shift in sensitivity. Her attitude amplified by the perpendicular placement of her right arm on her hip. "Calm down, Ms. Kaitlin. Your body is beautiful. And I don't have a body-type. *You* are my type…"

"I haven't been able to do much power-walking or gym activities since the baby, you know. Besides…" Kaitlin was on a roll. And Finn was- for the first time- utterly shocked by her defensive reaction.

He reached softly for her shoulders. *Let me address her a bit teasingly once again. It seems to work in easing her discomfort.* "Miss Kaitlin. Can you please just relax, and accept a sincere compliment?"

"Alright. I don't know what's wrong with me. Thank you,"

Kaitlin added, bowing her head. "You know? I love being a mother. No matter how I happened to arrive at that point. Argh! I don't even know what I'm saying. I don't even care if I have any damn extra kilos…"

"I was actually going to say…" Finn chipped in. "On the contrary to your comments about your body- you look fitter to me, and maybe even slimmer. Not fuller at all. And it's actually got me concerned- have you been eating well, Miss Kaitlin? I know you have to focus on Malin, and you're even breastfeeding. You need well-rounded nutrition."

He gauged Kaitlin for a reaction or a response, but she was just staring at him. Her green-turning brown eyes were sparkling despite the squint caused by the direct sun.

"That's actually what I meant when I said 'imperfect' earlier," he went on. "Human bodies are frail- frailer than our beings. We don't need to eat as much as you do. Nature tends to be enough to replenish our depleted energies. But you here: my imperfectly-perfect, human *friend*…." Finn teased, inching his smile closer to her face. "You need to take care of yourself more. You need to be strong first, in order to help make Malin strong."

"For my daughter…" Kaitlin finally managed. "You're right. I wasn't expecting that. I appreciate it, Finn. I'm sorry. I don't even know what my little outburst was about. I haven't talked to many non-babies lately, aside from Paul," Kaitlin chuckled softly, clearing her throat. "Paul- by the way- he's making sure I take care of myself. Don't worry."

Finn followed Kaitlin's eyes back out toward the waves. Any further exploration of an emotional confession had now felt evaporated. But they'd come this far for him to back out now. He had to try once more, at the very least. He had to lead Kaitlin to the discovery of her nature on her own- all through her own will.

"Miss Kaitlin. About the feeling you were talking about. Look. Our spirits…we can just feel each other. I know you think of me while I'm thinking of you, as well. That, too, isn't because of my status as a

81

jinn. That's simply my love…"

"Finn, I don't think you're listening," Kaitlin whimpered. "This cannot be. Whatever this is, it cannot be called 'love', or include anything physical- in any way shape or form. Please. I can't do it, nor be able to handle it. Can you understand that?"

Finn tried. He'd tried to understand when his first human beloved had used similar words to express her frustrated state, as well. *"I wasn't thinking when it was new- so new, and exciting,"* his Nordic paramour had said. *"But it's too deep now. And you are asking from me more than I can give- literally. I cannot throw away the support of my entire family- nor my sanity."*

Finn breathed in as much oxygen as he could to bring his human form back into the present moment. *Freya's over. I will no longer be a weakling in love.* Sure, he'd left Kaitlin alone as promised, assuring her silence in exchange for her then new puppy-Bo, as well as Paul's safety. But truth be told, he no longer gave a damn how Lar would react if she actually did risk everything and talked to the police about Tan. "She has no tangible evidence, sir," Finn had already rehearsed what he'd say. "Rest assured that our brother Tan and The Group, Inc. will not be compromised."

No.

He was now more concerned about his pride as a jinn- a being who didn't have to plead and chase after a woman in order for her to stand brave for their love. But most of all- he'd been worried about Kaitlin. Finn didn't care if Tan went to prison, but knew that Lar would. And he'd be pissed enough to go after Kaitlin. She would be in danger, and so possibly would Malin. He couldn't risk that.

"Finn?" Kaitlin asked in a strong pitch of voice that brought Finn's attention fully on her physical reality once again, standing up to pace around the wooden ledge. "Are you okay?"

She cares. "Y-yes. Sorry. I'm listening. I'm honestly just trying to take everything in myself. You think this is all some fun and games for me, don't you?"

"No, but I *am* curious. Why are you appearing before me now? You can't just come here and attempt to confuse me after time has passed and things have settled. Paul and I are mostly parents raising Malin now. And it's comfortable...I'm comfortable. I think I'm finally, comfortable..."

"But are you happy?"

"I don't care!" Kaitlin cried, her tears escaping their prison. "Can't you see that? I'm just so....so tired of having lived my life ...with everyone's expectations. Each time I've chased 'happiness', things always ended up with me in hot water."

Finn crossed his arms across his coat and attempted his best to repress the grin forming on his mouth. *She emblazes me whenever she gets heated like this.*

"...Always walking on eggshells," Kaitlin continued. "I can't... I don't care if I have to stay in denial, or if there's even an alternative reality to my raising my daughter with Paul. But I'm happy being a mother and being part of a family. Please- don't ruffle feathers now. Have you come here to tell me that our deal is off? Is that it? We're not keeping quiet anymore? What is this...?"

Finn only raised an eyebrow and proceeded to unfold his arms from across his chest. He leaned back on the dock to stare back out into the sea. *She's still fighting this.*

"You're still a paranoid rambler too, apparently. And, no, I didn't wait all this time and then just show up for you today for *this*."

"Can you blame me?" Kaitlin responded in a forcibly calmer voice, enunciating each word. "Gee, thank you, by the way."

"I'm sorry, Ms. Kaitlin," Finn took a deep breath and gazed into her eyes. "I didn't mean to hurt your feelings with an insult. I'm not Paul."

83

"Finn..." Kaitlin started.

"It must all be very complicated for you. I understand," Finn continued. "I just don't understand why even what starts out as a lovely conversation between us can somehow still manage to turn into an argument..."

"Just, don't bring Paul into this, please," Kaitlin said, lowering her voice to a whisper now. She cocked her head to the side "Okay? Please! It makes me further uncomfortable; I think."

"Well, I'm sorry, but he is in this. Sadly so, but he is," Finn placed his head on his knees, licking his lips. There it was again. That sensation he was just fully discovering. *Wetness*. Had he teared up once more? "Watching him with our daughter...It's...It's...."

"Wait. Wait, we don't know that," Kaitlin interrupted. "She could very well be mine and Paul's. I mean, this is awkward to talk about. But, come on. I thought it was *him* that night. You know. Because we weren't exactly *non*-sexual, and..."

"Okay, Kaitlin, I get the hint," Finn rolled his eyes. "I don't need details. I'm glad I was apparently foreplay to drive you into your husband's arms..."

"You're being ridiculous right now," Kaitlin raged. "Not to mention- unfair. How in the world can someone with the activities implied in The Group judge something as normal as spouses..."

"I also needed to talk to you, Kaitlin," Finn's tone meant business as he cut in. In all honesty he'd momentarily forgotten all about John Walker's return and his plethora of concerns with regards to it, the moment he'd set his eyes on her again in such proximity. But any further closeness between them would evidently not be happening that day. That much was clear. *I might as well warn her and call it a day. For now.*

"Not everything is about marital or extramarital relations, Miss Kaitlin. Something's happened and I didn't know who else to talk to, in all honesty. I mean, Bjorn's cool, but he's always out together with Anja.

And Meredith, well, she's…. busy lately."

"Why's she busy…." Kaitlin began to ask, but Finn cut her off.

"You think I'm relaxed, Ms. Kaitlin? You see me here today, and go all off on me, but do you think I have things any easier? That dead woman's father is apparently in town, searching for answers. Alright? Linette Peterson's father. He gave Meredith his card, the bastard. Reminded me a bit of how you'd discovered my business card last year, actually," Finn's anger eased with nostalgia.

"Her father? Wow, alright." Kaitlin's downcast eyes and blank expression weren't communicating anything to Finn in that moment.

"You know, you're right," she finally peered up at him. "I suppose I never did ask you about that. When did you put that card in my pocket last year? While I was at the gym? In town? At…oh God…at my house…?"

"Ms. Kaitlin, you're doing it again…"

"Rambling?" Much to Finn's surprise, she smiled, placing her hands over her eyes.

"Assuming," Finn went on softly, encouraged. "Being paranoid. As if I'm some creep stalking your every move…"

"I just meant…"

"While we were walking," Finn interrupted. "You were ahead of me for a quick moment. Gazing into the sky. That was my chance. I slipped it into your pocket. No- hocus pocus-or, magic- isn't that how you humans term it?" Finn laughed.

"Slick," Kaitlin teased. "Well, anyway. You were telling me about Linette's father? Go on please…"

"Yes. John Walker. Father of the year. Traveling across the world to mess us all up. All because of that damned Tan and his daughter….!"

Kaitlin's face was solemn. "So, Linette's father has come to help investigate her death…Well, good! I hope he helps them capture Tan, then! He deserves it! Don't you think? I mean, I'm sorry, but if you had nothing to do with her death- as you've claimed…"

"Of course, I didn't!" Finn exclaimed. "I don't kill, Ms. Kaitlin. And if you still don't believe in me after everything…then maybe I made a mistake in thinking I could confide in you."

"I know you didn't Finn," Kaitlin insisted. "I just don't understand why you'd be so concerned, then? Who cares if they catch Tan?" She crossed her arms over her chest.

"Kaitlin- the girl committed suicide, remember?" Finn raised a brow.

"Oh, right," Kaitlin nodded. "How could I forget Tan's convenient cover-up story? Either way…why are you worried about them questioning him?"

"He's weak!" Finn declared. "He'll blurt something crazy and implicate us in The Group in some way- even if indirectly. And they'll investigate the cabin, and we may possibly have to move out. Maybe even have to stay back with our families for a while. If our documents are discovered…I can't exactly afford…."

"Oh, I'm sorry. I understand it must not be an easy financial decision…" Kaitlin was trying her best to sound empathic.

"I was saying," Finn wrinkled his nose. "I can't exactly afford facing my birth family again after having left home…"

"Oh," Kaitlin quipped. "Wait…is Tan still in Oslo?"

"How did you know he was in Oslo?" Finn crossed his arms. "Ms. Kaitlin, don't tell me you've been chit-chatting with Meredith?"

"Just once or twice," Kaitlin stammered. "I wanted to see how she'd been after her forced abortion. And she was always a good friend. She found out about the baby and called to congratulate after…"

"Abortion, huh? Oh, yeah, she is a good friend to you, alright." Finn smirked.

"Finn, what are you trying to get at…?" Kaitlin inquired.

"Look, any way you look at it; Tan wasn't exactly boyfriend of the year. True. But he's no killer Kaitlin. Relax!" *I'm lucky she can't read my mind*, Finn thought. "And, yes, he's in our Oslo branch, now. Him and Meredith couldn't live together anymore. We arranged for him to fly back out to Turkey, but it was ultimately decided to be smarter for The Group to keep a closer eye on him..."

"Right," Kaitlin began. "But, come on."

"Tan hasn't- and will not- hurt anyone," Finn interrupted. "The girl simply killed herself, and her father will figure that out for himself and rest assured once and for all, hopefully. I just felt the need to share with you. Make sure your brilliant husband dear doesn't put his nose where it doesn't belong again."

Kaitlin placed both hands on her temples, rubbing them as she nodded back and forth. "Finn, we won't say anything. I won't break my promise. I hope you don't either. I'm trying to absorb all this. Look, I have to say this...Please don't visit Malin and I, especially when we're alone."

"What?" Finn queried.

"If you want to talk- I don't know- manifest, like you did today! Make sure she doesn't witness it. I don't want to traumatize my baby. Please. Be careful. Especially when she's sleeping and the house is so eerily quiet anyway. The other day-she cried!"

"Okay, Ms. Kaitlin. I believe this is now my cue to head back home," Finn muttered. *I can't believe this*. "First, I'm a thief. Then, I'm a rapist, and now apparently I'm a creep who'd want to scare and wake up my own..."

"Don't!" Kaitlin interrupted as tears began rolling down her cheeks. "Don't say the rest of that sentence, please."

"Kaitlin. Don't forget. You made that choice to call me after meeting me in the forest. A stranger. Hocus pocus or not- a mysterious card. You didn't question it. You invited me into your presence..."

"Finn...I'm sorry. But I'm so overwhelmed..."

"Don't worry," Finn stood up in a rapid motion of light that was able to bring him at least 100 meters or so away from Kaitlin's body now. "I don't need to lurk in secret, like a damned freak. You can always call me if you return to your senses..."

"Wait!" Kaitlin called out. "Same number?"

"You don't need a cell phone to summon me again," Finn locked his gaze on hers sternly. "Come on, go feed Malin, already. She needs you." *Just think of our embrace and picture me.*

"What's that mean...? I just call out your name?" Kaitlin called out somewhere in the distance now, as Finn sped away in beam form.

He mustered the courage to avoid the temptation to go back near her. He could tell she needed more time.

When I remain in your thoughts, my love, and not merely cross them: I'll appear. Keep me in your thoughts. Guard me. Guard this connection.

Inhaling the crisp autumn air, Finn decided to walk through the fog that had set in among the trees back in the Stavanger woods. Even with her denial and offensive accusation, he was radiating. He still felt too elated like a little child to transport back to the cabin in his orange energy form right away. Making one's way around nature always helped to clarify the fogginess of his own thoughts, he knew.

How could Kaitlin simultaneously be able to both fill and empty his cup? *How does Kaitlin have this power over me?*

A gust of wind caused his human frame to quiver. He pulled his black peacoat closer around his lean-muscled frame. *I'm weakening already.*

No. Finn decided Kaitlin wouldn't change him any further than she already had, giving very little in return. Stretching his arms out in front of him, Finn closed his eyes, allowing the brisk air to tickle his nostrils once again. Inhaling one major gulp of oxygen, he gradually allowed himself to shrink into a ball of black, feline fur.

I'll jump across the twigs better this way. Finn always had more fun in animal form, physically speeding across the crackling twigs in the forest. He preferred his physical being low enough near the ground to be immersed fully into both the soil and flora.

What did I think would happen? She'd jump in my arms again like that night, or surrender her lips to mine like in the cabin? Stupid, stupid Finn.

Had that much water really passed under that bridge of last year? Finn was never the one to give up on something that his entire soul and being was telling him had not ended. *We're far from over, my beloved*, he thought, opening his eyes to view the cabin he'd instinctively already ran toward- *you'll see it soon enough.*

He'd spent nearly an entire decade of what he'd calculated to be his nearly 60 years of life in human years manifesting in the same form of the 25-year-old man version of his spirit. Finn didn't personally know any sixty-year-old humans, but had observed their behaviors long enough to know that he'd certainly felt more energetic than them.

He'd first manifested for Freya, and had since gotten used to his human form. Lar had found it useful and encouraged it, as well. *These human gals will age their way out of The Group,* Bjorn had reminded Finn, the one time he'd caught him crying after his last human beloved had left his world behind and gone to the United States. *You would have fallen out of love with her had she stayed with you, anyway. Freya would have, in time, become more like a mother figure. Lar's maxims hold logical reason.*

Thinking and feeling were one of the beautiful commonalities his kind had with human beings. Yet the mixture of reason with the emotions in his ether would often plague Finn. And, this time, with Kaitlin; he was no longer sure reason could play any part in his persistence whatsoever.

That little girl has extended beyond any logical reason against us being together, he thought. Finn wasn't a jinn who cared much for details. As far as he was concerned, when their souls touched that night- their intimacy had been palpable beyond any reason. And, in one form or another, something was telling Finn that their connection would always carry on through Malin.

§

WITH THE REMAINDER OF HER LONG-HELD TEARS pouring over her cheeks, Kaitlin closed her eyes and turned her head to the sea, allowing the breeze to caress her longing face. She gulped one final, long breath in before pacing to the bus stop.

Kaitlin was feeling shocked, intrigued, and admittedly a bit flattered as well that Finn would approach her. To confide in, even after a whole year had nearly passed. *John Walker.* The name kept echoing in her mind throughout the bus ride to Stavanger- Kaitlin had stayed on to head straight to Hundvag island as fast as she could. She checked her phone. Sibel had sent her a picture of Malin napping peacefully. *Thank God.*

John Walker, she thought again as she proceeded to walk fast-paced to Sibel's place. Her ankle boots were now stubbing her toes, but she didn't mind. Where had Kaitlin heard of that name before?

That handsome actor who just died tragically while filming that movie about fast cars? Stopping for a moment to recollect herself once she'd spotted the white-painted wooden cottage-style home where Malin was waiting for her, Kaitlin scratched her chin. *Oh wait, that was Paul Walker. Like my Paulie. So, the name must have stuck with me.*

Kaitlin's disheveled hair greeted her whilst it reflected back at her through a sizeable glass portion of the blue-painted door, complementing the cozy-feel of the small but two-story structure with particularly angular roofing. *Luckily Finn saw me without this hat hair,* she thought, pulling her hair into a messy bun while attempting to ring the bell with the hat in her hand. Just how it had been able to hold through the soft ocean-side breeze was beyond her; her gift hat from Paul. Kaitlin shut her eyes and inhaled with sulky shoulders.

"Welcome, *annesi,*" Sibel's greeting, simultaneous to her abrupt opening of the door, took Kaitlin by a jolt-causing surprise. A glance at her daughter's angel face whilst she appeared at ease in Sibel's arms drowned Kaitlin's foggy mind in a whole other wave of emotions.

"My angel," Kaitlin reached for daughter. "You've woken up!"

"No, no, no," Sibel's voice was somewhere between teasing and serious as she took two steps backward. "We have to wash our hands when we come from outside, don't we?"

"Oh, of course, of course," Kaitlin blushed as she took a step in and removed her boots by the door. An exotic concoction of rich-red and brown designs adorned the rectangular ethnic carpet in the small corridor that led to the living room. "I guess I'll be air-kissing you too, then, dearest babysitter," she chuckled, mouthing *thanks* as she entered. The covered-floor felt especially soft beneath Kaitlin's tired feet in socks.

"Did you have fun on your little play date? Who's mommy's love?" Malin cooed, with the purest smile Kaitlin had encountered her entire life answering her. "Mommy will be right with you as soon as she washes her hands in the…where was the bathroom, again?"

"Our house has been forgotten already, kids," Sibel joked over her shoulder, as two young children- dressed more as if they were going to a holiday festival than relaxing in the house- came up behind her to greet Kaitlin. "But, I know, I know, that's partly out fault. Ever since I've gotten more involved with the Women's Club. Speaking of which, Ann asked about you…."

"Sibel? The bathroom?" Kaitlin rolled her eyes with a smile. Her friend had a tendency of becoming distracted easily. How she was able to have so much on her plate yet also have her house look so immaculate

91

was beyond Kaitlin.

"Right this way, Kaitlin *teyze*," Aylin pulled her arm with the free arm, as her other one was playfully tugging at her own fluffy jean skirt.

"Aren't you the sweetest little princess, *Aylincim*?" Kaitlin closed the door behind her and looked at her face closer in the mirror this time, ignoring her hair. The impeccably-designed bathroom with a dual washing machine and dryer had more guest towels stacked on top of one another than Kaitlin had ever seen in a house. A bar of soap was hanging on the wall with a blue, evil-eye stone attached that Sibel had explained to her symbolized 'protection against negative energies', or against *nazar*. Kaitlin mused whether she perhaps needed such a stone herself.

Was she meant to rip open the plastic around the soap bar, or was is just yet another decorative item? *Bingo!* A good-old soap dispenser Kaitlin was more accustomed to had also luckily been placed on the washing machine. *Mmm, this smells good.* She took a peek at the soap dispenser and a sinking feeling hit her stomach. The picture of ocean waves on its design immediately transported her thoughts to Finn smiling at her at the harbor, not even an hour ago. *Get a hold of yourself, Kaitlin. That was enough excitement for the day.*

"Momma…" Malin's voice sounded to Kaitlin to be coming from lower on the floor now right outside the bathroom door as she opened it to take a look. *Or just maybe even enough excitement for 17 more years or so.*

"I couldn't hold her back anymore, Kaitlin," Sibel was shaking her head back and forth sheepishly. "She practically leapt out of my arms to crawl to you. I have a feeling she'll be walking by her birthday coming up."

"Aww, don't crawl on the cold tiles in here, honey bunny," Kaitlin said, picking her up and inhaling Malin's neck. *Heaven,* she thought once again. "Hands all clean now, *mon lapin*. I've missed you so much."

"She really was a sweetheart today," Sibel said, turning her head in attempt to distract her son and daughter from their television-glued bliss. "We loved playing with Malin, didn't we?"

"Yes!" Aylin and Hakan said in unison, making Kaitlin chuckle. She wondered just then if she too would one day become yet another mother relying on technology to occupy her child's time in order to get any work done. "Thank God daddy wasn't here to see that. He would have gotten all bossy on us about catching a cold from tiles…"

Wait a second.

Kaitlin's stoppage in thought caught Sibel's attention. "Kaitlin? Are you alright? Come let's sit in the dining room and munch on my special pie before the hubby arrives to drive you gals back. I know, I know. You told me *no food*, but how often do I get to see you lately? This time I've added spinach, and I think…"

Kaitlin nodded, tuning out the rest of Sibel's speech as her body followed Sibel closer to the kitchen area. *Bossy. Boss.* "That's it!"

"Momma?" Malin eyed her inquisitively, hanging on to Kaitlin's shoulder for balance through a one-armed hold.

"That's right, my angel," Kaitlin pumped her fist in the air victoriously. "Momma's got it! John Walker was daddy's old boss back in Canada!"

"Dadda," Malin smiled, while Kaitlin returned hers with a nod.

Paul had said his ex-boss couldn't have been having an affair with Linette, or hurt her, because he saw her as his daughter. Kaitlin shook her head with a smile as she sat down on a wooden chair with Malin on her lap. *What if she really had been- if what Finn's said was true- his actual daughter?* Her sudden urge to share the discovery in her mind made a part of her wish to get home to Paul quickly already for the two of them to discuss this novel development. *I don't know how exactly to break this to him, but we have to do something! He has to contact him! We can help him!*

"Would you like tea or coffee, Kaitlin?" Sibel called out from somewhere in the kitchen.

"Umm, if it's that Turkish tea in those little glasses, then, yes please. I've missed those so much!" Kaitlin called out with an especially high-pitched voice. "You're too good to us today, *teyzesi*. Thank you, girl."

"Any time," Sibel's voice replied.

Whether or not Paul's old boss had changed his contact information, Kaitlin had no idea. She began making an increasingly fussy Malin hop on her lap. *How in the world could I be of help to lead this Walker man to Tan as his daughter's killer, without tipping Finn off?*

All Kaitlin knew in that moment was that everything couldn't have occurred without a reason. She had to help Linette's murderer to be brought to justice. *I'm a Libra, after all.* She had to help tilt the scales in the truth's favor.

"No such as thing coincidence, right? That's what these folks claim?" she verbalized in nearly a whisper, locking eyes with Malin's hazel gaze. Kaitlin smiled, squeezing her daughter's pudgy legs. "Maybe throughout all of this, I'm truly meant to help that Linette girl to rest in peace, my angel."

"Did you say something?" Sibel asked.

"Oh, no, no," Kaitlin called out. *What's that smell?* She noticed Malin's face get pink just then, with a frustrated yet uttermost adorable expression dawning across her cherub cheeks. *Oh, no.* "On second thought- Sibel? Sweety, when did Malin last have a diaper change?"

CHAPTER 9

THE PENITENTIARY

C-318

THE BUMPS FROM THE HAPHAZARDLY PAINTED walls in the cell encircled the prisoner like hawks, closing in on him as their prey. They then proceeded to rotate around the walls and fly out the window again. For as long as he could remember, the prisoner had amused himself with that particular imagery, lost in thought while his fingers would fidget with whatever he could get his hands on. He'd use gum and clippers to cut photographs from the local papers he was able to receive, and hang them up on his wall. They weren't allowed scissors or anything that could hurt anyone in there, not even themselves.

Why would he even have wanted to? He'd had his beautiful memories for company.

The lake. Today he imagined himself as a particularly large fish the hawks were fighting amongst one another to get their claws on.

"Fishy!" the little girl suddenly called out, causing the prisoner to smile whilst he closed his eyes and gave himself fully over to the daydream. Her legs had been dangling on the lake: the little girl with the strawberry-smelling hair. The view of the grand mountains in the distance complemented the memory in his mind.

"Be careful, my sweet," he called out. "Don't fall, now."

"Alright," she smiled, bringing her knees back toward her chin.

"But even if I do, you'll save me, right?"

"Of course," the prisoner responded. "I'll always protect you. No matter what."

CHAPTER 18

Oslo

THE CLICKING OF A WOMAN'S HEELS INCREASED IN proximity, along with his heartrate. "Nora?" Lar called out meekly, leaning closer toward the wall behind his head. He listened to the sound get louder once the elevator doors had shut. "Is that you?"

His shoulders were slumped lower than his sullen face as he lay across his dark satin-sheeted bed. It was ambitiously King-sized, to no avail; his lonely body curled up on the same side of it each and every night.

"Yes, Master," Nora responded from the other side of the thick wooden door. "I just got back from Vigeland Park. Can I come in?"

"You know you never have to ask, my girl. Come on in." Lar smiled. Nora had become his closest confidante in Norway. *Like the daughter I'll never have,* he'd often think, before dismissing it just as rapidly. Nora was only 24 years old, but much wiser beyond her years. She knew how to keep secrets. And with fair blonde hair and deep eyes, she also happened to be a statuesque Norwegian beauty- the perfect cover. Lar needed someone like her.

"I still cannot comprehend how you're so taken by those ugly statues they've got for the tourists out there- risking a cold in this temperature to walk among them, no less! Doesn't the Opera House or something have more appealing performances for you to check out?"

"It's one of its kind by a single artist, Master- and I like special things, as you well know," Nora's excited eyes matched her hand movements as she flopped down on the corner of the bed. "I mean, all those displays of human life…all the emotions- the beautiful and the ugly. Out in the open air for everyone to see. It's truth. And truth is beautiful," Nora winked.

"Would you look at that?" Lar chuckled, playfully patting Nora's arms. "Maxim 21 coming to artistic defense. I love it when the students can enlighten the teacher." He hadn't been able to quite pronounce the last word before beginning to cough into his fist.

"Master, are you feeling ill?" Nora asked in surprise. "Is that why you're in bed?" She opened the velvety curtains and trudged to sit at the foot of his bed, careful as her curvy body had been accentuated by a trendy yet tight skirt.

"I wish there were more exciting, or at least routine reasons- like a cold- for me to be here, dear Nora," Lar answered solemnly, his head rocking from side to side. "I'm still thinking about what was discussed yesterday. You know. About the dead girl's father paying a little visit here to the good old land of the Vikings. Did you talk to Anja?"

"Yes, Master, and I'm afraid she's been of no additional help," Nora replied with a sigh, twiddling her fingers and focusing instead on her new manicure. "I mean, I can't believe we're related sometimes. Not sure what she takes seriously in this life, come to think of it. She said there's nothing else except what she's told Tan, Master. Are you sure you don't want us to do further research on this 'John Walker'?"

"No need to waste your precious time, dear Nora," Lar responded after letting out a distracted sigh. "Nothing too suspicious to me about a man and his nature, attempting revenge or at least seeking answers."

"Stig told me this morning about the plan you two discussed last night, Master." Nora went on. "I believe it will work. I mean, it has to. For nothing must happen to Tan. I know how deeply you care for him."

"I hope you're right, my dear," Lar sighed heavily, caressing her cheek. "But it's not just that. Did you see the way he reacted? He's still so panicked. He doesn't trust me. Or doesn't feel safe here. I'm even beginning to lose hope in…in…"

"Hey, hey, Master." She leaned closer to wipe a fallen tear from his face just then. "Nonsense! Our family here is lacking a foundation if we are to ever lose hope, you know that. He will begin to see your love…he will. Master?"

"Yes?" Lar called out feebly, eyes focused on the smoke-gray wall across the room.

"Would you want me to…?" Nora began with hesitation. "I mean, I have so much respect, and I do not mean to offend you. But you told me you're not certain about Tan's…inclinations. Correct?".

"My dear Nora, out with it already, will you please?" Lar insisted.

"Would you like us to-you know-encourage him to join Stig and I? To, umm, get him acclimated toward, his own gender…"

"No!" Lar bellowed. He liked to believe he took good care of himself, even at age 45. Yet he knew he was no match for Stig's rock-hard abs and baby blues. "He may become, confused, if he does indeed recognize homoerotic tendencies stirring in his soul. What I feel, it's more than sexual, Nora. It's real. I don't care if he can never think of me in that way- I would never force him to even put a hand on me. So-no, no, no. That would not be right. My beliefs…My maxims…"

"Master, please calm down," Nora attempted to placate Lar's rambling by holding his shoulder. "I just wanted to help, if I could. I know your pure intentions. Stig and I both respect you to the moon and back. You did always take the mission very seriously. It is very much appreciated, believe me. You took me in when I had nowhere else," Nora's eyes began to tear up. "When my brother was, doing all that to me…. his own sister…and *mama* wouldn't believe me. No one in my family would believe me."

"You and I are not too different, my dear Nora…" Lar stroked her arm.

"Nonsense, Master. I am nowhere near the enlightened soul that you are, and…"

"What I meant was," Lar interrupted with a whisper, shutting her mouth with a soft touch of his finger on her lips. "…we have both suffered non-understanding and non-acceptance from our blood families, and have had to create our own."

"Yes, Master," Nora attempted a smile.

"Look, I appreciate your adherence to Maxim 24 on the tragedies of monogamous love and offspring creation into this already cruel world. You are a most dedicated pupil, Nora. But you must understand. Once and for all. I do not mean to lead Tan toward some bi-curious path of sexual exploration. Heck, he may even develop a crush on *you*, dear, beautiful Nora! We certainly can't have that, can we now? It'd anger Stig, too!"

Nora chuckled to join in Lar's own teasing expression. "You never worried about Tan and Anja? They're both human, after all, and could have possibly broken that maxim through bearing a child…"

"Your cousin, dear, was never his type," Lar shook his head. "Tan's into the silent, quiet types. Linette…Meredith- well, I just had to curb my jealousy with her since she is of the jinn, even though she was intimate with my foolish Tan. For, of course, as you know, dear Nora, avoiding pregnancy is always of utmost importance…"

"Yes, Master."

"In Stavanger," Lar continued, "Bjorn and Finn were not in human form during the activities, so they were physically out of Tan's way for the most part. Especially with Meredith's possessive, monogamous hold over him. But Stig? Let's just say you're lucky I require a connection beyond just looks to develop affections. That jinn of yours, by looks alone- could increase the rate of global warming…"

Nora fully erupted in laughter this time. "Yes, I admit I love my

Stig in all his forms. Oh, Master. Life blessed me when our paths crossed on that fateful day back at the university. I think I'm understanding you a little clearer with each passing day."

"How do you mean?" Lar smiled.

"Well, I believe this may all stem from your need for a partner in all senses of the word," Nora opined. "You want to be his first male lover- a human man. You would also be needing a human successor for The Group, in due time. I understand all that, Master. But, wait, then…perhaps…I may have to...Oh, God. No, I couldn't."

"What are you trying to get at this time, Nora?" Lar's curiosity had genuinely become piqued. He placed his hands over Nora's own which she had placed over her face. "No shyness necessary. Out with it."

"You are like my brother, Master, and I respect you too much. But if I must, for our mission…since, you know- he must already think that you and I are intimate… Perhaps I could get him to join you and *I* instead …"

Nora, stop it. I do not want you to seduce my poor Tan, for goodness' sake. In any way, shape, or form. Stay out of it! "You cannot be involved, period!"

"I'm sorry …" Nora stammered. "I just thought, if it were you, in place of Stig. I mean, heck, I would stay out of the way. I thought I could just stick to kissing, perhaps. You know? Muttering something about how guilty I felt doing this to Stig, and how you are the exception for all of us. Perhaps, if he could have this set-up as an excuse to be cuddled by you…more than me. He could then feel your touch, and it could enlighten him to his bigger mission. To be by your side. Expanding The Group beyond Europe…"

"Stop it all right this instance!" Lar bellowed, and Nora stopped talking immediately, retracting her body.

"I understand you want to help, Nora," Lar spoke in a softer tone after a moment of silence. He took a deep breath and leaned back against the fluffy pillows he'd plopped up against his mahogany headboard. "But, my dear, like I said. You are so beautiful. So precious. He would be swooning over you…"

"Nonsense, Master. Any attraction would be fleeting. Only until he realizes the beauty of your soul. Why, when he looks into your eyes, and as his body senses your soulmate-touch…"

"He needs to come to me on his own, Nora…" Lar nodded blankly, verbalizing the decision he'd made to himself long ago. The decision that had further felt in the core of his heart to have been the right one when he received that frantic call from Tan at the Turkish airport. "Master, help me," he'd sobbed into the phone, having just been ostracized away from the cabin by Meredith. *I'll never forgive that jinni for doing such a thing without consulting me.*

"For me, that will be the true test of love. Let's return to this topic at a later time, if need be. We must make haste. Upon Stig's return we will have our meeting in the dining room to discuss the little matter of throwing the police off. It'll otherwise be any day now when that girl's father will likely lead them to Tan."

"Why won't he just believe she would have committed suicide?" Nora wondered, staring blankly at the wall.

"Blood instincts can sometimes be stronger than our other five senses, dear Nora," Lar replied with a heavy sigh, picking up his smartphone. "Look, I'm ordering in some hors d'oeuvres…"

"With wine…" Nora inserted with a burgundy-painted smile.

"Oh, yes, with lots of wine," Lar returned the gesture. *As soon as Stig preemptively ensures the police off of his back, Tan will realize once and for all the lengths to which I would go to, only for him. He will recognize the true meaning of love.*

"Oh, by the way, Master, I was able to sort through the footage by the cabin door," Nora said. "I truly do apologize for not looking sooner. I should have awakened to the fact that he might have been a chosen one as well- as he's apparently been able to see our Meredith, unlike average humans. It must mean something. For indeed everything must happen for a purpose. If nothing else, perhaps this could mean he's meant to be a client. If convinced, the Canadian company listed on his card could certainly afford to…"

Nora scrolled through her smartphone screen for what felt to Lar like ages. He was growing impatient. "Yes, yes, dear Nora, have you got the footage or not?"

"*Her er det*! I've got it. See? It's hard to make out a face. But I was wrong- not some disheveled old man at all. Rather a handsome fella- around your age- no more handsome than you, of course."

"Let me see, my girl," Lar rolled his eyes. He knew that complimenting fellow brethren and sisters had been one of his own maxims, but sometimes his disciples could get to be too much. *It's beautiful they're so grateful for the lavish life and acceptance The Group is able to provide for them*, he congratulated himself, regardless. It'd felt nice to be appreciated- unlike many of the folks he'd called his family and friends back in the Emirates. An entire lifetime ago. *It's better to be loved for who you really are- not a false image.*

As Nora showed him the video on her phone, Lar could swear there'd been something familiar about the visitor. The man in the footage was eyeing his surroundings as he swayed back and forth in a long, dark coat atop tailored-looking pants and a sophisticated scarf. Gloved hands partially in his pockets. At one point he looked up at something- a bird, perhaps? Right before Meredith could be seen in her human form opening the door.

Lar paused the video and zoomed in. *No way!*

It couldn't be, could it? All of a sudden it had begun to feel to Lar as if a boiled pot of water was spilled across his entire body. The face had aged, naturally, yet it was certainly still most familiar. Unmistakable. Had his lifelong fantasy of reuniting with the love of his youth arrived in the form of such a nightmare? Could Abdul Jaan Vaziri-his *Abe*- be 'John Walker?'

CHAPTER 11

Trondheim

T HE WHITE PAINT HAD VISIBLY BEGUN TO PEEL OFF OF THE single-floor house, matching the unkept weed and dead rose petals scattered around the small front yard. *Linette deserved more than her lot in life,* John sighed heavily at the door.

"Come in," the distinctly-throaty voice opening the door comforted John. Annika Peterson looked feebler than he remembered, with a shorter and layered haircut that reminded him of a punk rock band from the 80's.

"No need…" she reached out her arm to dismiss John's efforts to take off his shoes as an upward glance had her blue optics meet his warm cocoa one. The woman he'd once loved as his closest confidante and later lover had still aged beautifully, as far as he was concerned, despite the unkept roots peeking from underneath her burgundy-colored hair and the added wrinkles on her forehead.

"Oh, Annika," John softly nudged her other arm closer into his body in an embrace so close Annika must have been able to smell his after-shave, for she asked him if he'd still been using 'Old Spice'. John nodded, and she inhaled the aroma with her eyes closed for increased effect, unable to pull her face away from the coop of his neck.

We'd always made each other feel safe and protected, hadn't we? An image of his wife Helen crossed John's mind just then. Her perfectly blown-out bleach-blonde hair and Botox-smile never causing a single wrinkle anywhere on her face, despite being well into her mid-40's too now.

"I'm a man of habit, you know me," John giggled as he added additional pats across her back for support.

"Yeah, yeah," Annika finally wriggled out of his grasp with a chuckle. "And I remember how I, too, was just a habit you couldn't break in your 20's, wasn't I?"

"Annika," John sighed, without surprise. He'd certainly run through about three different scenarios in his head on the short flight to Trondheim; all three had his ex-mistress, whom he'd left behind with a mere letter despite his seed in her body, upset with him. "I've told you. I'd married too young. And met you too late. Can I please come in?"

"Oh, yes, of course," Annika waved dismissively, forcing a smile despite herself. "The carpet's been lifted, so, ignore the messy floors, please. I haven't exactly had any interest in mopping up the place. And her room has mostly been left intact. Precisely as she likes...as she's left it."

The grandmother-inherited, raggedy house Linette grew up in was made up of two bedrooms, from what he recalled from his sneak-visits to her place. Yet he also recalled it having had more color than the currently noticeable myriad of dark greys and browns. John added another pat on Annika's back for emphasis, with a glance at her soured face then leading to him pulling her closer across his chest. He'd secretly missed the way her shorter height used to make him feel like someone's hero.

His once secretary, who had to quit after discovering she had been second fiddle to an already-married man. *I was such a cliché, and have done so much wrong- haven't I?* He'd ensured Annika that Helen and him had divorced, and that the people in the office weren't notified of it, for as long as she would believe it. Karma, of course, had a way of biting him in the buttocks; his usually ice-cold wife had decided to surprise him for his birthday at his job, and all hell had naturally broken

106

SELIN SENOL AKIN

loose after that.

"Can I get you something to drink? Some coffee, perhaps?" Annika said, leading him to the nearly bare living room space, with two sofas and a vintage TV set but little else. John attempted a smile. *Annika must be spending most of her time in her likely lonely world in her own bedroom.*

"No thanks. I had two cups on the flight. You've still got that cappuccino machine?" John asked with a raised eyebrow. He could never get himself to drink regular coffee from the pot, having grown addicted to the frothy milk over too many work meetings.

"I'm afraid I gave it to my neighbor," Annika shook her head, leaning her head toward the dark bedroom adjacent to the bathroom. "I'll show you her room."

The wooden-door had been left slightly ajar. John noticed the closed window blinds as Annika pushed through the door as if she were moving boulders. "I'm always afraid someone's going to pass by and peek in, you know? Her killer, perhaps?"

"Annika, you need to let light in," John shook his head and clicked his tongue against the roof of his mouth. Opening the shades, a Twin-sized bed with a pink quilt and modest glass work-desk made him smile, visualizing Linette doing homework. A set of black drawers on either side of her bed displayed so much dust John had to stifle a cough. "Do you keep up this place at all?"

"She's gone, John!" Annika broke down in tears on Linette's bed. "I should have made all the effort when she was still here. And, frankly-you should have been more concerned when she was still alive, too! Am I wrong?"

"Annika, listen to me," John started, plopping down next to her as the bed creaked. "We have to let bygones be bygones. You know very well I've done the best I could ever since she came to that job interview in Montreal, introducing herself to me. I never questioned her for one second. When she said she needed money, that you guys hadn't been doing too well…"

"My daughter didn't go to Canada to beg you for money, John!" Annika exclaimed between tearful sobs, her eyes now glued to the black dresser still adorned with two jewelry-boxes. "She was a damn good student. She was going to go places- even if you'd rejected her from your wife's precious company. She just had to try. She wanted to try. To give you a chance…To get to know you…"

"I know," John spoke softly. "I saw my mother in her eyes. She really took after '*Umiy*. Her dark eyes and ebony hair- soft and honest. I never questioned for one second this was our child. And I'm so grateful. Life gave me that chance. To be a father, albeit in secret. To get to know her electrifying spirit. To get to…"

"This was her favorite," Annika interrupted, getting up to pick up a still-ticking clock from her bookshelf. "She liked the classics in all forms. Insisted on this antique thing, did you know?"

"She was an elegant young lady," John nodded with a smile. "Even at the office. All the woman envied her. And those bastards always eyed her each time she walked in." He added a laugh.

"How much did you know about her last boyfriend- Tan?" Annika's voice grew urgent as she sit back down next to John, still holding on to the clock. "I'd get the strangest feeling about that one whenever he'd come over to ask to pick her up for their little dates."

"He created a scene at work one day when we'd been out to lunch," John nodded. "I never really even talked to that particular bastard in person. I mean- Linette would tell me about some problems he'd been having with his jealousy, and I remember mostly just shaking his hand when I met him once at this event we had, but that's about it. But this other guy from the office- Paul, who works here in Norway now, actually- had a particularly unpleasant run-in with him at the office, apparently. Did Linette ever discuss that with you? Anything about Tan's

108

temper?"

"No, I don't recall her mentioning anything about such an office visit," Annika looked genuinely surprised as she shook her head. "I mean, Tan always acted polite with me. Too polite, in fact, I recall thinking. Nothing like the casual way her previous boyfriends would speak with me. I remember thinking- *what in the world is this young man trying to hide, or overcompensate for*, you know? He tried to kiss my hand at one point!" Annika laughed; her eyes locked to the window overlooking the concrete street outside.

"I should have picked up on his questionable tendencies when she told me he'd followed her upon her return to Norway," John placed his face between his palms. "I haven't got a clue wherever the hell he stayed out here in Trondheim. But I questioned his old roommate back in Stavanger the other day. Some fellow Turkish kid named Serdar. Was very friendly."

"Any leads?" Annika's face was all business now. Traces of emotion had vanished, along with the subtly-peeking glimmers of sunshine outside. Thunder and rain were audible coming from outside the window.

"Because, John, you know I'm not buying this 'suicide' possibility they've thrown out there," Annika continued after John shook his head. "I told you on the phone. I mean- maybe I was in denial- but I really, truly believed she'd run off! That her new social life had her feeling too embarrassed to live with her good old *mama*. I'm such an idiot. Aren't I? I should have called the police sooner. I told myself they'd never listen. That she was of adult age, and I should respect her choices. I should have..."

"You called me, Annika!" John turned his entire torso to face his ex, caressing her cheek. "And I let you know she was alright. You can't blame yourself. I told you that she'd been keeping in touch with me. That she may have been staying with some friends for a while."

John needed his hands on his own forehead just then to give it a massage of comfort. "If anything, it's my fault. For never letting you know once the e-mails had stopped coming. I mean, I just assumed she'd outgrown me, too. With lingering resentment for missing out on her growing up, you know? Maybe I wanted to believe that. Needed to. And then I didn't want to worry you, and then…"

"Wait! About those friends, John…" Annika got up and started pacing around the small room. "Did you ever ask who they could be? Tan? I mean Linette only had two girlfriends that I knew of from the neighborhood- and both of them swore to me they'd had no idea where she could be. What did that roommate of Tan's say- had Linette ever stayed with them when she visited Stavanger? She'd always told me she was staying with her friend Gina down there whenever she'd fly out, but I'm not so sure anymore…"

"That's the thing," John began, fighting the urge to start chewing on the nail of his forefinger. One of the many bad, old habits he'd tried to quit over the years. "I went to that Serdar kid first, to ask about Linette and Tan. He didn't recall her having stayed over there much. Said he was told Tan and our girl had been closer when they were both here. That things had begun to dwindle between them when Tan moved to Stavanger. But Linette had given me two addresses- 'in the case' she 'soon' could not be reached at home here with you. That's how she'd termed it. She was reluctant to provide both- but after I raised my voice and demanded it was important that I had in my possession an address to contact her if she wanted those monthly payments to continue…"

"*Two* addresses?" Annika cut in.

"Well, sort of. Tan apparently befriended some outdoorsy folks and had moved out to live in a cabin. That was the second address aside from the apartment with Serdar …"

"A cabin?" Annika squealed. "Don't tell me the second address was a cabin!"

"Well, umm, yes," John went on. "Linette mentioned how she'd been contemplating moving to Stavanger permanently. How her cell phone also didn't get much reception from the woods whenever she'd visit Tan down there and…"

"John, what the hell were you thinking?" Annika's tears were rolling down her face once again. "I'd assumed she ran off with that boy or some other friend or whatever. But a cabin? You should have told me! It's right out of some scary movie! She couldn't even handle it if she chipped a nail! That was not her personality. John! Didn't it ever occur to you that some nut might have locked her away in the woods and…"

"Annika!" John grabbed her shoulders. "Get a hold of herself! Life isn't typically some horror story you evidently still enjoy binge-reading or watching. She sounded like her usual self. I realize it sounds weird- yes, I'll give you that. But she couldn't have been kidnapped, for God's sake…"

"As far as we know, John," Annika was relentless. "Only as far as we *know*! What if Tan- or whoever else was in that cabin- had been threatening her? Followed her back here?"

"I visited the place," John shook his head. "It seemed like a legit place. Met a nice lady who lived there- someone who Tan recently dated too, coincidentally."

"A lady?" Annika raised an eyebrow.

Was it just him or was Annika still a tad bit possessive? "A young lady. It was just her there, with this weird cat. Looked like she lived there alone. Didn't seem to recognize Linette's name. But she did know Tan. The two apparently broke up not too long ago. She still looked quite shaken up over the guy."

"Hmm, alright," Annika went on. "And? What did she say when you voiced your suspicion he's killed our Linette? Did she reveal anything that may be significant?"

"You know…" John said, placing his chin between his thumb

and forefinger. "Now that I think about it, I did later find it a bit strange that an ex-lover would not be more curious about how Tan could have been connected- even if potentially so- to a woman's disappearance or death? Come to think of it, she also just didn't seem too surprised to hear that my daughter was dead… "

"Well, she may have been following the news," Annika suggested. "Perhaps she was together with Tan when they saw the body discovery on the news together…and he told her…"

"I don't know," John shook his head. "Something doesn't add up. I think you may have gotten on to something here. I can't quite put my finger on it. But I may need to revisit that cabin. I still have to find that Tan, first. I mean, the Meredith girl seemed so nice- I didn't really think of what to make of anything while I was in there. And she looked so much like her…"

"Meredith. Was that her name? She looked like our Linette; you say?" Annika began to stroke the clock.

"Yes," John mumbled. He felt too depleted to utter even another word, yet he couldn't let himself go now. "We couldn't be the ideal parents for her in life, Annika," he eventually added, looking up from Linette's bed at his ex-lover.

"Maybe if she'd been raised with both her parents together. Raised with me in her life, from a much younger age. Maybe she could have made smarter decisions. About the company she kept. Her confidence. Her wrong choices on who to love…"

"Do you really believe that it is a choice, John?" Annika asked.

Staring blankly at the wall, John recalled his younger self once more- laughing in the forbidden embrace that had changed his life that summer in Dubai. *Why the heck has this country continuously been reminding me of him?* He'd only gotten around two letters from a Norwegian address before they'd stopped coming into his late mother's house in Montreal altogether. For all John knew, Lar may even have had returned to the Emirates by now.

"I'm not sure," he sighed with a shrug. "I'm afraid I may just be the last person to ask about love."

"Still, as a long-term married man?" Annika snickered. "I mean, yes, the heartbroken, pregnant woman I was at 22 would certainly agree with that, most definitely. But even now- after- what, how many years has it been since you and Helen have been married?"

"It's going to be twenty-five years on Christmas, actually."

"How's she been?" Annika raised an eyebrow. "She still doesn't know that Linette was…?"

"Linette never wanted her to find out- my precious girl. She said avenging her childhood wouldn't do anyone any good- and that I needed Helen to maintain her faith in me."

"And maintain her support of the company, too, of course," Annika smirked. "We couldn't complain much for years. I hated it, John. I hated the silence. Our necessary complacence. You must know, I hated accepting those checks from you. Knowing they were really from her…."

"Now, hold on there, Annika," John was adamant. "I worked a damn load of hours at that place, too! Everyone in Montreal knew about our software because of me. I was the face. I was the brains. In time-I earned a lot of that money!"

"She was the financier, John," Annika interrupted softly in a sing-song way. "It was the first time I'd realized in my life that I had to stop believing in fairy tales, and grow the heck up about the reality of the world."

Annika sat on her daughter's bed, picking up a rugged brown teddy bear with a red bowtie. "It was also then that I realized you didn't love me," she muttered. "When I called that day to let you know I was pregnant. *It's not mine. I don't have a child.*' I'll never forget those words."

"Annika, please…"

"You said it extra loud, just for her to hear," Annika clenched her jaw. "Just to show off some feigned, egoistical power over me. That the father must have been someone else, knowing I'd never then been with any man other than you. Knowing damn well that Linette was yours…"

"Life has cursed me enough, Annika," John shook his head. "Rest assured. Just when I felt blessed to have discovered her. Thinking life had finally given me a second chance. To be a father, to make things right. Only to have her return to Norway, and then go on to lose her for good like this. I didn't come here to revisit old wounds- only old memories of her beautiful being. And discuss how we can catch her killer. We're both already unable to heal this biggest slash on our hearts. Our daughter…"

"Did you see this one?" Annika had long gotten up to look through a small photo album.

"Uh, oh," John couldn't help but smile despite the purposely shredded-clothes and a wild pose struck by a teenage Linette. "Is this her celebrating *the russefeiring*?"

Annika nodded with a melancholy smile. "We had an absolutely gorgeous one of her from May 17th- the national costume suited her much more classily, of course. That one's framed in my bedroom. By my bedside…" She burst into sobs once more. "I'm sorry, John. I know you're trying to get some answers with a straight head. I didn't mean to go into everything today like this. I guess… I just needed to…"

"Shh…it's okay," John extended the entire length of his arm to comfort her frail torso. "We are in this together. We both lived this. The entire thing- the secrets, the loss, her memory."

He wiped a nearly-falling tear before it could reach his own cheek, darting a glance at her bookshelf this time. Pictures had proved to be too much for both of them to handle. "Let's see here," John started, running his hands through the spines of several books. "Our girl enjoyed

Camilla Lackberg novels, I see. I wouldn't have taken her for a mystery girl- more of a romantic fiction reader or some sort."

"She's become the subject of a real mystery herself, go figure," Annika turned her face to John with pleading eyes. "You promise me you're going to solve it, John? Promise me. And keep your promise- my one last request from you as her father. *Vær så snill?*"

"I will not rest until her killer is behind bars, for as long as I live, Annika," he kissed her forehead. "I swear on my honor."

John turned his full attention to the bookcase, his eyes latching on to a particularly-striking red spine. It'd been placed between some more Scandinavian authors that had been familiar to him.

Oh, hell no! The name he saw had surely been out of place- and enough to send the strangest mixture of shivers throughout his entire being.

'*Atlas for the Meaningful Life*'. John clenched his fists. *Written by Lar Iktar.*

"John?" he heard Annika call out as he closed his eyes, his rapid breathing only intensified as he took the book out to look at the cover- which only had a visual of a bonfire of some sort. He turned it to the back-cover. The entire portion of the hardback had been enveloped with a photograph he'd never thought in a million years he'd see.

I'm going to miss you so, so much, the tearful voice from the airport at the end of that summer echoed in his head. John opened his eyes, struggling not to drop the book in his hands. An older version of the same face of his forbidden love from youth was undeniable. Sitting on a burgundy armchair, in what appeared to be a luxuriously-carpeted living space.

Lar Iktar. What the fuck was your book doing in my daughter's possession?

115

CHAPTER 12

New York City

LINDA RAMSAY SOUNDED GENUINELY SURPRISED. "Sandy? Is that you darling?" Sandy had figured that would happen. It was a natural reaction, she supposed, for the woman to randomly hear from her daughter's longest friend.

Of course, it's me, lady. You saw my number show up on your phone screen, didn't you? Sandy knew she had to throw in a pleasantry or two before getting to her point. "Mrs. Ramsay! How are you? How's everything going?"

Sandy could never forget the last time they'd spoken, when Linda had phoned her with concern for Kaitlin's well-being in Norway. Afterwards, Sandy had called her friend right before entering the coffee shop where she'd apparently go on to have a jinn-encounter. *Finn-the-jinn was one great actor*, Sandy frowned. Making her believe he'd been a marketing recruiter named Matt Evans. *He should be in Hollywood.*

"I've been alright, doll," Linda's voice remained chipper. "Can't complain much. And yourself? How's New York? You know, my Aidan had left me a couple of brochures when he returned from that big meeting they have every year over there. At, what is it called- United Countries?"

"The United Nations," Sandy stifled a chuckle.

"Oh, yes, yes," Linda continued. "*Les Nations Unis*. He's always working so hard. Well, anyway. It got me thinking about how I need to visit before I become too old to travel, my dear- and see you on Broadway, too, while I'm at it! What show are you taking part in?"

Sandy cringed as she slapped her own forehead softly, thanking the heavens she couldn't be seen doing so from the other end of the line. She hated people associating every form of stage-acting in New York City with Broadway: especially since it reminded her how far she still was from her childhood dreams.

"Oh, you flatter me, Mrs. Ramsay," she remarked. "I'm not on Broadway yet. But I'm getting there. We're just about to wrap up 'The Cherry Orchard' by Anton Chekhov at this small theater downtown, if you could make it before next weekend. But, then again, I doubt you'd be traveling down here before first crossing the big pond- am I right?"

"Oh, of course, of course, my dear," Linda continued on the other side of the line. "Kaitlin holds the phone up to Malin's babbling, and I melt like ice cream. Can you believe her other grandmother got to see her before me! I told Kaitlin. I don't care how they supposedly had that unused ticket to Norway to see their son; Paul should have arranged for all of us to meet our precious Malin at the same time."

"I hear you," Sandy threw in for good measure, eyeing the clock.

"Kaity tries to console me, saying at least I'll be the one with Malin on her first birthday, but, still…This simply isn't fair when I'm…"

Sandy decided she had to get a word in at that moment, or forever hold her peace- and her plane ticket. *I criticize Kaitlin for complaining about her relationship with her mother, but I hear the woman speak- and I get it.*

"Umm, Mrs. Ramsay?" Sandy seized a moment of silence in Linda's conversation. "See, about Norway- I was thinking of joining you on your trip next week, actually."

"*Mon Dieu!*" Linda exclaimed. "That's wonderful. Does Kaity know? She didn't mention anything. How will you deal with your theatrical duties? By the way, call me Momma Linda- like you used to, remember?"

"Okay, I will," Sandy answered with a smile. "And, well, it just so happens that I'll be having two weeks off from the stage," she continued. "I realized it coincided with your planned trip, from what Kaitlin mentioned during one of our chats. It'd be a surprise for her, by the way- I haven't mentioned anything about possibly visiting. What do you think? Do you think she'd be okay with that? God knows I want to see my unofficial little niece already- especially for her first birthday." *It doesn't exactly look like I'll be settling down with kids anytime soon.*

"Oh, sweetheart, I think that's such a swell idea!" Linda sounded excited. "I'm sure she'll be thrilled. Heck- they're already used to hosting two long-term visitors from when Paul's parents were over there. I'm flying out Saturday. Did you buy your ticket yet?"

"Well, I already have my ticket to Amsterdam, actually," Sandy revealed. She'd been able to secure the last remaining seats on a Delta flight to Europe on promotion. There were no direct flights to Stavanger, which was only about an hour-long flight from the Netherlands. *Worse comes to worse, I'll just have fun in the coolest city in Europe,* she'd figured. "If you don't think Kaitlin would mind, I'll look for a transfer flight for the same day, then. Might even catch you on the same transfer flight- you're doing KLM? Lufthansa?"

"KLM, honey," Linda affirmed. "Amsterdam, yes. You know, I remember Kaitlin's dad and I had the loveliest time there on the canals. I never tried those special cakes they get high on over there. Zachary had insisted but…"

Sandy attempted to drown out the rest of Linda's trip down memory lane. Having lost her own parents in a fire when she'd been a teenager, and without any other siblings at that- Sandy had grown to create families for herself through her social circle.

It'll be good to see Kaitlin and her little bundle of joy. Sandy realized she could have told Kaitlin she wanted to visit- a surprise wasn't exactly necessary. And, yet, she knew her friend. Kaitlin would surely feel overwhelmed and say how she'd rather have Sandy over during a more 'suitable' time where she could show her around and tend to her more. *Yadi yadi yada,* Sandy thought with a smile. *No need for some perfect getaway. Momma's got other fish to fry as well.*

Linda's continuing conversation on the other end reminded Sandy of her friend whenever she'd get nervous, actually. *Kaitlin has more in common with her mother than she realizes.*

Kaitlin had blurted out the identify of Finn as a jinn, and despite pretty much ignoring the topic afterwards- Sandy was able to appease both her utter shock and fears through her own subsequent research. She'd simply become too curious to let it wait another off-season from her performances; she had to fly to Norway and find some things out for herself.

I'll leave grandma Linda alone with them as much as possible. I won't be in the way much, and Kaitlin shouldn't mind. She wouldn't, would she?

Who was she kidding? Sandy was also very single for the first time in a long time, and had grown particularly curious about the cabin Kaitlin had told her about. Sending her the woodsy picture of her and The Group, in fact, where Sandy had grown to find a certain jinn by the name of Bjorn particularly intriguing. *Bjorn Berg.* The Group, it turned out, actually had a website- a very simple one about paper that hadn't alluded to anything philosophical about nature and all the crap Kaitlin insisted these beings had been united around to 'recruit people', in her terms.

No. Nothing had been interesting about the website without any pictures of them, even. Sandy had a hunch it was a cover-site used for the few companies that truly did use them for lumber and paper. Just names. Some stock imagery of trees and piles of paper. A mission statement about socially-responsible logging and fair prices. And a telephone number. With a list of names. She'd casually found out from Kaitlin that 'the guy next to the blonde' in the picture- who was apparently some human chick named Anja- went by the name of Bjorn. And the rest had been history.

She'd found him on social media, and he'd confirmed his membership in The Group. Bjorn had apologized for Finn's actions, and invited Sandy over 'for coffee' and showing her around the 'wonders of Norway'. To make up for 'that whole thing'. Whenever she'd be visiting her friend Kaitlin, of course. Not just to meet him or anything. Only if there would be time.

Curiosity and some jinn-hunk's generic invitation wasn't the main purpose of her planned surprise visit, she reminded herself. *Of course not.* It was to see Kaitlin and Malin, and to lend a hand to her friend.

Besides, it wasn't as if she'd had some extraterrestrial abduction. Finn hadn't harmed her or Kaitlin. No one had been pressuring or threatening her. She was a big girl who could make her decisions on whom she'd felt intrigued by enough to get to know a little better. She could be open-minded, couldn't she?

She cleared her throat. *Friendship first.* This was to first and foremost be a baby visit. If there was time, she'd meet Bjorn for coffee.

And that was to be the end of it.

§

Sandnes

KAITLIN LOST COUNT OF HOW LONG SHE'D BEEN AWING AT THE POST-IT note. Paul had left it for her on the coffee machine again, just as he would do so- albeit more frequently- during their first year of living together. *Have a beautiful day my mermaids,* a smile brewed on the corner of her lips while she read it again to herself. He had also added a little caricature of two mermaids inside a heart- one an adult and one a little girl. *I wish he'd still do more surprises like this more often.*

The yellow post-it reminded her of the other, less pleasant one she'd discovered at their balcony in Stavanger after their new puppy, Bo, had been dog-napped by Finn. She shuddered, pouring herself another cup of coffee. *Then again- what surprises have I really done for him lately?* Paul was a domestic type who'd much rather be surprised with a novel dish than a new lingerie item from his wife, but Kaitlin had to be fair. *To each their own.*

Kaitlin's smile remained fixed on her face as she got up to answer the door. She knew it'd be Paul. He'd outgrown several redeeming features, yet ringing the doorbell to kiss his wife as she opened the door- despite having his own key- had also remained permanent. Besides, the clock on the wall pointed to 3:30 in the afternoon.

"*Salut, ma belle,*" Paul leaned over to kiss her on the forehead. His frozen lips and minty breath reminded Kaitlin how much she'd been missing a walk out in nature lately. Something she not only couldn't do because she had to watch Malin now, but also because Paul's face would turn various shades of pink and purple every time the words 'nature' would be mentioned. He'd vowed to ignore her 'interaction' with a 'wrong crowd' in Stavanger, reiterating how their new place in Sandnes needed to be their 'new beginning' as a family of three.

"The note made me smile, thank you," Kaitlin held on a moment longer than usual in her embrace.

"It didn't make Malin smile?" Paul pulled his face backward, flashing Kaitlin a pout.

"I know with us as her parents, Malin's bound to be a genius, but, alas, I'm afraid she hasn't started reading yet!" Kaitlin teased with a laugh.

"Cute, babe, cute," Paul rubbed his hands together after hanging up his coat. "You know I was referring to my drawing. By the way- is the heat enough in here for you girls? Can Malin nap well like this?"

"She was distracted by it and smiled, her daddy-highness," Kaitlin assured him. "We're warm in here, babe, don't worry. Come have a little snack."

"Let me look at our little love, first," Paul whispered, inching closer to the bedroom.

"Why don't you wash your hands first and be ready for her," Kaitlin suggested, not bothering to lower her voice. Though Malin didn't have much trouble sleeping through noise, parental instincts usually would have both of them whispering whenever they'd wanted to ensure she continue to get her rest. "She should be waking up soon, anyway."

"Look at that," Paul spoke through the door he'd slightly cracked open further. "She's sleeping with her stuffed mermaid. Coincidence?"

"Well, I may have added it there for her to wake up to. You know. Inspired by the note." Kaitlin beamed.

"You are my mermaid, for certain," Paul grabbed her face in his palms. "You swam across the Atlantic Ocean to come save me from my fruitful yet joyless life alone here in this Scandinavian paradise. Paradise is hell when you can't share it."

"I know, sweety," Kaitlin touched her forehead against his. "*Je t'aime*. Hey. Are you alright?"

"I'm alright," Paul mumbled. He walked to the kitchen counter and poured himself a cup of coffee. Watching him gulp it down without any milk surprised Kaitlin further on top of his particular sentimentalism.

"Babe, your heart murmur condition…" she began, but Paul waved a dismissive hand to her face. "Didn't that doctor say you shouldn't have more than one cup of coffee a day? And I think you missed your pill this morning, too."

"I'll take it before bed," Paul reassured her, "and this is my first cup today. I even forgot coffee at the office today, can you believe it? I read that e-mail from old John Walker when I woke up, and my mind's gone haywire the entire day, I suppose."

No such thing as coincidence, Kaitlin's heart sank so low that she couldn't distinguish whether the voice in her head had been her own thought or Finn's. *His words from my memory, or from possibly his current presence here with us.*

"Wow," she muttered with a shiver. Maybe Paul had been right. Maybe they did have to increase the temperature inside the apartment. "Your old boss, huh? What are the odds? It isn't Christmas or anything. Was it about his daughter?"

"His daughter?" it was Paul's turn to stare quizzically at Kaitlin. "Oh, you mean, Linette? Well, let's not assume. I mean, I don't know the exact genetic makeup of their bond…."

Oh, shoot, how would I know that? "Yes, babe," Kaitlin nodded, plastering on a smile, sitting next to him at the dining table. "I mean, you said he confided in you that he'd- umm- seen her as his daughter. And the discovery of her body was all over the news, right?"

"Kaitlin?" Paul looked befuddled. "You do know that Linette wasn't exactly some celebrity to have made global headlines with her death or body-discovery."

He pointed his cup toward Kaitlin. "Her open case is of course crucial, and yes- I saw a local article or two on it when I ran a Google search. But I just don't see how its coverage could have expanded beyond regional media."

"Well…who's to say John wasn't following Norwegian media, Paulie?" Kaitlin went on, with a playful eye roll. "If the man was indeed that close to her, wouldn't he have noticed she'd stopped corresponding with him? Not answered phone calls? Wouldn't he have maybe been curious to contact people that may have known her here in Norway? Or, heck, even perhaps run a search on Norwegian news himself, if all that had failed?"

"Babe, are you sure you don't want to send your resume to

Sandnesposten?" Paul chuckled, gazing at the windows. "I swear you needed to have studied Journalism instead of Marketing and all that fancy schmancy stuff...Hey, did you get the blinds in that corner too? Oh, good, you did."

"Ha ha, very funny," Kaitlin smiled, gazing at the window shades, only half-closed, as their view was of trees rather than their neighboring single-family homes. She congratulated herself on having acted fast, lowering them earlier 'for privacy'. Avoiding at least one additional tirade as the sky had already begun to darken for the autumn evening.

Kaitlin had to admit she missed leaving them completely open to view the lights of the city and the passing ships from their seaside apartment back in Stavanger. Gulping down a glass of wine or evening tea. "Paulie, relax, no ship-goer is going to eye us with binoculars," she'd insist.

The memory made her crave a drink just then- yet she couldn't bring herself to risk alcohol that could potentially harm Malin while breastfeeding. "I had, in all seriousness, sent my CV to *Stavanger Aftenblad*, remember? They all require Norsk, damn newspapers..."

"Mmm, hmm," Paul turned his eyes to the television relaying the news in English on BBC. "*Og du trenger å lære norsk, ikke sant?*"

"*Ja Ja*....yes, yes," Kaitlin rolled her eyes. "I *do* need to finally take those Norsk classes. I know, Paulie."

"You know? Come to think of it: you didn't ask what the e-mail said, Kaitlin," Paul continued after a minute of silence. "You just assumed it was about Linette. Have you been thinking about last year again? Is there anything you'd like to tell me?"

"Oh, I didn't even realize," Kaitlin stuttered. "Just hearing his name- my mind went back to poor Linette, I suppose. You're right. I have no clue. What did the e-mail say?"

"He's here in town, apparently," Paul's eyes were still glued to the TV, displaying commercials now for baby food. "Do you think we should begin introducing more solids to Malin?"

"He's here?" Kaitlin feigned surprise. *Father of the year*, Kaitlin remembered Finn's steaming voice. *Traveling across the world to mess us all up!*

"Oh, my goodness. What else did the e-mail say?"

"He just mentioned how he'll be in Norway for a while and recalled that I'd moved here, too," Paul shrugged. "Asked how we've been and congratulated us on becoming parents. That was pretty much it."

Kaitlin took a deep breath, running her hands through Paul's scalp. "I feel really bad about that girl..."

"Someone you didn't know?" Paul responded, eyeing her up and down. "Why Kaitlin?" he went on. "Because you've met her possible killer whilst playing around in the woods when you were bored last winter? That buff and tough guy who burst into our office back home with his jealous rage?"

"First of all," Kaitlin whimpered. "That hurt. You know very well my only intention had been accruing some income on the side. Second, well, maybe so. I mean, I just can't fight the feeling that we've somehow been involved in this whole murder mystery- albeit inadvertently- for a reason."

"For a reason?" Paul raised a brow.

"Yeah," Kaitlin went on. "Think about it. You, with your office connection to that girl from work. And me with...well, everything. I mean, maybe John Walker could even be thinking it was rude of you to not have at least sent him your condolences when all this first happened. Come on, Paul. You're usually the one all about these niceties..."

"I didn't want him to feel uncomfortable, Kaitlin," Paul insisted, turning the volume higher on the TV. "It's not some accident or heart attack. It's a mysterious death, with the possibility of a suicide. And suicides- even potential ones- sort of feel, I don't know, personal to loved ones. I just didn't think he'd particularly appreciate word about it from his professional circle- past or present…"

"Okay, okay. Keep your voice down. Malin will hear!" Kaitlin reminded him.

"I thought you wanted her to wake up!" Paul tilted his head. The smile that appeared on his face disturbed Kaitlin.

She turned her head from him to the baby monitor situated on the coffee table, showing only Malin's cherub face shift with her breathing in sleep. Normally, a nap longer than one hour would only mean a harder time for Malin to fall asleep at night, but for the moment- Kaitlin would just have to deal sacrificing her own sleep to tend to her daughter. It was better for her to rest while her parents tried to sort this craziness out.

The crying that interrupted their bickering just then had strangely felt welcomed, nonetheless. They needed their lifeline if their nerves were to survive making it through dinner.

Paul, not surprisingly, turned into a whole other man before her eyes, throwing Malin in the air. Despite Kaitlin having warned him for the umpteenth time to not 'do that' as she'd 'just woken' up and hadn't even gotten breastfed yet, she smiled along with Malin. Her daughter's joy had proved to be her cure-all.

After a brief breastfeeding session- and an even quicker diaper change- Malin had accompanied her parents' quiet dinner from her baby chair, munching on some baby carrots. Kaitlin's phone rang when they were taking their last bites. Seeing the word 'Mom' appear on her smart phone, Kaitlin clicked off the call.

"Who's that?" Paul raised an eyebrow.

"My mom!" Kaitlin replied with exaggerated slumped shoulders. "I'll call her back after dinner. I'm not mentally prepared at the moment to handle her…"

"You can't talk to your mom next to me?" Paul's voice was stern.

"Paul!" Kaitlin showed him her 'Recent' call list through gritted teeth. "See? That really was my mom. Are you really not going to trust me, after everything I divulged? After everything's been so beautiful here in this new town, with our daughter and..."

"I wasn't accusing you of anything, relax," Paul's voice was calm again. "I just wouldn't want you to be rude to her. The woman is naturally excited about seeing her granddaughter, babe. Speaking of which, my mother..."

"Paulie, we can't house my mother and your parents here at the same time; come on, we've talked about this."

"Well, we technically can," Paul insisted. "Maybe in the summer?"

"Your parents have your niece and nephew back in Quebec to play with. This is a huge deal for my mother- her first grand-child."

"Every grand-child can be special in their own way," Paul had begun, but Kaitlin wasn't hearing it.

I need a shift in tactic, Kaitlin thought. "I mean- God bless your mom for helping me for those two weeks, but your parents have already been here. We can invite them another weekend. And attend to them more fully and properly."

Kaitlin felt glad just then that her father had been out of the picture for as long as she could remember- she didn't think she could handle an additional person in the house. Her overbearing mother could be enough of a presence to compensate for four people sometimes!

"So, you're only okay, it seems, for them to take turns to see their grandchild, I suppose," Paul got up to open the refrigerator. "You don't want to have both sets of grandparents here to spoil Malin with. I understand..."

"*Tabarnak*, Paul. That is not what I said!"

"No cursing in front of Malin, remember?" his angry voice sounded purposely-softened to Kaitlin. She had grown accustomed, after all, to her husband's habit of doing so: in order to make Kaitlin look like the one overreacting.

Paul's phone rang to Elvis Presley's 'Jailhouse Rock', and Kaitlin breathed a sigh of relief. It couldn't have been Jeanette calling from her honeymoon, could it? She smiled, recalling how jealous she'd felt last year about Paul working side-by-side with his childhood friend. The woman had luckily recently gotten married to their fellow colleague- Tim- and Kaitlin didn't think she had any reason to be curious any longer.

Except, she was. "And, who's that now?"

"One second," Paul's face looked alarmed as he put his fork down on the ceramic plate and headed to their empty guest room. "I'll be right back."

She tried her best to overhear his conversation, but all she could hear was Paul chuckling loudly. *He wouldn't be so obvious had he been hiding something, would he?*

After a particularly loud chuckle, Kaitlin clenched her fists and got up to head to their bedroom. *So much for our hourly alone-time to watch TV together before bed.* Throughout dinner, she'd imagined putting on her silk pajama set rather than her usual cotton ones. It was a Friday night, after all, and Paul wouldn't be waking up early the next day. It was also their only day before her mother would be arriving Sunday. *Come on Paul, we could still sneak in a little something- if you're not hiding something from me, that is.*

Kaitlin contemplated whether to give up and head to bed, or completely pull-down the shutters to comfort Paul's paranoia about neighbors seeing them. Paul's footsteps began to inch closer to the room just then. He had a big smile on his face.

"Who was that on the phone, babe?" Kaitlin was intrigued.

"Honey…guess who's coming to dinner?" Paul beamed, arms on his hips.

"Sidney Poitier?" Kaitlin smirked.

"Sidney who?" Paul's toothy grin transformed into a grimace.

Didn't we watch that American classic together? Kaitlin pondered. *Oh, shoot! That was with Dean, wasn't it?* Dean Richards was Kaitlin's college boyfriend back at the University of Toronto, who was now married himself with two kids. He and Kaitlin would occasionally keep in touch online.

"It's an old movie, babe. Forget it." When was the last time she and Paul had been able to watch anything together- including much of the damn news- since Malin was born?

"So, tell me already!" Kaitlin pressed. "Who's coming?"

God, I hope it's not picky Lesley and her husband. I cannot handle another vegan-cooking disaster.

"...Isn't that such a cool coincidence?" Paul interrupted her thoughts.

"What is?"

"John. Mr. E-mail," Paul pulled a chair from the dining table, rolling his eyes. "Weren't you listening, babe?"

"Oh, right, right" Kaitlin immediately cupped her hands around her mouth as soon as she realized how loud her exclamation had been.

"He's apparently here to visit Linette's mother, from what he just told me," Paul's eyes were as wide-open as saucepans. "He said he'd tell me more in person over coffee. Of course, I insisted he dine with us instead. To catch up on Montreal and..."

This has got to be my opportunity to help justice to be served, Kaitlin was convinced as she tuned Paul out. *John Walker*. The man whose arrival had somehow seemed to have shaken Finn and The Group. He'd be there- in their apartment. Did she even need to think it? Finn and The Group- including Meredith on their last phone conversation or two- would often quip what Kaitlin was beginning in her heart to now believe as a universal truth. *No such thing as coincidence.*

CHAPTER 13

D ABBING HIS MOUTH WITH THE WHITE CLOTH NAPKIN BEFORE him, John's grinned at his dinner hosts. " Let me take you kids for a drink out on the town," he proposed. "It's the least I could do for that delicious dinner. I've never quite tasted salmon like that."

"Bon appétit," Kaitlin gleamed, gauging Paul for a reaction.

"You can surely get a babysitter, can't you?" John pressed. "The fresh air will do all of us good upon this stressful conversation…"

"Thank you, sir," Paul met his wife's gaze. "But, some other time. Kaitlin's mom's flight is arriving from Canada tomorrow afternoon, and we need our rest tonight." Paul said with a smirk, bringing on a curious gaze from Kaitlin. "We'll be prepping the house early in the morning before picking her up at the airport…"

"I understand, I understand," John cut in with a yawn. "You don't want to hang out with an old geezer like me on a Saturday night." He added a smile, but Kaitlin didn't exactly feel he'd been too eager for a night out either.

"Sir, honestly, Malin- God bless her- doesn't sleep too well," she tried to assure him. "She wakes up often and had only had one experience so far being babysat- by my friend. And Sibel was being polite, but I had a feeling Malin wasn't exactly a walk in the park…"

"Yeah, sir, she's got a temper, our Malin," Paul chimed in, meeting her gaze. "Engin filled me in later what Sibel may not have told you. Something about throwing a toy at one of the kids. Her temperament is seemingly inherited from her mother, but at least we may be able to get her an athletic scholarship somewhere," Paul erupted in hysterical laughter.

"Oh, yes, of course. She must have gotten that from me, Paulie," Kaitlin decided to play along in front of company, though she felt certain her clenched teeth were showing. "Since you're always such joyful and people-pleasing company to be around."

She made sure to link her arms with Paul's and throw John Walker a smile. His expression displayed more discomfort and shock than being impressed. "Right. Right. You two. You're a beautiful couple. Go easier on each other, will you? You'll regret it when you're older like me…"

"Sir, nonsense, you're not old at all," Paul yanked his arm free from Kaitlin's grip and headed toward the refrigerator. "We're still keeping the wine cool like you like it, from what I remember. You can have a drink here, instead…"

"He's right, Mr. Walker," Kaitlin added, clearing her throat. "Have a drink here. And, besides, you're definitely a classy gentleman. And you're younger than my mother, surely. What are you, like, 43 or something?"

"…Or something," it was John Walker's turn to burst into laughter, matching Paul's hyena pitch. How Kaitlin hated loudness as a quality in men in general.

"No drinks, thank you. I'll be out in a few as soon as I down this cup of coffee. Like I've said," John continued, following a big gulp of the hazelnut latte he'd requested earlier. "I'll be here for a bit longer after Oslo, trying to locate Tan. It's the capital; so hopefully the local cops there will be more help than the ones in Trondheim and here have been. I mean, I'm assuming they should all be in communication with one another, but I also figured there's no harm in pressing them in person. Then, if I don't have any luck in Oslo, I was thinking maybe I could add Bergen to the list. As my last stop to visit the local police there before my return."

"Oh, I'm sure the cops in Oslo will be helpful," Kaitlin's expression froze on an indistinct piece of lint on the leather couch she plopped herself on. *He can't be here in this room with us, listening in, can he?*

"By the way, I'm sure your mother is a lovely lady, Kaitlin, regardless of her age. If she's birthed you…"

"Thank you…" Kaitlin smiled sheepishly. The compliment jolted her out of her momentary reverie.

"Momma Linda is just lovely, for sure," Paul added in a tone Kaitlin couldn't make out in regards to whether or not it'd been well-intentioned or sarcastic. She knew he wasn't exactly fond of her 'judgmental' mother, and had occasionally referred to her as such.

"She's coming to see the angel sleeping there, I'm sure…" John Walker darted a look in the direction of her room, and Kaitlin wanted to capitalize on the moment.

"Let me go check in on Malin, gentleman," she whispered, tiptoeing closer to her closed door- decorated by a gray-hued wreath with felt, pink rocking horses glued on.

Sleeping like an angel, indeed, she thought, smiling as she inched closer to her daughter to observe the rise and fall of her chest. *And on her back this time. Paul should come and see this. I'm doing something right.*

"I wish I could have seen my Linette," she heard John's tearful voice erupt suddenly- more audible than he intended, she was sure. Kaitlin took a sneak outside the door to see his face buried in his palms. "I should have let you know she was my actual daughter before, too. Maybe you could have aided me in my investigation from earlier on."

"No use in mourning our uncontrollable pasts, sir," Paul chimed.

"I avoided coming here for so long, Paul," John continued. "Too long. I didn't want Norway to remind me of…well…anyway. Oh, I should have come after Linette. I thought she'd wanted a fresh new start. No contact. Maybe that's why she chose this dark route. Maybe I'm just kidding myself, and this has nothing to do with some guy. Maybe I'm the reason she truly did do this...the reason she sacrificed herself."

"Don't say that, Mr. Walker!" Kaitlin darted out the door faster than intended, glancing behind her to ensure Malin hadn't awoken. She heard her daughter murmur a subtle coo and move her head, but then she appeared to be lulled back to rest once again. *Good.* "The case may very well have been murder," she sat down next to Paul.

Kaitlin suddenly got unexplainable chills across her chest and shoulders. *Mind your own business, Kaitlin. You hate when people butt in to yours- so why are you getting so involved in this?*

"Kaitlin, you okay?" Paul placed a firm grip on her left shoulder. His hazel gaze was warm and genuine from what she could construe.

I'm simply incapable of being someone with a poker face, aren't I? "I just want to help Linette, Paul," Kaitlin continued. "I didn't know her, as you did, of course. But it all seems so unfair. Especially with Mr. Walker being here. How he couldn't openly admit her paternity for years in Canada, and she had to grow up without him in her life for the most part. And then, for her to be taken so soon. Just like that. I just...*"*

It was Kaitlin's turn to shed a tear, which she quickly wiped with the back of her hand.

"Seems you've given her the backstory, Paul," John smiled feebly. "It's alright. I appreciate it. You've got a heart of gold, Kaitlin. I appreciate your sentiments. You've chosen a good one, Paul Maverick."

"Yes, I have," Paul answered, not looking at Kaitlin. "So, sir, tell me again who you've questioned so far. I can't imagine anyone other than that Tan guy killing her either, but we need statements from more people to aid with evidence and to lead us easier to him..."

"Well, I went to that cabin she'd written to me about..."

Oh, shoot. Apparently, it's easier to locate without getting lost for everyone other than me, Kaitlin thought with a deep breath which had inadvertently caught a whiff of John's aroma. *This guy sure sprays himself a lot.* Not quite musky or earthy, though. What was it that she'd caught a scent of? Gardenias? Kaitlin smiled. Paul would claim it wasn't 'manly' enough.

"Cabin, eh?" Paul darted a stern look in Kaitlin's eyes.

"I only came across a young woman," John was oblivious to the couple's awkward glances. "She resembled my Linette a lot actually. Meredith Olsen, was the name. A strange but nice young lady. She said she used to date Tan. Can you imagine if he really does turn out to be behind this? I should have warned that young lady to be careful, as well…"

"Kaitlin?" Paul asked, slouching on his chair and crossing his arms. "Would you care to fill in Mr. Walker on everyone else you met at that cabin last year? You know? Since you want to aid in his investigation and all?"

Damn you, Paul! Kaitlin was sure her shock must have been stronger than the one which had become written on John's face.

"Your wife? How would she know these folks?" John Walker's eyes were as wide as the cosmos.

"You asked for this," Paul whispered in her ear. "You owe him the truth. Even if you still seem to avoid it with me when it comes to details."

"Not fair, Paulie!" Kaitlin hissed back despite her attempt at a whisper.

"Umm, alright," John cleared his throat, glancing at the two of them. "I have to take my cue to leave, finally. You two kids must be tense about heading to sleep already to wake up for the airport tomorrow. Maybe I can stop by another time before I leave, when it's more suitable. You can always call me if Kaitlin or you remember anything."

"No, no, sir, please stay," Kaitlin insisted. *Paul isn't exactly going to go easier on me if we're alone in the house.* "My mother's flight isn't until later tomorrow. I'm just trying to remember. Hmm. Well- Tan. I didn't even know his last name, to be honest, until you mentioned it, Mr. Walker. In fact, I didn't even know Meredith's last name was Olsen. I was just casually introduced to them after I'd been, umm, approached about a job opportunity. To translate for a group of friends who ran a business from that cabin."

Oh my God. Why in the hell did I have to get myself involved in this?

"Go ahead, Kaitlin," Paul pressed. "Tell him the name of the fancy Paul Bunyan with the blond hair? The headhunter himself…"

I can't. I don't want to say his name in this house. Kaitlin felt her heart about to leap outside her chest. "Umm, it was French. So, it's stuck in my mind. Du Feu, was the last name…."

"French, eh?" John leaned closer to her with a raised eyebrow. "Hmm. What could his first name have been, then? Do you recall? Something popular, like Jacques or Julien or something of the sort?"

"Umm, no, something with an 'F' sound, actually…. I think…"
He's closing in on me.

"Philippe? Felix? F…?" John was relentless.

"Finn!" Kaitlin's frustration was multiplied. She regretted it as soon as the name escaped her mouth uncontrollably.

Shit!

Kaitlin froze in her tracks almost immediately as she stood upright in her chair. Her neck began throbbing with what felt like thin but pointy stabs of metal.

"Hmm, alright, I'll try to see if that name pops up across any of the searches the police conduct," John sulked. "I should just give up. If the capital of the entire country doesn't help with the case, maybe it'll be a sign I really do need to let it go. I promised her mother. But, maybe we'll have to face the music. A lot of people can just commit suicide, I suppose…"

"You can't do that, Mr. Walker" Kaitlin's nature got the best of her. *No way you came all the way here to our house and it wasn't for a reason. I promised myself. Linette. I have to help your dead daughter.*

"There's more indication it was a murder cover-up, with the notes and her arm placement during burial if you ask me. Don't ignore your instincts, sir. You've come this far. And with Tan in Oslo- something is bound to come up!"

All this couldn't have been for nothing. Maybe…just maybe I've been going through hell among heaven to help bring justice to a dead woman's case.

The throbbing began strengthening just then. Warning her. *I'm not giving any further information. About The Group. Or indicating anyone in particular. Not that I really know too many details anyhow.*

An audible sigh from John Walker brought Kaitlin's attention back into the moment. His eyes were laser-focused on the thumbs he was now fiddling. "Oslo, huh? You know he's there? What would he be doing there?"

Kaitlin reveled in the silence for a moment. She felt the courage to look back into Paul's eyes again, gaging for a reaction. Nothing. "Meredith had mentioned something about him being in Oslo."

Paul stood up as he cleared his throat, murdering the eerie quiet with his rapidity. "You sure you don't want that glass of wine, sir, before you leave?"

"Ok, Maverick," John managed a smile. "I'll oblige. I could use one, I suppose, indeed. I'll call the cab right afterward back to the hotel."

"Scandic, wasn't it? By the airport?" Paul inquired.

"No, Radisson Blu. I mean, yes, the first night I stayed there but I wanted to be closer to the city center by the lake…"

Kaitlin's heart took a momentary leap as her mind raced back to her walks with Finn by the very same lake. *What was that?* A hair had painfully buzzed at the back of her neck once again. Her ears also began ringing just then.

Was this the way it always felt when he came near me? For the life of her, Kaitlin could not quite recall. *And I never realized? Or, never attributed it to him, at least?*

"Figured it'd be closer to that cabin Tan used to live in for me to investigate," John continued. Paul was nodding along with a shot of whisky he'd now poured for himself. Kaitlin's attention was piqued with the mention of the cabin. She forced herself to pay attention to the most uncomfortable conversation. "But apparently he's in Oslo now, according to Kaitlin. I wish Meredith would have told that to me too."

Your wife's thirsty too, Paul. She knew he wouldn't ask her whether she'd wanted a drink, as she was breastfeeding; yet a part of her still felt disappointment. She could have been offered a bloody cup of water at the very least, couldn't she?

"Serdar was also helpful, telling me Linette would come over occasionally, but that he'd try to stay out when she was. You know, to give her and Tan privacy…"

"Sirdal? Who's that?" Paul's puzzlement quickly disappeared. "Oh, you'd visited that macho guy's old roommate- right?"

"Serdar. With an 'R' at the end, yes," John explained. "These foreign names. I can never quite pronounce them right. I'd always thought Turkish ones would be similar to Arabic, but they're two very different languages."

"Arabic? You speak Arabic?"

"My mother and I are originally from Lebanon," John nodded. "I'm half-Lebanese. She'd talk to me exclusively in Arabic, before I moved out to stay with my Canadian father."

"Wow," Paul muttered, locking eyes with Kaitlin. "I never would have thought you were anything than fully Canadian, sir. That's so cool. So, Linette, I suppose, was only half Norwegian, eh?"

"That's right," John went on. "She took on her mother's maiden name. Annika couldn't even place my name on her birth certificate. I was a different man back then, Paul. I was very selfish. Helen's been good to me. Too good to me. But I wasn't fair to her any more than I could be fair to Annika- Linette's mother. I made her promises that I could marry her…when I couldn't. I always thought about convenience…Always convenience."

Kaitlin got up to pour herself some seltzer water while John downed his glass through wistful thoughts. "Would you like another glass, Mr. Walker?"

"No, no, dear Kaitlin, this is it. I see it's almost 11. I'm calling that cab right now, and you kids are going straight to bed."

"Nonsense. I'm driving you back, sir."

"You'll be doing no such thing, Paul. You kiss your sleeping angel and head straight to bed with your wife, you hear? Get your rest and pick up your mother-in-law tomorrow. Nothing more important than family…"

"But, sir, it's no trouble at all…" Paul insisted.

"What's all my money worth it if I can't be of any use at least to myself, let alone someone else?" John put on his coat and turned toward Kaitlin. "Thanks again for your hospitality. I'll be heading to Oslo after some sightseeing tomorrow- Helen's awaiting some pictures of those fjords. Call me if anything else comes to your mind…"

"Thank you again for the lovely gift, Mr. Walker," Kaitlin chimed, glancing at the wrapped-box on the table for Malin. "I hope Oslo goes well for you, and to see you before your return to Canada."

"Yes, we owe you a night out on the town, sir. Maybe Malin can fall asleep earlier when her grandmother is here, and she can allow us a night out before you leave." Paul chuckled as John patted his back by the door.

Maybe Oslo will allow him to reach Tan and help place him

behind bars where he belongs, Kaitlin thought as she waved him goodbye.

Then we may have something to celebrate. Maybe justice can finally be served.

"Thank you, kids. And thank you Kaitlin, for sharing what you've been through- I feel more confident heading to Oslo now. Oh, and one other thing, dear Kaitlin. Do you recall meeting an older man with that Du Feu fellow and the rest of them? A man by the name of Lar Iktar, to be exact?"

Kaitlin felt like she'd just been punched in the stomach. The shock of the name still pulsing through her veins. "Lar Iktar?" she managed to ask.

"Yes, Lar. I recognized the man from my youth- a photograph from a book Linette had among her things that her mother and I came across in her room. I wish I'd taken it with me, but I just dropped it from my trembling hands. He's my age, and I knew him a long time ago. He's apparently become a popular author now."

"You knew Lar Iktar?" Kaitlin repeated. The room appeared to be spinning around her. Had she accidentally spiked her water over dinner?

"We, umm, had worked together in Dubai back in our youth," John muttered. "My dad was a Canadian engineer frequently taking on projects in Beirut- it's where he'd met my mother, actually. Well- lo and behold- his company had a paid internship opportunity for college students that summer in the Emirates nearby, and I took it. As a young man, I wanted to get away from my mom for a while, ya know?" John smirked as he playfully nudged Paul's arm with his own, creating a look more of confusion than understanding of the comedic implication on Kaitlin's husband's face. *Sadly, no, sir- Paul wouldn't know,* she thought, fighting the innate, catty urge to tease Paul about his constant calls to his parents and sisters back in Canada.

She'd married a momma's boy- and was told by friends it was an endearing trait- yet Kaitlin had never thought so. Treating one's mom and women with respect and kindness- of course, she loved that. But insisting your mom and siblings visit for long periods of time in a house as a married man…

"Kaitlin?" Paul interrupted her thoughts. "Do you remember the name of that dish? The one we had at that Arabic restaurant in Spain?"

"Oh, the one we loved?" Kaitlin was trying to remember. What the heck were these two now talking about? What did a restaurant have to do with Lar Iktar, and what had she missed? "*Baba ghanoush*? Was it? The one with the eggplants, right?"

She sighed with relief upon seeing Paul nod excitedly. "You have to try the recipe one day, babe." Paul added- and Kaitlin's smile immediately evaporated.

"Yes, well, it was Lar's favorite at that restaurant where we ended up having lunch." John's eyes were now transfixed in memory, staring almost non-blinkingly at the kitchen counter. "At first, we were splitting the bill, but I caught him counting his money one time. And he didn't exactly refuse when I offered to pick up the tab after that. Lar was, I learned, from a humbler background despite having been able to land the same internship. He was from a working class family. Not very ambitious back then. So, imagine my surprise seeing how he's apparently made it to heading some company here in Norway."

"They mostly just called him Lar," Kaitlin shrugged, eyeing the door. "I remember I did find it strange they'd address him by first name. But, from what I was able to gather through talking to Meredith from the cabin; Lar was apparently an Adjunct Lecturer at some university up in Trondheim where she was also a student."

"Meredith is from Trondheim too, huh?" John clicked his tongue. "Look at that. Yeah, I looked him up on LinkedIn and other sites as well. No doctoral degree- just a Master's one from Oslo. But apparently, he became a hit with the students, and they continued giving him classes for years."

As if her utter shock that John Walker had met Meredith at that cabin in Stavanger wasn't enough, to now discover that Linette had a book written by Lar Iktar! This was getting stranger to Kaitlin by the minute. "I was told he was also behind their life philosophy- living in the woods and all. They all quoted him frequently. But I cannot imagine how- or why- your daughter may possibly have interest in...?"

"Why not, Kaitlin?" Paul asked with an exaggerated shrug. "You almost inadvertently joined them as their translator or what not, didn't you?"

Touché, Kaitlin hated when Paul was pesky and bitter- but more so on those rare occasions when he was right. Had Linette been lured into The Group by Tan? Or Lar? Perhaps it had been neither, and she was simply curious about the man from Tan's discussions. Heck- how much did Kaitlin really know about her? Perhaps she'd joined them first, and Tan was the one lured later on? Was Linette the type of young woman who'd be free-spirited enough to join some mischievous cult-like small business in the woods?

"I'm still in shock about this so-called paper business you speak of," John was shaking his head. "I'd thought that Meredith girl was alone in that cabin. Some young cat lady- alone after betrayal by her ex-lover."

"How do you think your daughter may have known about Lar, sir?" Kaitlin asked. "She had his book, right? And, Paul? What do you think- from what you remember of your late old colleague?"

Paul patted John on his back comfortingly. "Maybe she just heard of the book and purchased it coincidentally? You know what guys? I'm ordering that book right now. Maybe it could contain a clue. Sir, what was the name of that book Linette had?"

"I wasn't enough," John mourned. "She didn't know where she could feel like she belonged. I couldn't be enough."

"Sir?" Paul repeated.

"Oh," John looked up at him. "Sorry. The book. Yes. It became quite an influential book, apparently. Topped several European charts. *'Atlas for the Meaningful Life'*."

"I'm on it! Ordering right now!" Paul was tapping away on his smart phone. Kaitlin's heart sank as his mouth managed to ask her his subsequent question, though his eyes were avoiding hers. "Did you see it at that bookstore you visited the other day, babe?"

"Why, what about the other day?" Kaitlin snapped back, cursing herself almost immediately soon after as Paul raised his eyebrow. *I'm so terrible with this.* "I mean, I just couldn't really stay out as long as I wanted to, babe, you know? I couldn't even look around the bookstore much. Just sort of had my coffee, inhaled the ocean breeze, walked around a bit and immediately felt the need to return to Malin."

She smiled in John's direction for support. *Please say something.*

"Becoming a parent is the biggest thing to happen in life, isn't it?" John finally uttered, with melancholy, downcast eyes.

She'd only been a mother for eleven months, but already she couldn't imagine being away from Malin- who'd immediately felt like an extension of her soul through the formation of a new body. Ever since holding her bloody and wrinkly birth-face in her arms.

"They make everything worthwhile," Kaitlin patted John's arm, as he'd finally opened the door. "Somehow all the terrible things we've experienced seem to have occurred for a reason- for us to have gotten to the point where we became parents. Hold on to whatever memories you're able to with your late daughter, sir. And be grateful you had them, at least."

"I'd already missed most of her childhood," John responded, removing from his feet the plastic covers Kaitlin reserved for guests. "And now, I wasn't even able to be there at the end of her life, either."

"My own father missed out on most of my childhood, too", she

wanted to say, but stopped herself. How would she conclude that thought- with the cliché "…and look at how well I turned out?"

Kaitlin smirked. *Had* she turned out well? As far as she was concerned, it could certainly be up for debate.

CHAPTER 14

WITH THE SUN CUTTING THROUGH THE WINDOW PANE, Kaitlin's heart began to fill with hope. She could actually accomplish something today. "Please let me drive, babe," Kaitlin said, using the ungloved portion of her wrist to push back the chunk of hair that had fallen out from her ponytail. Sibel had agreed to watch Malin again while Kaitlin and Paul worked together to tidy up the apartment. She'd focused on scrubbing the guest room where Linda Ramsay would be staying the most. Housecleaning was one of the many overly-priced services in Norway.

"Babe, I know you've missed driving around town since Malin was born, but why today of all days?" Paul was working on their bathroom window the hardest. Foggy stains from inadequate sprays or wiping cloths had been one of the rare pet peeves the husband and wife had in common.

"Paulie, please," Kaitlin began. "We promised last night to leave that awkward conversation with your old boss behind us for these two weeks. That whatever happened with me and the cabin must have occurred so we could help him seek justice for his daughter."

"Relax, Kaitlin," Paul shrugged, though his face appeared to Kaitlin to be repressing his true feelings. "I won't be opening that can of worms. Don't worry. I was referring to how you don't have your license here yet and- well- Momma Linda won't exactly feel the joyous welcome we're intending for her with the local police on our *culs*."

"Well, trust me," Kaitlin sneered. "I've already braced myself for just about thirty or so separate indiscretions in my mother's mind she

144

could criticize me about." Keeping up the home or mothering Malin would certainly top the list, Kaitlin was convinced. "I want to show her I've been able to do this one thing right at least. Surprise her straight off the bat at the airport. I've handled that highway before, come on."

"Okay, but we need to warm you up with a practice, catch-up drive first," Paul said as he took off his plastic gloves and laid them on the top of their washing machine. "You know? It's been a while since you drove us to *Kvadrat* and back- and it's the same highway you'll be driving in later. How long does Sibel still have Malin?"

"I'd say about another hour and a half, or so," Kaitlin responded, eyeing their ship-shaped wall clock hanging on the hallway wall. "We can grab coffee and, I don't know, maybe a little something for my mom at the airport."

"You want to do the balloon and teddy bear thing again, I'm assuming?" Paul attempted a smile as he rolled his eyes. "I hear my dad still hugs the little fella to sleep."

"Ha ha, you keep laughing," Kaitlin teased, inching closer to Paul with an embrace that had her arms to his back pocket. *Right on his butt.* "But that was a special souvenir in addition to the flowers. The little girl teddy bear had the cutest bow and Norwegian-flag dress. To remind them of Malin? Hello! You've got to give me more credit than you do." She reached for the keys to their Audi and jiggled them out of his pocket playfully. "The house looks good, and I'm putting on my jeans. Let's go do this!"

"*D'accord, d'accord*," Paul reluctantly agreed, picking out his favorite button-down jean shirt from the closet.

"Remember the last time I drove us?" Kaitlin asked, smiling as she put on a designer belt on her jeans as well, making sure it'd be visible to her mom by tucking her turtleneck inside her jeans. "I was just about two months or so pregnant, wasn't I? You were warning me against strapping my seatbelt on too tight over my stomach. I also recall…well never mind." An intimate detail from one of their rare but sweet lovemaking sessions on the first night in their new place played out in Kaitlin's mind, making her blush.

"What?" Paul asked, cocking his head slightly to the side, only to subsequently open his eyes wide a moment later. "You mean when I was…in you…asking if I was accidentally touching…. oh my God!"

As they both burst into laughter, Kaitlin said a little prayer of gratitude to herself before heading out. *I hope our base remains this strong, God, so that no outside force can affect it. May I drive- and my mother arrive-safely, and may we all get through these two weeks with blissful memories. Amen.*

§

"WHICH FLOWERS SAY 'WELCOME' BETTER?" Kaitlin asked, her takeaway cup of mocha latte in one hand while the other was softly caressing the petals of two different bouquets.

The smile hadn't left her face for the past 45 minutes as she'd managed to drive them to the shopping center- where they'd gone into a store or two before getting coffee. Even finding time to check in on Malin via video call.

"The purple ones look pretty, and hey, look at that, they're on sale…" Paul casually remarked, swaying side to side with his eyes glued to his cell phone while Kaitlin was walking around the flower shop. *Ouch.* She had to admit she actually liked the mostly purple arrangement more than the multi-color one she'd also been eyeing. Yet the '*salg*' tag had turned her off from deeming it worthy to give to her mother. Especially since…

"Hmm, I don't recall looking for a sale item to welcome your parents last spring?" Kaitlin's eyes were still glued to the flowers.

"I didn't purposely seek a sale item for Momma Linda, Kaitlin." Paul's voice was stern as he neared her face. She'd always liked that he

146

was taller than her but only by a hand's length or so. Even in her average heels; he could kiss the top of her forehead yet never tower over her. "I just happened to observe that this lovely arrangement was on sale. What's wrong with that? Why do you have to bring my parents into this?"

"Whatever, it's okay, you're right, I like this one too," Kaitlin tried to brush it off and headed toward the cashier. She knew he'd react this way, yet something inside her couldn't help but comment whenever she sensed non-special treatment. She'd grown so accustomed to Paul having made her feel like the only woman in the world during their friendship-turned-dating days that when the pedestal she'd been placed on felt demoted to her, Kaitlin felt hurt. "Let's just pick Malin up and head to the airport already."

Paul shot her a vague look and remained quiet as she used their mutual credit card to pay for the purple flowers.

"*Tusen takk*!" he thanked the friendly cashier, exaggerating his smile- in Kaitlin's opinion. To ensure everyone around them that everything was alright, in his typical fashion- as far as she was concerned.

"If you want, I can take us to Sibel's faster, and you can drive us to the airport." Paul commented after their hand-holding yet physically distant walk back to the car had halted in front of their sports car. "Maybe we can even stop by that *Rimi* close to their house in our old neighborhood. You know- pick up something sweet to thank Sibel and Engin for watching Malin."

"Oh, I remember that *Rimi*," Kaitlin nodded excitedly. "I've got this, don't worry. Buckle up, flower man."

She met Paul's subsequent look with a truce-seeking smile. "Let's go!" he spoke once they were both in the car.

Was it true what Sibel had told her? Kaitlin was distracted while driving as carefully as she could. *We do truly marry an entire family*

147

rather than just one person, don't we? Even if they're far away they manage to affect marriages.

Kaitlin was secretly wishing she'd been driving to Sibel's without Paul, so she could vent to her friend over some of that Turkish tea again after picking up Malin, when Paul reached for the steering wheel. "What are you doing?"

Kaitlin shook her head and snuck a look to the rear-window just in time to see that she'd swayed the car too far to the right and almost onto the gravel. Luckily Paul had caught the wheel and turned it slightly to the left again in time. "Sorry, I was just thinking about picking up Malin and…We're almost there, I see the market after that next light, right?"

Kaitlin pressed on the brakes at the traffic light, and turned her face to Paul- who'd had his hand on his chin with his eyes closed. "Paulie? Right?"

"You could have gotten us into an accident, Kaitlin, or worse!" he blurted.

"I-I'm sorry, okay?" Kaitlin tried her best to fight back tears, taking in a deep breath as the light turned green. Her foot shook as she stepped on the gas pedal again. "I'm going to *Rimi*."

"Go ahead," Paul said mockingly. "It is indeed, there, yes. You know best!"

"You can stay in the car if you want," Kaitlin whimpered, pulling into the market parking lot. "I'll find a box of chocolates or something. Whoa…" The front bumper hit the curb as Kaitlin had to step extra hard on the brakes while pulling the Audi in between one of the only remaining parking spots that were available.

"What are you doing- speeding here like that? Elaine can park better than you!"

The reference to Paul's youngest- and most annoying sibling, in Kaitlin's opinion- was the straw that broke the camel's back. Kaitlin felt her fury reach a boiling point. "Oh, wonderful. Maybe you'd like to send her a grand arrangement across the ocean to congratulate her on driving better than your wife!"

"Really? This is still going to be about the flowers- is that what it is?" Paul was steaming. "Would you rather go pick flowers in that damn forest in Stavanger, Kaitlin? Huh?"

"I knew you wouldn't let it go," Kaitlin shook her head with disappointment. "Look, I don't want to see your face or hear your crazy voice overreacting right now. I need to stay calm when picking up Malin and later on the road."

Compared to her several drives in Toronto, Kaitlin did always feel relatively more comforted in Norwegian traffic. She especially adored how everyone yielded to the right of way at roundabouts without traffic lights. Nonetheless, one could never be sure, could they?

"You can drive to Sibel's by yourself then!" Paul reached across to unlock the doors from Kaitlin's driver's side. "I'll meet you there."

"Paul? Paul! You're not really going to leave me stranded in the car by myself, are you?" Kaitlin felt her hands begin to tremble on the steering wheel, her expression frozen in shock. Paul had unbuckled his seat belt and already opened his door.

"I already have." Shutting the door behind him and kneeling down to mutter through the half-cracked window, Paul fogged the window as he spoke. "You're lucky we're picking up our girl right now- I wouldn't leave her in the back with you as the driver later. I need a damn walk alone. See you at their house."

As he shut the door fast behind him, Kaitlin shut her eyes and released the long held-back waterfalls from her eyes.

§

"PAUL'S HERE, GIRLS," KAITLIN HEARD SIBEL CALL OUT. She splashed one final handful of water on her face and closed the faucet. Luckily,

149

she'd been able to arrive safely at Sibel's, despite trembling hands on the steering wheel. Once there, she'd excused herself immediately to a private corner to breastfeed her daughter- after washing her hands first, of course.

Kaitlin glanced at the forced smile in her reflection. Paul hadn't come yet, and Kaitlin was told by Engin that he apparently had texted to let them know he'd be walking over soon 'from a store'. She was sure he must have bought an additional- and unnecessary, if she could say so herself- present for the house. Kaitlin shook her head.

"We're ready," Kaitlin put on Malin's puffy coat and kissed Sibel on both her cheeks. "Thank you girl, once again."

"Anytime," Sibel's smile was reassuring. "And, please. Promise to come over for dinner with your mother, too."

"Will do," Kaitlin grinned, holding Malin's hands to wave 'bye' together once out the door. Despite the nerves in her stomach, she plodded carefully toward their parked car, where Paul was leaning on the hood with his arms crossed.

He had a knowing smirk on his face as he bit his bottom lip. Kaitlin knew that look. He'd concocted some sort of plan. *Why's the back door opened?* Kaitlin managed a feeble 'hey' to her husband. She knew he'd had an extra set of keys to their car, but was still unsure what he'd been up to. "*Salut,*" he responded, the smirk fixed on his face as he waved at Sibel and Engin at the door as well.

Kaitlin's jaw dropped, standing now before Malin's baby seat. An exquisitely-adorned basket full of a myriad of lilies and carnations welcomed her. She'd never imagined he'd go to buy something like this, with the way he'd stranded her. Kaitlin tried to shake off the memory of her excruciating wait at Sibel's- a wait for an arrival that had even for a moment had her fear would possibly not even materialize, had Paul persisted in his hurtful stubbornness.

The bouquet even included a teddy bear with its paws attached to

150

the handle. How could a person have been able to make her both dolorous and joyous- on the same day?

"You really didn't have to, you know?" Kaitlin spoke, buckling Malin in with her favorite rattle. Even their daughter had cooed something resembling an "oooh" upon discovering the flowers in their car.

The surprise in the car had shown her that the 'store' Paul had said he'd be walking from was apparently one of the premier, boutique flower shops in downtown Stavanger.

"It's okay," Paul was still avoiding her eyes as he picked the basket up to place it in the luggage compartment now, opening up space for him to sit next to their daughter. "We have an important guest to welcome, so, just be quiet and drive, will you?"

"Make sure her bib stays on, Paulie," Kaitlin said, kissing Malin's forehead and softly closing the door as she walked to open her own door on the driver's side. How she wished Malin could have been one of those babies who had taken to pacifiers for comfort during long rides..

"Don't worry about us, mommy dearest," Paul uttered, caressing his daughter's cheek as he was now settled next to her. "We're ready to welcome grandma. Just keep your eyes on the road and watch your speed, babe."

"Thank you," Kaitlin smiled at the rear mirror, trying to catch Paul's gaze before starting the car. He was only staring outside the window. "Paulie?" she added softer. "I mean it. Thank you. I wish you'd told me you were going to the store. I thought you stranded me back there. Well, you did technically do so, actually. I mean- what if I got into an accident on my own, driving under the stress of our fight like that?"

And not just an accident, at that, Kaitlin had thought as she fantasized for a good 10 minutes- still parked in the car after picking up the chocolates for Sibel and Engin. *What if I'd left you? Taken Malin and left you for good?*

Okay- so she knew that he knew the market's relative closeness to Sibel's house. But leaving her in that condition? How could he not care that she'd be driving over there in tears? Which she still had done so- lying to a concerned Sibel at the door that the tears were about her guilt over leaving Malin for a second time.

"That was tough love, *ma chérie*." Paul finally cracked a smile, meeting her gaze in the window whilst he cocked an eyebrow. "I've got to tell Malin her mom's going to be more like an older sister to her growing up." He added a wink.

Finn. Why did every little thing manage to seemingly remind her of him? *Out of my thoughts.*

"Oh, really?" it was Kaitlin's turn to give him a sly look. She had a hunch Paul's gesture had more to do with settling things down before facing his mother-in-law. *He loves looking like the more responsible one, always.* Perhaps even some indirect apology- which Kaitlin had to admit she would have preferred. Regardless, it was time to toughen up indeed, and get prepared for Hurricane Linda.

"Let's go pick up *grand-mère*, Malin!"

§

SOLA AIRPORT STOOD NEARLY EMPTY as Kaitlin and Paul took turns rocking Malin's stroller back and forth in the 'Arrivals' area. The black screens before them showed that the flight from Amsterdam had already arrived. *I wonder how many pieces of luggage my mom must be waiting for,* she thought.

The little bookstore with souvenirs she spotted around the corner reminded Kaitlin of their travels as a couple throughout Europe, mostly for various Statoil and technology conferences. Reading together on the airplane was one of the rare past-times the two of them had in common.

Kaitlin couldn't recall the last time she'd been able to read a book other than the crinkly-soft one with a bunny on it titled, 'I Love You This Much'.

Except the novel, 'Exquisite Captive', of course, which she'd been reading in Sandnes harbor. When a certain visitor had had her feeling like some such captive herself. Kaitlin had to physically shake off the image of Finn's burning smile that appeared before her eyes just then.

"Oh, there she is!" Paul called out several steps ahead of her with the stroller. "I see her, come on!"

Wearing a belted bubble-coat of an azure shade, her mother looked just like she'd left her back home. Despite the transatlantic travel and the subsequent transfer flight, with her coiffed hair highlighted a tone lighter than usual- her mother was beaming at them. She'd blown-out her hair in wispy strands again- swearing it hid her wrinkles, Kaitlin recalled.

"*Maman*!" Kaitlin hugged her, smelling one of the latest perfumes she'd remembered from the mall on her mother's neck. *I must smell like…*

"*Merde!*" Linda cursed as a running man had stepped on her foot, gazing after him long after the man apologized. "I thought life was supposed to be slower out here, you kids."

"It is an airport, mom," Kaitlin chuckled, unbuckling Malin to pick her up in her arms. "Come on. We'll talk more after I drive us home. How was the flight?"

"Paul, my dear, you sure you're really going to let Kaitlin drive?" Linda muttered, struggling to hug him from the flowers he picked up from Malin's stroller basket to give to her. "Are these for me? Thank you!"

Since when had her mother begun calling Paul anything endearing- anything other than simply by his name? *Since he's just welcomed her with his showy bouquet basket, that's likely when,* Kaitlin thought.

The warmth from her mother at least appeared genuine to Kaitlin when she picked up Malin. "Best for last," her jaw dropped as tears filled her eyes. Her mother just clutched her granddaughter, breathing in her smell- for a good minute until a security officer told them they had to part from the crowded area and out toward the parking spaces. "She has your cheeks, Kaity. She's even more precious in person."

"Paul- once again- are you sure?" Linda raised an eyebrow as they stood before the car. "With my granddaughter in the back?"

"Momma Linda, don't worry," Paul let out soft laugh, budging his mother-in-law's second bulging Burberry luggage into the trunk. "Kaitlin's been practicing a lot. Traffic is lighter here than in Toronto..."

"But she doesn't have her driver's license!" Linda was adamant. "She never listened to me back home, I was hoping that you'd be able to register some sense into her, Paul. With the increase in responsibilities now, she's especially...Ooh, be careful with the bouquet- make sure the luggage doesn't crush it..."

"Mom, I'm right here and you can tell me directly, you know," Kaitlin waved her free hand while hanging onto Malin, who was now eyeing both of her predecessors curiously. "A permit is perfectly alright and legal to drive with my licensed-husband next to me. *Unless he decides in anger to strand me to drive alone again*, she thought, yet quickly dismissed without dwelling. "And stop bringing Toronto into everything. Please. You know I never needed a car there, being so close to public transportation..."

"...And boyfriends that would drive you everywhere, too, of course," Linda muttered under her breath, ignoring Paul's eyeroll at her whilst taking his place in the passenger's seat.

As always, her mother could be counted on to bring her fantasies down to earth. *Is mercury in retrograde today or something?* Kaitlin thought, overwrought with disappointment already. She focused on her daughter's confused yet utterly disarming face in her baby seat. "Why's everyone picking on mommy today, my sweet?" she whispered.

"My kitty cat…." Linda cleared her throat as she tickled Malin. "Who's grandma's kitty cat? Who's grandma's…."

Kaitlin took the opportunity to meet her husband's eyes for sympathy, to no avail. "Let's go before the traffic gets rough, guys," she sulked into the driver's seat. "Mom, do you need help with the seat belt? You have the bottle I gave you, right?"

"Are you sure you don't want to sit up front, Momma Linda?" Paul added. "You must be exhausted. You can take a little snooze up front while I can deal with…"

"Nonsense. I came here for my precious granddaughter and I can handle her just fine," Linda said firmly as she positioned Malin more comfortably in the rear-facing child seat.

"Goo…." Malin laughed as she shook the rattle that was now handed to her, causing Kaitlin and Paul to finally share a smile.

"Everyone buckled in and ready to go?" Kaitlin peered behind her in the mirror.

"We are. Are you?" Linda chuckled, yet Kaitlin didn't have it in her to even feign either a clever remark, nor a laugh along with her mother.

This was going to be a long two weeks.

CHAPTER 15

T HE ENDS OF HER MOTHER'S BLEACHED STRANDS, the few remaining potato slices on her plate, or her peace of mind? Kaitlin couldn't determine which one had become fried more. Her thoughts traveled to her mom's motto of '…ladies must always leave the table a little hungry'. Before Linda's prying eyes now, Kaitlin wanted to spare one additional possible chastisement on her eating habits if she could help it.

Is that what I'm going to eventually turn into, as well? she wondered, cleaning up the table. *Will I criticize everything and everyone around me, mostly out of dissatisfaction with myself and my own life?*

"Thank you for that welcome dinner, honey," Linda patted her daughter's lower back. They'd both begun working on the dishes. "I'm glad to see that a new life across the ocean hasn't made you forget your roots."

"Well, I'm glad to have you here, mom," Kaitlin scrubbed the plate in her hand with a smile, her stomach letting out a little growl. She wasn't sure whether it was the two glasses her mother had drank or she'd been sincere; regardless, she'd gladly take the rare compliment from her.

"I can now attest to being a proud Canadian momma to see you've improved your poutine," Linda went on, drying the forks. "But that rice was a bit too soft again. I always tell you, Kaity, you add too much water when you…"

And, there she goes again. Her mother had reliably turned to her more familiar critiques. Kaitlin nodded, drying the dripping water from her hands.

"Can I help you here, ladies?" Paul rubbed his hands together playfully, walking over to them from the living room area. "I've gotten Malin distracted by those Teletubbies. Let me take over."

"Here, babe, you can get the coffee mugs and the rest of these forks." Kaitlin pointed out her remaining portion. "She's watched too much television today. I'll work on putting her to sleep earlier tonight."

"Okay, babe," Paul quipped, quickly picking up one of the pan lids she'd placed on the dryer rack. "Oh, no. Look at this one, Momma Linda. Your daughter's rice tonight was actually still better than her dishwashing skills."

Hearing her husband and mother exchange a soft chuckle, Kaitlin stopped dead in her tracks. She turned to gaze directly at them both. Seeing Paul hold up the glass lid toward the light to make his point to her mother, Kaitlin's stomach sank. "Grease stains galore..." Paul was going on, clenching his teeth as he shook his head. With his additional comment, even Linda had now stopped her snickering, instead locking sympathetic eyes with her daughter.

You defend my driving skills to my mom, only to subsequently ridicule my domestic skills to her? "Gee, Paul! Whose side are you on?" Kaitlin's feigned laughter served its routine purpose of a trusted shield.

"I'm teasing, babe," Paul insisted, pouting in her direction for a truce.

"Well, you know they say jokes can camouflage true feelings." Kaitlin raised her brow. "Boo..." she added jokingly, noticing her mother had been preparing to open her mouth regarding the matter.

Criticizing my mother's caprices as it suits you, but siding with her when ganging up on my domestic skills? Kaitlin vowed to get Paul back for this once she'd be in the company of his mother again. "It's okay, let me tend to Malin, you two," she managed before Linda could offer any word. "Excuse me."

Fighting back a tear, Kaitlin strolled toward her refuge, who must have sensed her approaching. "Ta…ta," Malin pointed to the silly, wiggling characters on the screen.

"That's right, my sweet," Kaitlin softly caressed her daughter's head. "Te-le-tub-bies. But, alas, it's time for my favorite Teletubby to go to sleep."

As Malin began to fuss and squish her face right before she was about to cry, Kaitlin picked her up gently, heading toward the crib. "Please, my love," she whispered into the crown of her head. "I know. I know. Mommy wants to cry, too. But sometimes we can't. We simply can't."

§

THE PASSAGE OF TIME HAD BEGUN TO FEEL LIKE IT HAD SLOWED TO A good hour of delay since Linda's arrival. She was happy to see her mother- despite their squabbles. Of at least that much, there'd been no doubt in Kaitlin's mind. Her mother was a connection to her past. Her roots. Her hopes. Her youth.

"This is that brown Norwegian cheese you spoke so highly of?" her mother interrupted Kaitlin's thought with an off-put face. *My issues*, Kaitlin smirked, mentally adding another connection. Her mother had seemingly acquired novel ways of remarking distaste at something related to Kaitlin and her life in Norway: things that she could not help but wonder whether she'd secretly agreed with as well. Had she been fair enough to the settled life? Did people see her as a snob?

"I hope you've slept alright," Kaitlin finally managed to utter. An entire hour seemed to have passed since Paul's alarm clock for his work departure had woken them up as well. Her mother was still eyeing an in-flight magazine she'd brought along with her while downing her coffee. Not much talking was being done, and Malin was still blissfully sleeping.

"It's funny, Kaity," Linda said. "I thought I'd be waking up at some odd hour with the jet lag- even earlier than Paul- but, nope. I guess I'll be needing some extra beauty sleep tonight. I plan to play all day with my granddaughter and show her the clothes I got her. And then- tomorrow- fjords, here I come!"

Babies don't exactly care for clothes, mom, she thought. *I hope you've brought something useful as well.* Kaitlin stopped herself. What was she thinking? Even to herself, she sounded like a spoiled brat.

"We can't wait to see them, mom, thank you," she smiled, drinking her last sip of coffee with a loud gulp. "Yeah, I wish I could join you on that boat tour you booked, but, alas, Malin could catch a cold and..."

"Yes, dear, no, no, you two stay home," Linda dismissed with well-manicured nails. "Of course, of course."

Bothered ever just the slightest that her mother seemingly hadn't even considered going on one of the region's most popular tourist attractions with her daughter and granddaughter, Kaitlin stood up and headed toward the kitchen counter. "More coffee?"

"No, thank you," Linda responded, distractedly walking toward the living room window. The off-gray shutters had still been closed from the night before. "The living room needs better light, and so do these plants." Linda said as she opened the shades. "And frankly, so does Malin. Didn't her doctor tell you the importance of Vitamin D for a baby?"

"Mom?" Kaitlin shifted her tone. "You did remember those supplements I asked for Mal, didn't you? Along with the Omega drops?" Kaitlin could never be too sure. Her mother had a tendency of asking her if she needed anything- even before she'd go for groceries when she'd been younger, for example- and yet come back without the very thing she'd ask for.

"Yes, of course," Linda replied defensively. "I haven't even

159

really opened my other luggage. Everything is in there, Kaity. Patience has never been one of your virtues."

"Lovely view, right mom?" Kaitlin tried to change the topic, placing her hands on her hips as she stood next to her mother before the window.

"Mmm, the trees are nice, yes," she muttered, cocking her head to take in the two neighboring condos in their complex. "So, each apartment has four families, correct?"

"That's right," Kaitlin nodded. "Although we're lucky the apartment below is empty at the moment: an artist who travels often. We just have an elderly couple next door and a newly married couple that recently moved in below them…"

"No babies for Malin to play with…" Linda said in a disappointed tone, heading to the guest room with Kaitlin slowly following close behind. She rolled her eyes and snuck a peek at her room to see whether Malin was still sleeping. The vision of her daughter's chest moving up and down allowed her face to ease into a grin.

"Well, the Aker's next door have a daughter around my age," Kaitlin informed. "They sometimes visit with their little baby boy. Maybe, as they grow up, they can also play together…"

"What lucky grandparents," Linda smirked. "To frequently be able to see their grandchild."

"Mom…" Kaitlin started to say, but her mom was on a roll."…Oh, darling. I must say the old place in Stavanger was simply – I can't quite put my finger on it- but more charming than this place."

Linda started straightening the creases from two neatly-folded sweaters she'd laid out on the guest bed. "Sorry. I know you and your Paulie don't exactly need any more friction. But you know your mom is capable only of always speaking the truth. I mean, that view of the ocean was something else."

"Well, mom, the green outside our window here is beautiful,

too!" Kaitlin stood firm. "We're still in nature. It's better for Malin to grow up with the backyard here. The neighboring homes have kids also, and more spaces for children. Anything beats the concrete in Toronto, don't you think?"

"Yeah, yeah," Linda dismissed with a Mona Lisa smile. "I suppose you're going to stick to your story about how y'all hurriedly moved out here for the two extra bedrooms. But, come on…your mother is not stupid, Kaity…. you can tell me…"

Kaitlin's heart skipped. Her panic was surprisingly able to momentarily triumph over her usual annoyance over her mom uttering the nickname she'd detested for years, thinking it childish. *Can she possibly know?*

"Paul's been losing money, hasn't he?" Linda finally filled the silence. "I mean, that place may have been smaller, but the rent was higher due to the location- was it not?"

Kaitlin's temples began to pound. "What? No! Mom, don't be silly. His paycheck hasn't dwindled. In fact- Paul's been looking forward to a raise come the new year…Argh, mom, I swear you've begun to drive me crazy already…"

"We can never run from ourselves, Kaity." Linda shook her head, placing the sweaters into the empty shelf space Kaitlin had laid out for her in the wooden IKEA closet. "No matter where you go, you carry yourself and your burdens with you. Like the turtle with its shell. You know that, right?"

Kaitlin couldn't believe what she was hearing. "Mom, why are you bring up all these depressing things right now?"

"You don't drink out here, do you?" Linda's face meant business.

"What?" Kaitlin protested.

"Your father," Linda continued. "I always tell you how you remind me of him, Kaity."

I'm sure he must have been more sensitive with his words, that's for sure, Kaitlin mused. "It's not fair how you always bring up a man I barely remember whenever you're trying to make some vague point to me, mom."

"Zachary didn't know how else to escape," Linda's eyes were now on the wall behind Kaitlin. "Not even himself. He drank and drank some more. Until he couldn't escape anymore. And then, of course, he escaped from me and the kids."

"Mom, I'm not my father." Kaitlin shook her head slowly. "I'm not trying to escape. Do you pester Aidan about his genetics, too?" She barely kept in touch with her older brother. His handsome, single, and fast lifestyle in Toronto hadn't really kept him connected much with his mother and sister other than an occasional holiday or birthday phone call.

"Aidan's been sober for an entire year now, Kaity." Linda stated matter-of-factly. "Didn't you see how much of that beer belly he's lost since your wedding?"

"He only showed his face on the FaceTime call to see his niece, mom," Kaitlin rolled her eyes. "I didn't exactly ask him to do a body show with the camera. I'm sure he's got plenty of his ladies working on that already."

"He'll settle down when he's ready," Linda dismissed.

Of course he'd be allowed what I wasn't, mother, Kaitlin mourned, images of her teenager years competing with her brother for their mother's acceptance flashing through her mind.

A wail from her bedroom next door alerted to her that Malin had awakened. "Let me get her," Kaitlin excused herself out of the guest room. As far as she was concerned, Malin had woken up just in time. A trip down their unhealthy family history was the last thing she needed.

§

AS MUCH AS SHE DESPISED BICKERING, KAITLIN HAD TO ADMIT A QUIET dining table irked her even more. Even Malin seemed to notice- not feeling the need to wail for attention. She was taking cyclical turns eyeing her parents and grandmother whilst munching on her remaining pear slices.

The doorbell ringing interrupted the awkward silence. "You want me to get that, dear?" Linda asked Kaitlin, who in turn looked at Paul.

"Who could it be at this time?" he raised an eyebrow, meeting Kaitlin's eyes.

"Well, it's only 8 pm. Maybe it's that sweet elderly couple you mentioned today, Kaity." Linda began to gleam, running a hand through her hair. "Maybe your neighbors saw me coming and wanted to wish me a warm welcome."

"I doubt it, mom," Kaitlin remarked with knitted eyebrows. "These Norwegians eat earlier than we do and some even head to sleep around this time."

"Maybe those two lovebirds had another fight?" Paul snickered.

"You never know." Kaitlin recalled how they'd listen to their other neighbors go at it when they'd just moved in, right before Malin's birth.

"Hel-loooo?" a familiar voice was audible from the other side of the door. *That sounds like...no, that's impossible.* Kaitlin plodded toward the door, standing on her tiptoes to look through the peep hole.

"Sandy!" she gushed, opening the door.

"Surprise!" Sandy's smooth, mocha complexion stared back at Kaitlin's shocked face.

"Oh, my goodness, what a lovely surprise..." Kaitlin hugged her friend, giving into the opportunity for comfort.

"You've made it, sweetie!" Linda called out. "Welcome!"

"Mom? You're not surprised?" she glanced over her shoulder, swaying side to side still in the embrace.

"I'll admit we've coordinated on this surprise, Kaity," Linda smiled. "Sandy and I tried to get on the same flight from the Amsterdam transfer to Sola Airport, at least. But, alas, we couldn't…"

"Yeah, your mom's flight was sold out so I had to take the next available flight out here," Sandy explained, exchanging greetings with Paul. The truth was- the flight she'd booked had simply been cheaper, but, they didn't need to know that, as far as Sandy was concerned. "We wanted to be here for her first birthday. Speaking of the angel- where's my little niece? Sleeping, right? I've missed her, haven't I?"

"Oh no, Sandy, dear," Linda cackled. "Kaity here hasn't been able to train her to sleep in an orderly manner for a baby, unfortunately. She's strapped in her high chair. Come see my little angel."

"Yes, my Malin's angelic, indeed, but she is imperfect like all us humans," Kaitlin retorted. "Which reminds me, ladies. Her doctor warned us about outside germs and her sensitive skin. Let's please make sure to wash our hands whenever we come to the house, shall we, dear guests?" Kaitlin shot Sandy a look imploring for sympathy. *Help*, she mouthed, to which Sandy smiled.

"Of course, honey, which way is the bathroom?"

"Right this way. I'll show you the towels." Kaitlin sure had been impressed by the set up she'd seen in Sibel's bathroom. She only wished that her guests would be dazzled by her own décor as well.

As a jovial time was spent in the living room, with Linda and Sandy showering Malin with attention, Kaitlin smiled. At one point, Sandy made sure the two locked eyes. "Can we talk?" she saw her friend mouth, to which Kaitlin nodded and tilted her head in the direction of her guest room.

"Oh, nice," Sandy eyed the minimalist set-up of the wooden table as soon as they stepped inside. A full-sized bed and a beige spinning chair also made up most of the room.

"Looks comfy?" Kaitlin asked, placing both hands on her hips.

"Girl, I was considering sleeping on the couch or on the floor even, had there not been room," Sandy flashed her dimples. "This is the Hilton, in comparison! Seriously! I vaguely recalled you mentioning two guest rooms, but I couldn't be sure, and I did come uninvited…"

"Hey, I'm just glad you're here, girl," Kaitlin assured her, plopping on the edge of the bed.

"Really?" Sandy asked softly, sitting down next to her. "Well, first things first. I really did want to surprise you, hon. And maybe try to be a bit of moral support with the baby and your mother undoubtedly requiring your attention."

"And Paul," Kaitlin smirked.

"Well, I hope he really is still asking for your attention in a myriad of ways, if you get my drift?" Sandy chuckled.

"I've missed laughing with you," Kaitlin grinned.

"I wanted to surprise you and deliver my baby gifts to beautiful Malin in person," Sandy began unzipping the front compartment of her sole luggage. "When your mom didn't say it'd be any trouble, I just figured…"

"Sandy! Nonsense," Kaitlin dismissed. "Why are we in a three-bedroom place if we can't have close guests like this from time to time?" She added in a whisper. "Better you than my in-laws."

Sandy's warm expression induced Kaitlin to go on. "And it's more than just okay. I'm happy you're here. Really. Just feel bad I can't maybe take you out sightseeing as much. It's hard with Malin…."

"Leave that part to your mom and I," Sandy held out both her palms. "We're here to help you out with Malin and around the house, yes. But we've also planned ahead, hon. A girls-only outing or two to sightsee- without you or Paul feeling any pressure to have to accompany us. I even have some numbers on me for car rentals, if need be. I'm just surprised she's been able to go this long without spilling the beans."

"You know my mom," Kaitlin glowered. "She must have been too distracted. Paul's become her new partner-in-crime. Can you believe the unlikeliest twosome to get along joined forces to critique my dishwashing skills last night?"

"Well, I'm here now," Sandy made a salute gesture. "I'm solely on your team, girl."

"Deal, my dear ally," Kaitlin tittered. "I'll let you shower and change. Let me know if you need anything. Toiletries, socks, pads, you name it...."

"Thanks hon," Sandy cut in. "I think I've got everything. But there is one thing that's been bugging me throughout the entire flight. Mind if I finally ask before we head to sleep?"

"Shoot," Kaitlin replied, peeking out the door to ensure all was well with Malin in the living rooms.

"The Group...from the woods in Stavanger," Sandy began, biting her lip.

"Sandy..." Kaitlin asserted.

"I know, I know," Sandy spoke rapidly. "But you have to admit. You left me kind of hanging after that whole Mr. Evans, aka Mr. Finn Du Feu, paying me a visit in NYC incident..."

"Girl, I told you," Kaitlin lowered her voice. "He just turned out to be someone who tried to seduce me out of my marriage. And I almost fell for it, under the professional pretenses. And then things became a bit- you know-complicated vis-à-vis that girl discovered in the woods. You know everything there is to know."

"A stalker-ish jinn-figure. I believe those were the words you'd used..." Sandy was nodding blankly, oscillating her body back and forth as well.

"Yes, exactly my point," Kaitlin exclaimed. "It wasn't the easiest thing for me to deal with, so I don't exactly want to invite that energy to our conversation. Like I said, he must have hacked my phone as well, learning your information from my frequent contacts list. Trying to get to me through my friends, since I wouldn't pick up his calls..."

"Right," Sandy's expression shifted. "Did he call those ladies-who-lunch or whomever you befriended here? Or that Turkish lady you befriended- what was her name- Cybill? Did he pay her a visit too?"

Did Kaitlin hear a tang of jealousy? Comparing her old and new friendships would have been like apples and oranges. "You mean, Sibel?" she squinted her eyes. "Umm, no, not that I'm aware of. I don't think so…Sandy what's up with all these questions? Are you preparing for a detective role or something?" Kaitlin tried to smile but her heart was pounding. *Is she really not going to let this go?*

"I'm just curious, hon," Sandy shrugged. "Especially now. Being in this country. It makes everything you told me about on the phone more real somehow. And all those mysterious circumstances you would talk to me about. They sort of just came to a halt. I feel left out, girl. As if there's something bigger than some creepy hunk crushing on you after you doing some translations for him- and you're telling your new friend here rather than me. You even said she'd been the one who suggested to you that they might have been jinns in the first place."

"Girl, are you serious?" Kaitlin was in shock. "Come on, Sandy. I'm the one who should be sensitive now, if it's going to be like that. I mean, I'm so happy by this beautiful surprise. But aren't Malin and I enough to hold your interest during your brief time here?"

"Kaitlin, I'm going to let this go," Sandy promised. "But not before I get something straight and off my chest first. Of course, I'm so happy to see you finally- and with your beautiful baby, too. In this beautiful country. In this beautiful house. But I also remember when you called me…after that night…"

Kaitlin's heart sank. *The night?* Whom she'd assumed to be Paul coming in after Kaitlin was already in bed. Penetrating her body with desire and heat grander than the fjords. Only for her to fall asleep afterward, and later awaken to witness Paul coming home late and for the first time. A myriad of thoughts pounded inside her head all at once.

"You know…" Sandy went on, upon Kaitlin's physical silence. "During the last month of your pregnancy? You called me in panic after you claimed foggy figures were closing in on you in your sleep?"

"Oh…" Kaitlin breathed in a sigh of relief. "That night. Yeah. Like I said. It's strange. I don't even remember calling you, hon. I honestly don't. Thank God for the time difference. I mean, I vaguely remember being scared because Paul was away at that London meeting and I was worried being pregnant and alone. I must have sleep- dialed you…"

"I asked my therapist back in the city," Sandy's tone was serious. "She said it sounded like sleep paralysis. But with your forest story, I began to fear for you, and couldn't be so sure…"

As Sandy spoke, it all flooded back to Kaitlin. It had been around two to three weeks before she'd given birth the previous fall. The truth was- Kaitlin had indeed woken up the following morning, still unable to shake off the strange dream she'd had. It had felt so real that she'd dialed Sandy; she knew the time would be earlier in NY.

She'd seen a pair of ghostly figures circle her room- so vividly as if it hadn't been a dream at all. The more she screamed and told them to go away in her dream- clutching her pregnant belly protectively- the stronger the blob of shapeless energy had darted straight onto her body. Kaitlin had felt unable to move, and could only recall praying and pleading. *Please, don't allow harm to come to my child. I beg of you. I'm going to be a mother. I'm going to be a mother.*

"You still have the same therapist, by the way?" Kaitlin asked, nodding. "How's that been going?"

"Good. Can't complain. I mean, I'm not sure how much progress I've made or not. But I like the consistency, ya know?" Sandy placed her hands in the pockets of her ripped jeans. "I've gotten used to people and jobs always changing around me. She's at least been one constant who knows my darkest stuff."

"And my dark nightmare too, now, I suppose," Kaitlin said with a stern face that quickly transformed into a smile. "It's alright. I'm never going to meet her."

"Oh, hon, it's anonymous even if you were. I just referred to you as a 'friend' with such a dream…"

"I guess I'm a little surprised as to why you'd even bring it up in therapy…" Kaitlin interrupted.

"Ok-ay. And now I'm officially regretting bringing it up tonight, as well," Sandy smacked her lips. "It's late girl. Let's get some sleep. Malin wakes up early?"

"She'll be up around dawn for milk- sometimes falls back asleep until 9 once she's had a mouthful." Kaitlin spoke, taking in a deep breath. "This needs to be addressed. I'm curious, too- especially because Finn traveled to NY to chat you up. Was there anything else that may have happened that you're not telling me?"

"Funny- I kind of wanted to ask you that some question, hon," Sandy replied with a raised eyebrow, before shaking her head 'no'.

The sound of car horns coming from the parking lot of the neighboring condo broke the rush of chill. Sandy gazed outside. "Not quite on the water like your old place, but still- at least you guys have a more spacious place of your own, girl."

"Well, almost. We're still paying the mortgage, but, yeah," Kaitlin managed in whisper as she looked out the window as well. "Sandy, I don't want to talk about Finn and The Group. I understand you have questions- many of which I'm not even sure I know enough to be able to answer anyway. And I don't blame you. This guy came up to you. You didn't ask for it. I get your curiosity, believe me. It's just, well, you know how the whole thing messed with Paul and I. I don't ever want to approach that point-of-no-return again; this time, I'm afraid we'll cross it. You can understand that, right?"

"I'll try my best," Sandy smiled, patting Kaitlin's back. "Sorry.

Being single again has got me interested in some adventure, I think."

"Thanks girl," Kaitlin relaxed.

"Starting with joining your mom on that fjord tour she raved about," Sandy enthused. "Sets off tomorrow morning from Stavanger, I think. We are allowed to check out the bigger city, at least, right? Did you know it's called Europe's oil capital?"

"Only through my visits of Paul's Stat Oil website on a daily basis, hon," Kaitlin smiled.

"Oh, my bad," Sandy smacked her forehead playfully. "Of course. Sorry. Dumb tourist mode here."

"It's all good, girl," Kaitlin insisted, glancing at the time on her phone. "Let me know if you need anything else in your room."

"Thanks. Goodnight," Sandy responded.

She's definitely acting strange, Kaitlin thought, tiptoeing to her own bedroom where Paul was snoring softly near the edge close to Malin's crib. She really hoped she was imagining it. Especially with her mom now sleeping in the other guest room. Handling any more potential jinn drama would certainly be more than she could handle.

CHAPTER 16

Stavanger

WITH THE COLD BREEZE SCRATCHING HER FACE, SANDY wrapped the oversized wool scarf tighter around her neck. The lean waterfall meandering down the majestic mountain before them was worthy of the awe that exuded from both herself and Linda Ramsay. Sandy craned her neck higher from behind a couple of tall riders in front of her. The tour guide was pointing out a visible family of goats that had gathered for some grass snacking.

"These fjords are to-die!" Sandy exclaimed.

"To die?" Linda looked worried, her reaction causing a nearby woman to eye her curiously. "Oh my, Sandy, you suppose this vessel could throw us overboard?"

Sandy rolled her eyes, feigning a half-smile. "I just meant that they're absolutely breathtaking, Momma Linda, aren't they?"

"Too bad Kaitlin and Malin couldn't join us." Linda's eyes went to her phone.

"Yeah, the wind draft would have been too harsh on Malin's skin, poor thing," Sandy mourned. "I did notice a few babies…"

"They're likely Norwegian babies," Linda snickered. "Kaitlin says their skin's tough like reindeer." The two women shared a laugh, until Sandy's face fell.

"Uh, Momma Linda," she took in a deep breath, knowing she couldn't avoid her truth any longer. "Can I ask you something?"

"You were thinking what I'm thinking right?" Linda guessed with eager eyes. "When the boat docks- let's shop at that store with the lovely display we passed by earlier. You know- at that corner after you got us the coffees? Those presents we gave to Malin last night weren't quite enough, were they? Especially me- I mean what kind of a grandma am I? Well, not a very creative one, that's for sure. I just didn't know what else I could have brought over, since Kaitlin's seemingly orders everything she needs…"

"Oh, no, don't say that," Sandy was taken aback. *Did Kaitlin make a face? Say anything to her mom? Was that cute GAP onesie-set in multiple colors and the electronic puppy not enough?* "Your presence here is worth more to Kaitlin I'm sure than anything else. And the gifts were simply lovely, Momma Linda. Especially that squeaky teething toy." *What the hell was that thing called?*

"Malin did seem to like Sophie the Giraffe the best, didn't she?" Linda breathed with a smile, locking eyes with a toddler boy with white-blond bangs. He was wobbling about on the stern, distracted by flags waving in the wind as his frustrated mom chased after him. "I miss the girls already. Let me call Kaitlin. See if she needs anything…"

"Umm, about that, actually, Momma Linda," Sandy insisted. "I realized- after today- it's doubtful we can leave Kaitlin to tend to Malin alone at home again. Just so we can sightsee more. That'd be sort of unfair, wouldn't it? So seeing that this adventurous boat ride was sort of an exception …I was wondering if…"

"You were wondering if…?"

"…If you'd mind me leaving you for just an hour- an hour and a half at max to take advantage of my short time alone in downtown Stavanger," Sandy rushed, sucking her lips. "You'd be- you know, shopping and walking around like you suggested, while I sort of go on a blind date with this Norwegian gentleman I've been chatting with."

"A Norwegian gentleman?" Linda's eyes lit up. "Oh my…"

"Now, don't worry," Sandy cut in. "I'll text constantly to keep you posted, and meet you right where the boats dock. Or at a store of your choosing."

"I suppose that would be alright," Linda hesitated.

"Thank you, Momma Linda," Sandy put her arm around Linda's jacket. "And let's not tell Kaitlin. She'll think I'm crazy. I've just been alone for a while- it's hard for married people to get it sometimes, you know?

"What's the fella's name?" Linda inquired. "Are you sure it is safe? Where will you be meeting?"

Can't say Finn or Bjorn. She may slip something to Kaitlin. Sandy's thoughts were louder in her head than the noisy kids running circles around them. "Umm," *Think Sandy think. Hansel? Nah. Sounds too German. What was that movie with that hunky actor playing some Nordic god? Th...* "Thor!" Sandy blurted out.

"Thor?" Linda sounded excited again. "Sounds like some blond, muscular fella. *Oh, la la...*"

"Yeah, if he's anything like his picture...." Sandy winked. "Oh, and, we'll be by the lake. Lots of people will be around. No worries."

"You know, my Aidan dyed the tips of his hair blond," Linda wagged a finger. "Can you believe it? Men highlighting their hair these days. I'm sure you see plenty of those in New York, but I don't know. It looks good on him though..."

"I'm sure it does," Sandy smiled politely. If she didn't know any better- namely, that of his reputation among their circle as a ladies' man- Sandy would have thought his mother was trying to set her up with Aidan. She nodded along, images of Linda as a mother-in-law crossing her mind as she indulged the woman in further chit-chat. She and Kaitlin would surely then have something in common once again to commiserate about.

How she'd missed the days of their mutual dating dilemmas back in the day. Sandy absolutely loved Kaitlin. But married life- and life abroad, too- had admittedly made their more recent conversations feel forced. That was, of course, until her whole forest run-in confession with the jinn and human brotherhood in the forest. Or the sisterhood or group or whatever the heck they were called. She was certainly intrigued enough to discover for herself.

After Linda finally promised Sandy an hour or so of free time to see Bjorn, she allowed the wind to sway her dark curls away from her face. Thanking the tour guide, the two women walked toward the cobblestone streets leading to Valberg tower.

"You be careful, dear, and please message me often," Linda air-kissed Sandy's cheek. "Shall I meet you at Skoringen? Kaitlin texted something about a big sale on summer sandals."

"Skoringen, it is," Sandy agreed. "Happy shopping, Momma Linda! See you sooner than you can say '*hei hei*' to all the store clerks in town!"

Sandy waved bye to Linda and took in a deep breath. She walked toward the statue Kaitlin would tell her about, and faced the wooded area peeking from behind homes in the near distance. Bjorn had texted her earlier, offering to walk with her from town, but she'd refused. She was a big girl. She could do this. How much worse could her unorthodox date be from some of the crazies she knew she'd attracted in NYC? All Sandy knew for sure was how much she'd missed being able to feel her heart pound as fast as it then was.

§

THE DARK NAVY SUIT FITTING HIM BETTER THAN THE GRAY ONE SHE'D remembered him in, the jinn-man Sandy knew to be Finn Du Feu welcomed her with a disingenuous smile.

The cabin hadn't proved to be too difficult to find, much to Sandy's surprise. From what Kaitlin had described, it had sounded as if it would magically appear before her eyes somehow once she'd been walking for a good while. "It was as if all time stopped," Kaitlin had quipped.

Bjorn had instructed her to keep hiking slightly uphill until coming across two tall, adjacent evergreen trees. She'd apparently then be able to spot the wooden, two-floor red cabin right then and there.

Sandy hadn't completely gone out of her mind- especially not for some jinn-guy. No. She had come prepared. A metal knife and a portable charger in her over-the-shoulder hobo bag- just in case the GPS system she'd enabled had gobbled up most of her cellular battery life- accompanied her.

"Mr. Evans," she focused on Finn once again. "Nice to see you here across the world. I do believe you stood me up for that job interview back in the States."

"Ms. New York," Finn smirked, squinting his green optics with curiosity. "Looks like Malin's brought you to our humble corner of the world. Please, do come in. Bjorn's told me you were in town."

"Thank you," Sandy replied as he took a step backward and motioned for her to enter.

"Have a seat," he continued. "Make yourself comfortable. Oh- but wait. First, we must take off our shoes."

"You want me to take off my shoes too?" Sandy cursed herself for carelessly deciding on Tweety Bird socks that morning. She should have realized Kaitlin's rather new home habit may have been widespread in this region.

"A pure and organized home can purify and organize the soul," Bjorn's voice neared them just then. Sandy felt the looming presence behind her- almost breathing warm air on her neck. She looked over her shoulder to see that he'd actually been at some distance, farther across the living room.

"Okay, guys, a girl can take a hint," Sandy wiggled her feet out of her Uggs, stalling for a moment before finally mustering the courage to face the jinn-man she'd been chatting up.

"Welcome, Lady Liberty," Bjorn said, sauntering toward her.

He's blonder- and hotter- in person, Sandy couldn't pry her eyes away from his baby blues.

"Thank you, Bjorn," she blushed, extending out her hand. "Nice to finally see you in person."

"Likewise," Bjorn took Sandy's trembling hand into his large, firm grip- electrifying the nerves traveling from her palms up through her arms and the rest of her body.

Jinns, at their original essence, are created out of the element of fire in comparison to our earth-decomposing bodies, Sandy recited to herself, recalling everything she'd taken notes on throughout their brief, virtual courtship discussions about The Group, Norway and life in general. Flirty comments and suggestive implications had also been part of the chats, Sandy had to admit. She felt the urge to ask, anyway. "How's your girlfriend, Anja?"

"Bjorn's told me your interest in The Group, if I've gotten it correctly?" Finn jumped in, clearing his throat. "I'm about to leave now, and I'll leave you two to hang out and chat more; you must be bursting with questions. But I just had to say, Sandy. I was very pleasantly surprised. To witness how sophisticated and open you are to a better way of living- much more than Kaitlin has been."

"Well, I am on a break between shows, and I wanted to give you ever the slightest benefit of the doubt, Mr. Evans- I mean- Mr. Du Feu," Sandy quipped. "You know- I figured that real, possibly temporary work could perhaps indeed await me here, marketing paper and all." Smiling at Finn, his blank stare back at her suggested he wasn't really getting it. *Is he not reading my mind?* she wondered.

"Surely, you're not going to come all the way to Stavanger- and frequent our secluded part of the woods to hang with us- to discuss work, are you, Sandy?" Finn asked, raising an eyebrow. "Bjorn had me under

176

the impression that you were interested to find out about our life philosophy here in general."

"I've shared some of the maxims with her, *mec*," Bjorn nodded toward Finn, continuing his stare into Sandy's deep-set brown eyes. Her forest of timber had surely felt like it had been lit on fire.

"The introductory ones in the Prologue?" Finn asked. "Before the start of Part 1: the Authentic Life?"

"Oh, yes," Sandy stated. The relaxed expression she noted on both jinns' faces emboldened her. "I was under the impression- and excitedly so- that Bjorn was to give me a signed copy of Lar Iktar's book here today, actually. I'm genuinely interested in reading more. And, don't worry. No side-job necessary. Not even made-up interviews. Apology accepted."

"Apology?" Finn asked with a slick smile. "Oh, but it's all worked out well that we had that little meeting in New York, hasn't it? Why be sorry for such a beautiful catalyst- to now see you here in our humble abode, excited to learn more about our ways?"

Sandy blushed as she mouthed 'okay' with a smile, eyeing her surroundings and deciding to plop down on a cushiony, velvet armchair with dark legs. "It's lovely here," she managed to say, rubbing her hands before the cinders emanating from the furnace. The grand living space only consisted of a matching armchair on the other side of the fireplace, before an oval table separating them from a rather large, L-shaped leather couch that looked like it could seat five people.

"I suppose it's what you also did with Kaitlin, and you didn't apologize to her either, did you?" She added a smile to appease the look of anger that had momentarily appeared in Finn's gaze.

"I'll apologize if it makes you feel better, Sandy," Finn spoke, putting on a black coat as Bjorn sat down on the coach near her. "We wouldn't want you to feel any way but good."

I really needed some extra work, Sandy thought solemnly. *And,*

yeah, he's cute, but this attitude- what the heck had Kaitlin in so deep?
"Oh, Mr. Evans, you apologize- yes- but your jinn heart doesn't seem to be in it."

Sandy threw in another smile for good measure; though she'd brought that knife along, she didn't exactly want to end up in the papers back home. What would they call such an article? 'Rising star found dead in Norway'? Sandy dismissed the morbid thought. *Besides,* she mused with further sadness; *perhaps I wouldn't be called anything except some random 'dead body'.*

"That New York sense of humor, I like it". Finn winked, "Sandy would get along with our Anja, wouldn't she, *mec*? She should be home soon."

"Not too soon I hope," Bjorn smirked from the couch. He extended his hand to Sandy, closing in on her with his taller frame.

"Qu'est-ce que c'est...*mec*?" Sandy looked back-and-forth between the two men.

As Bjorn looked curiously at Finn- she got the impression that he didn't speak French like his housemate. *Duh, Sandy*, she told herself. *Not everyone would know French in Norway.*

"It's a Norsk impression, similar to 'my man'," Finn indeed responded, causing Bjorn to smile understandingly now. "You have such slang in New York, too, from what I heard over there on my little business trip. Well, it was nice to see you again," Finn rushed to put on some brown loafers. "Sorry, I've got to get going. Enjoy your time, you two."

As she waved at him, Sandy noticed Finn had stopped right before he was about to leave from the door. "Have you and Malin played yet? How is she?"

"Ma...Malin?" Sandy asked, confused. "Kaitlin's baby girl? Oh, she's a delightful child. She truly is."

"Isn't she?" Finn smiled. Sandy was about to ask him how he

would know, but Finn was already gone; without any distinguishable footsteps to attest to his departure. Had he materialized into some invisible jinn form? Sandy still had too many lingering questions.

"You're radiant in person," Bjorn glared into her eyes, towering over her even sitting down.

"Likewise," she muttered through rosy cheeks. "I mean- nice to meet you, too."

What the heck are these jinn buddies conjuring up? Sandy dismissed the concern as soon as her eyes locked into Bjorn's sky blues. "Thanks for satiating my curiosity about your jinn world….and your clan."

"Don't mention it, Hurricane Sandy."

Sandy turned around to see that Bjorn's icy glaze was now inches from her face, stinging her warm brown eyes to the very depths of her core. *Could ice burn?*

"*Though speak'st aright. I am a merry wanderer of the night,*" he whispered. "Come, let us wander around this cabin as an apology tour. We host bearing sweets. Would Lady Hermia like some coffee?"

"Mr. Shakespeare," Sandy's jaw dropped. "As a lady of the stage, I must say, I'm impressed by your thespian knowledge."

"Our education is yet but one of many ways in which we've all evolved our spirits, and awakened our minds here in the community." Bjorn insisted with sparkling eyes, getting up to sass toward the kitchen. "Milk and sugar are alright?"

§

"*HOW LONG ARE WE SUPPOSED TO HANG OUT HERE, FINN?*" Meredith directed her thought with a bark at Finn's feline form, meters from the cabin now as they circled each other in the flora.

"*I give that Sandy girl, let's say, no more than thirty minutes or so before she gets scared and runs for the hills."* Finn smirked. *"Bo! Come here, boy."*

The tawny puppy had been playing with a twig behind a nearby rock as they conversated. Already a young teenager in human years, Bo stood bigger than the black cat who'd been helping his mother in raising him. Meredith never talked about his father, and Bo never asked. He spent his time on earth learning about humankind- even practicing manifesting in flesh form a couple of times. Though he felt most comfortable as his jinn self- an orange beam playing in the woods by reflecting all around- he did occasionally like to accompany her to town in various forms.

Finn offered to walk him on occasion, but Bo would laugh it off along with Meredith. He'd learned by now that it would seem strange to humans to see a cat and dog walking alongside each other like a family. Real cats and dogs, he was told, weren't known for getting along much.

"I still don't like this, Finn," Meredith darted her thought at him once more, nuzzling Bo's neck. *"It's not fair to Anja. She loves Bjorn."*

"You and your romanticization," Finn mocked. *"She's just grown used to him. And, come on- you know she's been staying in Sirdal more than she's had to lately, working on the recruitment of that human male of her own."*

"You're the last jinn to talk about the 'romanticization of love', aren't you, Finn?" Meredith smirked. *"I know Kaitlin's still occupying your thoughts."*

"It's not like that," Finn insisted. *"It's about Malin. Our connection."*

"What about...?" Meredith began but could not bring herself to complete. Staring at Bo, she returned her son's smile. *Looks like we'll be lingering in this river called 'denial' a bit longer yet.* She kept her last thought to herself.

§

SANDY WASN'T SURE WHETHER SHE'D INCESSANTLY BEEN LICKING her lips as a result of the rising fireplace heat, or the embers blazing throughout her entire body upon eyeing Bjorn. *He- and his biceps- aren't too different from the imaginary 'Thor' I made up in my head,* she thought with a smile.

"I don't really drink coffee, thank you," Sandy glanced down at the floor for just a moment before Bjorn was suddenly centimeters from her face. She jolted backward with a yelp.

"We both know you like coffee, Lady Liberty," Bjorn smiled with a tilt of his head. "You met our brother Finn, after all, at a Starbucks-didn't you?"

Touché, Sandy thought. "They sell other things there besides coffee," she teased back. *Now I'm beginning to see how Kaitlin must have felt with Finn. These folks are too damn good at this.* "Okay, you got me, you got me," she let out a little laugh. "I just didn't want you to bother with coffee, you know, since..."

"Milk? Sugar?" Bjorn insisted, licking his lips as he looked Sandy over from the tips of her toes to the top of her head. Whatever he appeared to be insinuating, Sandy was enjoying it.

"A little milk and two sugars, please." Sandy cleared her throat, feeling her cheeks redden.

"Two sugars, got it," Bjorn eased up with a smile. "Coming right up. Please. Enjoy the fire. Make yourself comfortable."

"I know I'm not supposed to..." Sandy started, easing into the leather couch. "Have so much sugar, that is. Not healthy..."

"Your life, your choice, Lady Liberty," Bjorn turned to wink at her across the kitchen, where he was waiting for the machine to pour the coffee on to a bold red cup. "We never judge here."

Her attention traveled to a cabinet underneath the widescreen television set, which had been playing various European music videos with exaggerated costumes. Sandy recalled Kaitlin filling her in on the details she'd experienced in the cabin- notably the members' lack of personal things, since they apparently shared one another's rooms as well as lovers. *Interchangeable*. She couldn't afford to ignore that part- no matter how she'd missed this feeling of excitement with a male. For Bjorn, was she merely interchangeable with Anja? *Sandy, you're tripping,* she thought to herself.

What could possibly be in there? Her focus returned to the wooden furniture before her. *A tea set? Cutlery? Guidebooks on how to entrap humans?* "I'll just take a little peek," she muttered under her breath as she slowly stood up.

"Pecan pie?" Bjorn's voice made her flop back down in her seat. *Shit.* "Sorry?"

"Pecan pie?" Bjorn repeated closer, locking her deeper into the cushions, his ice-blue gaze a dagger. "We have a fresh batch from this morning I could quickly heat up for you in the oven if you'd like."

"I, umm...would love some actually," Sandy chirped. She figured it'd be best to stall for more time. "It's one of my favorite desserts. Thank you."

"No sweat," Bjorn winked as he returned to the kitchen area.

No sweat, yeah right, Sandy thought, gulping a deep breath with her eyes closed. *That was close.*

Wouldn't a pecan pie need a couple of minutes to heat up? Weren't jinns also made of fire? *Can't Bjorn just heat it through his touch or something?* Sandy shook her head with a smile. This wasn't some magic show at the Cirque du Soleil.

Stretching her neck toward the kitchen to ensure Bjorn wasn't on his way back again, Sandy opened the cabinet doors. She spotted little else but stacks of folders, some candles, and what appeared to be a green leather-covered photo album. She quietly took it and set it on her lap.

Here we go, she inhaled the aroma of the dessert along with the deep breath she'd gulped for her motivation. *Better be quick.* The first two sheets of printed photos laid underneath the stretch of plastic film displayed similar group photos to the one Kaitlin had shown her. *These folks sure love that forest.*

Bjorn and Anja- whom Sandy recognized from the forest picture Kaitlin had shared with her- were hogging the camera in various poses. A vision that stirred a surprising pinch of jealousy in Sandy. She quickly turned the page to now spot a handsome, older man dressed in an overtly-flashy dark purple suit. He was sitting at some urban café setting with two blondes and two waif brunettes in exaggerated make-up situated around him. Who was this man? Charlie- and those had been his Angels? *Hugh 'Lar' Heffner?* Sandy snorted, remembering the name of The Group's leader praised by Bjorn.

Reaching for the smartphone in her pocket, Sandy took a speedy snap of the particular photograph. She almost dropped both it and the heavy album upon hearing Bjorn.

"It's ready, I'll be right there. Sorry to keep you waiting," he called out, making Sandy close the album shut, but not quite put back in its place. His voice sounded like it'd still been in the kitchen.

"No problem, thank you," she called out. *I came so far,* she told herself. What harm would sneaking a look at one or two more pages really quickly cause?

She randomly opened the photo album from the middle this time, shocked to see two entire pages filled with various pictures of one of the petite-framed women with the blonde hair. Posing with Finn in some photos and a black cat in others. The woman's face looked vaguely familiar, but for the life of her Sandy couldn't quite put her finger on where she might have seen her before. She had just turned the page to see a picture of the same blonde with her arms wrapped around Finn in a passionate kiss by a bonfire, when Bjorn's gaze startled her senseless.

"Curiosity killed the cat," Bjorn said as he set a tray with her dessert plate and coffee cup on the table. "I've already stirred the sugar.

Let me know if it tastes to your liking."

"I…I was just trying to pass the time during my wait," Sandy closed the cover of the album softly, hands shaking. "I should have asked for permission. I'm sorry. Lovely pictures…."

"That's alright, thank you," Bjorn replied nonchalantly, sitting beside her. Sandy didn't quite know what to make of his relative ease just yet. "I agree- they're lovely memories. You must have come across the picture of Master Lar there with some of the gals from years back. I think we keep the more recent stock at the HQ."

"HQ?"

"The headquarters," Bjorn explained. "In Oslo. That's where Lar lives. With our main sister, Nora. She's of your kind. Really nice. You may get to meet them if you play your cards right."

"Well, that sounds really nice," Sandy stammered, not sure if she liked the part about playing her cards right. She wasn't exactly trying to be initiated into some sorority or anything like that- was she? *What the hell am I doing?* Sandy repressed the strange sensation in her stomach. *Too late now.* "I highly doubt I can have time to visit the capital. I'm only here for around twelve more days or so."

"Life works in mysterious ways, Sandy," Bjorn drilled his sky eyes into her soul. "I'm really proud to be a member of The Group and all it stands for, and memories are one of the most beautiful purposes of life. Yet nothing can quite be as magical as the moment, don't you agree?"

"I think I do," Sandy spoke. To her own surprise, she believed it. Why else would she be in the cabin with a jinn- and in secret from Kaitlin and her mom at that? Either she was being adventurous- living in the moment, or absolutely insane. Sandy truly hoped it wasn't the latter.

"Finn gets a bit touchy sometimes, seeing his ex in the albums," Bjorn explained. "I always tell him, 'Just get rid of her pictures and let it go, brother,'…You know? I haven't been to Oslo in a while actually. I miss Master's presence. He's taught me so much…"

Sandy turned her attention to the coffee. "Thank you for the lovely hospitality," she chimed in. "But I don't know how much longer I can stay here. I've got to head back to town. And I was wondering whether you could…? Well, never mind…Sorry."

"Could we- what- Lady Liberty? Create sweetened coffee with a snap of our fingers? Heat coffee instantly with our energy?" Bjorn laughed in the sexiest way Sandy had witnessed someone do so in a long time. *Kaitlin wasn't kidding about their nickname fascination.* She was sure her cheeks and chest had become crimson, judging by the sudden heat she felt on her cheeks. Along with the butterflies in her stomach.

"You've got a lot of questions," Bjorn reached for her cheek. "And that's beautiful. You're not repressing yourself, unlike your friend. Questions like this actually make us happy. I'm proud of who I am. And your questions show interest…At least in our kind, I mean…"

"Bjorn," Sandy's curiosity had only peaked. "How many humans know about you? About your kind, I mean."

"We've been revealed in the Quran, but we've been around since the beginning of time- created alongside humans," Bjorn explained. "Many of us do indeed practice Islam, but not necessarily all of us. I'm not by any book much, to be honest…"

"Oh, same here," Sandy chimed in, unable to yet return down to earth from the sky in Bjorn's eyes. "In fact, I've always described myself as Agnostic. That's…you know…where we believe in a Creator, but…"

"Shh…" Bjorn whispered, tucking her thick curls behind her ear as he inched closer to Sandy on the couch. "You're making small talk now. I know what Agnostic means. We're not at some lecture on a campus, sweet one. It's ok…You don't have to be nervous…."

"Well, I just thought, you know, we were trying to get to know each other better," Sandy couldn't lean back any further, nor did she want to.

"You forget, I already know your kind, Lady Liberty. Don't you think it's time you get to…experience mine?" Bjorn smiled softly.

"What's that supposed to mean?" Sandy pursed her lips.

"Isn't that what really brought you here?" Bjorn smirked. "Curiosity? What was that song about the fabricated fairy tales about us? *I'm a Genie in your Bottle?*"

Sandy was sure some of her spit had splattered across Bjorn's face as she burst out laughing. "You mean, 'I'm a Genie in a Bottle'. It was a 90's pop song. Yes."

"*You've gotta rub me the right way…*" Bjorn joined her laugh. "That's right. It's coming to me now. Back at the University it was really popular."

Hadn't that song come out in the late 1990's? Sandy remembered herself dancing to Christina Aguilera as a pre-teen. How could Bjorn have been a college student then? "Bjorn? How old are you?"

"Oh, snap, songs and pop culture trivia always date us, don't they?" He chuckled. "Let's just say that in our years- I believe I've got a decade or so on you. But not in my body in this realm."

"So…your spirit ages, but your body remains the same?" Sandy's mouth was opened.

"Depends on how we maintain our spirit," Bjorn explained. "Aging works differently in our realm. Regardless, believe me- had we not been living this casual and relaxing existence out in nature, I don't believe I could have been able to manifest with the youth and vigor of this human version of my energy."

"How about Finn?" Sandy figured she'd ask for Kaitlin, too. She was additionally doing research, wasn't she? "Is he the same age in jinn years?"

"Your curiosity has mostly been piqued by Finn, I see," Bjorn stiffened his jaw. "No problem…"

"Wait, what? No!" Sandy did not even want to entertain the

186

possibility of something that would ruffle feathers with her best friend.

"No, no you're far more interesting!" Sandy blurted. "What I mean is, umm, you've been very welcoming and open with revealing about your kind more than…"

"Oh yeah?" Bjorn's smile had returned. "Tell me again…how interesting I am…"

Sandy giggled as Bjorn whispered close to her ear. "I'd love to create a current so strong, as to blow away all the particles of sand from your 'Sandy' body. You can be my beach. I'd love to wash over you with my waves…"

"Oh, damn. I'll give it to you- that's some poetic stuff right there." Sandy giggled through goosebumps. "I'm sure you throw such lines out there for the other girls as well. You're quite the charmer, Mr. Berg…"

"None of them were ever named Sandy," he winked, arms interlinking with hers. "More importantly, if I'm the charmer then who's the snake? No- it is doubtful that any Sandy in any part of the world was ever held tightly by the serpent of desire…In which case, I believe that'd make you my charmer."

Oh, my God, we're discussing his serpent already! "Bjorn, it's getting hot in here, I admit it. But this may be a little bit too fast for me…"

"Why the shock, sweet one?" Bjorn's relaxed attitude was enough to simultaneously turn Sandy on and annoy her. "I know why you're here," he continued. "I admire your bravery. It's alright. It's just us here at the moment. I want your trip to Norway to be worth it. No shame in fulfilling our curiosities among our community."

"Th-thank you, Bjorn," Sandy stammered, struggling to inch her torso farther from Bjorn's increasingly closer position on the couch. "My trip already has been sweet, so far. Really. I've seen my best friend and her beautiful little baby girl. Went on a little boat cruise of the fjords earlier. I've…"

"Yes, tourist. But you'd more enjoy being a tourist of another kind, wouldn't you?" Bjorn pulled back, squinting his eyes on her with a sly smile.

"Oh yeah? And what kind would that be?" Sandy tucked a thick strand of her curls behind her ear.

"A tourist of my kind," Bjorn whispered, nearing her body once again. "A tourist of my flame…The powers of my animal form. Or my spiritual presence, housed by a human body vessel to provide you with the ultimate experience on your trip…"

This guy's saying he can indeed change form, I guess. Bits and pieces from Sandy's intensive online research floated through her mind. *That's kind of hot…Shit!* She could not let herself get into this supernatural maze of a date, she decided. *I cannot get on this grandiose roller coaster, when I've been known to get lost even in amusement parks.* "Bjorn…"

"No passport or ticket necessary for a trip to paradise here on earth," he interrupted. "Stop thinking. Stand up…"

"You're very cute," Sandy said, inhaling a large gulp of air. "And I've loved talking to you in person now too, after our chats. I just…think I should call it a day for today. Kaitlin's mom is in town, too, actually. The old lady is waiting for me, she'll be worried. I can come back another…"

"Shh, I promise I'll get you back to the city center in no time," Bjorn placed a finger on Sandy's lips. "I just need 10 minutes of your human time- from what will equal a lot longer and deeper than that in mine. Can you be open-minded to the pleasures your soul will feel in the next minutes, Lady Liberty?"

Bjorn's sudden yet subtle brush of full burning lips on her own took Sandy by surprise, but also managed to send the sweetest shiver of pleasure across her entire body. *Damn it, why couldn't I rebound from that Quinn loser with some random human local dude at some bar?*

"Close your eyes…and don't be afraid…." Bjorn's whispers and intensifying gaze were now accompanied by a strangely soothing possession over her entire body. Sandy realized she could not physically move much at the moment.

"You're going to dump me because I don't buy you gifts and take you out?" her ex-boyfriend and neighbor Quinn had drunkenly embarrassed her to their entire Battery Park building. "Forget you, girl! You're going to regret this! I'm going to find a real woman who doesn't constantly need a man to make her feel special."

Take that, Quinn.

"Shh," Bjorn grabbed her chin as her kissed her once again, this time with his hands traveling her entire body. "You are more special than you realize, Sandy Burns. You're going to be the toast of the main stages before you know it!"

"How dost thou know'est so much, Shakespeare?" she teased, allowing herself to give into the temptation she could no longer avoid. *He's even found out my last name.* Sandy cleared her throat as she heard barking somewhere in the near distance outside. "You *rogue*. Will you be expecting Anja or Finn back soon? Or- what was that other girl's name- Meredith? Anyone?"

"Would you like to see upstairs?" Bjorn asked in a cool tone. "You may be more comfortable there. Not even your friend Kaitlin saw upstairs. You'd be the first."

"What's upstairs?" Sandy tilted her head.

"No crazy dungeon or anything from whatever cautionary tale you may have grown up or auditioned with, Lady Liberty," Bjorn snickered. "Just my room. Along with two other bedrooms and our grand bathroom- we've actually got a sauna in there. The human flesh particularly has a liking for the sweat it induces…releasing the toxins."

"Release is good…" Sandy cooed. *What the hell am I saying?*

Had this jinn-man slipped something into her coffee? She didn't physically feel drunk or high- yet she was disarmed like she'd never remembered herself being with a guy before- especially on a first date.

"I'm merely responding to your true nature, Sandy," Bjorn responded to her thought. Luckily, Kaitlin had revealed their mind-reading powers to her- otherwise Sandy was sure she'd be shocked enough to run for the hills. Literally.

"Oh yeah? And what does my- nature- say to yours, right now?"

"You want something different," Bjorn went on. "Correction. You *need* something different. An experience. To make you feel alive. Purposeful here across the world for something more than a visit to a friend and taking nice pictures to share on your little Instagram page. All I'm asking for is 10 minutes...and I can join your spirit in passion- in my most raw and natural form. Can you trust me? I will not violate your body. I promise. You will be safe with me- safer than with that Quinn or any other boy back home."

"My spirit?" Sandy gulped. *Screw you, Quinn.*

"Come, let's head upstairs first for some privacy," Bjorn motioned her to the stairs he was now strutting toward. "I mean- it doesn't matter to our community here- but I can imagine you would not yet be comfortable..."

"Privacy...yes. Thank you..." Sandy didn't have a chance to utter another word as she found herself in Bjorn's arms in a whooshing flash. They were both now on a large-bed with silky sheets, and a small window displaying the moon that had grown higher in the darkening sky outside. "Whoa...did we just, fly here? Teleport?"

"You can say that, yes," Bjorn gushed. "I wanted to give you a little preview. Did that scare you?"

Sandy shook her head with a smile. Surprising herself that she'd genuinely meant it. She had curiously not gotten scared. Not even one bit.

"Look at my view every night," Bjorn motioned toward the window. Come. The woods look lovelier from the second floor."

"It's so peaceful," Sandy awed at the sight of trees and sound of crickets. "Back in New York, I'd have to endure listening to my friend Lisa's non-stop chatting to be able to travel in her car upstate to the Catskills, like we'd done once or twice. But it wasn't as breathtaking as this place. I can't explain it, I mean…I don't see anything particularly extraordinary…but it feels…"

"What do you want to see? Kaitlin had a thing for waterfalls. How about you, Lady Liberty? What's your favorite part about the natural world?"

The ocean. Sandy closed her eyes and imagined herself in Coney Island during the previous summer. The salty waves rushing over her body. The seagulls….

A sudden shriek of an actual seagull abruptly pulled her from her daydream. "Oh my God," she shrieked when she opened her eyes, witnessing that the moon-glazed, darkened silhouettes of trees outside the window had transformed into an ocean with subtle waves brushing the sandy shore. "Where did we go? Bjorn, this is spectacular!"

"We're still here. We are capable of making our desires materialize when we believe them and give into them fully, Sandy. The jinn merely have ways to tap into theirs more quickly."

"Thank you!" she found herself turning around to hug Bjorn, yet only ended up hugging the air. She shrieked and leapt off the bed. "You've become a gh-gh…"

"In allowing for maximal naturalization, I could no longer maintain my human flesh, Sandy," Bjorn gauged her for a reaction, and continued upon her stunned silence. "I'm merely my jinn form. But if this scares you, I can return us both into your regular plane and dimension of the cabin. And you can return back to town if you'd like…"

"But I saw you," Sandy felt sure she was stuttering. "Yet I could not touch you. H-how could that be?"

"This is my way of making you feel safe," Bjorn spoke softly. "A jinn cannot physically violate or alter a woman's body, sweet one. Anything beyond a kiss isn't really possible between our kinds. Even then what you're actually feeling is our dense heat on your lips, rather than skin like with a human."

"I'm speechless…" Sandy managed to utter.

"If you allow me," Bjorn carried on. "I can reach down to make love to your soul, and you'll feel it. Not as much as a fellow jinni would, of course. But, you game?"

"Would this be…. some…temporary possession?" she asked bluntly. *I've come this far, I might as well.*

Bjorn motioned her over back to the bed, smiling with a reassuring motion of his head. As Sandy blushed and sat down next to him- she found herself surprised that she could still make out the silhouette of Bjorn's regular muscular, fair-haired and icy-blue eyed self. He hadn't become transparent like some ghost she'd seen in a 'Casper' movie as a child.

"Enough talking and thinking," Bjorn took in a deep breath. "Is your soul ready, to experience the beyond?"

"You didn't answer my questions…" she teased.

"Oh, but Lady Liberty. We've already possessed each other. Let's just make the most of it before I take you back to town. A beautiful memory. Ready?"

"I'm here, aren't I?"

"I have to hear you say it…" Bjorn pressed.

"I'm ready…" Sandy whispered.

"Say my name…"

"I'm ready…Bjorn Berg." Sandy obeyed.

A sudden orange beam of light took Sandy's breath away. She

rolled her eyes backward, with a pleasure of intensity she'd never experienced before. She indeed did not feel any penetration of any physical sort. Yet something inside her washed over with titillating warmth that managed to spread millions of tingles traveling at the speed of light to every single nerve and neuron of her body.

Sandy extended her hands toward Bjorn's alabaster face. yearning to pull it close to her own for a reassuring kiss of intimacy. She could not do so. All she could do once more was to enjoy as the orange beam of light immersed into her being, with the now familiar tingles causing Sandy to release a vocal sound of pleasure.

"Are you okay?" Bjorn whispered in her ear.

"It's not fair," she moaned. "This has all been so exquisite. But I can't kiss you anymore. I can't feel you."

"You're right," Bjorn stated. "I'm afraid there are limits to crossbreeding intimacy. We can touch and kiss once we manifest as humans, but we cannot make actual love unless we're in our natural states. I am only allowed the continuation of that sensation with a fellow jinni."

"How about Anja?" Sandy asked, unsure why she was thinking about Bjorn's relationship with her then.

"Don't worry about her. Sweet Sandy, have you ever wanted to float? I can levitate you…."

Before Sandy could utter any word, he did just that based on her smile. The walls around Sandy began to spin as she witnessed her body slowly being lifted toward the ceiling. From the higher perspective, she could observe that aside from the multi-pillowed and adorned large bed, there had been little else in the room except an armoire and a small, beige vanity table with a matching stool. Then, she spotted it. A women's hairbrush.

"I still wouldn't want to be more unfair to her." Sandy licked her lips. "I know I wouldn't want my boyfriend- jinn or human- making out with another woman."

"You're not a stranger," Bjorn insisted. "You can even become one of us if you'd like. We'd have to consult with Lar first, but I'm sure it can all be arranged. Anja's a part of our ecosystem. She has friends of her own in Sirdal. Don't concern your pretty head with all that anymore."

"Umm, Bjorn?" Sandy's dark curls were lingering in the air, with her body suspended in a horizontal position. She glanced downward to lock eyes with her magician. "Can I come down now?"

"Oh, of course," Bjorn chuckled, unhurriedly lowering Sandy onto the bed. She took in a deep breath and sat up the minute she'd done so. In a flash, Sandy whirled near Bjorn by the vanity mirror.

"Holy gumballs" she exclaimed, causing Bjorn to raise his brow with a slick smile.

"I think I preferred your Shakespearian vocabulary, dear Thespian," Bjorn winked at her. "Hey. Look toward the mirror now. What do you see?"

"I see myself. I don't see you." Sandy shrugged.

"Would you like to do so, before you go? See me- that is-in my favorite form?" Bjorn grinned.

"Well, I suppose I have experimented thus far…"

A sudden slithering took Sandy by surprise, yet strangely didn't scare her one bit. She allowed for the smooth and cool skin of Bjorn's instantaneously slithering form to wrap itself around her body. Despite the reptile reflection she saw, she didn't feel snake skin, but rather more of the fiery energy. *Oh, thank God,* she thought.

How she'd be able to shake off the disturbing memory of having allowed herself in some perverse embrace with an actual animal form-Sandy didn't even want to think about it. She simply smiled at Bjorn, holding a good thought in her heart she wouldn't be regretting this later.

CHAPTER 17

Sandnes

THE SUBTLE KNOCK ON HER BEDROOM DOOR JOLTED KAITLIN UP in bed. How long had she been staring at the ceiling here like this? With Malin successfully napping, she felt disappointed in herself for missing the opportunity to do further blogging on the computer. She peered at the screen. Two mere paragraphs on the importance of a new mother asking for help to make time for herself peered back at her.

Kaitlin had titled the article 'Moments'. She closed her eyes and transferred her thoughts to her trip to the bookstore and coffeeshop downtown. *The momentous freedom of one's arms holding something other than a stroller, or a slouchy shoulder bag heavy with diapers...*' A sound from the other side of the door halted her typing. "May I come in?" Paul whispered, pushing the door slightly ajar after Kaitlin hummed a short, welcoming tune. Hitting the 'Save' button, she closed the lid of her laptop and eyed him with a grin.

Her husband was wearing a navy-blue cashmere sweater with a white collar sticking out. Even on their worst days, Paul would manage to look handsome to her in whatever semi-formal outfit he would come up with for work.

"She's been sleeping for a while." Kaitlin's eyes glanced up at him, toning her voice down to a youthful pitch- Paul's favorite. *It reminds me of the innocence inside of you when you talk like that*, he'd say. "How was work, Paulie? You hungry?"

"Same old," Paul made himself comfortable on their bed after changing out of his work clothes. He moved closer to the edge of their sizeable bed, with knees touching his chin. "Some guy tried convincing me to change our health plan today," he shared, staring out the window in a position matching Kaitlin's own. "I don't even know how security let a solicitor in. He was quite a persuasive fella. Oh, and I've brought back half of this huge beef sandwich I had for lunch, so don't sweat dinner tonight."

"Well, I've prepared soup- Malin's tried a few sips, too. You can have that with your takeout." Kaitlin lingered her gaze on Paul with a smirk. She knew her husband had a tendency to be coerced into buying one house item too many each time they'd be approached by particular salespeople. And he insisted that *she'd* been the spendthrift one. "So, did you take the bait?"

Paul shook his head. "The bait? Oh, you mean about the health plan? Nah, don't worry, babe. Nothing can beat our own Statoil plan. I just jotted down some of my information to be polite. He said he'd send over some brochures."

"Oh, that's good," Kaitlin remarked. "We'll throw them out if they send us any such junk mail."

"Yeah, we'll be contributing to the local recycling efforts, babe." Paul added with a coy laugh. "So, what was it you wanted to tell me?"

"Well, you'll tell me if I'm exaggerating, right?" Kaitlin began after taking in a deep breath, urged on by Paul's nod. "I kind of feel-unattended, somehow. By our guests, I mean. You know. Not special. I mean: both my *mom* and best friend- for God's sake- from the other side of the world, nonetheless- pay a visit. They supposedly want to see me and Malin. And here they are- their second day here really, and they're apparently over us enough to go sightseeing…"

"You know, I'd been meaning to talk to you about that," Paul's pursed lips took on a serious tone.

"You were?" Kaitlin asked.

"Yeah," Paul continued. "Here I thought they would have paid me to be their private tour guide after work hours and on the weekend- but look at them, making the locals richer."

Paul's widening smile annoyed Kaitlin even more than his off sense of humor with her mood in the moment. *He means well*, she reminded herself. She rolled her eyes playfully and tossed a pillow in his direction in the same manner. "I'm serious, Jim Carrey."

"Babe," Paul spoke after taking a long breath in and placing his head affectionately on her outstretched leg. "They're only here for two weeks or so, and time is money. And this is Norway. *Norway.* We're damned lucky to be living in this natural paradise that many people dream of visiting; we both know this. I'm sure they would have preferred to go with you, but we both know Malin couldn't go on that windy boat ride just yet..."

"They're not exactly from war-stricken, desolate places, Paulie," Kaitlin continued with a pout, caressing his wavy brown mane. "Canada and the States both have natural wonders, as well. I just thought they'd want to stick around the house with me and Malin for a while longer at least. You know? Play with her while I took care of things or something. Or, heck, maybe even help me out a little..."

"Babe, look at me," Paul suddenly sat up on the bed, putting his open-palmed hand out before Kaitlin's rosy face. "I hereby solemnly swear to increase my child-rearing duties in the evenings and on the weekends. I will do so gladly, and you will not feel the need for the position to be filled by your mother or..."

"Cut it out," Kaitlin teased with the pillow once more. "This is not about them servicing me. This is about them- oh, I don't know- at least waiting another *day* before displaying more touristic interests than Malin, maybe?"

"Okay. This does it. I'm taking you ladies to the museum on Saturday before they close early. *All together-* and that includes the fourth little lady, our sleeping beauty herself," Paul kissed her softly on the forehead. *"D'accord?"*

Kaitlin smiled. How could a man who could irk her with atmosphere-high expectations manage to then woo her with seldom-expressed but wise, tender words when she needed them the most?

"D'accord," she agreed. *Maybe I'm the one with lofty expectations.*

"I like when you talk to me like this..." Paul bounced his eyebrows, whispering on her neck. "You know? When you open up to me, I want to open you up in other ways..."

"Oh, yeah?" Kaitlin thought for a good few seconds to reply with something seductive, but her particularly-heightened hormones throughout her pregnancy and since becoming a mother didn't allow her to be able to wait any longer. She grabbed Paul by his white t-shirt and kissed him hungrily. *The soup will just have to wait.*

The sound of soft wails coming from the crib just then had them both chuckle breaths of air into each other's faces. "Oh, no, I think her highness is waking up from her afternoon nap."

"I guess she doesn't want a sibling anytime soon," Paul quipped. Kaitlin smiled teasingly, straightening her blouse as she walked to tend to their daughter. Paul's reference to a second child already- when Kaitlin hadn't exactly been able to adapt just yet to having become a mother- would have irritated Kaitlin, had she not been as heated for any action she could get. Whether Paul thought it'd be for a second child, or their routine, occasional intimacy using protection- she couldn't care less at the moment.

"Shh...." Kaitlin rocked the crib gentler than she'd thought she would have to, noticing Malin had luckily drifted back off to sleep. Darting a suggestive look over her bare shoulder, Kaitlin gauged Paul's gaze. He was eyeing her slouchy sweatshirt with a smile. *Time for the kill.*

"You know, babe," Paul whispered, inching closer to her and pulling her rapidly toward him onto their heap of decorative pillows. Kaitlin giggled and Paul had to jokingly place his palm on her mouth. "Perhaps we should send Sandy and your mom on a random touristic venture every day, actually. If Malin's nap time is going to last long like this..."

"Well, you *did* come home a bit earlier today," Kaitlin glanced up at her husband with wide eyes, caressing the subtle brown scruff on his cheeks. "And her nap is lasting longer than her usual 45 minutes as of late. Perhaps the stars have aligned for us today."

"When does that tour-boat get the ladies back to town?" Paul inquired in a serious tone. He'd promised to pick them up by the port in Stavanger.

"Oh, it already has," Kaitlin replied dismissively, continuing after seeing the puzzlement on Paul's sturdy face. "Sandy messaged me something about an extra hour or two of shopping or whatever else they're apparently doing in town."

"Kaitlin, didn't you tell them the shops will be closing up early? And I do need advance notification of when they're ready for me to pick them up. The traffic at this time..."

"Paul," Kaitlin grabbed his white t-shirt, rolling her eyes. "They'll be just fine. They'll message us. Can we just...?"

"Oh?" Paul blushed. Taking another look at the crib to ensure Malin was sleeping, he added, "Can she hear us?"

"Paul!" Kaitlin's voice grew increasingly frustrated.

"Okay, okay," Paul raised his arms in the air, his childish tone making Kaitlin smile as she let him kiss her and start running his hands all over her body.

"I surrender, my lady. I'm all yours."

§

199

ROCKING MALIN BACK AND FORTH IN HER ARMS, Kaitlin exhaled with her breath creating a fog on the window. When had the temperature dropped so low? The heater was supposed to be automatic.

Where the hell are they? She'd already placed the chicken cutlets in the oven after feeding Malin her usual mashed fruits with shredded walnuts. Though their gratifying time making love had induced hunger in both of their growling stomachs, they promised to delay appeasing their appetites further than a few sips of soup. Until Paul returned back home with their guests.

Kaitlin hadn't been able to fully wallow in her contentment from the evening after a peek at her phone. Neither Sandy nor her mother had texted her for a good hour later than expected, and Kaitlin had begun to get worried sick. A million horrid thoughts had begun to circle around her thought space. She had even just begun to picture Finn making himself appear before Sandy again- as he had done so in New York- when Malin had woken up, and Kaitlin actually sighed with relief at the distraction of tending to her daughter.

"Where is grandma?" Kaitlin asked Malin, carrying her toward the kitchen to look at the oven timer. *10 minutes left.* "They better come here soon, because momma is starving!"

"Momma," Malin smiled, clapping her hands.

"That's right, my love," Kaitlin responded, just then noticing Malin's hands traveling to cup her breasts. She chuckled. "You want more milkie-milkie?"

"Mmm," Malin seemed to agree, as Kaitlin sat them both down on the leather couch. Lowering her slouchy top further down on her breast, along with one of the several nursing bras she'd intermittently been using around the house - she allowed Malin's lips to drink her milk.

Though it had begun as a frightening novelty- and a painful one for her sore nipples, at that- Kaitlin had quickly come to appreciate the increased closeness she felt with her daughter each time she witnessed her angelic countenance depending on her for nourishment. *Another miracle of life*, she thought with a smile. Wasn't that how Finn had also coined it?

A rather haphazard turning of the keys woke both Kaitlin and her nursing daughter from their reverie. Malin began to cry at the interruption as Paul opened the door with a tired looking Linda and rosy-faced Sandy in tow behind him.

"Girl, we are so sorry!" Sandy quipped, taking off her shoes.

"I heard you ladies had a long shopping fest after the tour, eh?" Kaitlin teased. "You've forgotten all about poor old me and Malin, here, haven't you?" The sound of the timer signaled that the cutlets were ready just then, and Kaitlin tried to provide some solace for her daughter. "It's dinner time for us, sweetheart. We can't all be nursed. We're hungry too."

"Kaitlin," Sandy's face crunched up in a sentimental expression. "Halt all talking, dear, sacrificial yet beautiful mother you. This vision of seeing you breastfeeding your little one. Too beautiful for words, hon."

"It's the best thing in the world, girl," Kaitlin beamed.

"I've missed my angel…" Linda began to rush toward Malin still in Kaitlin's arms when she was stopped.

"Your hands, mom," Kaitlin's tone meant business as she pulled Malin away.

"Kaity, you're serious about all this- I'm impressed," Linda gave her daughter a look-over as she headed toward the bathroom, before adding, "…since when are you this clean…?"

I'll ignore that, Kaitlin dismissed. "Ladies, we were worried sick. What happened after the fjord tour?"

"Did a handsome Norwegian gentleman lead you astray with flatteries, Momma Linda?" Paul bobbed his eyebrows suggestively. He'd mostly kept quiet the drive, reminiscing the earlier moments with

201

his wife.

"Oh, nonsense, Paul dear," Linda waved her hand back and forth in the air. "Not me, but, oh, I think perhaps our little New Yorker here might just have gotten flattered, alright."

Sandy shot her a look dirtier than sewage as Linda nudged her arm playfully. "Aww, nah, not really," she tried her best to laugh it off, despite ruby cheeks.

"Sandy? What's up?" Kaitlin eyed her friend intensely, handing Malin over to her now clean-handed mother to embrace.

"Nothing, girl. Just a local guy friend I'd made online. I'd promised a quick coffee to meet him in person while in the area."

"You made a date here with a stranger online?" Kaitlin was very confused.

"Not a stranger," Sandy began, before turning red. "Umm, well, not really. We know some folks in common. Bjorn was cool. I mean, umm, Thor. Everything was casual."

"Thor, or Bjorn?" Kaitlin asked softly, lifting her brows.

"Thor. These Nordic names. Crazy. We'll talk later." Sandy raised both eyes up in a way that implored for Kaitlin to drop it for the time being.

"Huh…" she uttered before heading to set the table. "Oh, yes, we will."

Dinner was bound to be interesting.

§

THE AIR IN THE GUEST ROOM WAS GETTING HEAVIER THAN A CIRCUS of elephants exercising. Sandy wondered just when Kaitlin's face would soften up and she could witness her usually-sympathetic friend again. She hadn't said much throughout dinner, either. *It's not like I made out with her own jinn-buddy or anything,* she released a heavy sigh.

"Details- Sandy. Now!" Kaitlin barked.

"What?" Sandy shrugged, playing with her chipped nails. "I just met a friend in person while in the area. I didn't leave your mom for too long, if that's what you're getting at. She really wanted to check out the local trends…"

"Girl, how long have I known you?" Kaitlin folded her arms. "I think you know exactly where I'm getting at. I know when you're lying. I mean, Bjorn? Please don't tell me you went to that cabin…"

"Cabin?" Sandy made a puzzled face. "Oh, *that* Bjorn! Please, hon. How many Bjorns must there be in this country- why would you assume it'd be that Bjorn you met?"

Kaitlin twisted her lips, and took in a deep breath. Her lingering gaze on Sandy was revealing enough.

She reads me too well. "Small world, eh?" Sandy attempted a smile. She wasn't feeling sure how much of everything she could reveal without apparently setting off some third global war.

"Sandy!" Kaitlin was shaking her head.

"Hon, after Finn approached me in New York, you know I got curious about their kind," Sandy began. "After what you told me- it all strangely made sense. How bizarre everything had been. And I went to their website- and asked some questions to Bjorn. About Norway and their lifestyle. He remembered who I was right away- I guess Finn shared his little game in New York. So, yeah, we've just…you know… been talking online, and, it was magical, Kaitlin. I was, like, lifted. And he…slithered."

Oh, shoot, Sandy instantly regretted spilling so much already.

"Sandy!" Kaitlin stormed. "What in the world are you saying? Lifted? And who slithered? What exactly did they slither? Did you join in whatever kinky group stuff those damn…"

"We were alone, Kaitlin," Sandy's eyes were nearly glowing as she cut in. "And it wasn't what you think. It was pure, almost. We, like, soared…"

"You – what?" Kaitlin grabbed her scalp. "Soared? What the hell are you saying? Did he give you drugs?"

"I…I think I have to rest, Kaitlin," Sandy was feeling her head pound like drums.

Kaitlin turned her eyes toward the ceiling, placing both hands on her suddenly flushed cheeks. "Did you sleep with this dude? Someone you'd just met after meeting online?"

"No. Well, not exactly. I can't explain it. But it felt so right! A once in a lifetime opportunity…"

"Oh, it felt right, did it?" Kaitlin demanded. "Sandy-Bjorn's a jinn. Finn's a jinn. They're jinns- remember? Have my experiences not meant anything to you?"

"Girl, you know I've been single for a while now," Sandy was wagging her hands all around herself. "And it was a harmless little kissing and things of that nature. Well, a different form of nature, I suppose, you can say…"

"Knowing everything I lived through," Kaitlin placed both hands on her hips. "All the fears, losing my new dog, being followed and even harassed on the phone: you purposely went to hang out with one of them?"

"Finn was just leaving right as I came in, Kaitlin," Sandy rushed. "Now, I know you're thinking this is crazy- and I can't blame you. But firstly, I just had to demand an apology for messing with me with his little job-search skit, you know? And, he did. He also asked about Malin." She gauged for Kaitlin's reaction. She'd been feeling like there was something Kaitlin wasn't quite telling her, and Sandy wasn't one to be able to rest without getting to the bottom of things.

"Sandy…please tell me you're joking about all this," Kaitlin whimpered, shaking her head side to side. Hearing Malin's giggles from the living room comforted her, but she couldn't hear her mother or Paul. Were they listening? She lowered her voice. "You left my mother alone

204

to go to a cabin you know is inhabited by otherworldly beings?"

"Kaitlin, wait, please just hear me out fully first," Sandy pleaded.

"No, please, you listen first, Sandy," Kaitlin demanded. "I'm sorry, but this is way beyond even meeting some random Norwegian guy from a dating site or whatever. Are you aware of the trouble you could have gotten yourself into through the jinn world? I got to know Finn a little bit and all- but Bjorn? He just seemed like a partier to me. And isn't he still with Anja? Why would you? What were you expecting?"

"Nothing!" it was Sandy's turn to interrupt, albeit with imploring eyes. "I didn't-and still don't- expect anything serious with him. Think of it as- I don't know- method acting, or something."

"Oh? And what role were you preparing for exactly- a TV show about a woman victimized by mystical creatures?"

"Kaity?" Linda's voice sounded close.

"Does my mother know?" Kaitlin asked. Sandy shook her head.

"We're going to continue this tomorrow," Kaitlin went on. "Look, I'm glad you're alright, and that you and my mom are back home in one piece, girl. I just hope this hasn't opened some door...some connection with their kind and with us here somehow."

"We're coming Momma Linda!" Sandy called out, adding to Kaitlin, "I told you. Bjorn's cool. Please, trust me. No one will be in danger of any kind."

§

KAITLIN STILL COULDN'T SHAKE SANDY'S WORDS OFF HER MIND, slicing some tomatoes to accompany the avocado toast. *Slithered.* She had peered at the clock by her nightstand almost hourly into the morning. Her inability to fall into a deep sleep had her jealous of Paul's loud breathing next to her. She had almost been afraid to fall asleep, as she snuggled her body closer to Paul's.

What was it about the word that had been bothering Kaitlin? *Why did Sandy have to get us further into this jinn mess?* she thought. She

205

remembered storming into the Stavanger cabin after finding out Finn had visited Sandy in NYC. Anja and Tan had been half-naked and nonchalant around one another. Without their significant others present. Well, there was that damned snake but.... *Wait a minute*!

What was it that Sibel had told her? About these jinns being able to take on both human and animal forms? John Walker had told her he'd seen Meredith with a cat. And she'd seen a cat walk along with her a couple of times- strange, as stray cats were an anomaly in Norway. *"Cat got your tongue?"* Finn's voice echoed in her head. Could it be? Anja's snake with the sky-blue eyes must have been Bjorn. Could Finn's animal form of preference have been a cat?

"Good morning, ladies," Sandy said softly somewhere behind her. Kaitlin didn't respond. *Why is this happening again?* Why were these beings somehow attracting not only Kaitlin, but people around her as well? *Will I ever be free?*

"Have you shaken off your jet lag, Sandy?" Linda momentarily halted wagging a toy at Malin on the playmat in the living room. "I think I was finally able to sleep better last night. My first two nights were terrible."

"I hope to sleep calmer soon, too, Momma Linda," Sandy replied, eyes darting into Kaitlin's back. "Can I help with breakfast?"

"I still cannot believe you, Sandy! What the hell were you thinking?" Kaitlin fumed, turning around as Malin cooed loudly in their direction.

"Sorry, baby," she continued in as soft a tone as she could muster. "Mommy used a bad word. It's just your dear aunt Sandy here has not exactly been making smart decisions lately..."

"Oh, gee thanks, K," Sandy rolled her eyes as she plopped down on the dining table. "Very mature of you to use the little angel to throw daggers in my direction. I'm sitting down- come direct them right at me. I deserve it. I'm listening. Shoot."

"Kaity!" her mother cut in. "I told you. I'm a grown woman. I was fine shopping around town. Sandy was very responsible with her messages while she was on that date. Go easier on our guest, please…"

"It's okay, mom," Kaitlin rolled her eyes. "We'll talk with calmer heads after breakfast, hopefully. I just hope Sandy hasn't- ahem-wrapped herself in any trouble." She added a smirk.

"Pun intended?" Sandy smiled with relief, walking next to Kaitlin.

Despite her anger, Kaitlin couldn't help herself. "Yes, pun intended," Kaitlin chortled as she buried her face in her hands. She couldn't stay angry with her friend for too long.

"Okay, I'm going to tell you all the details…" Sandy spoke quietly, working on mixing pancake batter. "Including the, ahem, *wrapping* part you claim not to be curious about."

"Do I first need a cup of coffee for this?" Kaitlin deadpanned.

"You just may," Sandy retorted with a smile. "You might also want to add a shot of whisky or Bailey's to it while you're at it."

"You'll have it in my place," Kaitlin sighed. "I can't drink while nursing. Remember?"

"Girl, look," Sandy placed her on Kaitlin's. "I'm sorry I fibbed a bit about my plans following the fjord tour. But, come on, at least I got to see everything firsthand. It was an out-of-body experience- and, I think, literally so…. I felt like he was encapsulating me without my feeling his flesh in that moment, though I could certainly see him."

"You didn't feel his flesh?" Kaitlin clenched her eyebrows.

"Yeah," Sandy's eyes were wide. "I mean, how do these beings impregnate women, for God's sake, for the continuation of their kind? I have no clue."

"Girls," Linda spoke over Malin's toy rabbit being stuffed on her face. "Do you need help?"

"Almost there, mom!" Kaitlin called out, smiling back at Sandy.

"Let's spare her the juicy details."

Sandy nodded and continued. "He made love to me- almost- I suppose. Yet, in our human, normal sense- he didn't, really. I didn't physically feel anything, and even he assured me I couldn't be violated."

That hit a nerve in Kaitlin. "He…didn't physically enter you?"

"No," Sandy shook her head. "Sorry to be completely up front and raw about it, girl. But that's what I mean. It was strange- scary a bit, yes. Yet also, sweet, somehow. He said jinns using their human forms to make conventional love to a woman was forbidden, or something like that. He was able to move me- without physically violating me-if that makes any sense. Well, I suppose he did violate my soul or thoughts or I'm not sure what exactly…"

Hold up. Her thoughts speeded a mile a minute as Kaitlin drowned out Sandy's ramblings.

"I can barely keep my eyes opened…" she recalled telling her husband, when she'd thought it was him who'd come to bed late that night.

"I just need you to keep your legs opened…" he'd responded, making love to her, only for her to later see the real Paul entering their room with an apology for coming in late. Kaitlin had certainly felt herself made love to in the normal, physical sense- hadn't she?

She'd avoided the long-burning question in her mind for so long. The doubt was a most unwelcome addition to the guilt she'd already been feeling. For her unintended infidelity, and even for the experience of being violated. Perhaps it hadn't been infidelity- or even trickery- after all? Not in the traditional sense, anyway.

"When you open up to me… I want to open you up in other ways…" Paul's voice from their most recent love-making spoke in her mind now. Maybe Paul and Finn merely enjoyed using similar foreplay lingo. Was it just Kaitlin? Was it all a coincidence? *Malin.* Her daughter's name triggered another question heavy in her heart, and

Kaitlin knew at once what she had to finally gather the courage to do.

"Sandy, I know how you can make it up to me," she faced her friend head-on. "For your little lie to go hang with your jinn lover-boy and leaving my mother stranded. After breakfast, you need to cover for me while I head out for a while."

"Head out?" Sandy asked, befuddled as she placed the pancakes on the plates. "Are you okay? What's going on?"

"Sandy!" Kaitlin demanded. "Listen! It's urgent. It'll be my turn to explain later, alright? There's someone at the local lab Sibel once told me about. I need to, umm, make a quick check-up appointment."

CHAPTER 18

Oslo

LAR IKTAR LOOKED OVER HIS ONCE FAVORITE DISCIPLE. "Finn Du Feu. You've arrived in Oslo again, at last." He shook his head softly with pursed lips. *Look how weak that woman has made you.*

"I came as soon as I could after your summon, Master," Finn bowed his head. "Stig has filled me in with some of the details. Has he completed his part of the mission?"

"Yes, he has," Lar assured him. *This mission will toughen you up once again, my dear Finn.* "And with success, too. Not to worry. Come sit down. Let's go over the details for your portion of the task. I'm sure you'd want to head back to Stavanger as soon as you can." *Tan may return with Nora any minute.*

"You don't need to worry about hiding Tan's presence here, Master," Finn gazed straight at Lar, beaming closer to him in an instant. "I know he's in Oslo. I saw him. And you. A while back. When I was here to track down that Emilia girl for the other branch."

Why did I get myself involved with these mind-readers? Lar cursed his luck. It had been the fastest way to success for his company- he reminded himself.

"My clever Finn," he cleared his throat and took in a deep breath. "Yes, Tan is indeed here. Meredith never asked my permission to send him off to his home country. She's lucky I haven't kicked her back out into the Trondheim woods. We do not turn our backs on our brothers or sisters. Of any kind."

"With all due respect, Master," Finn placed his hands in his pockets. "I've known what Tan had done since the beginning. He'd shown me Linette's diary entry, and I heard him mourn his crime. But I kept my mouth shut. I admit I didn't want to miss the opportunity to pursue Kaitlin Maverick. I must ask- and, forgive me – but, why were *you* quiet about Tan?"

"You've already wasted too much time, Finn!" Lar bellowed. "Enough with this insolence! This is not about Tan. It's that Kaitlin woman. We must ensure she's left dependent on you, and then on us. She *must* be made into a member of our Group, already!"

"But, Master…." Finn attempted.

"No way out this time," Lar continued. "No way you can convince me again to leave her be otherwise. You've gotten the woman involved too damn much. This is the only way we can keep her under our control…"

"But, Master, she's raising a child, our child…"

Lar threw his head backward to fully allow himself a gregarious laugh. *He's lovesick to think that it could even be possible. This is how Tan was too, with Linette.* "Is this what you came here to Oslo for?" he inched closer to Finn. "To convince me to approve of your blasphemy to the maxims that have propelled us to our awakened existence? Your blasphemy even to the righteous path of your own kind? What would your mother think? That baby is not *your* child! You are a jinn! Get a hold of yourself! Has your family before The Group taught you nothing?!"

"Master, please don't say that," Finn was shaking his head. "I know what the books say. But I feel it. I feel she is my child. She has to be! She looks straight into my eyes. She sees me. When no one else does- unless I'm tapped into their particular energy field. Malin does. She spots me right away. She's mine. She's Kaitlin's and mine."

"Very well…" Lar started more calmly. "It looks like I'm going to have to take the fatherly role here, aren't I, young Finn?" He took in a deep breath before yelling. "She is not your child! It is unnatural and impossible to cross-breed!"

"Master, I know you mock my intelligence," Finn was adamant. "And I do not intend for any disrespect. But I simply must insist there's got to be a loophole. Some exceptions. We are both created by God, after all. Humans of the soil and us jinns of the flames. Surely there can be some instances where…"

"Nonsense!" Lar wagged his finger in Finn's face. "No matter what games your powers are playing on your logical reasoning- there's no way you could have done more research than I on the matter, Du Feu. Do you doubt my intelligence? Do you downplay all those years I spent working day and night on my degree? I've researched nothing but religion, philosophy and mysticism for over six years here in Oslo. *Six years!*"

"Of course, Master," Finn bowed his head again. "Surely you're more educated than I. It is not my place to question your studies or …"

"Why do you think I was so relaxed with your pursuit of human women?" Lar continued, pacing with his hands tied across his back. "Hmm? And Meredith and Bjorn's pursuit of humans as well? It was precisely *because* I knew no interbreeding could naturally occur between jinns and humans, and therefore our Maxim 24 on children in The Group would not be violated!"

Finn became silenced by Lar's advocacy against children. He gulped several, audible deep breaths. Swallowing his tears as he avoided Lar's eyes for as long as he possibly could.

"The child can stay with that grandmother you mentioned was here, or that annoying girl who got to Bjorn," Lar finally filled in the silence in a calmer voice. "What was her name, Sandy? Or even that Turkish woman Tan had suggested two years ago, whom I shot down upon realizing she wasn't meant to be a part of The Group. Non-targetable. Too damn righteous and strong-willed."

"I understand," Finn's eyes were downcast.

"If you insist on waiting for her little girl to grow a little older-fine, I'll allow you that," Lar continued softly. "But sooner or later, you cannot avoid the inevitable, Finn Du Feu. Neither can you ignore your mission, unless you want things to change around here."

"I understand the part about Kaitlin, Master," Finn kept his eyes closed to hide tears more than out of deference. "But precisely in regards to that little girl; I have to ask you to reconsider one more time. Master, I feel it. I feel that parental, fatherly urge I'd always heard about…"

"Master, may I cut in?" Meredith manifested herself next to Finn in a flash of orange beam.

"Meredith! What in the world are you doing here?" Lar put his face in his hands, turning his head between her and Finn. "Why have you allowed her to accompany you, Finn? You've gone so astray from your original purpose in coming here to accept your mission."

"She insisted she come with me, Master…"

"Master, please, may I have a word with you?" Meredith cut in. "Finn's right. I did insist. I know you're cross with me, and wouldn't have otherwise accepted my visit, had I first planned it with you, but…"

"If this is about Tan…" Lar began shaking his head.

"We do not swallow back bacteria we've spit out, Master," Meredith gulped. "It is not about Tan. In fact, I was hesitant to join Finn today if it'd even meant Tan would be here. Luckily, I see he isn't…"

"You're still a poetess, I see," Lar smiled.

"She's also been reading more than doing outreach with those new South Asian clients, Master," Finn shook his head teasingly.

"You need to focus less on my hobbies…and people's children," Meredith hissed. *And more on your own.*

"Mer…" Finn warned her in his mind.

"Master," Meredith breathed, adjusting her shoulders after meeting Finn's domineering gaze. "I'm tired of having to be in hiding. Treating Bo as if he's some stray dog we've been taking care of around the cabin. He's growing up so fast. Enjoys manifesting in flesh, as he's learned from us. We cannot force him to always remain in canine form. And a teenage-boy cannot share a small room with his mother…"

"You knew what you'd be getting yourself into when you violated the Maxims!" Lar's voice was firm. "Rules are rules for a reason- Meredith. They're meant to optimize our lives. You see? This is living proof- a cautionary tale- so I should be glad, I suppose."

"With all due respect, Master, I didn't exactly get pregnant on my own." Meredith eyed the floor.

"You two- do not for a moment think that, just because I am a human, I am an idiot," Lar gazed between Finn and Meredith once more. "I meant I can now use you two- both of you- as an example of what *not* to do with the rest of your sisters and brethren."

"Master," Finn began, rolling his eyes. "Meredith's convinced about something, which I'm not even sure about."

"Oh?" Meredith snickered. "Yet here you are, apparently so *sure* about Malin!"

"I know you two violated our maxim at our annual bonfire festival, you sin-jinns!" Lar yelled. He recalled the video of both of them looking distressed- and then at each other- while everyone around them had been dancing. "You are lucky I still need both of you- and have respect for your accomplishments over the years. Or you'd both be banished!"

"Master," Meredith began.

"Silence!" Lar demanded. "Deep down, I know you're a smart young woman, Meredith. And not only for the great accounting and recordkeeping you've been providing us with over the past five years. You didn't come to me when you and Finn decided to console each

214

other's sudden loneliness in your jinn-energy forms. Or when you decided to have that child."

"Master, I honestly don't even remember how much I'd had to drink…" Finn was stammering.

"Nor did you do so when you and Finn decided you could banish poor, confused Tan from the cabin," Lar's eyes were still locked on Meredith. "Now how dare you come to me to ask for a favor?"

Lar didn't want to think it- but it seemed that Meredith had more in common with Linette Peterson than their facial features. *My poor, poor Tan.* He could still recall her vivid laughter in his mind. He'd heard her with Tan on that phone conversation he'd tapped.

"Sweety, that man is a weirdo!" Linette had said. *"If I didn't know any better, I'd think he wants to jump you more than me. All that talk about nature and ascension? I don't think I can really join a group like that. Are you sure he hasn't been ascending high on some psychedelics, instead? Cocaine perhaps?"*

But he was thankful he'd resisted the urge to shut the computer off in anger. He'd listened all the way until the end.

"Well, I'm sorry my friends aren't apparently on par with your ex-boss Walker, Lin. Lar is a good man, and that means more to me than being some fancy boss at some fancy job with some…"

From there- he'd tuned out the rest. Tan had defended him. He'd passed his test. His love for Lar was real- and perhaps it could even be deeper than Tan realized it. Once he could wake up to recognize it.

Fluffy, superficial people who would never understand. They had to be rid. Or at least be left behind- like his mother, back in the Emirates. The world needed to be rid of its viruses. Heaven on earth could only then be closer to reality.

Linette had been the major hindrance in his ultimate path of fate with Tan Kuvvet. Lar Iktar felt it in his heart. He'd lost love once in his life, and he was not about to do it again. Life was giving him a second chance. A do-over to be able to live his heart's desire.

"Master, Linette will come around, don't worry," Tan had urged. "I love her, and am very jealous as you know. But The Group is my family. And here it's different. I will be alright. As long as she can accompany me in my beautiful, purposeful life here."

"She cannot!" Lar had bellowed. Tan's sexuality- his true one would flourish soon in due time- Lar knew in his heart. His attraction to women like Linette wasn't the obstacle- Linette herself was. And she wasn't worthy of The Group, nor of Tan. The girl was fluff. She was not worthy of higher enlightenment.

"I looked deep into her eyes, lad," he'd convinced Tan. "I looked at her soul. And I'm sorry, but I didn't see it. I didn't see that spark. I know you care for her, and see potential in her. But she has none. It's only your earthly desire for her that is clouding your higher judgement. She cannot help you achieve your ascended purpose. You have to let her go..."

"Master, I can't...Her and I have this chemistry, I know, I know, you don't condone it but..." Tan had cried. But Lar had cut in.

"It's only an earthly body addiction- it is not real love. Do you want to live here with us as your new family, lad, or not!?"

"Yes, Master," Tan had bowed his head. "I'm sorry."

"...*Weirdo...*" His blood boiled as her mocking tone resounded in his memory. If Jaan had indeed been her father, she'd nowhere near inherited his sensitivity. No. Linette Peterson was certainly not worthy of Tan. *Or of being alive.*

"Master, are you alright?" Finn interrupted his thoughts. Meredith had positioned herself next to him, eyeing Lar too with utter shock on her face.

How much did they hear in my mind? Lar hated the leverage these jinns would always have over him- despite their lower position on the professional scale. He hated how much that inadvertently meant that

216

even he had to relinquish some control to their kind, and allow some of their caprices. "I'm alright. I was just thinking. Alright- Meredith, you can be more public about your son. But- since you're both here- I'll be handing over the mission for you to complete together; you both have to complete it thoroughly as your ends of the deal. Is that clear?"

"We're ready to listen and heed, Master," Finn bowed his head, and Meredith followed suit.

CHAPTER 19

Stavanger

SERDAR KORKMAZ WAS BEFUDDLED. He'd woken up from his rare daytime nap in sweats, with an even rarer nightmare of sorts. *Töbe, töbe.* He shook his head in all directions in shock as he paced to the bathroom sink to splash cold water on his face. His reflection told him his thick dark beard was in need of a shave, but he didn't have the energy. *Delilah likes it like this anyway*, he smirked.

What was he doing, thinking about his latest girlfriend? He had to call his mother or sister back home. He knew they'd always believed in divine messages coming through visions during sleep, and this rare one had been so vivid that Serdar was convinced it had to mean something.

What had at first appeared to be a small cat chasing him around the apartment had suddenly turned into a roaring lion, pouncing at him until cornering him in the spare guest room. The lion had kept clawing at him until Serdar had somehow shrunk in size enough to hide on the top shelf of the built-in closet. Once he went into hiding, the lion had given up and disappeared out of sight; Serdar had woken up precisely at that moment.

What was it about a lion? Or, a closet? Was it something about shelves? Or that shelf in particular? Serdar messaged for his sister at Boğaziçi University in Istanbul to call him when she had the chance. In the meantime, he had to appease his still rapidly-beating heart, as well as his curiosity. He walked to the guest room and pushed the door ajar slowly. The Full-sized bed with various bookshelves to give it a cozy atmosphere- and, admittedly, to impress the ladies- didn't reveal any trace of the lion that had jumped on it in his dream.

Delirdim sanırım, he thought with a smile. He truly must have gone crazy to have even considered something he saw in his sleep to be real. Yet there he was, being pulled toward the oak doors. He walked to the nearly-empty closet, opening the doors rapidly this time. Standing on his tiptoes, Serdar reached his neck to observe the shelves where he'd seen the smaller version of himself hiding from the lion. *Tan was taller than me, wasn't he?* He realized then that the last full-time inhabitant of the guest room- his ex-roommate- hadn't ever had to stand on his toes like that. *That lucky bastard.*

Serdar was just about to go back to his room to check out a message notification from his cell phone when something caught his eye from the dusty corner. Something brown. A book? He stood on his tiptoes again, this time extending his arm further in. He recoiled in fright as his fingertips touched upon something solid. *What the hell is that?* Unable to reach back far enough, he rolled a chair with wheels from the nearby desk to stand up on it.

There we go. He carefully reached for what he saw to be a cardboard box and placed it on his bed, letting out a sigh of relief. Where had it come from? Serdar was surprised to see that the top hadn't been taped shut or anything. An old cologne, a couple of notebooks, an empty cloth bag, two picture frames showing Tan with his family. *Damn, why did he leave these here?*

"Were these here?" he asked out-loud. How could it have been that he'd never seen a box like this before? But then again, he didn't use the guest room much. Serdar picked up a sheet on the top of the pile and turned it over to see writing.

TAN

LEAVE LINETTE ALONE ALREADY. WHEN WILL YOU GET THE HINT? YOU GUYS ARE OVER. ALLOW HER TO MOVE

ON, ME AND HER HAVE MORE IN COMMON THAN YOUR HARD HEAD CAN UNDERSTAND. SOMETIMES I REGRET NOT TAKING YOU OUT BEFORE. AT OUR OFFICE BACK IN CANADA. THE PAST IS IN THE PAST. YOU TWO MAY HAVE BEEN AN ITEM IN MONTRÉAL. BUT NOT HERE IN NORWAY. GO FIND YOURSELF ANOTHER GAL. OR ELSE.

PAUL

Serdar immediately threw it back into the box upon reading. Who was Paul? *Oha, bu ne ya?* The paper appeared to be from some company called 'Statoil'. Serdar had no clue why some guy would threaten Tan, and why Tan would keep such a note. Something that apparently went back to his days in Canada, at that.

What was that golden piece of metal also peering out at him? He couldn't help but sneer at the outdated smart phone. Blackberry? On second glance- he saw that he'd been wrong. It was a Nokia. He didn't recall Tan using these- maybe they were his old phones. He saw the charger alongside it, and connected the phone to an electrical outlet for a good 10 minutes to see if it'd turn on. It did.

A black-and-white photograph of Tan hugging that ex-girlfriend of his was on the home-screen. Serdar rolled his eyes. *I don't know if it was this crazy bitch who convinced him to go out to live in the woods, but good riddance.* Luckily Serdar had moved on from those days. He'd gotten his degree and become the manager of the local Radisson Blu hotel. He didn't need a roommate to afford rent any longer. He could invite his girlfriends over the past couple of years without worrying about asking Tan if Linette would also be over.

He scrolled through some old pictures and messages. *What in the world?* Most of the pictures had been of Linette- even in selfie mode. One would almost think this had been Linette's phone. He clicked on 'Messages'.

"Hvor er du???" was one message that caught his eye, sent by 'Momma'. Tan's mother in Turkey would certainly not have texted him in Norsk. He scrolled down after some promotional texts, as well as one

from-Tan! "I miss you."

This was Linette's phone! Serdar recalled her father stopping by, inquiring about Tan. And now, to find Linette's phone. After a strange dream leading him to it, nonetheless. What in God's name was going on? Had it been some astrologically retrograde period? Tan had moved out of their apartment so abruptly, and acted so mysteriously after leaving that Serdar had barely had the chance to ask him anything.

He scrolled back up. And then, he saw it. The last text. *Oh my God!*

MA CHÉRIE,

WHY DID YOU DO THIS? YOU THOUGHT YOU COULD GET RID OF ME BY ESCAPING TO THE OTHER SIDE OF THE WORLD? YOU THOUGHT YOU COULD LEAD ME ON FOR MONTHS AND MONTHS EVERY BLOODY DAY AT WORK, AND THEN SIMPLY LEAVE WITHOUT EVEN A PROPER GOODBYE?

PLEASE, AT LEAST GIVE ME A PROPER EXPLANATION. IT CANNOT BE COINCIDENCE WE ARE BOTH IN NORWAY. WE CAN AT LEAST BE FRIENDS. PLEASE, LINETTE. YOU KNOW I CAN BE BETTER FOR YOU THAN TAN. JOIN ME FOR A WALK THIS EVENING. BY THE LAKE. ONLY TWO WEEKS TO GO UNTIL CHRISTMAS. JUST SEEING YOUR FACE WILL BE A GIFT ENOUGH FOR ME, AT LEAST. I WAS ALWAYS THERE FOR YOU IN MONTRÉAL. PLEASE, BE THERE FOR ME NOW. JUST THIS ONCE. I REALLY NEED TO SEE YOU. IF YOU WANT—I CAN PICK YOU UP FROM WHERE YOU'RE STAYING HERE. I CAN EVEN TAKE YOU BACK UP TO TRONDHEIM. I'LL BE WAITING.

LOVE ALWAYS,

PAUL

§

Sandnes

SHE'S STILL NOT BACK? Paul shook his head as his fingers sought the keys in the back pocket of his trousers. He turned the door knob slowly. *Maybe she fell asleep along with Malin.*

Kaitlin's friend Sibel had invited them all for some lunch, after which he'd been told that Sandy and Linda would be taken on a tour of the touristic candle factory nearby. They'd drop Kaitlin and Malin off to rest. Malin did tend to get fussy when out for too long outside of home environments, Paul had to admit.

He peered through the rooms to see he'd been the only one home. Paul sighed, feeling his stomach rumbling. He'd just opened the refrigerator when the house phone rang. *C'est bizarre.* They'd mostly kept the wall-mounted phone in the new apartment for emergencies, as him and Kaitlin tended to be most frequently contacted through their smartphones. Taking out a carton of orange juice, Paul reached for the receiver. "Hello?"

"Hei!" A cheerful, young voice answered in an accent Paul could not distinguish. "I'm calling from Quality Lab. Is Kaitlin Maverick there?"

"Kaitlin isn't here right now. May I take a message?" Paul asked, furrowing his brows. *Why didn't she provide some lab with her cell phone number?*

"Very well!" the voice responded. "We- well, I- because she was so shaken, so, off the record, I just wanted to give her the news straight away! To let her know that those results with the samples she provided us with have come back quicker than we anticipated. The paternity match between a…let's see here…a 'Paul' and a 'Malin' have come back nearly 100 percent. Of course, no match can be 100%, but we can assure here that in circumstances like these…"

The woman went on at the other end, despite the fall of the receiver from Paul's hand. "Hello? Are you there?" The receiver was dangling, just like his arms. He could swear he felt the room spin around him, and had to place his weight on the wall.

"I'm here," he managed to pick the receiver back up. "Sorry about that. Alright, I'll let her know. Thank you."

"Alright, sir, thank you," the voice went on. "We appreciate your service with us. The bill-along with the typed results- will be mailed out to this Stavanger address I see here on file. We hope you have a nice day."

Paul couldn't hear himself think, sitting down at the dining table. He took a gulp straight from the carton, and several drops spilled on the glass table. *Merde!* He hurled the carton toward the sink, splattering more juice across the kitchen counter.

Turning of the keys caused Paul to let out a chuckle. *What's my dutiful, darling wife going to say, I wonder?* He closed his eyes and steadied himself on the table.

"Oh, hey, Paulie," Kaitlin entered, pushing in Malin's stroller. "Look sweety, daddy's home. Isn't daddy going to help me with this stroller?" She tried to meet Paul's gaze. "Paul?"

"You got a phone call, Kaitlin." Paul's profile was frozen like a statue in the kitchen.

"Alright," Kaitlin sounded confused, closing the door behind her. "And? Paul! Can you help me with Malin, please? What are you doing in there?"

"What were you doing behind my back, Kaitlin?" he turned toward her in a calm voice, chewing his lips. "I think that's the real question of the day."

"What?" Kaitlin wriggled Malin from her stroller.

"Dadda!" Malin cooed, as Paul's gaze lowered onto hers, filled now with tears.

"I am, my angel," Paul kneeled behind her on the mat where Kaitlin had placed her. "That's me. I am."

"Paulie, are your hands clean?" she called from somewhere in the bathroom.

"Oh, my hands are clean, sweetheart," Paul's voice maintained its soft demeanor. "Are yours?"

Kaitlin walked to pick up Malin. "I have no idea what you're trying to get at, Paul. Seriously. I've had a long day. And Malin needs a diaper change. Excuse us for a sec..."

Maybe I've excused too much. Paul followed his wife and daughter into their bedroom. Had the other man been in here? Or had the affair Kaitlin was apparently worried about- enough to apply for a paternity test- been back in Stavanger? And who was to say that it had even been one man? Paul shuddered.

"Paulie?" Kaitlin's face was fallen as she patted down the final Velcro on Malin's diaper. "I'm very confused."

"Oh, I can imagine, Kaitlin," his arms were crossed. "I must have confused you so much. So much so that you likely sought clarity in another's arms."

"Excuse me?" Kaitlin asked, until a look of understanding immediately replaced her look of worry. "What phone call were you talking about, Paul?"

"Quality Lab," Paul said with a forlorn smile. "They wanted to give you the good news. I am indeed my daughter's father, Kaitlin! Congratulations! Your affair didn't reproduce a love child."

"*Mon Dieu,*" Kaitlin cupped her mouth with her hands. "That was- a misunderstanding. I gave them Sibel's address and number. That was her house number, wasn't it? And since when do their privacy laws allow for..."

"Fuck privacy laws," Paul inched closer to the bed, teeth clenched. "That young woman may have been a novice, but she was God-sent."

"Paul," Kaitlin whimpered, looking down at Malin. "Please stay

224

calm. Of course, you're Malin's father. I never cheated on you. See? This is proof- you heard it yourself!"

"Kaitlin I never *had* any bloody doubt, until today!" Paul pounded his fist on the bed. "Are you kidding me? Are you stupid? And do you think I am, as well?!" His nostrils flared as his blood-boiling words continued. "Why the hell did you feel the need to even *take* a paternity test, Kaitlin, if you never cheated on me?"

"It's not what you think," Kaitlin was recoiling away from him on the bed, arms around Malin. "I experienced something during my sleep..."

"Either you've truly gone mad and you're hallucinating- thinking you're the second Virgin Mary or something now, or you must have suspected someone," Paul's teeth were inches from Kaitlin's face. "Which one? Which one of those nature-loving, yogi, fancy paper-making gang or bang or whatever members was it, Kaitlin? Tell me!"

"Paul, please..." Kaitlin cried. Malin began to wail. "You're scaring Malin. I swear to God, it is *not* anything like you are obviously thinking and implying. Let me explain, please."

"My wife," Paul began, wagging his finger in Kaitlin's face. "My fun-loving wife, full of energy and an active drive ... gets more sex from me again...I mean, I tried! I tried, damn it! She has everything she needs under our roof.... We finally have a baby.... And....and she.... she...goes and feels the need to take a paternity test to prove her husband is the father? How ...the fuck...do you think you're going to get yourself out of this one...?"

"Paul...I didn't...cheat," Kaitlin enunciated each word in a squeaky voice, trembling. "You have to listen to me.... babe, I love you."

"How could you do this to me, *babe*?" Paul began whimpering now, his hands rubbing his face with three deep breaths. "And you're going to continue to lie about it...when science and all that high school stuff about the birds and the bees is so clear-cut and obvious...I'm beginning to think your lying just may be worse than the actual indiscretion…"

"It…wasn't anything….voluntary, Paul," Kaitlin's words poured more than her teardrops. "You have to believe me…"

"What! What, were you- raped? Is that what you're trying to tell me now?" Paul was shaking his head.

"Not exactly sure how to even say this…" Kaitlin started shaking her head and took in a deep breath. "But…I was…haunted. I didn't know how to tell you earlier. About, their nature…The Group, from those woods, I mean."

Paul stared at her for the longest minute of Kaitlin's life. Finally, he began to laugh. "Oh, you were, haunted, were you? So, how does that work…like …you're telling me, what- a *ghost* fucked you?"

"Paul…. stop making fun of me," Kaitlin cried over Malin. "You have to admit there have been crazy things going on…ever since last year and Linette's body being discovered. We really, truly have to talk…but calmly…"

"Oh, no you don't…" Paul said softly, with his voice increasingly rising after each subsequent word. "You don't get to cheat on me- right under my nose- and then tell me what to do. You don't cheat on me…and then say it was with some ghost or whatever…and then tell me to calm the fuck down…"

"Paul…please…stop…"

"How could you…how *could* you!" Paul screamed into her face as he yanked Kaitlin's ponytail and flung her on the bed. She shrieked in pain as the side of her cheek hit the wooden headboard and her skin began to throb.

"Malin is right there," she squealed quietly. "You could have hit her."

"Well, I didn't!" Paul kissed Malin's cheek and stood up, pacing around the room in tears. "I wouldn't. I can't even hit you- though you sure as hell deserve it. I'm not the monster, Kaitlin. Ask yourself- who is the real monster?"

"Shh, it's okay, honey bunny," Kaitlin buried her tears nuzzling Malin's head, rocking her daughter back and forth. She heard Paul's keys and his walking toward the door. "Where are you going?"

"To a brothel, for revenge!" Paul deadpanned, only to then start laughing hysterically. "Back to the office to bury myself in work! You know, I'd come home early, thinking I may catch you girls back from Sibel's. It wasn't worth it."

As the door shut loudly behind him, Kaitlin continued to rock with Malin, humming a lullaby. She no longer felt sure of anything. Scratch that. She wasn't sure she could even feel at all.

CHAPTER 28

TYPING UP THE LATEST CARBON EMISSION STATISTICS ON THE company's corporate social responsibility practices had been proving more difficult than Paul expected. His trembling fingers had only managed two typed pages, rather than the ten or so he'd envisioned during his drive back to the office. "You better work, work…" he'd hummed the recent Britney Spears song on the road, refusing to think about anything else. He couldn't afford a crash. Malin would need him. *My daughter,* Paul wiped a falling tear before it could reach his cheeks.

A rush of people walking past his office door in full chatter-mode alerted Paul to his stomach growling. Was there a birthday celebration he hadn't been told about? Whatever it was- he was hoping there'd be leftovers for him to snack on, and fast.

His hand went to his telephone. Kaitlin hadn't called. Paul wasn't surprised. In time, she'd learned better than to interrupt his time alone to relax and think. He didn't want to hear any more excuses or lies.

"Paul?" he heard his friend and colleague Tim whisper on the other side of the door following a subtle knock. "I'm coming in."

"Tim?" Paul got up to open the door. "Of course, but, what is…going on?" He turned toward the reception area to see that the commotion had accumulated there. Was that a cop he saw?

"Are there cops here?" Paul asked as Tim shut the door. "I thought I saw someone in uniform."

228

"Two cops, to be exact, Paul," Tim lowered his eyes on the floor. "I'm afraid it's about you, mate."

"Me?" Paul's heart sank. "Whatever for?"

"Beats me." Sweat beads had started to form across Tim's forehead. "I tried to ask, but all I heard was that they'd had a warrant. They're coming here as we speak. Leslie's just making sure the warrant and their identifications are legit. I wanted to warn you ahead."

"Tim," Paul cackled, shaking his favorite colleague's shoulders. "You need to relax, my man. How's Jeanette? How's everything?"

"She's good, she's home. Paul, I'm serious," Tim's expression remained stern. "What do you want me to tell Kaitlin?"

"Tim, I haven't done anything..." Paul had just started to say when he heard it. Two powerful knocks.

"Paul Timothy Maverick?" A low male voice called out. Tim wasn't exaggerating.

"Paul, we know you're in there," a different man's voice added. "If you cooperate, there won't be any trouble."

Through the frosted glass, Paul could make out that several people had gathered behind the cops. He couldn't remember the last time all eight or nine colleagues in his division had crowded outside his office door. Except that one time his childhood friend- and fellow colleague, Jeanette- had thrown him a surprise birthday party during lunch hour.

He wished she could be there right now. But then again, maybe it was for the best. Jeanette would certainly have caused a bigger scene, asking the officers more questions than Paul could muster to do so for himself.

Not a peep was uttered by anyone 'casually' passing by his door just then. The presence of police officers at work had been enough to unnerve everyone senseless. He took in a deep breath and locked eyes with Tim, his heart pounding. "I have nothing to hide."

Paul straightened the collar of his jacket and opened the door.

229

"Yes, officers. How may I help you?"

"We have a warrant for your arrest," a pudgy officer held a paper out in front of Paul's face. The words had already begun to blur before his vision when he was able to make out a familiar name highlighted in yellow marker: *Linette Peterson*.

"A warrant?" Paul stammered, allowing his weight to crumble toward his desk and grabbing onto the edges for dear life. "On what grounds?

"You can learn more at the station," the taller, younger-looking officer responded.

"We've uncovered new evidence possibly connecting you to the death of Linette Peterson," the older one revealed, mouthing "It's okay," to his now confused looking partner.

"Linette?" Paul asked, bewildered.

"You have five minutes to gather whatever you think you may need to take with you," the younger one continued, his arms crossing his chest. "Charger, your phone, some immediate cash…"

Paul grabbed an empty bag from underneath his desk. Throwing in his charger, wallet and cell phone, he nodded with acceptance and managed to turn his head toward Tim despite his disorientation. "Help Kaitlin if she needs to come to the station, will you, please? At least until this ridiculous misunderstanding clears itself out."

Tim nodded with downcast eyes. "I didn't know your middle name was Timothy, my man," he tried to smile. "You can count on me."

"I'm ready, gentlemen," Paul held his chin up. "Honestly not sure what this is all about, but I'd love to help you on the case."

The younger officer shot him a sympathetic smile. "You do know we're taking you into pre-trial detention. As a suspect, not a witness."

With trembling hands, Paul leaned on his desk to collect his breath. *When it rains, it really pours*, he thought. *This has got to be the worst day of my life.*

CHAPTER 21

THE SIGHT OF THE DOORBELL BEFORE HIM SET TIM HAGEN'S nerves on fire, as if pressing it would set off a bomb rather than cause Kaitlin Maverick to welcome him. Taking a deep breath, he did what he had to do. His oldest mate from work had asked him, after all, for this difficult but necessary favor.

"Tim," Kaitlin indeed answered the door with an unsure smile. "What a nice surprise to see you here."

"Hi, Kaitlin, may I come in?" Tim asked, spotting a cheerful woman around Kaitlin's age, as well as an elegant older lady he assumed was her mother from what Paul had shared. "Hello, ladies!" he waved. Linda and Sandy introduced themselves from further inside the living room, eyeing him curiously. Tim fought back a tear as he recognized the adorable tot crawling around on a mat, looking up at him with a muddled expression. *Poor girl must have been expecting her father.*

"Of course, come inside," Kaitlin didn't meet his eyes, ushering him toward the living room. "Where's Jeanette? I didn't realize you guys had returned from your trip. How were the Maldives?"

"She's good, and, yeah, our holiday was exquisite. Quite beautiful," Tim's voice was stern as he reached for his shoes.

"No need," Kaitlin waved her hand dismissively, heading to the cabinet drawer to offer disposable shoe covers. "Tim, is everything alright? Is Paul still at work? How is he?"

"I need you to sit down, dear," Tim smiled softly, pulling out a chair from the dining table. He lowered his voice, leaning closer to Kaitlin. "Perhaps you'd like to discuss this alone."

Kaitlin took a seat next to him, throwing a blank look at Sandy and her mother behind her. "That's alright. You can say whatever it is here."

"Now, before I start," Tim took in a deep breath. "I'll kindly ask you to remain calm. Paul is just fine, and I believe everything should soon be working itself out..."

"Is Paul at the hospital?" Kaitlin asked, with a face displaying how a myriad of fatalistic possibilities must have been running through her mind at warp speed. "He was here this afternoon. He later, umm, returned to work. I haven't heard from him since. Tim?"

"Earlier today," Tim began, gazing at the floor, "...my first day back at the office- I'm afraid I was a witness to something. Two officers accompanied Paul to the local station, you see, and..."

"Oh, my God..." Sandy exclaimed.

Tim looked up to observe that Linda had placed a hand around her mouth as the other caressed her granddaughter.

"He's okay," Tim attempted his best to keep his tone assuring. "He just asked me to tell you in person. You know, as he was being led for, umm, some questions. So, I just wanted to..."

"Some questions? Where exactly was he taken?" Kaitlin finally spoke with dismay. "Tim? Please!"

"Oh, maybe Jeanette should have come with me," Tim said, slapping his own forehead. "Women are so much better at these things, aren't they? She's still shaken at home. I couldn't get her off the couch."

"Sir, could you kindly tell us what the matter is, please?" Linda marched toward Tim now, her arms crossing her chest.

"I'm not sure, ma'am," Tim's voice was shaky. "The officers let me know his family would be notified, so they should be reaching out to you soon. Ma'am, please sit down."

"I will not sit down, sir, without you please telling us what exactly is going in with my son-in-law?" Linda insisted. Kaitlin had joined Sandy on the mat next to her daughter. "He isn't in some sort of legal trouble or anything, is he?" her mother continued. "Has he been accused of something?"

Tim locked eyes with Kaitlin, now staring up at him like a lost little girl. "Kaitlin, he's gone to answer some questions and give a statement," he spoke gently, taking a seat on the couch. "He's at the Sandnes *politistasjon.* I'm really not sure what they're grilling him about, to be honest. But I'm sure it'll all clear up real soon and he'll…"

"Sandy," Kaitlin whimpered. "My phone. Can you…?"

"Kaitlin, they have his phone," Tim interrupted. "It's no use. Believe me, I've called as well. At the very least they're going to be keeping him there overnight. Something about a lawyer was also mentioned. I'll go there first thing tomorrow morning for further details…"

"Oh, Jesus sweet Christ…" Linda began to make exasperated circles around the kitchen.

"You're taking me there with you tomorrow, Tim, you hear?" Kaitlin begged.

"Kaitlin…" Sandy inched closer to the couch, a confused Malin bobbing up and down in her arms. "What's going there in person going to do? Malin needs you…"

"Momma…" she cooed just then, causing Kaitlin to finally erupt in tears. She extended her arms to take in her daughter in her own embrace, sniffing her head as she swayed.

"Canadian!" Linda called out, as if she'd had a sudden epiphany. "Paul's a Canadian citizen. How the hell can they take in the citizen of another country?"

"I'm really not sure, ma'am," Tim stammered. "But I promise you, that's what I'm going to try my best to find out tomorrow at the station. We have to…"

"What if they don't tell you?" Kaitlin was adamant. She felt more confident somehow with her daughter in her arms. "I'm his wife. His family. What if they only tell me? If you don't want to accompany me, I'll go on my own."

"She does have a point there, sir." Sandy shrugged her shoulders with a half-smile darted at Tim.

"Very well, Kaitlin," Tim nodded. "I'll drive you there. I can't have you in that environment on your own. I promised Paul. Everything will be alright."

§

IT WAS HARD TO BELIEVE THAT THE HORIZONTALLY-LARGE BUILDING could unravel the questions in her mind, but Kaitlin had to try. Throughout her life, she'd tended to regret things she hadn't done- even more than the mistakes which she had. She would get to the bottom of things at the police station, and then contact Paul's professional legal advisor, Mark Goldberg, immediately.

"You need to be calm-and strong- for Malin!" Her mother's pep-talk back home before their drive ran through her head. She looked over the dreadfully-painted building. *"Your milk can stop with a sudden rush of stress; did you know that?"*

"How would you know, mother?" she'd responded, dressing Malin on a maximum of three hours of sleep. "I thought you said you couldn't breastfeed me, and that I was bottle-fed for a long time..."

"Exactly," Linda had answered, staring at her shoes. "It happened to me. That's how I know."

"You mean..." Kaitlin had stammered. "When my father..."

"That's right," Linda had nodded. "It all happened in one night. Everything changed in one night."

"Are you ready?" Tim's voice halted her thoughts from the driver's seat. "I'll walk in with you girls to the reception area."

234

He turned over to pat Malin's head. Linda had insisted she take Malin with her for the police to see. "They'll have pity seeing his child," she had said. *His child.* Kaitlin fought back forming tears with all her might.

A blonde woman in uniform eyed them behind a desk as they entered through the glass doors. *"Kan jeg hjelpe deg?"*

"Engelsk, vaer sa snill," Tim returned her cordial smile. "My friend, Kaitlin Maverick here, would like to inquire about her husband, Paul. He was recently taken into custody."

"Oh, right," the woman responded with understanding, her high pony tail swaying as she stood up to retrieve a folder from the shelf behind her. "Paul Maverick. I remember, yes. He was brought in today."

"Officer, where is my husband now?" Kaitlin questioned. "We haven't been told anything. Why has he been taken? He wouldn't commit a crime of any kind. I don't understand."

"Beautiful girl," the officer responded, solemn eyes locked on Malin. "Mrs. Maverick, I'm Officer Erin Jensen. My colleagues, Daniel and Hans, are leading the investigation into Linette Peterson's case and looking into your husband's arrest."

"Arrest?" Kaitlin cried, meeting Tim's solemn gaze. "Officer, do you mean to tell me that my Canadian husband- a law-abiding, respected computer specialist at Statoil for years- has been arrested?" Kaitlin's eyes flooded with tears. "Tim? Say something? What is going on?"

"Mrs. Maverick…" Officer Jensen began with raised eyebrows.

"Paul is not some convict!" Kaitlin cut in. "He won't even let me take extra napkins from restaurants, or step on a bug! Isn't there some bail or anything? This is absurd!"

"Kaitlin, he's not convicted or anything, don't worry," Tim patted her shoulder with a weak smile. "The officers are merely leading an investigation at the moment. You heard her."

"Being arrested and being convicted after a trial has officially found someone guilty of a crime are different things…" the officer lectured. "He's technically on remand. And, no, we do not have a bail system in Norway."

"Well, sorry for my confusion," Kaitlin answered with wide eyes. "Neither I nor my husband exactly have experience with police stations and criminal trials. How can he be arrested?"

"Perhaps it would be best if we wait for a lawyer; we've offered him one, but he expressed preference for his own. But I will allow you this," the officer exchanged glances with Tim, inhaling a big gulp of air. "Your husband has already been notified he may call the Canadian Embassy in Oslo first thing tomorrow. Regardless, I assure you, with the evidence we've obtained, we can certainly arrest him according to Criminal Procedural Code, section 171 and section 106 of the Foreigners Act…."

"May I please just see him?" Kaitlin pleaded, rocking her body back and forth as Malin started to cry.

"I'm afraid visits are not allowed for inmates still in police custody for some time," the officer shook her head, biting her lip. "He was relocated to Stavanger *fengsel* a short while ago. It's a correctional facility nearby."

"Correctional facility?" Kaitlin whined. "Is that a prison?"

Officer Jensen nodded. "Because of strong evidence recently uncovered, we were able to place him there until an official case could start here in Sandnes, right at the Jæren District Court. "

"What evidence, ma'm?" Kaitlin implored. "Put forth by who? What could my daughter's father possibly have done? We were pretty much always together."

"I feel for that little baby you've brought with you, Mrs. Maverick," Officer Jensen attempted a smile. "I want you girls to go home for her safety." She eyed the periphery as if to ensure no one had been dropping in on their conversation. "I'm not supposed to share this, without officer Daniel Lindberg calling you first. But I will tell you this much. The cell phone of the late Ms. Peterson was discovered by an old acquaintance of hers- do you know her case?"

"Linette!" Kaitlin exclaimed through quizzical brows. "Yes, my husband's old colleague. She had an imposing ex-boyfriend from what I know- Tan. Shouldn't he be the one in question?"

"Well, from what I know from my colleagues in Oslo, Mr. Kuvvet has been cooperative so far," Officer Jensen shrugged. "We've also come across a threatening note your husband allegedly sent Tan. Around the same time period we now believe Ms. Peterson could possibly have been murdered."

"Ma'am, we always believed Linette to have been murdered as well!" Kaitlin shrieked, caressing Malin's head. "Paul himself was really upset when we learned the police were considering it may have been a suicide."

"The note Mr. Kuvvet received was written on stationery your husband uses at work," the officer took in a frustrated breath. "It included, I believe, the Statoil company logo with his name and information at the corner. There was also a disturbing text message originating from your husband's phone number to Ms. Peterson. From the same number that's still active under his name."

"A note?" Kaitlin screeched. "A text message? Ma'am, it's been years. Where were those assholes- sorry, acquaintances- with this supposed evidence years ago?"

"Mrs. Maverick, please remain calm," Officer Jensen outstretched her arms, making a playful face to Malin to distract her. "I assure you; we'll continue to do the best we can to ensure the authenticity of the evidence. But I must tell you the text message was sent on December 11, 2010- which was roughly the time of her death according to our Forensics Team. The date also coincides with when she disappeared, according to the statement by her mother. So, for the time being, you can understand we have to preventively keep him under custody."

"Tan Kuvvet is a liar!" Kaitlin exclaimed as Malin began to mewl. "If the girl supposedly committed suicide and left a note attesting to that, then how can anything like this even be considered as a possibility?"

Officer Jensen shrugged. "Anything can happen, Mrs. Maverick. We've seen it all, including forged checks and handwriting- with regards to that suicide note. Rest assured, we'll get to the bottom of it. In the meantime, we must do our job."

"I'll take you girls back home, Kaitlin," Tim caressed the baby. "It's just a preventive measure. It'll all be sorted soon."

"I hope you do consider that forged handwritings may also be a possibility for someone framing my husband," Kaitlin insisted. "This misunderstanding will clear out soon. It has to. Paul? A murderer? It's ludicrous."

"I hope, for you and your daughter's sakes, Mrs. Maverick, that it really will," Officer Jensen pressed her lips together. "Please try to see everything from our side. We have to take all necessary precautions and measures with regards to this case. We have your number. Please be patient."

§

THE OFFICER'S VOICE RAN FREQUENTLY IN KAITLIN'S MIND over the course of nearly a week since Paul had gotten arrested. *"Threatening note…Disturbing text…"*

How could they have jumped on Paul so quickly like this? Was a mere company logo enough to convince them? Anyone could have obtained the stationery from Paul's office. *But none would likely have had Paul's supposed motivation and connection to Linette from Canada,* the voice in the back of Kaitlin's mind reasoned.

"Girl, it's been six days," Sandy was going on somewhere behind her in the direction of the kitchen. "You have to eat better- and regularly so."

Kaitlin managed a smirk. She barely blinked, staring at the window across the couch and not the view behind it. *It's funny,* she thought. *I've been recalling the so-called evidence more than Paul's latest, emotional words to me.*

"Ma chérie," Paul had managed to mutter when she was finally able to talk to him; over a ten-minute phone call he'd been allotted the morning after her police station visit. A visit where she hadn't been allowed to see him in person- but merely drop off some extra cash and change of clothing. She'd barely been able to whimper his name upon opening the collect call, allowing him to air out his thoughts instead. "Let me get this out first, because the call may get dropped."

Kaitlin closed her eyes. A single tear managed to escape from her eyelids with her recollection.

"Know that I'm okay, in a comfortable little room here. I'm more worried about you and Malin. You have to keep your hopes and spirits up. You have to stay strong. I'm not perfect- and not a minute goes by here without me feeling like scum for not treating you very nicely the day of this ridiculous arrest. I certainly wouldn't have wanted that to be our last memory together before this injustice. But I saw that paternity test- and what did you expect me to think? I don't know how, but somehow, I believe you- though none of your explanation made sense. I know your good intentions, and I realize how your mind may have gotten clouded, feeling alone in a new town."

"You have a husband in jail, for goodness' sake," Sandy interrupted her nostalgia, joining Kaitlin on the couch with a plate of grapes and sliced bananas. "What's going to happen if he doesn't come out soon like he insists? What if this is not some 'procedural misunderstanding', girl? What if it lasts six months? Six years?"

"...I ask now for you to believe me, too. I would never hurt Linette, or even that lowlife Tan. I hope he pays soon for this false accusation- and burns in hell- that's for sure. But I would never hurt anyone on purpose. I know in your heart you believe me..."

Kaitlin opened her eyes with a deep breath and popped in three purple grapes simultaneously in her mouth. "Sandy...I can't think about that right now. He'll be home soon. He has to be. Mark Goldberg is the best lawyer we know. He's assured me it's all under control. He's already applied for a defensive testimony, and said he doubts they can have enough to be granted an extension for another four weeks to keep Paul in there. They're going to realize this has all been a misunderstanding. That he has been framed. This is Norway. And Paul is the last man on earth who would ever be in jail."

"...And yet, that's exactly where he is, hon," Sandy retorted, adding a smile. "You suppose he really could have been the last man on earth, then, eh? Maybe Finn and Bjorn aren't the only jinns, and most of the men we see roaming the streets have actually been of their kind?"

She patted Kaitlin's back after hearing her friend groan. "I'm just trying to make you smile. I'm apparently not doing a good job. Girl, look. You just have to be prepared for anything. You know? I mean- I know, for me, I'd never thought I'd have myself a little supernatural fling here in Norway, and an outer-body experience at that. Oh, boy."

"I can't even smile right now, girl," Kaitlin sighed. "Thank you for trying. At least your experience has shown me I'm not crazy. You've seen the jinns, too. And your- ahem, experience with Bjorn- opened up my eyes about impregnation and...well, I'm just glad my Malin is fully mine and Paul's."

"I really wish you would have confided in me about that night earlier," Sandy scratched her chin. "You never told Sibel either?"

"Girl, we went over this," Kaitlin looked at the ceiling. "I

240

couldn't tell anyone. It's been so hard for me to come to terms with this. I didn't feel comfortable sharing something I didn't understand myself."

"Well, I'm glad my experimentalism was able to help solve the mystery in your mind, I guess, " Sandy said, subdued. "You could have at least confided in a therapist, girl. I'm telling you- mine has done wonders for me back in New York."

"Has she convinced you to be more adventurous with jinn lovers as well?" Kaitlin teased.

"Ouch," Sandy bit her lip. "I'll let that one slide. But, look, in all seriousness- you've always got to have a plan B, Kaitlin. That's what I always say." She plopped her body on the leather sofa and sat up straight, assuredly patting her thighs.

"Plan B?" Kaitlin squinted her eyes.

"Yes!" Sandy insisted. "Let's say he doesn't come out. What's going to happen? Guilty or innocent- the fact remains that he *is* where he is. We have to think realistically here, hon. Surely you can't keep up with the mortgage on this place. Would you not want to return to Toronto with your mom, or heck even crash in with me in New York for a while? We have to prepare for the worst, so as to make sure that you and Malin…"

"Thank you, but let's not jump the gun just yet," Kaitlin cut in. "Paul must have thought of an emergency plan for the mortgage. He's always been the one for our 'Savings' account I wasn't allowed to touch. Saying it was for a rainy day."

"Well, I'd call this a bloody monsoon," Sandy nodded.

"You can say that again," Kaitlin agreed, checking her phone. "Mom and Malin should be back from their little walk any minute."

"Can I ask something else before I let you get some rest?" Sandy asked.

"Shoot." Kaitlin answered.

Sandy took in a deep breath. "Have you considered the other sad possibility?"

"You mean, that he stays in there for a long time?" Kaitlin raised an eyebrow. "We're going to resolve this. I don't even want to think that…."

"No," Sandy cut in, inching closer to her friend. "I meant the possibility that Paul really could-you know-actually have been the one to do something to Linette?"

"What!? No, Sandy," Kaitlin began to laugh in a way Sandy could only construe as wild. "Paul? A murderer? He could be the most annoying, perfection-seeking husband sometimes. That's for sure. But, that? No. No…."

"Just throwing it out, there, sorry," Sandy held her hands outward. "Don't shoot the messenger, girl. I've seen documentaries about the boyfriend or husband being a killer, where neighbors always said things like 'he was so soft-tempered' and 'we'd never expect this from him'. You'd know better- you're right. If you've never seen any violent tendencies from him, it's probably out of the question…"

Violent tendencies. Kaitlin's mind rushed, beyond her control, to the image of Paul's arm pinning her to the bed. Reaching across Malin's head and almost crushing his weight on her in the process. His rage of jealousy momentarily stronger than his usual inclination for protection and softness.

And then another image materialized in Kaitlin's memory. Their cemetery visit in Trondheim. Paul had mentioned his guilty conscience, standing over Linette's grave. "What if I go to jail, Kaitlin?" he'd asked her. Paul had just been feeling bad over indirectly confirming her boyfriend's suspicions that day back in Canada, hadn't he? Of encouraging him indirectly toward his murderous choices. That had to have been it.

"No, no…" Kaitlin's mouth was saying as her head shook side to side. In that moment, she couldn't be sure who she was trying to convince.

CHAPTER 22

November 25

THE METAL-LEGGED PICNIC TABLE WAS WOBBLY, almost crumbling under the weight of gifts for Malin's big day. *They're overcompensating*, Kaitlin smirked. A sparrow hopped before the pharmacy-purchased bags, eyeing them with an aimless gaze. Kaitlin could relate. She had no idea how long she'd been twirling the string of the crown-shaped balloon with her fingers.

"Are you okay?" Sibel put a reassuring arm around her. Kaitlin did her best to return her friend's smile, rocking her body back and forth on the princess-theme adorned park bench.

"These decorations are spectacular," Kaitlin nodded. "The kids are having fun. Malin hasn't cried once yet. Heck, I think I'd even go so far as to call this party a 'success', but, alas…"

"….*Nazar!*" Sibel chimed in, completing the sentence with the Turkish word Kaitlin mouthed in return as she nodded. "You've gotten to know me too well, my friend," Sibel's smile continued to be full and crescent-like. "Exactly. Let's not jinx it. We still have the cake to get through. And you told me about Mrs. Ramsay's pickiness."

"My mother!" Kaitlin whispered, placing a palm on her forehead after darting her mom a look, who was luckily distracting Malin with one of the simpler balloons tied to the metal bars of the swings. "You're sure the French café didn't include nuts of any kind, right?"

"Just vanilla filling and strawberries, as promised!" Sibel leaned back on the bench to spread her body more comfortably. "Same with my

243

brownies."

"Good, because mom would have had a fit-literally!" Kaitlin laughed. "The brownies were delicious, by the way."

"Go easier on your mother, will you?" Sibel grinned. "She's no picnic. I can see that, too. But I believe she means well. And she's the only one you've got; you know what I mean? I miss mine back home terribly. The woman's still too afraid to get on an airplane to come see us. I cry at the airport each summer upon our return."

"You're right," Kaitlin sighed. "Mom's been on the edge ever since Sandy hung out with that Bjorn guy at the cabin, leaving her waiting alone for her return. It's become this rift at home, and mom feels both left out and strangely also caught in the middle of it all."

"Are you sure you're not also on the edge yourself?" Sibel asked, wrapping her arms around her body with a shiver. "We've been lucky with some autumn sunshine today, but this wind isn't looking like it'll be letting down."

"I think I'm alright as I can be, under the circumstances," Kaitlin got the hint. "Why do you ask?"

"You seem a bit shaky," Sibel shrugged. "I haven't seen you like this since- well- you know. The whole Finn the Jinn thing before you guys moved. Is there anything else you'd like to share?"

"I think I'm just emotional having to celebrate this milestone without Paul," Kaitlin said. "You know?"

"If you insist," Sibel responded, looking at her fingernails. "I do keep thinking about what happened, though. About what your friend Sandy did. Why would she go to that place- knowing all the things you lived through last year?"

"Argh, don't remind me," Kaitlin shook her head. "She's been so good with Malin and everything over the past week, I'm beginning to forgive her for stirring things up. But, yeah, we should get the kids to eat quickly." She stood up to stretch her body. "They'll run around a bit afterward- I suppose- but let's call it a day soon after before they all catch a cold..."

Rummaging her chapped hands through her brown-leather shoulder bag, Kaitlin's fingers decided on her phone rather than the hand cream that had initially initiated her little search. "Malin won't remember these days, but at least I should take some more lovely pictures to show her when she's older, you know?"

Kaitlin noticed Sibel nodding with her eyes glued to the concrete ground. "Albeit, she'll notice that her dad is missing from the photos," she added.

"Kaitlin..." Sibel stood up and joined Kaitlin's closer look at the kids. They were now all huddled around 'Clown Sandy'- who was putting her acting skills to optimum use, pretending to be terrible at juggling to make them laugh. "Malin will see how her mother has been a warrior...how she has been so strong for her..."

Strong for her.

Finn's caring words to her by the seaside shot through her mind like a light-beam, and the smile that formed on Kaitlin's lips became brushed by a falling tear. Watching Malin being pushed on the baby swing, she allowed herself to imagine an alternative scenario- long denied.

Paul can't be here, but can you? Kaitlin closed her eyes as she took in a heap of air. *What if Paul is never able to return? Can you help me with her? Help me feel supported? Less lonely?* She opened her eyes to see that Malin had now locked eyes with her, causing Kaitlin to instinctively start walking to her giggling daughter. Malin was swinging faster now in the way of the breeze. Inching closer, Kaitlin motioned for her mom that she'd 'take it from here'.

Ok, today I'm giving in.

"Momma..." Malin babbled as Kaitlin refastened her daughter's top jumpsuit button. She tried her best to fit her full buttocks into the child swing situated next to her daughter. Kaitlin closed her eyes, and now included his name in her conscious thoughts. *Finn. There you go. I'm saying it. I need to feel your presence. I'm admitting it. Finn. Finn. Finn.*

A current blew her wavy auburn hair toward the right of her, in the direction of an empty swing. Hadn't their neighbor's grandson been swinging there a moment earlier? Kaitlin could have sworn she'd caught a glimpse of his distinguishable ginger-hued head of hair. She faced Malin to follow her eyes, and, surely enough, was able to trace them to the empty swing. Swinging faster now, instead of slowing down.

And then- there he was. Wearing the same black coat he'd worn at the harbor. Face tilted, with tender eyes viewing the both of them. The sparkle in his green eyes gave Kaitlin goosebumps.

She couldn't feel her legs just then. Nor did she sense any danger to her baby. Kaitlin smiled back, and simply allowed the moment. Surrendering felt like heaven. She just let them swing there. Side by side. Grateful for Finn's choice of silence as well.

"Kaity, Sibel's gathering everyone for the cake!" her mother broke the tranquil quietude in a sing-song tone.

"We're coming, mom!" Kaitlin thought she could hear his voice whisper something to her mind, yet she couldn't quite make it out. *What was that, Finn?* She was still transfixed by the evergreen shade in his optics.

I don't want to take away from the special day. Just know that you two will never be alone. For as long as you allow it. For as long as I live.

And just like that, he was gone.

She realized she felt something for the first time since Paul had been taken in. Her mother, Sandy, and even Sibel, too- God bless them all- were being more attentive to her than ever. Yet for the first time since Paul had been away- Kaitlin suddenly didn't feel alone. She grinned as a tear fell across her red lips.

A frustrated wail from Malin told her it was time to depart from the beautiful reverie. The entire party and the entire park at that could dissipate in that moment for all Kaitlin cared. She could have stayed in that moment forever.

"Ok, baby," she got up to wiggle Malin up from the slots for her legs. "Let's go get some of that cake, now!"

"Hon?" she heard Sandy's voice call out somewhere behind her. Before turning around to walk back toward the onlookers, Kaitlin allowed herself to close her eyes and inhale deeply again.

Thank you.

§

PAUL MAVERICK WAS LOST. Before him stood the older of the two officers who'd dragged him- albeit politely so- from his office into custody. He'd opened the square slot from the green metal door of his cell, only to confirm a date on his documents. He slumped hard on his single-bed, situated across a wooden table and chair set. Grimacing as his thigh slammed against the wooden frame.

The table had a box of raisins from the breakfast brought to him and little else- he'd hated oatmeal, and had expressed as such to Kaitlin on the two or so occasions she'd tried preparing a bowl with cinnamon. *I'd take Kaitlin's any day now.*

The table was next to a toilet. The room looked to Paul to be a cross between a small college dorm and an emergency room at a hospital. *Not too bad*, he supposed. He hadn't exactly had any prior ideas about what a prison cell would be like, of course. He'd even go so far as to compare it to a motel room, had it not been for the toilet in his face, right next to the desk. At least the stand-in shower would comfort him, Paul prayed. Through the bars on the rectangular window above his head, his eyes glimpsed a bird fly by. *Freedom.*

"Sir, may I have a word?" he implored, noticing that the man was still lingering outside his door, overlooking some papers. Paul framed his face into the square opening. "Please? Just one word?"

"I'm afraid you've already used up your phone call with your wife yesterday, and lawyer this morning, Paul." The officer's loud gum-chewing was one of Paul's pet peeves, yet at least the additional noise now ensured him he wasn't alone.

"No, I meant a word with you," Paul insisted. *This needs to be heard.* "This misunderstanding is the biggest injustice, sir. I can't even begin to think of how this would look in the papers, for Norway's prestigious society and well-reputed justice system."

"Some real-deal evidence was uncovered, bro," the officer snickered. "Norway's reputation isn't exactly going to become ill-reputed because we're simply doing our job. I'm afraid it isn't looking too good for you at the moment. At least until you can have a trial, man."

"I've been framed!" Paul yelled. *Bro? Man? How much American legal drama does this guy watch?* "The whole thing about text messages and letters- it's all bull! Can't you guys see that Tan has framed me? He and his friends from that cabin are the ones who haven't left my wife and I alone since last year. Tan's had it in for me since Canada, where I used to work with..."

"I have to get back," the officer interrupted. Paul could hear snickering noises from who he assumed were his neighboring jail mates. "You can express all this to your lawyer tomorrow for him to type up your defense. I don't think you'll want to talk to me without him present, anyway. Now, if you'll excuse me..."

"Sir, what's your name?" Paul had to try.

The officer raised his eyebrow. "What's that now?"

"Today's my daughter's birthday and I can't be with her," he continued. "Can you try to imagine how excruciating this whole thing has been? A one-year-old girl's father can't be with her because a murderer planted so-called evidence against him. And, mind you, did so in *his* old apartment, among *his* belongings. Has anyone even asked Tan why he had Linette's phone in the first place?"

"Save it for the judge, Paul," the balding man with icy eyes said, adding a smile. "All suspects claim innocence. The investigation is still ongoing, and I'm sure Tan's statement is also being evaluated for validity as we speak."

"With all due respect, sir, kindly don't mix my tragic situation here from some Nordic Noir you must have read or watched, lately!" Paul couldn't help himself. "Google the news for yourself, you'll see that…"

"Do you want to get extra points off the cookie jar for insulting an officer, now?" The officer's snickering made Paul want to punch his jaw even further. *How about injuring a stubborn and unjust officer?* Paul took in a deep breath. *I can't afford to make needless enemies here if I want to see my daughter again.*

"I apologize," he caved in.

"You can curb your anger problems through yoga," the officer continued. "Even more rehabilitation services will be made available to you after the trial if you get convicted- and would be serving a more settled sentence."

"Lovely," Paul sucked on his lips.

"I'll see you tomorrow for your official statement, under your lawyer's supervision." The officer had turned to walk before stopping in his tracks and re-lifting the metal covering. "It's Officer Daniel Lindberg, by the way."

Alright, Colombo, Paul thought with an eye roll. "See you tomorrow, Officer Lindberg."

"Oh, by the way, they've told you, right?" Officer Lindberg added with a grin. "Once a week the inmates are allowed to lunch under supervision at the cafeteria. Maybe you can socialize, make a little friend."

"I don't plan to stay here long enough for that," Paul held his chin high. "The truth will unravel and I'll be released, sir. You'll see."

250

CHAPTER 23

THE CHIRPING OF BIRDS AND THE SUN'S RAYS ENTERING the window signaled ideal weather for taking a walk. Yet Kaitlin's eyes were fixed on the heap of books before her. What was she to do, if there indeed had been anything? *I'm married, with a child, and alone,* she thought. Would freelance gigs and Paul's savings be enough if things took a turn for the worse and he got sentenced? *Am I doomed to age alone? Raise Malin as a single mother?*

A tear fell on top of a red hardcover, and she realized she hadn't heard her daughter in a while. "Malin?"

"Momma," Malin cooed slightly in the distance, playing adjacent to the couch.

"My sweet pea. How did you get over there?" Kaitlin watched in amazement as Malin smiled her all-knowing smile, and allowed her sweaty and chubby fingers to stick to the leather sofa like spiderman on city buildings. She pulled herself up, shot a look at her mother over her shoulder, and took a bold step.

"You're walking!"

You're walking, and your father isn't here to witness it. That had done it. Kaitlin's tears began to flood her eyes. Drops of both pride and heartache.

"You have got to change those curtains to something brighter," Linda entered the living room with laser focus on the periphery instead of the momentous occasion occurring before her. "At least until Paul comes back and, well, maybe we should wait until he returns before you go on makin' extravagant expenses. You never know how long his savings will last you. You need to finally get yourself a real job! Wait…what is going on? My Lord. My baby!"

"Mom! Are you going to get this, please?" Kaitlin squealed, gesturing with her hands for Malin to take another step toward her.

"Get what honey?" Linda looked back and forth between her daughter and granddaughter- who was now standing still in place, arms-free and looking all around her with mischievous delight.

"The camera, mom! Or your phone. Quickly!"

"Oh, of course, of course." Linda grabbed her phone from the kitchen countertop. "I'm filming, my sweet pea." Her hands were shaky as she tried pressing the button to capture Malin on her smartphone. "I see the red circle- am I doing it right?"

"Yes, mom, that means you're recording, don't worry," Kaitlin scratched her cheek.

"Aww, my goodness. Okay, video, this is Linda on a visit to wonderful Norway to see my daughter and amazing granddaughter. Malin's just turned one year old and today she's taking her first steps right here…"

"That's right, grandma." Kaitlin smiled for the camera. Tears rolled down her cheek as a proud-looking Malin giggled, taking two more steps and grabbing her mother's hand. Kaitlin turned her head to catch her mother's gaze, mouthing 'thank you'.

And then, she heard it in her head. *I saw it, too.* Simply that distinct tone. Without any burning sensations or any hairs raised. No longer alarming, as it had now become familiar.

Finn. Kaitlin closed her eyes, cuddling Malin in her arms while allowing the voice and presence to seep through every inch of her being.

I'm here with you. Both of you will never be alone.

§

THE CLOCK ON THE WALL TICKED FASTER THAN HIS HEARTBEAT. Paul sighed. *Will I die in here? For nothing?*

"Let's make this quick, Paul," Mark Goldberg shook his leg rapidly in the interrogation room. "You know me. I need my cigarette."

"The patch hasn't worked, huh?" Paul smiled, leaning back against the metal chair, arms folded across the sweatshirt Kaitlin had dropped off for him.

"I'm afraid my demons have become stronger than my saviors," Mark chuckled, going through various papers on the table in front of him.

"Thanks Mark for agreeing to help me on such short notice," Paul smiled. "I was utterly shocked. I mean, speaking of demons- can you believe that lying bastard?" he fumed. "Was there any response to that supposed message I texted Linette?"

"I don't think so, no," Mark kept his eyes on his shoes.

"Question anyone from my old work place, Mark, and they'll attest to my character, and Tan's as well," Paul insisted. "He created a storm that day- demanding to see our CEO John Walker and Linette- steaming when I tried to calm him down…"

"I know, Paul, I know," Mark placed his pen on his ear. "We've been through this, and I'm already nearly done with this defense statement. Just let me know anyone else I should contact…as witnesses on your behalf."

"If I knew more details of my so-called 'crime', maybe I could." Paul placed his head in his hands.

A knock on the door startled them both. He could make out the slick smile on Officer Lindberg's face a mile away. "Welcome, sir," Mark nodded as the officer pulled out a chair. Paul followed suit, forcing his gaze on the puffy-cheeked man's eyes, doing his best not to get distracted by the gum in his mouth that was apparently to be a fixture with him.

"Gentlemen, before we get to that statement, I've got an update from my colleagues in Oslo," Daniel Lindberg folded his hands on the

253

table. "Mr. Kuvvet has apparently been further cooperative with regards to that box discovered. Said he couldn't get himself to look through old things Linette left behind; she'd occasionally stay over with him in Stavanger, from what the old roommate, Mr. Serdar Korkmaz, has also confirmed. Furthermore, Mr. Kuvvet used to rent an apartment in Trondheim that has since been rented out to a new tenant- hence, we cannot search it."

"And her cell phone?" Paul snorted and met Mark's gaze, who in turn gestured him to stay calm. "Why would Linette leave her cell phone at her boyfriend's place in Stavanger, if I've supposedly lured her out to meet through a text- precisely using our phones? And how would her body then be discovered in Trondheim? Sir, none of this makes any sense. I mean, why am *I* here?"

"Her body had been dead a while when my colleagues in Trondheim discovered the victim. At this time, we are not ruling out that the corpse may have been moved across cities," Officer Lindberg shrugged. "Mr. Kuvvet insists Linette didn't like to take her cell phone with her much when she went out. That she enjoyed her private moments to clear her head from time to time, without being contacted. And when she disappeared, he said he assumed she'd left Stavanger in a hurry; upset over some big fight they apparently had."

"Mr. Lindberg," Mark intervened right as Paul was about to protest. "My client and I are also intrigued by the reason why, then, would other personable items of Ms. Peterson's not have been left behind as well? Surely the young lady wouldn't be staying with her boyfriend with only one outfit and a cell phone?"

"We are aware there seem to be some discrepancies," the officer shook his head, popping a loud bubble in his mouth. "My team is still on the details of Ms. Peterson's irregular lodging patterns, trying to piece together testimony from her mother as well. But, Mr. Goldberg, substantial evidence momentarily trumps over discrepancies, as you can imagine. Your client's information is on that threat note, and that suspicious text message was discovered to have been received on her cell phone the night we believe she disappeared for good."

"What about Tan's anger as evidence, over some obviously faked note and text?" Paul clenched his teeth. "Surely your team can interview anyone back in SAP Canada over his actions that day when he stormed in…"

"When asked about his behavior in Montreal, Tan defended himself with the logic that it'd be natural for him to 'overreact with jealousy' as her then boyfriend," Officer Lindberg continued. "In his own words. Yet awfully 'unnatural' for you to react with such possessive anger- allegedly, of course- as a mere colleague…"

"My anger?" Paul cut in, leaning his face closer. "His behavior was acted out before countless witnesses. And the supposed anger that I've been framed with- was, what- expressed through some forged note? Or fake text message? This is like a child's game!"

"What my client is expressing frustration with, Officer Lindberg," Mark cut in with a soft tone, "…is the unsubstantial quality of a text message, allegedly received years ago by an unused cell phone, being considered as evidence. Alongside an unproveable note discovered…"

"Were fingerprints looked up for that bloody note?" Paul interrupted. *I think I can defend myself better than Mark without his cigarette.*

"Paul, please allow me to speak first…" Mark had begun, before Daniel cut in.

"Funny you should ask," Officer Lindberg smirked. "They have. And they match yours."

"That's impossible!" Paul stormed, as Mark lowered his face in his hands.

"I never wrote a threat note to that liar!" Paul went on. "Someone must not only have copied my handwriting, but also used paper I touched. I'm always jotting notes down at work, I..." Paul paused his talking as his stomach felt a sudden kick. "Oh, hell no!"

"What is it, Paul?" Mark whispered, closing in on him. "If you've remembered something, we can ask for a moment alone before calling Officer Lindberg back in, and..."

"That health plan solicitor!" Paul remarked. "He came so randomly the other week. I found him sitting in my office, in fact, before I'd even entered that morning."

"Health plan solicitor?" Daniel scratched his cheek.

"I'd found it strange that he'd be allowed in Statoil," Paul went on, eyes focusing on the green-painted wall behind the officer's back. "Especially since the company has its own health policy in place with all us employees. I even shared this with Kaitlin. I was trying to politely turn him down, and he insisted on me jotting my personal e-mail and number on the corner of the notepad I use with the company info. Said he'd make sure to send over some brochures or whatnot. That paper must have been used as the note. We need to find that solicitor! All our offices have cameras!" Paul turned to Mark. "Please ask my boss- Lars Phelps- for camera footage."

Daniel Lindberg folded his arms. "Wow, that's quite a story."

"It's the truth, sir," Paul banged his fist on the table. "Please do contact Mr. Phelps. He's the head of my division and has access to all the security records. Between 9-10 am sometime within the last two weeks. I can't remember the exact day. You're bound to see that man. I was so disinterested then- I hadn't even asked his name. But you guys can identify him! He used that paper to frame me- to write my supposed letter. I just know it!"

"Why would some health plan solicitor want to frame you for murder, Paul?" Daniel was shaking his head, staring at Paul's fist.

"He wouldn't," Paul was nodding. "But Tan Kuvvet certainly

would. He could have been working for him."

"Oh, sweet Jesus," the officer got up and pushed his chair back in. "Mr. Goldberg, kindly include this health plan guy in Mr. Maverick's statement, then, and fax it over to me at your earliest convenience."

"Sir, I visited that Trondheim cemetery, with my wife," Paul stood up behind him. "Ms. Peterson was my colleague and my friend…"

"You need to stay seated, Paul," Mark got up to motion him downward.

"You've surely heard of that old adage about murderers tending to revisit the scene of a crime or places that remind them of their victims in general," Daniel said at the door.

"How about the cabin, sir?" Paul ignored the accusation. "Have you searched the cabin?"

"The what now?" Daniel turned around to ask. "Paul Maverick, I'm afraid you're becoming accustomed to not letting me leave rooms without further questions and statements."

"Tan may be playing nice in Oslo now- but you can even ask my wife or former boss John Walker, currently here in Norway, to tell you about the red cabin in the Stavanger woods," Paul stood firm. "Tan didn't just leave his apartments directly for Oslo- he'd also been staying in cabins with some shady people until recently. Some semi-business/semi-cult folks. My wife has even met him and his circle. They apparently stayed interchangeably at cabins and various locations around the country all the time. Places owned by some rich guy- Lar Iktar. Some author or lecturer or guru or whatnot…"

"This is all hearsay at the moment, and I'm afraid…"

"Ask my wife and Mr. Walker for the confirmation of this truth, as well as the exact location of the cabin closest to here that we do know of," Paul cut in. You can find Mr. Walker's number from my…"

"Mr. Walker's a part of the investigation, Paul," Daniel said with a shrug. "Don't worry. We have his information. Now get some rest…"

"Sir, before you go. Do you have a child?"

"Paul, this is not necessary," Mark began.

"I beg your pardon?" Daniel smirked.

"A wife? A family? Anyone who depends on you?" Paul's eyes were filling up.

"That's none of your business…"

"Sir, think of them and how they'd feel if someone had set you up, like I've had done to me," Paul stared directly into Daniel Lindberg's eyes. "If your little girl had to grow up asking where her dad had been in her birthday pictures when…"

"A son. My little boy is six," the officer revealed, biting his lip. "He's with his mother. She doesn't let me see him much. So, believe me; I'm used to unfair, if that's where you're getting at. We'll just let the law and evidence decide what's fair for you. If you're innocent like you claim, then in due time…"

"Unfair doesn't have to be accepted," Paul pressed with pleading eyes. "We have to fight, don't we? To be allowed to see our children, with our clear consciences. Our most natural human right."

"What do you want me to do, Paul Maverick?" Daniel replied.

"Have that cabin searched- you're bound to realize Tan's the real killer."

"We can't just search somewhere without a warrant…"

"If he's a part of this investigation, as you've said, you must know by now that Linette was John Walker's estranged daughter," Paul pressed. "John has her old e-mails to him. About how Tan had been scaring her. Please, sir. I'm as sure as my momma's name there's got to be something in that cabin."

"I've already chit-chatted here with you for too long, buddy." Daniel nodded. "But I will talk to Mr. Walker about this cabin you speak of. I'll also inquire about that security footage. I'll see what I can do."

"Thank you for your time, sir," Mark nodded.

"You will not be disappointed, Officer Lindberg," Paul stated. "Thank you. You'll see I'm telling the truth."

"Don't thank me," Daniel smiled. "This isn't for you. It's for that little one I saw in her momma's arms when she came by."

§

TOSSING AND TURNING FOR WHAT FELT LIKE HOURS, Paul stood up in the creaky bed with a jolt. Had he developed a stuffy nose? The cell was heated rather well, he had to admit. No. He remembered better now that he'd taken a deep breath in. He couldn't breathe in his sleep rather because of his neck- being pressed almost as if flat onto his pillow. A voice now accompanied the strangulation sensation he'd felt.

"You shouldn't have done that," Paul heard whispered in his ear.

"What the?" he asked into the empty space, touching his neck. With his heart pounding, Paul closed his eyes and counted to four, breathing from his belly. When he opened his eyes, there stood someone before his door- shaking his body and rendering him helpless.

The being in front of him was in the form of a man. Slightly transparent, though not as much as a ghost he'd seen portrayed in movies. "Who are you?" Paul demanded, despite his quivering voice. "How'd you get in here?"

"Don't you remember me, Paul Maverick?" the muscular man with wavy dark hair chuckled.

As Paul pressed himself further into the corner of the bed, he squinted more carefully at the figure. It all came to him clearly then. "My number?" he'd asked the solicitor at his office. "Sure, it's +47 12 11 84 71."

"You've got your number memorized, sir?" the man had asked.

"Well, I've had the number for over 10 years now, so it's sort of become tattooed in my memory," Paul had revealed.

"You!" Paul exclaimed loudly now. "The health insurance guy. It was you- wasn't it? You managed to hack into my phone, and fabricated some retrospective message sent to Linette's number."

"It's a good thing you never signed up on that health plan," the being cackled. "Your poor wife would have had to pay extra monthly fees for nothing. Why, with you being here and all."

"How did you do it?" Paul's mouth was hanging opened. "Who hired you? It was Tan Kuvvet, wasn't it?"

"You should have been this clever earlier on in your life," the figure cackled. "You and your wife had been warned never to mention the cabin to the authorities in any way, shape, or form. Did you forget? Or has Kaitlin never specified that for you?"

"Tell that Tan he's the one who should explain himself," Paul muttered, teeth clenched. "Explain how he could try to pin me as the bad guy, while he was the one that murdered his girlfriend."

"You don't know anything about our brother Tan," the figure commented.

"How can you be alright in the framing of an innocent man, whoever you are?" Paul's eyes filled with tears. "Whatever you are."

"Brothers look out for brothers," the voice hissed. "Be they of the humankind or of the jinn. The name's Stig, by the way. Remember it. And keep your mouth shut. Think of your family." The figure was then instantly centimeters from his face in a flash of light. *The jinn?* Paul closed his eyes in fear. *Please God let this be a nightmare. Let this being leave me alone. Amen.*

Paul slowly opened his eyes, encouraged by the sudden silence. The figure was gone. He looked all around the room to see that he was on his own once again. Walking over to the sink by the door, he splashed some water on his face. The water was running slightly brown, but Paul didn't care. In the mirror, he stared at the red vessels visible in his eyes. *I need to get some sleep.*

Paul was still shaking as he forced himself to close his eyes and dive into slumber; despite his horror, alongside the loud snoring from the inmate next door. Pulling the scratchy covers up to his chin, Kaitlin's imploring voice came to his memory. *"Please, Paul, you have to believe me."*

He shuddered. Paul had scolded Kaitlin for being naïve with that forest group, yet that was exactly how he himself knew he had acted with the mysterious solicitor in his office. Had he been some ghost? Some figment of his imagination? Somehow, Paul was leaning more toward the former, as he hadn't exactly witnessed anything of the sort before.

He focused on his daughter's smile for comfort. *My daughter. Our daughter. I could have allowed her mother to explain. I could have done so many things differently.* Paul hugged the covers extra tight. *Maybe Kaitlin wasn't lying about these beings,* was one of his last thoughts before drifting off to sleep.

CHAPTER 24

PEERING AT THE MAJESTIC TREES AND WILD FLOWERS still holding on to life despite the approaching winter, Sibel zipped her orange coat all the way up to the neck. *I have to see this place for myself.*

Kaitlin had been dismissing her questions lately, but Sibel knew when her instincts were on point. The eerie feeling when she received that letter from Quality Lab, confirming Paul as Malin's father, only underscored her general hunch. She recalled how she'd told her friend about the DNA services she'd used with the Lab to help in a family inheritance case with a local relative. *Kaitlin definitely must have thought this jinn could also have been the father.*

She'd refused to believe it could be true, but Kaitlin hadn't been very honest with her. Life had taught her one could give others the benefit of the doubt and be kept out in the loop for so long, before they had to take some matters into their own hands. Sibel had long decided that people ultimately could only trust their own selves.

The strong aroma of pine cascaded from her nose down toward her entire being, and Sibel understood what had mesmerized both Kaitlin and her friend Sandy about this part of the woods. She spotted the red cabin. It looked more to her like a tourist-trap disguised as a woodsy-styled motel than an actual, humble cabin. Did the local government know about this place? Too many questions were running through her mind. But Sibel had to focus on the task at hand.

The kids were in school, the house had been tidied, and dinner had been prepared hours earlier than her usual. Today, Sibel was determined to get some answers. For herself. For Kaitlin. *For Merve.*

"*Bana geldi o akşam*," she remembered her former colleague back in Istanbul speaking to her with glassy eyes. "He came to me that night," she'd said. What Sibel was convinced must have been a jinn in disguise as her ex-boyfriend. An ex-boyfriend who'd long forgotten about her, in reality, and in another part of the world. She'd known Merve for years at that time- no way her friend could have suddenly started hallucinating otherwise.

Sibel inhaled and let out the icy air in a fog of smoke in front of her pursed mouth. She applied extra chap-stick on her lips and placed the tube back into her pocket. Her fingers touched the small Quran she'd also brought along with her. No jinn or whatever else she could potentially encounter in this place could harm her, as far as she was concerned.

Sibel was adamant about her Islamic faith, despite leading a secular lifestyle with the occasional drink and hair she enjoyed blowing in the wind rather than wrapped inside a hijab. She liked to think she respected everyone's choices, and expected them to respect hers in return. Except for friends lying to her to potentially carry on some secret affair- and with a jinn, at that. Sibel rolled her shoulders backwards three times, knocking on the door with a heavy sigh.

Nothing.

Sibel peeked through one of the windows with a plaid curtain only partially covering the foggy glass. She thought she could make out some creaking noises, but- alas, there were no footsteps nearing the door. Nor did she spot any movement or stirring through the glass that would point to a source of any noise. Maybe the inhabitants were out somewhere? She inherently doubted that for some reason.

She could make out burning fire in a furnace in what appeared to be the living room. *No way these beings would leave the fireplace on in a wooden cabin and not be home,* she thought. Yet weren't jinns made of fire? Why would they get cold? Perhaps it had been for the one or two humans that also inhabited the place. Or their skin could become cold when manifested into their human bodies.

Sibel shrugged. Whatever the reason, she knew they were inside. And the chills she felt course through her body made her sense they'd seen her, too. She smiled to herself, saying a little prayer in her mind as she took a few steps backwards. A prayer for them to leave Kaitlin and her family alone. A prayer also that Merve was in a good place now- wherever she was.

§

PULLING THE CURTAINS FARTHER TO THE SIDES OF THE WINDOW, Meredith watched the woman walk away. "We weren't seen," she said blankly.

"Why would you have wanted her to?" Finn raised an eyebrow. Adjacent to Meredith, he too was in his energy form. "Some buddy of Kaitlin's. Who cares?"

"What do you suppose separates which humans can see us, and which ones can't, Finn?" Meredith's focus lingered on a red cardinal that had landed on a branch.

"Something about a fragile soul and a sensitive mind," Finn dismissed. "*Maman* had often dismissed my questions beyond that."

"Are you sure she didn't say- a fragile mind and a sensitive soul- instead?" Meredith wondered. "My own folks were more into reason and the sciences. But I remember meeting your mother. Back before all of this, when we were barely even teenagers. I remember respecting her, because her spiritual knowledge had always made sense to me in my heart."

"What does all this matter, Mer?" Finn made a face, beaming to the kitchen.

"Are we the bad guys here?" Meredith continued, closing her eyes as she pondered the response to her own question.

"What?" Finn turned to face her.

"I always read about 'the bad guys'- in human books." Meredith turned around to meet Finn's gaze. "Finn, do you think it was worth it?"

"What do you mean?" Finn pouted. "Mer, I really can't take any negative energy today."

"We conspired in putting an innocent man behind bars- and for what?" Meredith eyed the floor.

"Oh, *mon Dieu*," Finn rolled his eyes, directing his attention back to the fridge. "Well, you know what Master says, Mer. 'Innocence' is a relative term. Paul may have not murdered Linette Peterson, yes, but who's to say he's some innocent man overall? Hey, do we still have some of those buns leftover from the last batch?"

"That's ridiculous reasoning, Finn," Meredith shook her head, walking over to the fridge and taking out the appetizer she'd baked earlier. "If that logic held truth- couldn't the same thing be said of anyone? Including Lar? Who is he really for us to believe every word out of his mouth? What gives him the authority or legitimacy to do so? Is *he* an innocent?"

"Where's all this coming from?" Finn started munching. "You're lucky Master can't hear our non-human communication on his little camera recordings."

"Come on, Finn," Meredith shook her head. "I know you've been doubting some things lately as well. Tan's made a mistake- a big one. Committed a crime. And, you heard Master's thoughts that day. Lar's in love! So Tan is accepted, while a woman's dead. And now- Stig, you and I have united in planting false evidence and altering phone records to commit another crime. For what- to protect some secret crush?"

"You never expressed such concern about that Linette girl before, Mer," Finn raised his tone. "Where's all this coming from? And we have committed no such crime, as we are on a greater mission…"

"A crime against purity, against good- Finn!" Meredith closed her eyes again. "An innocent man is behind bars. A father. What is our mission, really? A mission against the course of nature for humankind?"

"Are you finished?" Finn cracked a smile, continuing after Meredith returned it. "You should have been born as my sister decades ago, you know that? Or just lived with us at least. *Maman* would have loved you. She would have taught you French, and you'd have improved her Norsk…"

"Please don't even joke that I could be like a sister, Finn," Meredith's gaze burned firm into Finn's eyes. "That night you've been ignoring? That night bred something bigger than both of us. That night bred *life*."

"You are not only jeopardizing your presence in The Group by talking like this, but also trying to punish me," Finn wagged his beam in the shape of a finger in her face. He fought back his tears- it was easier for him to do so without being in human form. "I see how it is. It's alright. You're punishing me for Malin. And for Bo."

"Not everything revolves around you, Finn, or even me," Meredith remarked. "We have to be more responsible in our lives from now on." *I don't want to be a bad one. Bo cannot grow up to hate his mother.*

§

THE KNOCK ON THE BEDROOM DOOR SHOOK KAITLIN FROM HER CHAIR. Had her mother returned with Malin so soon? Sandy could have let them in, but hadn't she been napping? "Kaitlin?" her friend's voice on the other side of the door was soft.

"Oh, sorry, hon," Kaitlin let out a laugh. "I was typing away here. You're up. Come on in."

"Yeah, I couldn't really doze off too well. Can I have a quick word, girl?" Sandy twirled a curl of her hair which had fallen across her face. "I don't mean to disturb the minimal time you have to yourself without having to tend to Malin, but..."

"Of course!" Kaitlin closed the lid of her laptop. Panic set in her heart for just a moment, before she quickly sighed with relief- remembering she'd saved the document.

"I wanted to say I'm so proud of you," Sandy sat on her bed. "You've really been developing that blog, and being so strong overall. How was it like to finally see him for the first time since, you know, the arrest?"

Kaitlin had attempted the best to make sense of the strangest experience she'd felt in her life, aside from the nightmares of her pregnancy and-of course- that night back in their Stavanger apartment. The police marching to and fro as she and her husband had been trying to get out the right words in the visitation room. Their rare, later-approved visit. Malin crying more than she'd been giggling, situated on Paul's lap as he fought back tears of his own. Kaitlin had been trying to release it all into her journal-writing lately.

"It was a place where I never thought I'd find myself in a million years, Sandy," Kaitlin stared at the wall. "We exchanged pleasantries. He insisted on his innocence. Convinced me to reach out to John Walker for help. Said this nightmare would be over soon. You know. The expected. And then, just like that- we were told our hour was up, though I'm sure it'd only been around 45 minutes or so."

"You are more courageous than you know," Sandy was in awe. "Have you contacted Mr. Walker? Has he agreed to help?"

"Yeah. He said he was fuming in the beginning," Kaitlin eyed the plain-carpeted ground. "But that he eventually figured it couldn't have been Paul. He said visiting the cabin and then learning about The Group from me pointed him even more to Tan and those folks. He promised to confide to the Oslo police about the cabin."

"Oh, that's good, that's good," Sandy blinked rapidly. "There's one more thing, hon. Look, I know my trip out here began, well, with Bjorn and that whole thing. And I know it's been kind of awkward between us. Yet I'm glad I was here with you through this. I know your mom's extended her trip and all, but I really don't want to have to leave you like this now."

"I can't believe it's time for you to return home already. You're going to continue to update me on your busy life in the city, I hope?" Kaitlin put an arm around her friend, as Sandy returned her smile with a nod. "I wish I could see you in those Chekhov plays. Those were amazing reviews. I'm proud of you, too."

"I know," Sandy smiled. "Aside from my romantic choices, of course."

"Hon, I'm sorry if I overreacted a little bit," Kaitlin said, pursing her lips.

"Well…Maybe a little bit." Sandy winked.

"I've just been so sensitive with…well…you know. And to hear that you purposely walked into the fire…" Kaitlin shook her head. "Literally…."

"You can say that again," Sandy rolled her eyes.

"But thank you for coming, Sandy," Kaitlin grinned. "I may have gotten a teensy-weensy bit nutty over the whole Bjorn thing, but I'm sure you can understand. Just so glad you were here."

"Please come visit me in New York," Sandy insisted. "Little angel here needs to experience an airplane. You girls will get through this. As for me? I know I need a good psychotherapy session again. Promise me you'll check out a therapist here as well. I'm sure they have some who use English."

"Girl, for the last time; I don't need therapy," Kaitlin rolled her eyes with a grin. "I'll be alright. I've got mom staying with me, remember?"

Sandy instinctively inched close, as if Linda could overhear. "Precisely; is her demanding presence here not a better reason for some therapy?"

"You do have a point there," Kaitlin chuckled. "I'm going to miss you."

"I'm always a phone call away," Sandy beamed. "And I know you are too, no matter the distance. That's more than we can say about a lot of friendships."

"Concurred," Kaitlin held out a hand. "I promise to at least consider seeking a professional to talk about all of this. As for you, young lady- don't think you're off the hook, yet!"

"Uh-oh," Sandy feigned an annoyed face.

"I do hope you'll be choosier with candidates to date from now on." Kaitlin smiled.

"You sure you don't want to hang out again before you leave?" Bjorn's voice from their phone conversation the previous night replayed in Sandy's head. *"I thought we had a nice time, what about you?"*

"It really was nice, for sure," Sandy had responded. *"Which is exactly why I sort of don't want to ruin it with potential awkwardness the second time, you know? I want it to remain a beautiful memory. I think I need that."*

"If you insist, my hurricane Sandy," Bjorn had teased. *"But you just may run into me ever so casually at that New York City Starbucks. Only if you want, that is."*

"I think I would like that," she'd responded before hanging up.

"Concurred," Sandy smiled back at Kaitlin. Feeling happy without overthinking the future was enough choosiness for the time being.

§

AN AMBULANCE SIREN STARTLED KAITLIN AWAKE. She sat up straight in bed, panting. Weren't their windows supposed to be soundproof? She didn't know herself to be a particularly light sleeper. When had she dozed off? She vaguely recalled a scene from the latest 'Dexter' episode she'd been watching alone in her bed lately. The insides of her ears were still throbbing with pain as she removed the headphones she'd fallen asleep with. How long had she been asleep? What time was it? The bedside clock answered her- 4:30 AM.

Reaching for the water bottle on her nightstand with a parched mouth, she took a sip only to discover that merely a few drops were left. *Merde*. Instinctively, she treaded slowly toward Malin's crib. Kaitlin smiled. Her daughter was sleeping on her back, snoring ever so subtly, clutching her stuffed mermaid. A smile crept on Kaitlin's face as her toes searched for her fuzzy slippers in the dark. Stretching her arms over her head, she stood up and opened the door as quietly as she could on her way to the kitchen. She took a step back to hear her mother snoring away in the guest room. Luckily the doors were more soundproof than their windows.

Taking out another water bottle, Kaitlin welcomed the chilled air from the fridge, but not the surprising warmth she immediately felt on the back of her neck. She shut the door, staring at it in shock with heavy breathing. *Please, no, no.* The bottle shook in her hands. Kaitlin placed it on her neck to ease the heat. *I can't now, no.*

"*Ms. Kaitlin,*" Finn indeed whispered in her mind. Kaitlin couldn't get herself to face away from the refrigerator door. She took in a deep breath, keeping her eyes on the floor while inching back to her room. *No, no, not now, no.*

"*You called for me at the birthday party,*" Finn was audible again in her head. "*I loved that.*" Kaitlin took a leap toward the corner wall of her living room closer to the bedrooms, allowing her back to be comforted by the sturdiness. She slowly opened her shut eyes, eyeballing every corner of the space around her she could make out with the moonlight. *Malin.* She realized then she didn't have the luxury of being frozen and scared when she had a bigger duty of ensuring her daughter was alright.

Kaitlin paced to her room and shut the door behind her, sitting on the corner of her bed to keep a closer eye on her daughter.

"With nature, you'll never feel alone, Ms. Kaitlin," she heard him again, letting out a yelp and immediately covering her mouth. *"When your mom leaves, you'll be completely alone. Take Malin and come stay with me in the cabin."* Kaitlin jumped back toward her pillows. She contemplated picking Malin up in her arms, but didn't want to wake her up.

You wouldn't hurt her, would you? No, you wouldn't, she directed her thoughts, half asking and half demanding. *Even though she isn't yours.* Kaitlin clutched Paul's pillow across her chest, looking all around to see if Finn were visible. Nothing. He was still not showing himself.

"Do you think human tests have any meaning for me?" Finn voiced again softly. *"I am guided by what I feel. As well as by nature. The stars. Look outside."*

Despite herself, Kaitlin obeyed. She turned her head out toward the window. The shutters were opened wide, revealing a clear sky, dark blue with a myriad of stars and formations. *You opened the blinds when I was getting water?* For some reason she couldn't quite fathom, Kaitlin smiled.

"Did you know that stars don't shine? They burn. You burn me more than the heat I'm created out of," Finn whispered closer to her face now. Kaitlin turned to meet the eyes she knew she would.

"I will not give up on us as easily as you have," Finn's green beams were indeed intense on her as he whispered out loud now. Kaitlin could make out his silhouette next to her body. He was wearing his usual professional attire, albeit in a bit more relaxed style. His white, button-down shirt almost glowed as he sat on the side of the bed closer to the window. "I promised I'd look out for you and Malin- and I will, no matter what. She's your extension."

"Why did you really come into my life, Finn?" she whispered. "I know what you are. But *who* are you, really?"

"I am simply a being of enchantment, enchanted by the enchantress," Finn smiled. Could she be able to feel him if she reached out to try? Kaitlin felt back the urge, despite recalling Sandy's experience with Bjorn. *No.*

"My enchantress. Do you not see? I am not the one leading you astray. You're the one doing the leading, You're my star, Kaitlin. I follow you. I can't help it."

"Please," Kaitlin begged. "Paul's in jail, for nothing. The Group should be happy. What else do you want?" Tears were rolling across the pillow in her arms.

"Exactly," Finn went on softly, shrugging as he grinned. "Technically, you'd think my mission would have long been completed. But it hasn't. For our souls haven't. Our souls are incomplete without one another, Ms. Kaitlin. Do you not see?"

A murmuring sound from her daughter had Kaitlin throwing the pillow off her hands and onto the floor. "Malin!" she inched near, rocking the crib and humming her back to deeper sleep. She remembered something Sibel had said just then. Something about a prayer? She didn't know the exact words her friend had advised, but she had to try the best way she knew how. Despite her friend's different religion, they were all praying to the same God, after all- weren't they?

Kaitlin closed her eyes. *Please Lord, up in Heaven. Please allow him to part from this house. Please allow my daughter and I to sleep in peace. Amen.* She gradually lifted up her eyelids, noticing the heaviness in her heart had begun to dissipate. Her neck cooled off once again. She took in a deep breath, grinning as she gazed at the stars outside. Walking to the window to close the blinds, a new tear slipped from her eye as Kaitlin realized she didn't want to do so. A part of her wanted to fall back asleep looking at the stars.

The sunshine. No. The sun would bother Malin's eyes as soon as it rose. She couldn't. She just had to fight this 'nature' sometimes- the one regarding the self that Finn also spoke of. Kaitlin felt like she'd finally gotten it.

Wiping the fallen teardrop, she yanked the blinds shut.

CHAPTER 25

W AS IT JUST HIM OR HAD MORE DETAINEES been standing on the lunch line that day? A balding, older man called out in Paul's direction, wiping a runny nose with the back of his hand. "Maverick?"

"That's me," Paul cringed.

"Your lawyer is waiting for you in room 208," said the man.

"But, what about lunch?" Paul was befuddled, gazing down at the corn cob and beans before him on the tray. Not exactly appetizing, but it'd beat going hungry. Had he even lost a kilo or two around the waist since getting locked up?

"Trust me, brother," the man said with a smirk. "You're going to regret delaying rushing straight over there if you prefer first to eat this slime old Astrid has been preparing.

"I heard that, Eirik," the rosy-cheeked server said loudly with a smile.

Why had his lawyer arrived at this time? What had Eirik meant by regretting not heading there straight away? Paul noticed that Astrid-whom he'd chatted with a few times and had gotten to know as a kind lady with silver hair- was now smiling at him assuredly. *Could there be good news or something?*

"Alright, I'll set this here," Paul eyed both of them, laying the tray down on an empty lunch table.

"If that food's been paid for from his account, can we have it?" a loud, tattooed detainee Paul had gotten to know as 'Michael' roared in laughter, with his clique of around five other similarly motorcyclist-looking buddies. Luck would have it, even the Norwegian jail system managed to remind Paul of his rather nerdy high school days, lunching alone.

"Can I head there now?" he wanted to make sure he wasn't disobeying any regulations.

"Go already, loser!" one of Michael's buff buddies yelled, bringing on a high-five from someone else at the table. Paul just smiled, noticing that Eirik was now quiet and simply shaking his head in disappointment.

"Alright, everyone," he began. "I'm leaving, I'm leaving. Bon appétit." As an officer escorted him to the room, Paul's heart felt like it would soon be leaping out of his chest as he walked.

§

"*FEMTEN MINUTTER.*" The lanky officer remarked as he opened the door. Paul saw Mark Goldberg shaking his leg rapidly and twiddling his thumbs, smiling like a little boy with a secret.

"*Takk,*" Paul thanked the officer, who shut the door behind him after he went in to sit across his lawyer. "Mark…All is well, I hope?"

"Do you know a colleague by the name of…Jeanette Andrews-Hagen?" Mark was grinning as he confirmed the name from a folder of papers in front of him.

"Oh, no, don't tell me something's happened to Jeanette, too," Paul began, slapping his hands on the wooden table. "Somehow women I work with end up…"

"Mrs. Andrews-Hagen is just fine, Paul," Mark continued. "Lucky for you, she's apparently also become a witness in your case after being relayed the details."

Jeanette? A Witness? Paul was confused as a first-grader in an algebra class, but he'd take whatever he could get. "Great. But, how so?"

"That message the late Ms. Peterson supposedly received on December 11, 2010?" Mark picked up a pen to point it at Paul. "Well, Mrs. Andrews-Hagen provided an alibi for you and has presented it to the cops, Paul. You may recall that December 11th is her birthday, and she's shared a video of an office party from that exact evening's celebration."

Wasn't that the party when I'd had too much to drink? Paul's heart was racing with both excitement and curiosity. He could actually recall the event clearer now that he really thought about it. Kaitlin had just turned down one of his romantic offers at that time, insisting that they remained friends.

Kaitlin. His wife's name brought an image of his favorite, guileless smile from her in his mind. *Is our fight going to be the last memory she's going to have of me from our marriage?* Paul buried his face in his hands. *If I overreacted that day- and she really hasn't been unfaithful- will she be driven into someone else's arms now that all this has happened?* Paul shook his head. *No*, he decided. She'd understand. How would any father be expected to react to his wife feeling the need for a paternity test?

"Paul?" Mark interrupted his thoughts.

"Oh, sorry," Paul took in a deep breath as he smiled. "I was just trying to remember that evening. It's coming back to me."

"Well, lucky that your friend- and technology- have remembered it for you," Mark began to nod, eyes glimmering. "Paul; there's dated and timed footage of you doing karaoke to some love ballad."

"Evidence?" Paul's eyes felt like they'd be leaving their sockets soon enough.

"I must say; your voice wasn't half bad, Maverick," Mark nodded, clearing his throat before going into song mode himself. "It's a quarter after one, I'm all alone, and I need you now…"

"You're not so bad, yourself, Goldberg," Paul chuckled. He

couldn't believe what he was hearing. "Am I getting this correctly? You mean to tell me that I may soon be...free?"

"All signs are pointing in that direction," Mark beamed, crossing his arms and leaning back against his chair. "Well, the investigation is still continuing, so I believe it may only be a release under probation. You would have to report to the facilities regularly. It may take a day or two to process. And for the head of the local commune to make a decision whether this is sufficient to at least trump over the supposed 'evidence' against you. They contacted me to first ask if you can confirm Mrs. Andrews-Hagen's statement. So, I have to ask, for legal purposes, can you confirm that, on the evening of December 11th,..."

"Yes, yes, I confirm!" Paul shot up from his chair, tears forming on his glittering eyes. Had his prayers been answered? *Thank you, Jeannie.*

§

Oslo

TAN KUVVET HAD JUST GOTTEN THROUGH THE VERY THING he once had nightmares about. He'd had to put on quite a show of ease and comfort, sitting at that table across the police officers. Playing the part of the vengeful boyfriend, upset at how a 'suspect' like Paul Maverick could have murdered his 'big love'. Could it all have been that easy? Or was this the calm before the storm? Tan had learned long ago that good days often preceded bad occurrences for him.

"You did a good job, lad," Lar caressed Tan's shoulder. "You were so calm and collected in there."

"Are you sure, Master?" Tan said through rosy cheeks. "I was sweating like a dog under my suit."

"Your brothers have come to your aid," Lar continued. "As far as the police are concerned, Paul Maverick is guilty of murdering his unrequited crush from work. Logical. Easy. Simple as that. Even

Meredith has helped with planting evidence in Serdar's closet."

"Mer?" Tan's eyes widened. "She's helped? But, wait, wait," he thought of something else. "How did Meredith and Finn enter the apartment? Isn't it impossible for the jinn to do so unless a human's allowed for them in?"

"Anja," an all-knowing smile appeared across Lar's face.

"Anja?" Tan was confused.

"Let's just say she's been working on your old buddy Serdar," Lar smirked. "Used a different name and cover-up life story. You know the deal. She can be very convincing."

"Anja's dating Serdar?" Tan couldn't help but laugh. His joy was quick-lived as another thought occurred to him. "The poison? The box?"

"She took care of all that, my boy," Lar leaned in closer. "I made sure those tubes got back to me before Serdar discovered them, so the police wouldn't suspect anything. And Finn and Mer worked on the rest. Though I didn't quite tell them about the cyanide in those extra tubes."

"I'm...speechless," Tan chuckled with relief.

"They catalyzed Serdar to reach for our little updated version of the box you'd kept under your old bed. Placing it in a corner of the closet to make it more convenient for him to find," Lar continued with a sly smile. "We had a plan B in case Serdar had thrown it out, but he hadn't. It ended up working out perfectly. I must apologize, lad, for never having helped you with ridding it all this time, or at least guaranteeing it'd been disposed of. Truly. Never thought it'd become significant. I never thought the police would look beyond our cover of suicide. And certainly never that they'd trace your whereabouts and come digging for dirt here in Stavanger..."

"Serdar barely cleaned," Tan attempted a laugh despite his shock. "That little robot vacuum of his must not have given it away if it ever dusted under that bed...I'm in disbelief, Master. All this trouble, just for me. The brethren and sisters have come to my aid, despite the awkwardness of last year. They've forgiven me for what I did?"

"For what?" Lar winked. "The past is the past. You're always safe here. You know this."

"No one would do this all for me," Tan sniveled.

"And I wouldn't do this for anyone else," Lar's eyes locked on his, wiping a tear. "Do you know now, finally, how special you are for me?"

"I do, Master," Tan smiled, wiping the rest of the tears with a nervous chuckle. "I'll miss you in Stavanger. Are you sure it's a good idea for me to stay with Serdar for a bit?"

"A week will go by in a flash," Lar nodded. "They've already gotten your statement here. You won't incite suspicion. Serdar would have gotten suspicious if you hadn't accepted his invitation to catch up after his little discovery. You just have to go and act like everything's normal. Act like you're thankful to him for this discovery, and you can finally rest at peace knowing your ex's killer is behind bars, so on and so forth."

"If you say so," Tan shrugged. "I'm just so grateful."

"Can you do me a favor, at least, in return?" Lar grinned. "Just a small one?"

"What is it, Master?" Tan cleared his throat.

"Can you call me: Aresh?"

"Aresh…" Tan squinted.

"You don't like it?"

"It's a perfectly nice name, Master," Tan shook his head. "But, your name…"

"*Lar* was never my official name, lad," Aresh smiled. "I never really knew my father. My mother named me. She had emigrated to Dubai from Tehran. My full name was Aresh Jahan. As a teenager, I was able to make some influential friends, and legally adopted the name 'Lar Iktar'. I'd read somewhere that 'Lar' meant 'teacher'. I always wanted to grow up to be some sort of mentor, I suppose."

"You certainly are that, Master," Tan blushed. "The best."

"I haven't told anyone my real name here," Aresh looked into Tan's eyes. *Not even Abe knew. Jaan.* How Aresh had fantasized that the two of them were meant to be, back then. That his first name sounded like Aresh's secret, yet real last name.

"I was raised as an Arab despite my Persian heritage, and wanted to fit in. Yet even 'Iktar' turned out to not be 'Arabic' enough. I stuck with it, though. I always wanted to fit in, yet somehow never could."

"I understand, Master," Tan gazed out the window, chewing his bottom lip. "I know the feeling all too well."

"You fit in here, Tan," Lar inched closer behind him, joining his gaze at the city view. "Look at me, lad."

Tan turned around slowly, and saw that Lar was holding his heart. Scratching his cheek, he turned his eyes back toward the window. "I think I like being there, Aresh."

Lar closed his eyes and thanked God. He chuckled and took in a deep breath, patting Tan on the back. *Steady does it.* His hand could finally feel more at ease, lingering on his beloved's body.

Slow and steady.

CHAPTER 26

FIXING THE COLLAR OF HIS CRISPLY-BUTTONED, CRÈME-HUED shirt, John Walker caught his reflection on the elevator mirror. Slicking back his raven hair with a shaky hand, he took a deep breath. Was he ready to see him after all these years? It almost didn't matter. He had to face the truth head on, for Linette.

He'd waited for Tan Kuvvet to leave the premises before going to Lar's suite and ringing the door-bell. How he had to fight the unsatiable urge to punch his daughter's murderer straight in the face, watching Tan walk past him. But John knew he had to be careful, and patient.

"Jaan?" Creases had formed around them, but Lar Iktar's eyes were the same pitch-black olives as he'd remembered them. Strangely capable of both burning and easing his soul at the same time upon staring.

"Surprised to see me old friend?" John smiled, lowering his eyes to the delicate, sparkly tiles. How small the world indeed was. To see an old flame not to socialize, but in connection to the murderer of your child. How could the tender young man he'd gotten to know that summer be capable of such insensitivity- to harbor a fugitive from the law for a horrendous crime? "May I come in?"

"Surprised, indeed," Lar's mouth was still open, while his eyes studied all of John. "Welcome, please. Of course. And to what do I owe the pleasure of this blast of air from the past?"

"I can stay just here, if that's alright," John kept his shoes on by the entrance, as the door shut behind him. The truth was he felt tired as hell and wanted nothing more than to flop himself on one of the armchairs or leather sofa overlooking the city through full-length windows. Not that they looked particularly inviting. As John had come to expect from this self-made millionaire he'd read up on: much in his suite appeared to be expensive frills for show, rather than for comfort.

"Well, I came across your book. And heard about your lectures in Trondheim- fascinating. Do you continue to teach here as well? You've been doing well for yourself, I suppose," John placed his hands in his trouser pockets as he looked around the space. "Would you believe I was in the region for a holiday, and stopped by to congratulate you and say hello?"

"I've learned long ago not to over-fantasize," Lar blushed. "I haven't taught in a while. I prefer the cultural environment here in Oslo, with more creative endeavors. It thrills me to be near where they hand out the Nobel prizes…Well, come, have a seat, please. You don't have to take off your shoes. I can have the place cleaned up later. Have a drink."

"Maybe next time," John rocked back and forth. His eyes rested on a framed art piece displaying a countryside view by a river. "Nice reproduction. Is that Monet?"

"He was the best in his field, wasn't he?" Lar's eyes glanced over the painting before darting back to John's face once more.

"I'll get to the chase, old friend," John began, smacking his lips. "I visited the roommate of my daughter's ex-boyfriend- Tan Kuvvet. I believe you're familiar with your little recruit? And with my daughter?"

"Yes, I have heard of Linette's case," Lar shook his head. "Such a shame. To first hear that you've fathered a lovely woman like that. Only to then learn that she was murdered by an ex-employee of yours, and left to rot among the trees, the poor thing…"

"Cut the *hra'*," John pounded his fist on the wall. "I know it was

Tan. Where are you hiding him?" He had to admit it had initially shaken him senseless when he heard about Paul's arrest. John was human, after all. He had considered it for a good minute. Could Paul Maverick really have fooled them all? John remembered the shy smiles he would throw his daughter's way at the office. Could his crush have developed into a deadly obsession over time?

It had taken Kaitlin's frantic phone call for him to return to his senses. The cabin! Of course he had to tell the police what he'd discovered on his own as well, confirming much of what Paul's wife had told him. About Tan having lived there after Trondheim- with that Meredith girl- and then mysteriously running off to Oslo.

Meredith had implied it was because of some romantic betrayal. But John Walker remembered Tan. He'd witnessed his empty yet controlling eyes in the presence of his daughter. And, mostly, he'd talked to his sweet Linette. Sharing all her concerns about her on-again/off-again boyfriend and the way he had been treating her. *No*, John had decided. It couldn't have been some typical break-up. Meredith had obviously discovered what Tan had done. Conducting all these little schemes to save his butt. With the help of this two-faced man before him.

"How can you conceal my daughter's murderer, Lar Iktar?" John folded his arms. "And I won't even begin to wonder *why* you're doing so..."

"I beg your pardon?" Lar placed his fingers on his throat, with a shocked expression. "Are you suggesting that someone other than Paul Maverick may have murdered your daughter? And, *Ilahi*, that I'm somehow responsible for hiding...?"

"I'm not suggesting, Lar!" John hissed; teeth clenched. "I know!"

"What exactly do you think you know?"

"Exactly what you yourself confessed to- in conversation with your new little lover boy, Tan. That's what!" John reached toward his back pocket to take out a tape recorder.

"How did you…?" Lar was rendered speechless, taking a step back.

"The police have been helpful," John said with ease. "Evidence continues to pile against Tan Kuvvet and in favor of Paul Maverick's innocence with each passing minute. The details are irrelevant. I know. We all know."

The truth of the matter was, John hadn't had anything recorded on his small, dated cassette player. Except an interview he'd had with a former business partner a while back. He'd come to rely on his bluffy trick to get confessions out of some associates back in Canada. Obtaining Lar's address, John had lingered around the building long enough to see him with Tan. Connecting the strange philosophies Lar's book preached, along with the nature of the way Lar looked at Tan that had been all too familiar to John; he had developed a strong instinct.

Sure enough, here Lar was. He'd panicked, and unknowingly confirmed his suspicion. Just as John knew he would. "I showed them your little book," he continued with a knowing smile. "A book I interestingly came across in my late daughter's room with her mother. An officer from the Rogaland region was there too, coincidentally. Officer Lindberg recognized me right away from the case- and shared with me some things he's discussed with poor Paul in prison. The details he gave…I just knew Paul couldn't have done it. So they helped me…as part of the investigation. I read some of the chapters, Lar. You preach it yourself, don't you? That there is no such thing as coincidence…"

"I cannot believe all of this," Lar shook his head, maintaining his composure. "How much did you hear?"

"Even if I hadn't overheard you and Tan- it wouldn't have been long before I'd have figured it all out, Lar," John replied. "You always did have a certain style, and type."

"Please, Jaan. I'm begging you for mercy…" Lar kneeled, hanging on to his ex-lover's knees. "You're not 'John Walker' to me.

You're Abe. Abdul Jaan. Remember Dubai. Remember our love..."

"You incited *murder*, Lar!" John was in tears. Somehow, he had to admit a part of him wanted his old flame to deny everything. "Regardless of whatever sick justifications for it in your twisted mind-that still makes you an *accomplice* to my daughter's murder."

"I didn't know who she was..."

"It doesn't matter!" John bellowed. "My daughter, or anyone else's innocent daughter. Does it matter? This is a sin...a sin."

"Our love was a sin too, wasn't it?" Lar wept. "According to dogma, anyway. Yet we made it through..."

"It's not the same thing, Lar," John clenched his jaw. "What I had with you was- alright, very special, yes. But it was a summer thing. A one-time fluke. I was a curious and confused young man, okay? I *didn't* go on to create a damn frat-house system all over Norway. I'm shocked how many people have bought into your insanity."

"Don't you belittle what you don't understand!" Lar raised his voice, inching closer to John by the door. "We run a business. We help people. Please-don't take this to a whole other realm now. The issue at hand here is..."

"What don't I understand?" John barked. "I don't care about anything except the loss of my daughter. Is that something your brain can understand? Mr. Philosopher?"

"Abe..." Lar's falling tears implored, voice trembling.

"Speaking of realms, how in the world did you get yourself involved with the jinn realm, by the way?" John questioned. "Kaitlin Maverick shared some things with me. I first laughed them off, but putting two and two together reading your book- I realized she must have been right..."

"Abe, the jinn are creations of Allah, like us..." Lar began in a calm voice.

"When I met you, you were a forward-thinking young man,"

John interrupted. "Discussing liberal politics with me. Talking about how traditional societies need to have an open-minded and more lenient approach with their youth, if they didn't want to lose them to hopeless despair and extremism and all that…"

"What makes you think my organization isn't forward-thinking, Abdul Jaan?" Lar distanced his face and hands from John's knees, drooping his head. "Have you read the reviews for my book? Many find my maxims to be more enlightened and awakened than…"

"The jinn, Lar!" John raised his voice. "How'd you get yourself involved with them in this little cult you apparently created?"

"A cult?" Lar stood up slowly. "Jaan, you know how I feel about you. But let's not cross any offensive lines here, alright? Please. I'm mostly a business man. My brothers and sisters provide services and paper for…"

"Services…," John smirked. "I'm sure."

"I'm going to ignore what you may be trying to imply," Lar said. "You asked a question- so please listen."

He went on after John indicated with his hand to 'go ahead.'

"I had a jinn friend I never told you about, if you must know. He was around my age as a child, and growing up he gradually introduced me to his circle. Gradually more of them have felt comfortable over the years to come up to me. Whisper to me the beautiful maxims we co-wrote together, never caring about humankind's modern copyright laws and the such."

"The jinns whispered to you?" John raised an eyebrow.

"We mutually mourned how some families don't appreciate free spirits, capable of making their own choices in how to live and love- jinn or human," Lar went on, nodding. "So, as you see, I've created a beautiful arrangement for years now. And just because you may have gotten upset with me for the confusion our love apparently caused you over the years: The Group doesn't deserve all these offensive comments.

Especially since you see them yourself."

"I'm offending you now?" John cut in and stated firmly though gritted teeth. "Wait a minute- what do you mean by my 'seeing them'?"

"Meredith Olsen," Lar chuckled. "Shy little Meredith. She's a jinn. Most humans cannot see her- neither in her raw energy form, nor in her animal or human manifestations. But you did. That means you're not too different from me. Or Tan."

"Don't you dare try to bring me to the same level as you two," John lowered his voice through clenched teeth. "I'm not the criminal here."

"Tan is a troubled young man," Lar said. "Now, I'm not defending his actions, or mistakes. I'm just inviting you to shift your perspective. Please don't allow the past to…"

"Our past has nothing to do with this," John took a step back. "Besides, I'd be careful if I were you. I'm the one with the gun here." He reached into his back pocket and brought the silver revolver closer to his hip to show Lar.

"You're not seriously contemplating shooting me, are you?" Lar remained still. "You already killed me!"

"What are you talking about?" John was confused.

"Ever since 1990. Damn you, Abdul Jaan Vaziri! 'John Walker'! I've been dead inside for over two decades now!"

§

Dubai

July, 1990

"THE SUN RISING HIGHLIGHTS THE SPARKLE IN YOUR EYES, did you know that, Abe?" Lar's smiling eyes met Jaan's. The call to prayer became louder from the mosque's minaret in the brisk morning air.

"You should be a poet, boy," Abdul Jaan gushed, ruffling Lar's

287

thick, wavy mane of obsidian. *His eyes are darker than mine. And even darker than our sin.* "Do you suppose we'll be going to hell for this?"

"Hell can't possibly be hotter than your embrace. Come here…" Lar curved his lean but sturdy arm around Abdul Jaan's close-shaved head, playfully tugging him toward his chest.

"I'm serious, you tease!" Abdul Jaan attempted to wiggle his way out of the lock.

"So am I," Lar spoke firmly, pulling his arms back toward his own body, trembling with the cool dawn wind. "Look. How can love be sinful? Right? Many like us exist. Why would Allah have created so many of his beings like us- only to hate us? We may not be his favorites, I'm sure, since I bet he prefers reproduction for the race he created to go on. But I know he still loves us as long as we love wholeheartedly."

"I hope you're right, philosopher," Abdul Jaan smiled, cheeks sharing a shade of scarlet along with the sunshine. "This view is remarkable."

"Do you?" Lar's eyes were pinned still to Abdul Jaan's.

"Do I…what?" Abdul Jaan was still focusing on the clouds.

"Love me," Lar wasn't fazed. "Wholeheartedly, I mean…?"

Abdul Jaan sighed as he finally turned to face Lar. "We're still young. Let's take this slow, okay? You know I'm returning to Quebec next week. You're going to forget all about this out here."

"No, I won't," Lar was adamant. "Believe me. It's not like that for me, Abe. I promise you. Hey… look at me."

Abdul Jaan ran his shaky hand through his head, regretting just then how he'd shaved his longer brown hair before flying abroad. How he wished he could have been a woman sometimes. To be able to hide his confused eyes behind a scarf, at the very least, like the one his mother wore to cover her hair.

"Abe?"

"Sorry, yes. I'm looking." Abdul Jaan took a deep breath and turned to face his seducer. The one he wouldn't admit to anyone- not even himself- that he'd allowed to lead him astray.

"I promise, Abe," Lar stroked his chin softly with a subtle graze that sent beautiful goosebumps throughout Abdul Jaan's body. "I will never give up on our love for as long as I live."

§

"IT'S BEEN AGES, LAR," John was shaking his head as he listened to Lar.

"Jaan, I do not condone murder. But I've built my entire empire in this country based on being accepted for who one is," Lar explained with a wistful tone. "Tan was pouring his heart about how his girlfriend couldn't love him for who he was, and how he always felt the pressure to change. I...I didn't know what else to do. I didn't know her. I'd just met her once when he brought her to one of our parties. She was lovely. Absolutely lovely, but kept mostly to herself. I didn't think she was as into him as he was into her. I thought maybe she was using him. I... I didn't get to know her. I didn't know her family's situation. How could I have known? I just remembered my own youth. Feeling so lost..."

"You just wanted to screw him, too, didn't you?" John burst out.

"It's not like that..." Lar took a step back toward the living room. Where the hell were Nora and Stig? If he got killed, he was hoping they'd take care of his body, before Tan saw him in that condition. Just in case he hadn't traveled to Stavanger just yet and had to return to get something. "What are you saying? You must calm down, Jaan. Put that gun down, and sit down. Let me get you something to drink."

"That's why you have done all this, isn't it?" John was nodding rapidly to himself. "To build a cover in one way or another to realize your hidden fantasies? That's why you wanted to get rid of Linette- so Tan could be free to get with you."

"Abe, I am deeply in mourning over your daughter, as well, but you cannot possibly be telling me our summer was some one-sided fantasy...."

"I was overseas for the first time!" John smirked. "Away from my mother's control. I thought I was being adventurous, or rebellious or something. I didn't know what we were even getting ourselves into, until it was too late to back out at that point..."

Lar fell silent. "Adventurous. Rebellious. Okay," he finally spoke, gradually raising his tone. "Then why did you sleep with me the second time? And the third? That night before your flight? We are both mature adults here. At least be honest with yourself and realize denial helps no..."

"That's enough!" John pointed the revolver back at Lar. "It doesn't matter what I may have felt or not felt over twenty damned years ago, Lar. You're an accomplice to murder! Directly or indirectly- I'm not certain of the details at this point- but you helped him, to kill my daughter!"

"Okay," Lar's voice was solemn as he closed his eyes, holding his hands out. "Go ahead. If you're going to deny our love and my mission to help others like us- that it was all in my stupid imagination – go ahead! Kill me! Please! You may feel better. A life for a life. Just put me out of my misery, Abe! Go give the evidence to the cops if you want- but I don't want to die in prison. I'd rather be killed at the hands of the one I love- it'd give everything more meaning."

John slowly lowered the pistol through his sobs. "I will not commit a sin in vengeance for another, boy. Don't worry." He hurled the revolver toward the door.

"Come here..." Lar opened his arms to invite an embrace. Something about the way Jaan had still called him 'boy' excited Lar beyond his wildest dreams. To his surprise, it was welcomed, as John buried his head into Lar's chest. He smiled for the first time that evening.

"You have to aid in the investigation," John mumbled through tears he'd begun to wipe from his face now. He framed his hands around Lar's jawline. "It's the one responsible thing you can do. I need your word."

"I understand…" Lar uttered. "I suppose what must be done, must be done. This was my fate."

"How can someone as romantic as you have gotten himself involved in the dark forces?" John attempted a smile.

"The jinn are not dark forces," Lar shook his head. "On the contrary- they are merely somewhere in the middle. Like us. We are all being tested on this earth, albeit in different realms."

"Alright," John snickered. "So…tell me. Why Tan? Do you love that young man?"

"Look. Yes, I care for him. And it's real, Abe. It's not about sex. It's pure, raw emotion. Maybe even like a son I've never had. Maybe you can understand, with your late daughter…"

"Don't you dare compare your sick crush with my biological…." John was waving hands in front of him.

"You're never going to get it," Lar sighed. "I realize it now. It's okay. But this is for the greater good. You see? It's brought me to you. I've loved *you*. I've *been* loving you- still, all this time- the most. And always will…"

"Promise me, then, you'll do the right thing," John spoke softly and placed his fingers upon Lar's cheek. Aside from the increasing stubble, the years hadn't toughened the supple skin underneath. He knew he had to do everything he could to be convincing. But oh how John hated the comforting way that touching Lar Iktar again had begun to feel.

"I've missed this," Lar smiled. "Can't you stay here in Oslo with me? I can let the kids run the business among themselves. We can get our own little place. Be ourselves."

"Lar, that's a fantasy, come on now," John stiffened, darting his eyes to the floor with a smile and taking his hand off of Lar's cheek to run it through his own hair. "I've got my software company- it's doing well. I can't risk it. And Helen- my wife- she's been good to me. She needs me. More like a friend to me all these years, in all ways, as you can imagine."

"Tell me you think of me whenever you…" Lar's eyes gleamed with excitement.

"Shh," John subtly placed his fingers on Lar's lips. "You know I do. But, come on. We're grown adults. With our own businesses, as you've said. Besides, Montreal isn't exactly the Middle East, either."

"Oh, I see now," Lar's smile evaded his face. "You're free there to date other men on the low, too. Yeah? Why come here to be with me, right? Live the life you want with hot Canadians while you don't risk your reputation, or your wife's support and friendship. Why quit living in hiding, right? Why risk anything for happiness?"

"Lar…please don't push my buttons," it was John's turn to speak firmly. "You're lucky I'm not turning *you* into the authorities."

"What would you tell them? You couldn't prove anything. Tan made that choice to inject her with cyanide."

"My daughter was injected with cyanide?" John whimpered. "And I suppose you provided him with it, didn't you?"

"Let's suppose for a moment my financial transaction was somehow unearthed and proven," Lar pursed his lips. His tears were gone. "How would they prove I'd given it to Tan to use in killing Linette? He could have had other purposes for it. I could never get arrested as an accomplice, either…You're not recording all this now, are you?"

John took a step back, shaking his head with a solemn face. "You've really thought about all of this. That sweet, dear young man in Dubai. He's actually thought about how he'd be able to get away with everything. And just a moment ago you were begging me to kill you, since you didn't want to go to prison. Look at you now, mocking that the police would even be able to imprison you. I could never live with you and see that young man in your eyes, knowing what I now know about you."

"I'm still the same Lar…" Lar responded softly. "Your boy…Just blinded by love."

"Not anymore…" John shook his head.

"Well, I see you would never take a chance to live with me here, anyway," Lar nodded. "It's okay. I get it."

"Just like you don't want to risk your inflated ego and high off your book purchases," John crossed his arms across his chest, securing the pistol in his back pocket. "And all the youth you're luring into your home and God knows where else."

"Unlike you, Jaan, I don't have intercourse with anyone! Openly or in hiding," Lar exclaimed. He started crying again, burying his head in his hands.

"You're joking," John wasn't sure how much more could manage to surprise him in one day. A part of him knew he had to head back to the police station already. Yet he also had to know.

All Lar could do was look blankly at John's eyes- not into them, and then at the floor. "If you only knew…"

"If I only knew what?"

"Forget it," Lar said in a quiet voice. "Go, Mr. Walker. Thank you for sparing my life. I've already told you I've been as good as dead all these years. Living on a sold fairy tale to young folks. Hoping at least they could live their dreams, since I never could. I could never again be…with anyone...in that way."

"Are you serious?" John had grown to trust his instincts, and the childish look in Lar's eyes didn't appear to be lying. "My God. Lar…"

"Just go to the authorities, Jaan. I mean it. Tan needs to be in prison for what he did to your daughter- you're right. Technically- he could have not committed a murder, yet he did. You're absolutely right. As for me, I'm already in Hell. Don't you worry…"

"Can I trust you won't hide Tan...or warn him?"

"You have to. For once in your life- trust me, John Walker." Lar took in a deep breath. "I will even help you. With turning Tan in."

As John headed to the door, he turned around and took a deep breath. Walking rapidly back towards Lar, he pulled his yearning torso into his and kissed the lips he'd missed as much as the desert misses rain.

Lar pulled back, and stared at him in shock.

"By the way, it was," John added in a whisper. "It cannot be now. But it *was* real. I want you to know that."

Lar's falling tears wet his lips, pulling John in to kiss him once more. Their souls relishing in the joy of acceptance and release.

"*Wadean,*" Lar gripped John's hand longer than he knew he should. He must have also squeezed it a bit too much, he supposed, as John smiled while mouthing 'ouch'.

"Sorry," Lar smiled. "Fire can burn."

"And burns can last forever," John winked. He turned to glance over Lar- and their youth- one last time. "I'll see you."

"I'll see you." Lar nodded. "Write me back this time if I ever e-mail you, will you? E-mails should be easier to respond to now than letters were back in the day."

"I'll do my best," John winked again before shutting the door behind him. Pressing the button on the elevator, he inhaled deeply as he watched the elevator doors close before him- knowing Lar was watching from the peephole.

He reached into his back-pocket for the plastic pistol. *The man has become a bestselling author and rich businessman, yet he can't recognize toy guns.* John grinned "Your father is not perfect, but he's no murderer, Linette," he whispered to himself, fixing his tie and brushing his hair back.

John inhaled the crisp air as he walked out of the building complex and onto the bustling Oslo street. He looked at his wristwatch.

Oh, good, I still have time. He'd get a cup of coffee and do a little sightseeing to collect himself from everything that had just transpired in Lar Iktar's suite. Right before his appointment with the police.

Tan Kuvvet. You'll be getting what you deserve. Very soon.

CHAPTER 27

USING THE COMPASS IN HIS HAND TO SHOW HIM THE DIRECTION toward Mecca, Aresh 'Lar' Iktar laid out the silky prayer rug he'd kept under his bed. After performing his washing ablutions, he chanted, 'Allahu Akbar', and went on to prostrate his head on the ground, reciting the remaining prayers he'd memorized since childhood.

He stood back up again. "*Amyn*," he ran his hands over his face as he gradually finished his prayer. "Forgive me, *Ya Raby*," he said, palms open toward the ceiling. "Not for my inclinations- with which I've been characterized since my youth. With only the purest of intentions for the men I've loved. The ones given to me by my nature- the most powerful force you've created. The force of all life on earth and beyond- the visible and invisible- with which I cannot compete, nor control."

"I ask for forgiveness for what I'm about to do," Lar continued, closing his eyes. "I've led a young man who trusted me toward a dark path. Unknowingly. And I cannot warn him now to run from his fate at the hand of the Norwegian police. I promised Jaan. But that is not the only reason. I cannot carry this burden. I was selfish. Forgive me, *Ya Raby*. Forgive us. I hope Tan forgives me, too. I pray he can get the minimal sentence, and will do everything in my legal power to ensure as such. I will get him the best lawyers, and support him until he can come out of that jail a free man. Norwegian sentencings aren't extreme- if we are meant to be, we can truly be together then. Free, and with a clean conscience. And if he comes out and kills me for having left him to his fate, I'll accept that as well. But I will no longer interfere…"

Aresh splashed water on his face and wiped his scruffy face with a nearby towel. Folding the prayer rug and slipping his feet back into his silk slippers, he sat on his bed and looked at the bottom drawer of his nightstand. They were all in there. Well, he counted two bottles missing. He knew Tan had used up one of them to murder Linette- could he have dropped the other one by mistake in nervousness that night? Tan hadn't ever said anything.

He shrugged. Stig had now ensured that all fingerprints had been cleared of the tubes. All except that of Tan's. With her charms, and status as a human, it was now up to Nora to 'discover' this 'latest' evidence on her housemate, and present it to the police. *Those lucky cops,* Aresh smirked. They'd barely had to do anything in their investigation, and God knew they must have been getting a load of money for all of this.

"I will repent," Aresh whispered to his reflection in the mirror. "I'm doing Tan a favor. He will learn to forgive me in time, and realize we both needed this cleansing." It broke his heart that the timing of everything had to happen this way. Right as he and Tan were growing closer. *Will my heart ever experience lasting love?* Aresh released all the tears he'd been fighting back. Maybe he had to earn it first.

He wiped his tears and took in a deep breath. "I will earn love."

§

TAN SMILED AT THE SIGHT OF HER NAME ON HIS CELL PHONE. *Could it be?* Master had told him she'd helped with the framing of Paul Maverick as well. *For me.* "Meredith…"

"Run, Tan," Meredith's voice meant business.

"What?" Tan wasn't expecting anything of this sort.

"Lar and Linette's father," Meredith continued. "John Walker. They've teamed up somehow. I think they used to be close friends or whatever back in the day."

"Close friends?" Tan's voice was soft.

"Whatever! Tan! Are you not getting it? Lar's helping out his old friend now. He's not covering your back now that John Walker's gotten to him. He's playing innocent- allowing you to be implicated in a murder and a cover-up. The cops will probably be coming for you any moment now. Are you in Lar's suite?"

"Mer, sweetheart, relax," Tan sounded surprisingly calm to Meredith. "I'm in Stavanger. I was just with Serdar. Clever plan, by the way: you and Finn. I really do have to give it to guys. Thank you. I've already thanked Stig." *Lar wouldn't betray me. Would he?*

"Where are you right now exactly?" Meredith pressed.

"I wanted to see you so badly being here, but I wasn't sure you wanted to see me, so…" Tan's voice trailed off.

"Tan!" Meredith insisted. "Can you meet me near the cabin, as soon as you can, then? Far out where our favorite boulder was. You know the place. Where we used to…"

"Oh, yeah baby. I remember those days when your heat would lift me and I'd…"

"Tan, this is no joke!" Meredith urged. "I'm trying to help you, you crazy man. Though I'm sure I'm even crazier for trying to help you, after everything…"

"Okay, okay," Tan's voice turned serious. "But, wait a minute. Mer- you know I always have love for you, my girl. But, how do I know you're not luring me out to the woods again yourself? I mean, forgive me, but the last time you invited me out there, you kind of forced me to go to the airport! To fly out back to Turkey!"

"Why would I lure you now, Tan?" Meredith insisted. "Think about it. I was shocked then at your obsession with that girl, yes. I felt deceived. But that's all water under the bridge. A year has passed."

"Lar wouldn't…" Tan shook his head. "He wouldn't turn me in. Besides- what would he say to the cops? What evidence would he give? And, anyway, he sees me as- I don't know how to quite say this- but I've realized he sees me as, special."

"Oh, and you must have felt so flattered, haven't you, Tan?" Meredith retorted, rolling her eyes. "Don't be a fool, honey. Look, I'll just say it: John Walker was apparently his long-lost first love. I mean, I hate to break it to you. But I know more than you right now. Something about handing some tubes and bottles of remaining cyanide or whatever to the police…with only your fingerprints remaining."

"John Walker was his long-lost…what?" Tan's tone shifted. Lar had handed the cyanide to the police? Why would he have done that? The very cyanide that Aresh- whatever his name actually was- had given to Tan himself?

"I'm afraid it's true." Meredith had to face the reality that she'd missed his voice. Even when his warm tone toward her felt to be more out of lingering, platonic affection after everything they'd shared together in that cabin. Still, after her anger had subsided upon finding out what he'd done to his ex-girlfriend, and how she'd merely been her lookalike replacement- only Meredith's emotions were left. They hadn't gone anywhere. If anything, with Finn's refusal to accept the reality of Bo, Meredith had only yearned more for their now-faded romance.

"I overheard Anja talking to your housemate, Nora," she explained further. "And I heard some things, got suspicious, and was able to tap into their thoughts. It all became clearer to me."

"Suspicious…" Tan's nerves started becoming queasy.

"It felt to me like Lar's loyalty is to him: over all of us, actually." Meredith was feeling exasperated for a multitude of reasons at once. "Nora talked about Lar's sympathy for John Walker, discussing all these ways in which he's been trying to obtain some sort of closure and justice for his daughter's death."

"Loyalty…" Tan muttered, nostrils flaming. The cold, harsh reality hit him now like a freezing gust of wind. *Aresh must be presenting the cyanide tubes as evidence. No way Meredith could have known about the remaining cyanide otherwise. She isn't lying.*

"I know you wouldn't have hurt her had Lar not pressured you, Tan." Meredith went on. "I see that now. Lar's shit for what he did to you! And to me, too…So, you have to believe me. I'm wholeheartedly on your side here."

"What did he do to you, Mer?"

He didn't allow me to live my nature- my motherhood- freely. He threatened me if I revealed his real father to Bo- a father foolishly in love with a human whom he'd rather pretend he's fathered a child with.

"Mer?"

Meredith shook her thoughts off her mind. "Tan, you may be running out of time. I'm sure they've all got dabs on where you can be here in Stavanger. Please. Hurry to the woods, I'm waiting. I want to help you out."

"I'm already in the truck," Tan said, starting the ignition. "I trust you Mer. I'll see you there in a bit."

John Walker…his long-lost love. Meredith's words trilled at the back of his mind, and Tan turned off the engine. Could Aresh have tricked him? After everything? *No*, he thought. It couldn't be. This was ludicrous. Master had probably said whatever he thought he had to, just to get John Walker off of their backs.

The cyanide. Tan remembered his kryptonite. His crime weapon, the remainder of which he'd stupidly left behind at Serdar's place. His mom would always tell him there was an angel on one shoulder and a demon on the other that'd be watching his every move throughout his life- deciding at the end of his life whether he'd be worthy of heaven or hell. A tear rolled down his stubbled-face as he remembered something from that night. He couldn't take any chances. In case Meredith was right, and Aresh had really betrayed him. Tan would not be taking the blame for everything alone and rot in jail. There could be a better way to end the suffering, and still listen to the angel on his shoulder. To make things right. Taking his cell phone from the glove department, Tan dialed Serdar.

"*Bilader*?" Serdar picked up. "*Hayırdır*? Something wrong?"

"*Serdar'cım*, I forgot to ask you if you'd noticed anything else in that box or closet before handing it over to the police?"

"Oh, you mean those unused condoms?" Serdar chuckled. "Sorry, *bilader*. You can imagine Delilah's made me use them up already. I was lucky they hadn't expired! Wait…at least I think they hadn't expired…"

Where the hell did Anja come up with that name? Tan rolled his eyes. "*Yok, yok*. I'm glad those went to good use, *koçum*. I meant if you'd noticed a pair of socks rolled into each other?"

Serdar was silent for a moment, before erupting in laughter. "What? You don't have enough socks?"

"I know it sounds funny," Tan laughed. What had Lar said about the box- that The Group had indeed located it under the bed where Tan had left it, before moving it to the closet? Maybe they never noticed the extra tube he'd kept hidden separate from the other batch. Just in case he'd ever needed to grab another one quickly and discreetly that night, before rummaging through the entire set in the box.

"There was something, I- umm- had also left behind. But it was kept separately from that damn box. Can you do me a favor, *bilader*? Can you check under my old bed for an orange pair of socks? There's something inside…"

"One second…Those socks better be clean! Oh, I see!" Serdar finally exclaimed. "Let's see here. Holy, crap Tan. I feel something hard here. I see a glass vial. Oh, shit, is this that liquid ecstasy stuff?"

Allah'ım! His instinct in regards to what he had to do now felt affirmed. Tan closed his eyes gratefully, inhaling in nostalgia. Linette had looked beautiful in her black slip with the spaghetti straps she knew he liked. "This apology dinner better be good," she'd teased. "You owe me big time." Tan hadn't exactly ever murdered someone with a syringe of poison before. Despite reading up that one vial would be enough to immediately kill someone of Linette's body type- Tan couldn't be too sure. He'd needed to secure the back-up. Just in case.

"Tan?" Serdar raised his voice. "Hey, maybe we can get high together when you come back tonight. It's okay, man. I'm not going to report this thing to the cops, if that's what you're worried about. You crazy?"

"Yeah, yeah, GHB," Tan lied. "Ecstasy. I need it today, actually. To use with a friend- a young lady, you know? I'm getting a syringe for us from the pharmacy now. I'll stop by to pick it up from you in a bit. I'll get you some more later to do it together, though. I promise. "

§

"MOMMA…" MALIN WAS POINTING SOMEWHERE BEHIND KAITLIN AS she sat opposite her daughter on the playmat. Kaitlin's heart sank, feeling her chest flush. *Please don't show yourself to her anymore,* she ran in her head and closed her eyes.

"Dadda!" Malin added, and Kaitlin had just begun to wave her hands to indicate 'no', when she heard it. A familiar giggle. Kaitlin turned to see that her husband had opened the door slowly. Pointing a finger in front of his mouth to indicate keeping quiet to their daughter.

"Oh my God…Paul!" Kaitlin cupped her hands around her mouth, standing up with a jolt and taking two slow steps forward. Malin followed suit, waddling to her legs.

"I'm home, girls," Paul smiled through tears. Kneeling down after setting aside two large bags of his belongings, he welcomed both Kaitlin and Malin with open arms while they rushed toward him.

"You're walking now, my angel," Paul inhaled Malin's head, causing her to blush with a cross between shyness and pride.

302

"How is this miracle possible?" Kaitlin was shaking her head through her tears, her heart leaping out of her chest. "Mark didn't tell me anything!"

"He wanted this to be a surprise." Paul placed his forehead on hers, giving her a deep kiss on the lips.

"Please tell me the nightmare is over," Kaitlin inhaled his scent-welcoming the fresh soap smell.

"Well, I'm not out of the woods yet," Paul admitted, taking Malin into his arms as he stood up. "I have to report to the precinct regularly, and am not allowed to leave town....Have you gotten even lovelier my princess? Oh yes, you have…"

Kaitlin took in the scene she'd missed to the very core of her soul. It'd broken her heart each time she walked to the market or somewhere and saw a little girl on her father's shoulders. She placed her hand on her chest as she flopped down on couch. Was this a dream?

"I also have to see a psychologist, apparently," Paul continued, pacing around with Malin. "But, anyway- more on the details later. I talked to Mark, who talked to Walker. Apparently there's also some new evidence against Tan now!"

"Are you serious?" Kaitlin's eyes were gleaming. "That is amazing news! Wait- psychologist?"

"I'll tell you later," Paul went on. "John apparently first led the cops toward Tan himself- sharing Linette's old e-mails he'd luckily saved. I believe I have you to thank for that, *ma chérie*. For convincing John of my innocence."

"Your ex-boss is a man of reason, Paulie," Kaitlin shrugged. "He told me he didn't suspect you for longer than five minutes."

"What did he ponder in those five minutes, I wonder?" Paul scratched his chin with a grin. "Just kidding. Look, babe, apparently Tan's gone to Stavanger to hang out with his old roommate or whatever. I was told a couple of cops would discreetly be waiting for him by the cabin this afternoon. They apparently first headed to his old apartment, where the old roommate told them he'd just left for the cabin after picking up some things."

"Babe, I understand about Tan," Kaitlin was still puzzled. "But how were *you* able to leave? Without Tan having been caught yet. I mean, this is a miracle. And I'm so grateful, but it also feels like someone's going to pinch me any minute and I'll be waking up."

"Jeanette." Paul beamed, sitting next to her with Malin on his lap. "Can you believe it?"

Kaitlin's heart sank. "Jeanette?"

"Turns out- Tan murdered that poor girl on Jeanette's birthday," Paul nodded, twirling Malin curls with his fingers. "There was a party for her and the entire office was invited. There's a video. With my singing. Thinking about you, actually. 'I need you now'. Remember that song? Well, it ended up being my alibi. Can you imagine, the police have heard your husband's voice?"

As Paul placed an arm around her with a smile, Kaitlin forced herself to return it. "Wow." Despite the woman's recent marriage, she still couldn't help the feeling at the pit of her stomach whenever she heard the name of her husband's childhood friend. *Jeanette.* "That's great, Paulie. How fortunate."

"You girls stay put, I have to do something," Paul said, kissing her forehead.

"Where are you going?" Kaitlin asked. "Don't you want to eat something?"

"I want to look that bastard in the eyes as they arrest him," Paul's forehead wrinkled. "I sure as hell am not going to pay him a visit in prison. So this is my only chance to ask him how he could do this. Work with voodoo or whatever to make those spirits come to his aid...."

"Paul? What are you saying?" Kaitlin's jaw dropped as her heart began to pound. Had she heard that right? Had Paul just said- spirits?

"Lars Phelps apparently shared footage of me talking to myself in my office, scribbling on a sheet of paper," Paul went on, placing his hands on his hips. "Can you believe that? Remember that health plan solicitor I told you about? Yeah. I think you can see where I'm getting at. Evidently, that's also why I need to see a professional. But, it's alright. I'll do anything as long as I can be home with my two girls."

"The jinn!" Kaitlin bit on the nail of her thumb. "You...know?"

"The what?" Paul raised a brow. "I don't know what those things are called, babe. But they visited me in jail, too. Come to think of it, that's how that figure referred to his kind as well. *Jinn.* Yeah. And he didn't look like some Disney character, either. I would have sworn it'd been an inmate who'd somehow broken into my cell, had I not literally seen him materialize."

"You saw him materialize? Oh, Paulie," Kaitlin grabbed her scalp.

"He awakened me from my sleep! I felt the presence on my neck, Kaitlin. It was the strangest thing. And I thought of the damn paternity test...and considered maybe- maybe how if something like that happened to you too, how you might have thought..."

"Babe," Kaitlin began, waving her hands, but Paul interrupted her with a soft brush of his finger on her lips.

"Don't worry, I'm not bringing this up now. Today's a happy day, damn it, and I'm not going to let anything ruin it. We can have our entire lives to discuss details, if we must."

"Oh, must we now?" Kaitlin smiled through her pout. "Can we not have some B.P and A.P, clean slate? A fresh chapter in our lives?"

"B.P and A.P, what now?" Paul was confused.

"Before Prison and After Prison," Kaitlin placed her head on her husband's shoulder. She inhaled the aroma of the laundry detergent on his sweatshirt.

"We'll cross bridges when we get to them." Paul chuckled.

"Good to see your imagination's still on fire. I hope you've been writing while I've been away."

"I have, Paulie," Kaitlin smiled up at him. "Sandy's been motivating me. Mom mostly complained I should stop, and get a 'real job', but, you can imagine how that whole thing goes."

"You'll work if you want to," Paul's expression turned stern. "I don't ever want my wife to feel she has to work out of economic desperation. No matter what happens to me, know I'd do everything in my power to ensure you and Malin's well-being."

As Kaitlin mouthed 'thank you', she couldn't help but take in another sniff of his clothes. "I was so glad to see they were treating you well over there. It helped ease the entire craziness a tad bit."

Craziness. Kaitlin could no longer ignore her urge to know. Even if a part of her wasn't sure she was prepared to potentially hear a familiar name. "So, that jinn. Who was he? Did he introduce himself? What did he want?"

"I don't recall a name," Paul shrugged. "He threatened me because I told an officer about that cabin. Warned me to keep my mouth shut."

The door-bell rang, and Kaitlin knew her mother had returned from the corner grocery store. She turned to smile at Malin. "Grandma is back, my bunny. Shall daddy hide somewhere and surprise her?"

"I'm already on it, girls," Paul snickered, tiptoeing toward the bedrooms in an exaggerated way that made Malin giggle with delight.

"Kaity?" Linda's face was stoic as Kaitlin opened the door. It was all she could do not to burst out laughing with joy. The prospect of genuinely surprising her mother was fun. She needed this.

"Yes, mom?" Kaitlin stepped aside, stifling her laughter. "Welcome in, *madame*. How was your outing?"

"Kaity, I heard a man's voice," Linda placed a shopping bag down on the floor. Her eyes eyed the living room like a detective.

"Malin?" Kaitlin played along. "Baby, what do you suppose grandma heard? Could it have been the television?"

Malin replicated her playful shrug.

"You better not even think of bringing a man friend or whomever the hell with Malin in the…" Linda's finger in Kaitlin's face transformed into a full-on placement of her hands on both cheeks when she saw Paul's head, peeking from the bedroom door.

"Paul, dear? No way!" Linda was ecstatic, as Kaitlin's smiled through tears now. "*Mon Dieu!* Malin's got her father again! Hallelujah! But wait… Is this for real? How?"

"By the grace of God, Momma Linda," Paul grinned with arms opened wide, welcoming his mother-in-law with a hug. "I've obtained a strong alibi, and that Tan Kuvvet guy's murderous evidence has surfaced, biting him in the you-know-what."

Kaitlin swayed side to side with Malin in her arms. She thanked God her mom would be present to babysit Malin while she'd join Paul in that forest. No way she was going to miss that moment; to see Tan face the justice he deserved.

Kaitlin's mind began to focus on another thing while she began to get dressed. A single tear brushed her cheek as she smiled. *Paul's seen them too.*

She fought the urge to entertain what had begun to lurk in the back of her mind; namely the question of why Paul hadn't, then, seen Finn at the Ball, sitting at their dinner table. Could some people start seeing jinns later on in life? Triggered by something life-changing, like an arrest, perhaps? But then again, he had seen Finn in his photograph. Had Finn simply not manifested in human form at the ball, and only she could perceive him that evening?

She made a mental note to ask Sibel about it later. She and Paul had to get to that forest and hopefully witness justice being served. With Tan in handcuffs.

It could be closure for both of them. Or not. Kaitlin had no idea what awaited them in that forest. But it sure felt good to have someone who believed her by her side.

CHAPTER 20

KAITLIN SWORE HER HEART HAD BEEN BEATING LOUD ENOUGH for Tan to hear. She dug her nails on her husband's arms through his jacket. "He wouldn't hurt us, would he?" she whispered. They'd made it just in time, shortly after the two officers themselves.

"He looks unarmed," Paul shrugged, exchanging knowing glances with Officer Lindberg. He and his partner had made their presence known to them in the near distance when they arrived, each crouching down strategically behind a tree. Kaitlin had already spotted their parked car closer to town. "I doubt he'd try anything funny after he sees the armed police, but let's continue to stay back anyway."

"Maybe we should go home," Kaitlin whimpered, staring at Tan talking to Meredith in the periphery of the cabin. She wanted to call out to the jinni she'd once considered a friend, but also knew it wouldn't be appropriate to stick her nose into a potentially dangerous situation. Besides, the cops couldn't exactly hurt someone of her kind, could they? Were they even able to see her? Kaitlin could not be sure.

"Paulie, you've already seen him. They won't let him get away. I don't want this to get ugly."

"That woman resembles Linette…" Paul muttered, gazing at Meredith. "Is that Meredith Olsen?"

Kaitlin couldn't believe what she was hearing as she nodded. *He's seeing her, too. Just like John Walker.*

"Tan Kuvvet, stay where you are," Officer Lindberg called out, pointing a gun out toward his back. "Keep your hands raised and turn around, now!"

To everyone's surprise, Tan, who hadn't uttered a single word or attempted to make a run for it, slowly began to lift his arms up in surrender.

"It's all for a reason, right?" Kaitlin found herself blurting out. Tan didn't appear at all surprised by her presence there with Paul. He gave them a blank look before turning back toward Meredith, who was now staring into Kaitlin's eyes.

"Kaitlin…." Meredith sighed.

"Let me handle it, babe," Paul whispered to Kaitlin.

"No such thing as coincidence, right?" Kaitlin raised her pitch, competing with the loudness from particularly strong wind gusts that had begun. "How could you frame someone innocent? You're the one who belongs in that prison!"

She inched her body closer to Paul, who took a step forward and darted his eyes at Tan. "Look at me, man. The jails of Norway weren't that bad. Surrender, and try your trap for me out for yourself. Time's up. It's time for you to pay for messing up all our lives."

Tan turned softly to Paul with a boyish smile, reaching his hand to his coat pocket. "I already have been."

"I said; keep both hands raised where we could see them!" Officer Lindberg pressed, further stretching his armed hands toward Tan.

"Tan, I never wanted things to turn out this way," Meredith whimpered. "You were supposed to start over back in your country, with your family. I could have visited you there. You were given that second chance…why?"

"I don't think I'm as courageous as you, Meredith," tears were rolling down Tan's stubble. "You're so brave to question Master…Master of Illusion, was more like it."

310

Wiping his face, Tan continued. "I chose to hide back in Norway. I thought I would be safe with Lar. I thought following him had always made me brave...but I was just a coward. You always did deserve better, Mer."

"Save the tears for the jail visits, Tan," Paul intervened.

Now it was Kaitlin's turn to rein her husband in. "I think that's enough, Paulie. He sounds like he's about to surrender."

"I still don't trust him," Paul snarled, whispering to her ear. "He's got something in that pocket."

"I know you're never going to really visit me if they take me to jail," Tan's gaze lingered on Meredith. "I know, and I can't blame you."

"I'll always visit you...even if I have to do it invisibly. Stig's done it to Paul Maverick," Meredith turned to face Paul. "You have to understand, Mr. Maverick. Lar Iktar has all of us on a string. Even Tan."

"Stig..." Paul whispered to Kaitlin. "That was the name of the one who visited me. I remember now. Familiar?"

"No," Kaitlin shook her head.

"Tan, you're no good," Meredith leaned closer to Tan, caressing his cheek. "But you're my weakness. God damn it, you're my weakness, you idiot! You can become a better man in time. I see that potential in you. I believe in you."

"You're warmer than any human I've known," Tan responded, inching his forehead to touch Meredith's. "I know you won't believe me- but I really did love you. Your dedicated heart- you reminded me of a part of my own self. A part I'd buried. After her."

"Tan..." Meredith wept.

"Never lose your beautiful heart, *min nydelig jente.*"

"Tan Kuvvet, stop talking to yourself and put both hands in the air! Immediately!" Officer Lindberg demanded. "Paul...Mrs. Maverick. Kindly step further back. Hans? We may need backup."

"I'm on it, sir," the younger officer responded, pulling out a walkie talkie.

"I owe you an answer, Mer," Tan whispered, pulling out a syringe from his pocket, as Kaitlin let out a scream.

"Tan...what are you doing?" Meredith whispered in shock. "You should know needles don't affect me."

"*Linette,* Mer," Tan continued, with a blank expression. "It sure affected her... You had asked me how I did it, remember? How I killed her? I owe you the truth. Only you, and no one else. One injection into her neck, and it killed her instantly. Cyanide. It didn't hurt her much. Her spirit became free, purified, in peace. She didn't even smell, you know that? In the back of my old truck, driving her body to Trondheim. And, don't worry, Mer. It's faster than you'd think. I've practically memorized the precise spot on a human neck..."

"Oh my God," was all that Meredith could let out.

"Holy shit..." Paul said, standing in front of Kaitlin now as he eyed the policemen carefully stepping closer and closer to them.

"Maverick," Officer Lindberg insisted. "We asked you and your wife to step aside."

"I know, sir," Paul called out. "I just want to make sure Tan here gets into that car without doing something stupid..."

"I wish you nothing but the happiness you deserve," Tan continued to cry, stroking his face with the syringe.

"No!" Meredith was in tears. "No."

"Put your damn hands up, or we will have to..."

Tan could hear the cops somewhere behind him, but it didn't matter. He'd decided his fate on his drive to the woods. He knew what he had to do to be free of his sin. Running from it had only been delaying the inevitable.

His mother had told him this was a sin as well. But it couldn't possibly have been worse than what he'd already done. He'd taken an innocent life, and had to pay. He had to be cleansed. Everyone would be better off without him. Aresh would get over it- why, with his old friend back in his life and all. Tan shook his head. Everyone would forget about him soon enough. Except maybe Mer.

"*Min nydelig jente*…My lovely girl. When you warned me today- I knew it was only you who'd ever truly loved me."

"Tan!"

"I thought Aresh loved me," Tan wept with distant eyes. "As a son, a brother, however the hell, I didn't even care. But apparently not as much as he loved John Walker. I just wanted to be loved, Mer. Was that so hard for this world to understand? *How could you, Aresh?*"

"Aresh?"

"But you were right. It turned out he too would be ready to sell me out the minute *he* returned. The one he tried to replace with me, I suppose. I, out of everyone else, know how unfair that is. How unfair it was for you…"

"Master's name is Aresh?" Meredith wasn't sure what was confusing her more in the moment.

"I know you always felt you had to compete, dearest Meredith," Tan's attention was purely on Meredith's face. "But Linette was gone. It was different. I wish I never had to resort to calling him in Turkey- allowing him to take me back under his wings in Oslo. For what? I was lifted high, only to be dropped down again."

"Tan, you're going to get through this," Meredith spoke. "Forget Lar- Aresh- whomever. You saw how we all had your back to help you. You're not alone."

"Who the hell is Meredith?" the younger officer asked.

"How I wish I could have been born on this earth as one of your kind. Maybe I could have been stronger. Better." Tan leaned in to kiss Meredith's cheek before taking a step back. He pointed the needle to his own neck.

313

"Tan...don't do it," Meredith countered shakily. "Just confess and...maybe you can have a shorter term. Please. A lighter sentence in a lower-security prison. It'll be alright."

"This is the only way to make things right," Tan breathed, turning his head softly in the direction of Kaitlin and Paul with downcast eyes. "I'm sorry...all of you."

"Throw that syringe on the ground right this..." The officer couldn't finish his sentence before Tan, holding the needle in his fist now, injected the vein in his own neck with a strong thrust.

In almost an instant, all the faces around him slowly began to become obscure as he fell onto the dirt, hitting his head on a rock. He didn't feel much pain. He supposed his head would have hurt more, had he not already dosed his entire nervous system with the same amount of the poison he'd used on Linette. She'd been a tall beauty, after all. Their builds weren't too different from each other.

Linette.

All faces had indeed begun to blur in front of him, yet his eyes could not close as he took his last deep breath, and saw hers: Linette's angelic face was as clear as the light encircling her entire body in a flowing, silky dress as white as snow. She was smiling at him. Satisfied.

§

KAITLIN STOOD FROZEN IN PLACE, TEARS RUNNING DOWN HER FACE AS the ambulance doors shut. She'd never seen a deceased body before- nor did she want this young man she'd actually conversated with to be dead. Tan had deserved to pay the consequences for murdering an innocent woman, but Kaitlin would much rather have seen him placed behind bars than this alternative.

She had tried her best to avoid the image of his dead body being placed into the body bag-but to no avail. Kaitlin couldn't look away. His arms had naturally flopped on top of each other before the bag was zipped up. *Hadn't that also been how the skeletal remains of Linette's arms were discovered*? she pondered. Karma was truly a strange thing.

"Let's get out of here, babe," Paul called out, right before one of the officers began to talk to him about something. Kaitlin took advantage of his distraction and turned her attention to the sullen young jinni-woman before her.

"Are you okay?" Kaitlin asked, trotting toward the fragile young woman in tears. Meredith still had yet to stand back up after she'd crumbled on the ground along with Tan.

"Meredith," she leaned down to console her. "I know we haven't really talked much over the past year. But I want to say- old friends are memories, you know? I'll never forget how sweet you were with me, trying to help me out with everything, and, well, if you ever want to talk, about Tan..."

"Kaitlin, I'm sorry. I'm so sorry," Meredith's sobbing only intensified as she placed her face onto Kaitlin's shoulder. "I've messed everything up. I thought I'd been warning you about your husband. Woman to woman- despite our different forms on this planet. Yet, my Tan...I could never imagine it'd all come to this! Now he's...gone. It's all my fault!"

"Shh, it's alright," Kaitlin reached for Meredith's back. To her surprise- she could feel skin and bones. *She tried so hard for Tan, didn't she?* "You loved him. No matter how he treated you. Or what he had you do. You two had some connection, I just witnessed it tonight. Before his tragic decision to..."

"He never had me do anything," Meredith shook her head side to side. "It was all Lar. The order. His maxims. His bloody maxims. And my stupid, stupid jealousy over his past."

"Meredith, what are you talking about?" Kaitlin tried to cut into her sobbing. "I meant the way he talked to you, and the forced abortion..."

"I didn't get an abortion, Kaitlin!" Meredith blurted, finally meeting Kaitlin's eyes. "Tan asked me to- yes- but only because of Lar's pressure. I had to cover the birth from you, from Tan…from everyone, until I could make sure my son was safe."

A Golden Retriever in a heavy light brown coat came over to Meredith, catching Kaitlin's visual attention though certainly not her cognitive one. *How in the world could she have given birth without anyone noticing?* she thought. *Is that why she wanted to help Tan- she decided to forgive him as the father of her baby?* How in the world could a jinni get pregnant from a human if a human apparently could not do so from a jinn?

Her world felt like it'd begun to spin around her. Kaitlin dug her fingers into the dirt on the ground.

"Kaitlin! Let's go! What are you doing?" she could hear Paul shout somewhere in the distance. But his voice was more like an echo to her, as Kaitlin's focus was now intensely on Meredith and the dog.

What the hell? Kaitlin made a disgusted face at the sudden image of Meredith licking the dog on the cheek. The dog's warm brown eyes met hers once more- causing tremors throughout her entire being. The eyes were all too familiar. They belonged to a puppy she'd once been given as a gift, yet one that was taken from her too soon. By Finn.

"Bo!" Kaitlin exclaimed in tears. "It's Bo, isn't it?" She looked excitedly at Meredith, who nodded and smiled. All sense of logic and quest for answers momentarily halted as Kaitlin reached out to pet his now longer coat.

"Oh, I'm so glad you've truly been alright, Bo. Finn wasn't lying. My, how you've grown…" Bo nudged his head on Kaitlin's arm and let out a bark.

"He remembers you, Kaitlin." Meredith grinned. "We kept the name you gave him. Finn insisted."

Kaitlin's breath quickened. "You've…raised Bo as your own- with Finn? Am I getting this right?"

"Bo still talks about you, you know," Meredith's grin hadn't left her face. "Especially when we try to play the human game 'fetch'. He was a mere puppy in your arms, but he was a child in our years. So, he remembers."

As Meredith let out an uncharacteristically loud laugh, Kaitlin felt her stomach drop. "He mentions me? Mer? Can you- talk to him? As a jinni?"

"Well yes- that too- but also due to our other bond, Kaitlin," Meredith squinted her eyes quizzically. "Don't you get it? Bo's my son, and also a jinn. I told you- I never aborted my baby. I just carried out my term shorter and easier. Away from human eyes. In my canine form."

"Bo's your son?" Kaitlin stiffened. "Wait. And Tan didn't know? Or? Wait, wait. First of all- how did *we* end up with Bo, then? How did Paul end up receiving him from his colleague…?"

"Kaitlin, leave that dog be. Come on, let's go already!" Paul commanded, his voice inching nearer.

"He's not Tan's to know. I'm sorry, I know this is awkward. We consoled each other…just that one time. Look, I'll explain everything one day, Kaitlin." Meredith stuttered. "Go! Don't keep Paul waiting."

"Who? What? Wait, Meredith, please call me, at least," Kaitlin insisted. "We're both mothers now, apparently. We can talk everything out. Please. Promise me."

"I promise," Meredith whispered. "Now, go, Kaitlin. Go to your husband. Hold on to your love. And don't let go." Tears were streaming down her face again. "I pushed him away. My poor Tan. And then placed all the blame on him for being stuck in the past. All the while, I was the one focused more on his past than our united present…"

"You don't have to justify his mistakes," Kaitlin began, turning to meet Paul's eyes closer to her now. "I'm coming, babe. I was just…"

Her heartbeat raced; the sound of barking and animal limbs pounding on the dirt as they ran off into the distance astonished her.

"Kaitlin, you're still shaken," Paul kneeled and placed a strand of Kaitlin's hair behind her ears. "We have to go home now. I saw the other dog too- they ran off. I didn't see where she went, but I guess Meredith joined them also, huh…"

"They- they ran off?" Kaitlin asked, shock still pulsating through her entire being. "Bo…"

"Maybe once Malin is a little bit older, we can consider a puppy again," Paul smiled endearingly. "It seems you've been missing animals for comfort. I know, I know. I've missed Bo, too."

§

AS IF THE IMAGE OF TAN'S DEAD CORPSE ON THE DIRT HADN'T BEEN enough to haunt her, Meredith's voice echoed in Kaitlin's sleepless mind. *"We consoled each other…We kept the name you gave him… Finn insisted."* Kaitlin's tossing and turning had already made Paul try to lull her back to sleep twice. She ran her fingers through her hair as she sat up on the bed. Had she gotten any sleep at all?

"Babe," she heard Paul ask. He was still lying down while Kaitlin looked outside the window.

"I just can't get the image of Tan crumbling to the ground after his self-inflicted death…" Kaitlin told him. She couldn't yet bring herself to entertain the alternative picture she was also getting in her head- a picture of Meredith and Finn together.

She hadn't been able to figure out how- and even if- she could be able to tell Paul what she'd just discovered about Bo. Kaitlin had to give it to Paul. He had become more open-minded lately, with his own jinn experience. Yet she wasn't exactly thinking Paul would welcome the animal manifestation part of what she'd discovered. Worse, Kaitlin was

318

sure he'd insist that she join him in getting therapy. *Sandy would approve of that,* she thought with a snicker.

"Life is funny, isn't it?" she continued with a blank expression.

Soft snow had begun to fall, and she couldn't wait for Malin to wake up to witness it. But not just yet. Her daughter had to sleep a tad bit longer- long enough for Kaitlin to reason through some things with Paul as much as she could.

"Tan tried to convince everyone that Linette had committed suicide, only to end up committing suicide himself."

"We fucked up, Kaitlin," Paul blurted, bringing Kaitlin out of her reverie. She turned puzzled eyes toward her husband.

"Wait, what?" Kaitlin inquired. Where was this coming from? She'd witnessed him express seething anger in various ways before- yet, interestingly enough to her, never through cursing like this.

"We messed up, big time," Paul continued. "We messed up in non-typical ways. There was no grandeur, or any illegality in our mistakes. No. But we did screw up. Mainly because we couldn't appreciate what we had. Not consistently and consciously enough, anyway, to continue making the effort. To continue to express it. To choose to fight for our marriage above any other possibility. Without any alternate plans conjured up in our heads …"

"Alternate plans…?" Kaitlin quizzed in a soft tone. *Perhaps he feels Jeanette was 'the one that got away' for him?* She'd be lying if she said she wasn't a little bothered by Jeanette's alibi helping out Paul.

Paul stared at her, poker-faced. If he'd felt an attraction toward anyone else during their marriage, he wasn't going to give any hints- that much was clear. "Moving back to Canada? Leading separate lives? Anything. Anything could have been an alternative. You could have joined those group of forest weirdos- claiming to me you'd 'found your calling in life' or some crap or other. I could have not been able to forgive you for…for it all. And then, well, God knows what would have happened."

Kaitlin was about to respond, but Paul's hand caressed her lips before she could do so. "I don't want to think about any alternate plans, babe," he continued. "This is exactly my point. All we have is now. All we have is this. You. Me. Malin. Our new home here, far from our extended families. But we are at the core of our lives. You and Malin are at the core of my heart. And I hope we can always consciously make the effort to believe each other. And in turn, always be able to be honest, too. No lies. Not even white ones. For I think we've seen how even those 'white' ones to spare each other's feelings can hurt even more when they come back to bite us in the- you know what..."

Kaitlin's tears drenched her lips further as Paul laid a soft kiss on them. For the first time in a long time, she was actually speechless.

"Being locked up in that place...did something to me," he continued. "I'd judged you without considering how it may have been like in your shoes. It's hard for me to explain- believe me. But I think I get it now. I just wish one day you can look at me like you used to again. Like you did when you jumped for joy as you accepted my marriage proposal. Like you were the happiest girl on earth..."

"Paulie...I am still that girl," Kaitlin reached for his hand. "When you prioritize us like this, instead of the house or obligations or all those things. Yes- I'm aware of the importance of duties, too. But I just have an aversion to them because of my different upbringing from yours. And I just want those things to take a backseat to what I feel is more important. The dynamic may be different now- but when I see our daughter smiling at her daddy, like *she's* the happiest girl in the world? *That* reminds me of my own happiness, if my mind can ever just shut up sometimes. *That* makes me the happiest woman in the world..."

"Babe, but why would you even assume sometimes that you're not my priority- along with Malin, now, of course- just because I'm tending to work or my parents or, well, anything else?" Paul wrinkled his forehead. "Do you truly believe that my natural inability to pay attention to you 24/7 is some sign of a lack of love?"

That was a fair question, Kaitlin supposed. Was Paul right? Had the root cause of all her recent drama somehow been her incessant need for attention? *Am I really like that? If so- why?* Kaitlin sighed, and simply allowed her head to fall onto Paul's shoulder.

"I think witnessing Tan's end has also affected me more than I care to admit," Paul continued. "A once tough guy, saying all those things. Before going and injecting himself. We can never know how our end will be on this earth."

CHAPTER 29

New York City

OBSERVING THE HANDS OF THE CLOCK MOVE WITH TICKING noises in the eerie quiet, Sandy positioned her body lower, slouching on the blue leather sofa. Tapping her fingers on the wooden armrests, she made eye contact with the new blonde and thin receptionist Freya had apparently hired while Sandy had been away.

She attempted a friendly smile. It wasn't returned, and the receptionist turned her focus back to the computer screen in front of her. That was too bad. Sandy was sure they'd been seeing a lot of each other-especially after her Norway experience. Sandy truly needed some extra direction and healing through talking everything out.

"Dr. Olsdotter will see you now," little miss sunshine stated without so much as a half-smile.

"Thanks," Sandy made sure to exaggerate her own smile. She was hoping it'd give this lady a cue to try to improve her social skills.

The stairs she descended led to three wooden doors adjacent to one another. Freya shared the space with two other therapists and Sandy would often feel a bit nervous her confessions inside would be audible next door. She was assured the walls were soundproof. "Besides," Freya would add, "…my colleagues have enough they listen to on a daily basis and they're not interested in eavesdropping on anyone else's patient, believe me". Her door was always slightly ajar- signaling it was available for Sandy to 'come in and relax' as she pleased.

"Sandy, welcome back from your vacation!" Freya exclaimed in her usual, warm tone, though she was still typing something away on her laptop. "How was Europe? Which countries did you travel to again? I don't believe we went into detail on your last visit."

"Hi, Freya," Sandy smiled as she took her usual seat on the sturdy arm chair before her therapist, situated next to a small wooden table with a box of tissues. "Well, it wasn't some big, European tour- though Lord knows I would have loved to do that. I haven't seen any of the continent except Norway now! But, yeah, I can't exactly afford it, as we know…"

"Norway!?" Freya asked, her blue eyes and delicate facial features highlighted further by the silky, crème-colored headscarf she was wearing. "Oh, wow- where in Norway?"

"Umm, Sandnes. It's close to Stavanger," Sandy started, placing her jacket around the back of her chair. "Well, Stavanger isn't really well-known either, I suppose. They're in this place called the Rogaland region in the south where…"

"I know Stavanger, Sandy," Freya's eyes were as wide-open as pancakes now, her clear gloss-sparkled thin lips turned upward in a grin. "I'm just so surprised- I mean, I know we don't talk about my personal life. But I happen to be from there."

"You're kidding me!" it was Sandy's turn to be surprised. "What are the odds? You're Norwegian, Freya? I always assumed…Well, I don't know what I assumed. I mean, I can tell- obviously- you're a Muslim woman. And so I thought maybe, oh, I don't know- you were one of the rare, fairer peoples of the Middle East or something?"

"Okay, that's a fair- no pun intended- and not atypical- assumption, I suppose," Freya chuckled. Had Sandy offended her? If she had- Freya luckily didn't react in a way to indicate as such. It appeared that she was accustomed to such curiosities about her background.

"Sorry, I don't mean to sound offensive," Sandy said. "It's just, I didn't see many Norwegians with…"

"I'm used to it, don't worry," Freya laughed softly through

solemn eyes. "You're not the only one taken aback at first. I'm a convert, actually. I'm from Stavanger, but I converted to Islam several years ago, after moving here to New York and obtaining my license to practice psychotherapy. It was a personal choice- one with which I'm very happy. So now, with your permission, can we get back to you?"

"Oh, that's wonderful!" Sandy exclaimed. "I'm happy for you. Oh, sorry. Back to me, yes. I apologize. Where was I…"

"You were just telling me about your visit to Norway…"

"Oh, yes, yes," Sandy nodded, staring at the tan-colored wall behind Freya. "Wow, I still can't believe you're from Stavanger. I loved your hometown."

Sandy continued after Freya nodded with a smile. "I went there mainly to stay with my friend Kaitlin from back home in Canada. She lives there with her husband, and they just had the most adorable little baby girl. She's my best friend, and I wanted to pay her my long overdue visit. Congratulating her on the baby was the perfect catalyst for that…"

Freya jotted down some notes with a pen on a yellow notepad on her lap now, her swivel chair having been brought closer to Sandy. "Why else did you want to go to Norway?"

"Sorry?"

"Well, you used the word- 'mainly'- to explain your intention to visit your friend who just had a baby…"

Shit, she's good! "Oh, well, okay. Freya, you know me by now. And we only have an hour. So, I'll get straight to the point. I mean- I thought this was the perfect opportunity and timing to go, because I'd just experienced something here. I never really told you about it…it was some bizarre job offer I received at a coffee shop. But I felt it related to something else that I *did* tell you about…"

"Oh? Please. Do remind me…" Freya encouraged.

"Do you recall that time I was expressing concern for my friend- who saw vivid nightmares toward the end of her pregnancy, scared for her life?"

"Yes, I certainly do," the therapist nodded. "Was that this same friend in Norway? Kaitlin- was it?"

I hope this isn't violating some anonymity codes. "Umm, yes, yes it was. I guess it's okay to use her name here, right?"

"Of course, Sandy. Everything here is confidential," Freya assured her. "Now, please go on. How did you feel your friend's nightmare experience related to your coffee shop experience? Or to the need you felt to visit Norway?"

"Well, I know we briefly discussed that occurrence she went through in relation to her calling me in her sleep- which she barely even remembers- and in relation to sleep paralysis, as you scientifically explained to me…"

"Right…but not everything can be explained scientifically," Freya said with a shrug. "At least not immediately. I'm well aware. So, please tell me everything."

Freya must have caught her confused expression because Sandy noticed she added almost immediately. "I mean, you know- you did call your coffee shop experience 'bizarre', and all."

"Oh, right, right," Sandy let out a breathy sigh. *Here goes nothing. I'm paying for this- hoping Freya helps me figure this out more than Kaitlin has been able to.*

"So- basically, at that coffee shop- a handsome man came up to me, introducing himself as Matt Evans. He said he liked the folders I had before me on the table and that his paper company was looking for someone with great organizational skills, blah, blah, blah…"

"His paper company…" Freya's face suddenly turned an even whiter- shade than her already fair skin, Sandy noticed.

"Umm, yes, I know it sounds weird. Paper. Whatever, right? But you know, I've been having trouble paying the bills with the mere acting gigs I'm able to get. I was lucky to have found my affordable ticket to

Norway- though I did have to transfer about three times…."

Sandy went on to relay an overview of the events that followed-from her recognition of Kaitlin showing her a picture of the mysterious Finn in Norway, to both their relative experiences with two different 'jinns'. She paused to take a deep breath, checking the clock to make sure they'd still had time left for Freya to be able to put in her two cents.

6:52. The digital clock on Freya's desk reminded Sandy it'd soon be time to make the payment and leave, as their allotted hour was already almost up. *Shit.*

"Sorry, Freya," Sandy rubbed her face with both hands. "I know that was a lot. Sorry to just spring it on you like that. I must sound crazy-talking about 'jinns' and all that. But I've been told they're common knowledge in your religion, so I guess that further comforted me to spill it all out to you. And look at the time, I just…"

"Sandy, you have nothing to be sorry about," Freya pulled her rolling chair closer. "If anything, I'm sorry I didn't piece together certain details from things you told me during our sessions earlier."

"Certain…details?"

"All I can say at the moment is- jinns are real," Freya took in a deep breath. "I've…Well, I used to have a client who came to see me a few times before she disappeared. She'd found my comments on a website discussion board about the topic- and had desperately needed someone who'd believe her. Other therapists she saw in the city sadly mistook her story as hallucination, schizophrenia or even mania: a variety of names we have in our profession for, yes, very real mental ailments. But- jinns cross into our beliefs, and, well, long story short- I was happy she'd found her way to me. I was so happy to see the relieved expression on her face when she told me, and I believed her story about her jinn experience. And now, you. Here, you are…"

Sandy shed a tear and returned Freya's smile. *Thank goodness this woman gets it.* She reached for the box of tissues for the first time since beginning to see her therapist- wiping the tears that had begun to accumulate underneath her eyes. "Thank you for sharing that too, Freya. What great coincidence…."

"I'm no longer sure I believe in coincidence, Sandy," Freya said, her eyes burning a hole on the ground. A brief moment of silence occurred before she finally snapped back. "Did the jinn you mentioned- not sure about the names, you just called them 'my jinn' and 'my friend Kaitlin's jinn'- contact you again? Since your…special experience at his place?"

"Oh, you mean, Bjorn?" Sandy asked. "No. He said he'd visit me in New York if I wanted. But I'm not sure he's as into me as Kaitlin's jinn is into her. He still makes his presence known to her from time to time, from what I could tell. She refuses to talk about it much lately, especially since becoming a mother."

"Bjorn…" Freya nodded. Was that a spark of recognition Sandy sensed in the woman's eyes? She must have imagined it. It'd been a popular enough name in Norway, as she'd learned. *Much popular than Thor, anyway.* Sandy smiled, only to pout with another thought. "I never seem to keep any man's attention on me for too long, Freya. Human or jinn…"

"Why did you think that just now, Sandy?" Freya asked. "Belittle yourself from the point of view of another's attention on you, or lack thereof? I want to focus on you- and I want you to focus on yourself, remember?"

"Of course, of course," Sandy said, looking at the time again. "Well… thank you again for making me feel less alone in this. I don't want to take any more of your time. I hope we can discuss this further in two weeks when I see you next."

"Next week," Freya cut in. "I feel this is a lot on you- and requires additional support. Are you free next Friday evening as well? Tell Sam at the front desk to schedule you in. If she says she can't, tell her I insisted she make room."

"Will do," Sandy smiled. "She must be new…"

"You never shared the name of your friend's jinn, by the way?" Freya inquired as she stood up.

"Oh, you mean Finn?" Sandy asked with a shrug. "Yeah, I call him Finn the Jinn. Rhymes, doesn't it…"

"Finn…." Freya's voice trailed. Sandy thought she'd sensed a quiver when she mentioned Finn. Come to think of it, Sandy noticed Freya had also started to stare blankly now at the door behind her.

"Freya? Are you alright? Does that name sound familiar? Was that the same jinn who targeted that client of yours or something?"

"Oh, sorry," Freya shook her head with a grin. "No. Merve- she'd never been to Norway." *Merve- the poor Turkish girl who'd come here to New York to make something of herself, away from her family's support. Like I tried to do. Only I was able to free myself from Finn's mental possession. And she was never able to do the same from her own jinn. I should have been able to help her more…maybe she wouldn't have run off.*

"Freya?" Sandy was lost.

"Sorry, my thoughts travelled back to my former client," Freya assured, lowering her voice to a whisper. "I want to make sure you get through this alright. And your friend Kaitlin, too. You should thank the stars that Bjorn is no longer targeting you. You do not want to be the target of a jinn's affections in a romantic way. Believe me. Kaitlin must be more careful and protected against that Finn."

"My Norse goddess." Freya could still hear his whispers in her mind. Luckily, they were from her memory this time, and not from ailment.

"Freya?" Sandy asked, wrinkling her forehead. "Any message you want me to give to Kaitlin? I mean, she's in Norway. Do you do phone sessions? Do you suppose her situation could become dangerous?"

It surprised Freya Olsdotter to see how easily lying had become for her. *Lying can tragically become second-nature when you're forced to rely on it for survival.*

"It would be better for me to see her in person," she said. "But, in the meantime, yes. It would be good if you could convince her to have a brief phone- or even virtual- session with me, if you can. Did she ever go to therapy herself?"

"I don't think so...I tried to tell her to..."

"I'll try to be a little clearer, Sandy," Freya interrupted. "It's not that Finn himself is dangerous, per say..." *He's learned to leave me alone. I've been able to free myself here in New York. I have gotten myself up-risen literally from the ashes.*

"It's Kaitlin's...condition, I'm more concerned about."

"Her condition?" Sandy's voice rose.

"If she's gotten in so deep as to not only see the jinn, but to continue being targeted...with emotional connections and lingering visits having been established, from what you've described? I'm afraid that shows me she hasn't been receiving the mental care she needs. She's more in danger from herself...and, I'm afraid it can have long-term consequences for loved ones around her as well."

Sandy covered her opened mouth with her hand. "Wow."

"Sometimes, some people missing a reliable rock to turn to fill that void with the dangers of the abyss, Sandy...." Freya nodded, turning the door knob. "I'll see you next week, if I can."

"Thank you so much for tonight," Sandy had turned to walk back up the stairs, when she stopped herself. "I think I see where you went with that, by the way. Just curious if I've gotten it correctly, Freya, to understand my friend. I think you're implying the void she must have felt within her marriage, with her husband being away. But remember, this all started for my friend *before* her husband went to jail..."

"Well, then, perhaps her husband's void wasn't the one she was subconsciously trying to fill." Freya shrugged with a smile, closing the door as she said, "I'll see you."

With the door shut behind her, Freya leaned against it and slid her body to the ground. An entire slew of tears accompanied the memories she'd repressed for too long.

CHAPTER 38

MALIN'S BABBLING FROM THE OTHER SIDE BRIGHTENED PAUL'S entire face as he opened the door. "Let's see who it could be." He immediately picked his daughter up from Kaitlin's arms. His wife appeared tired but accomplished, smiling as she stood in front of her mother.

"Welcome back, babe," Paul said, kissing the tip of her nose. Sibel had invited her mother along with Kaitlin for a 'goodbye' lunch this time. "How was that luncheon ladies?"

"Spectacular," Linda exclaimed. "What lovely hospitality!"

It had delighted Kaitlin to have her mother off of her back. All until the drive back home allowed her comments to continue as per usual. "Promise me you're getting that license." ("Yes, mother.") "Sibel and Engin live in a single-floor but private home, while you two are still technically in an apartment." ("We like it, mother.") "Wouldn't Oslo be full of more job opportunities for you Kaitlin- couldn't Paul transfer there?" ("We'll see, mother.")

Kaitlin's loud sighing was immediately replaced by a smile at the vision of Paul lifting Malin in the air, blowing raspberries on her stomach. "I already missed my girls too much in those excruciating weeks," Paul said in a babyish voice. "You girls left me alone for hours on this lovely Saturday. Don't make daddy miss you any more than he already has. Alright my sweet pea?"

"Daddy..." Malin cooed in the air, overjoyed as Paul gave her little throws in the air that always managed to freak Kaitlin out more than her daughter.

"I was more convinced this time-Hundvag Island is absolutely stunning," Linda said, coming from the direction of the kitchen with two plates of apple slices. "Come on, kids, get your vitamins. Malin needs more solids than ever in her mere diet of smashed peas and rice now."

"Mom, you know I try my damn hardest…"

"An apple a day does indeed keep the doctor away, Momma Linda," Paul interrupted her with a smile, mouthing 'thank you' to Linda as he took a plate with his free hand. He placed Malin on the floor, who ran quickly toward Kaitlin.

"That Sibel woman can bake, I tell you," Linda went on with a smirk. "By the way, Paul, does Statoil have an office in Oslo?"

"Mom…" Kaitlin warned, changing Malin into a different shirt.

"Well, we did open a relatively new office building there in 2012," Paul started, "…but there's more work for me here at the headquarters, since…"

While Kaitlin did her best to drown their conversation out, she felt the little hairs on her neck stick frozen in mid-air, as she'd gotten accustomed to. Yet this time a chill ran down her entire spine to her lower back, which had not been the usual case. She heard a male voice echo in her mind with a whispery tone. *"Mountain air."*

She immediately thought it strange that the voice was simultaneously familiar, yet also not so much. *Finn?* She asked in her mind. There was no response- neither in her head nor in her feelings.

Strange.

"I need exercise!" she blurted loudly, causing Malin, her mother and Paul to all look at her at the same time.

"Kaity?" Linda broke the brief moment of shocked silence. "What's going on? Are you okay?"

"Mountain air." The reverberating whisper was clearly perceptible inside her head once again.

"I just need to stretch out my legs, I think. Driving isn't the same thing. You know? Mom, can you help Paul with Malin while I go for a little hike?"

Paul and Linda exchanged concerned looks, but her husband finally nodded in her direction. "I understand, babe. I think you're feeling a little overwhelmed, knowing your mother will be flying back soon. Do you want me to drop you off somewhere, if you don't want to drive far? And, Momma Linda is right, we do have to schedule that road test, just in case…."

"No, thanks, babe," she cut in softly. "I'll just take the Line 29 bus out to Dalsnuten again. Remember the last time I'd done that? It was a nice change. Got me out of my head, you know?"

"She climbed a mountain by herself?" Linda asked Paul quietly, raising an eyebrow.

"Before Malin, yes," Paul smiled dismissively. "It's not a very high one- not like Preikestolen or Kjerag. It's much safer. More like hiking. She'll be okay. Don't worry. I got this."

As Paul patted Linda's back and joined Malin on the mat where she was now focusing on stacking some toy blocks, Kaitlin nodded at him. She threw her husband a smile, while frowning inside. Her most familiar companion had, after all, always been her own mask. *Malin's the one to be babysat or supervised*, she thought with a pout, walking to her room to change into the thick polyester sweatpants she'd used on their little hikes throughout the region. *Not me.*

"Mountain air"

Kaitlin stared at her reflection in the closet mirror. *I need to feel free.*

§

THE HEART-SHAPED POND STOOD STRIKING AMONG THE ROCKY terrain. More flatland than mountains, the clear, azure sky stretched vast before her. Kaitlin lowered her eyelids, extending her arms out to the side while exhaling the chilly air.

This place was familiar to her. She could handle this. Neither a simple walk around the quiet premises of their condo, nor some bus ride downtown or even driving around for additional practice would be enough to satiate Kaitlin just then. She needed adrenaline. She needed her body to really work.

The gym? *No*. She knew in her soul it hadn't really been able to help excite her either. Her eyes spotted only a group of teenagers and two or three couples around the hiking trail. The heart called to her. "Finn?" she asked into the emptiness around the pond.

Why am I thinking about him when looking at something heart-shaped? Like some teenager girl with some crush. This man- this being-isn't some rockstar or college sports star, for Goodness' sake. He's messed up. He's so messed up. This is so messed up.... But then again, aren't I? Aren't I messed up?

Reaching for her backpack, she pulled out two mini-bottles of Bailey's. She'd stacked some from the liquor store the last time she'd been downtown. Luckily, Kaitlin never had a drinking problem. Despite drinking or smoking a cigarette or two on occasion, her body had never developed any substance addiction traits. *Not like my father*, she thought. Her mother's words echoed in her head.

"He didn't know how else to escape. He drank and drank some more. All until he couldn't escape anymore. And then, of course, he escaped from me and the kids."

It felt nice to get outside, alone with only her thoughts to accompany her. *And nature,* Kaitlin thought with a melancholy smile, downing the first bottle.

"Mountain air". She heard the voice once again. Alright, maybe she would also possibly be accompanied by a certain friend she couldn't really talk to anyone else about.

334

Kaitlin could still hear Sibel's voice at the back of her mind as she paced herself to the top of the trail. *"Before, you couldn't be held responsible, Kaitlin. A jinn had chosen you- and you didn't know. But now you do. So, I'm sorry, but as your friend, I have to be honest with you...and encourage you to do the right thing. Even if you don't necessarily like it."*

Sibel didn't understand. How could she? She had the perfect damn marriage, as far as Kaitlin was concerned. The perfect family. No one could understand.

Kaitlin stopped by the first cliff overlooking the town below, catching her breath as she stretched her hands toward her knees. The clouds caught her attention, appearing in different shapes and forms as they spread out low in the sky. Kaitlin could make out the town below as she sat herself close to the edge of the cliff, dangling her legs.

Gulping the second liquor bottle, Kaitlin feigned a 'cheers' into the air. "Here's to you, Norway!"

Her mind felt hazy as she stared back out at the low-hanging clouds. Did clouds have weight? Would they feel heavy if they fell on her? Would she tumble down the hill? Or would she hit her head somewhere as she fell down? How heavy her feet felt like they were getting.

"Kaity, don't do it!" The same voice reverberated and pushed her backward on the cliff. She was able to make a silhouette of a man-jumping on her body to throw it backward and down onto the ground, away from the edge. The blurred vision before her suddenly transformed into Finn's emotional eyes- solidifying from flame-sparkles into his human form. His body on hers now. Looking as if he was about to lean in for a kiss.

"I...I don't know what happened," Kaitlin stammered, breathing rapidly. "I swear I wasn't trying to...I wouldn't.... Malin... I couldn't do that to her. I couldn't leave her, Finn. I wouldn't. No. I just...got dizzy…and…"

"Shh- don't try to speak," Finn instructed in a whisper. "Take three deep breaths. I want you to count with me. One…"

"How do you know so much about what the human body needs to feel better…?" Kaitlin whispered, after taking in a long breath. She caressed his cheek. "I wish you could always be like this. In this form. One of us…"

"Ms. Kaitlin?" Finn asked quizzically. He couldn't hide his smile. "Are you drunk?"

"I think I was drunk before I ever had a sip," Kaitlin giggled. "My hero. You saved me. Call me Kaitlin again. Just Kaitlin…"

"Okay, sweet, dear, drinking lady," Finn helped her sit up straight. "As adorable as you sound right now, I think we need to get you to rest in the comfort of your own home. Obviously, you haven't been feeling very well today, if you even contemplated…"

"Please, Finn…" Kaitlin's smile turned into a whimper now. She allowed his outstretched grip to linger on her arms. "Please…can we pretend everything is normal and accepted? Just for a moment? Act like some normal couple?"

"Okay. Kaitlin," Finn's warm touch returned the caress of her hand, which was still on his cheek. "It's going to be alright, my dearest. You're going to be alright. For Malin. She needs her mother strong. Look, I'm sorry if I've caused you to become…cognitively… anything less…. I just couldn't stay away. I'm so sorry…"

"Finn…" Kaitlin felt his falling tear on her cheek- burning her skin as if she'd received a minor jolt of electricity. Yet she didn't mind it one bit. "Nothing about any of this has been ideal. Or fair- to anyone. But- somehow- I wouldn't have had any of it, any other way…"

"I wouldn't want you in any other way than the way you already are," Finn spoke, gazing into her eyes. "Maybe not on this realm. But in the ideal, beautiful one in my heart- you are *mine*…"

The intensity of Finn's words couldn't compete in that moment with the intensity of his eyes. Almost orange now, as if a forest fire was scorching his soul.

"I see the real you...I don't feel afraid. I don't know what this is...." Kaitlin smiled through her tears.

"Well, it may never hold a chance in the conventions of the real world. But I believe there's a word for this, Kaitlin." Finn smiled in the silence that was in juxtaposition with the firecrackers exploding inside her.

"Ahem," Kaitlin audibly yet playfully cleared her throat, turning her face toward the town below. "A beautiful, special friendship. Yes. I believe that's a lovely way to coin it."

"Friendship...on fire, you mean," Finn winked at her. "I believe that's how some define the word 'love'."

Encouraged by her smile, Finn's entire being pinned Kaitlin's body back to the rocky ground. He kissed her, the back of his hands holding her head slightly off the ground with protection. Kaitlin didn't flinch. She let him. *It doesn't feel wrong*, she thought as her lips moistened with floods heavy enough to quench the fire.

How can love be wrong? Finn's thought mirrored her own, pulling back to smile at her.

"I can't believe you lured me out here for a kiss," Kaitlin grinned. "You're a strange one, Finn Du Feu," she said with a slick smile. The way she'd seen him do so many times.

"Kaitlin?" Finn's expression changed. "Wait. Lured? What are you talking about?"

"I heard you...." Kaitlin shrugged. "You said 'mountain air'. You called me out here. This is my favorite trail in these parts- and the easiest for me."

"I didn't...call out to you," Finn shook his head in slow movements. "I just heard you call my name, and felt you'd wanted some company...What are you staring at? Kaitlin!"

"*Mon Dieu...*" Kaitlin gasped at the silhouette of a man in the near distance. A fellow hiker? His tall, sturdy frame began walking towards her, smiling with almond-shaped eyes staring straight at her. Becoming more familiar by each passing second.

"Kaitlin- now you're beginning to scare *me*!"

Kaitlin made out Finn's distinct voice, while she stood up and walked toward the man.

"There's no one there..." Finn continued. "No being, not even of my kind over there.... I would see..."

"*Don't fall,*" the man warned with a gentle voice, holding out his hand.

"Daddy?" Kaitlin squealed suddenly. She was looking into the soft eyes of the man she had not seen since she was five years old, as Finn remained behind her, observing with uttermost disbelief.

'EPILOGUE'

ZACHARY RAMSAY SMELLED THEM AGAIN. The strawberries. *How ironic*, he thought with a smile, watching his daughter eat them from the pink-hued fruit bowl on the balcony table. *This time it's the actual fruit and not fumes from her belongings.*

"Can we go to that lake again next weekend, Papa?" Kaitlin asked, dangling her bare feet from her stool, where her rose-painted toes weren't quite able to reach the floor yet.

"We can certainly try, *ma belle*," Zachary chuckled, wiping her stained cheek with the crumpled tissue in his hand.

"Dad?" Aidan waved his hand in front of his father across the plastic table. "Come back to the present, please."

"Sorry, Aidan," Zachary sighed, rubbing the growing gray stubble on his chin. Had it been a time for another shave? He didn't want that amateur worker doing it for him again. They'd taken that privilege from him the last time he'd attempted to do so. Something about there being too much blood. He wasn't suicidal. It had just been an accident.

He was simply distracted.

"It's alright, father," Aidan nodded, folding his hands as he heaved a deep breath. "I know you haven't been able to get any closure with Kaitlin, as you have been with me through my visits. Your doctor says this is all normal. You will be alright. Not to worry."

"Linda doesn't know I'm in rehab, right?" Zachary's eyes turned serious, placing his hands atop his son's. "And she hasn't told Kaity, either?"

Aidan didn't have the heart to tell his father the truth. That no one would realistically stay in an alcoholic rehabilitation center for so many years, and Linda was no exception. His mom had once seen Zachary with the girlfriend he'd made during his first stint in actual rehab, and that had been it. She was convinced he'd left her with two small children in order to 'frolic' with another woman, and assumed that's where he'd eventually remained after the divorce papers were signed.

"Yes, that's right," Aidan overheard the nurse on the phone on the other side of the door. "Patient Ramsay in room C-318. He hasn't been getting much sleep lately. The prescription refill should help. He becomes awfully dangerous to himself and aggressive to everyone without it."

"What's that prison guard going on about again, Aidan?" Zachary shot Nurse Laura a look from the window. "She's always watching me. It isn't enough I'm serving my life with this sentencing. The least she could do is allow me a drink. If I'm to die here, I can die with one moment of happiness at least. Couldn't I?"

Aidan smiled, wiping a tear before it could freefall and risk being seen by his father. "No drinks, dad," he smiled. "Just a few more months here without alcohol or drugs, and you'll have paid your dues to society. You will be out a free man again. You will see."

A few more months. That's how he'd been coining his father's passing years in the institution. Luckily, Zachary wouldn't really protest or question it. One moment, he'd assume he was still in rehab. Another - a prison. The routine had become familiar, and familiarity bred warmth. So did secrets. Aidan reached to caress his father's cheek. "I promise you. I will not give up on you."

"You've become a better man than I was, son," Zachary allowed his face to be cuddled. "What's this scent you're wearing? Is it a new cologne?"

"I haven't sprayed anything father. It may be the soap."

"Smells like strawberries," Zachary's eyes lit up with excitement as he stared at the wall behind his son. "I like it."

EXCERPT FROM BOOK 3 OF *THE CATALYST TRILOGY:*

'THE NESTLINGS'

Malin Maverick was content. Staring at her satin vision in the mirror for nearly half an hour now, the corners of her candy-red lips curved upward. *This is the perfect dress*, she thought. *I just hope my mystery date agrees.*

Lucinda- her friend and classmate- had come to the rescue to save her from her state of despair. "Girl, as confident as I know you are, I refuse to let you attend this dance alone," she'd said. "Robert told me he's got a friend from the neighborhood who's apparently seen you around. He's about our age and ruggedly handsome from his photo."

Those brown eyes. The photo had looked familiar to her. Like déjà vu of someone she'd met before, though of course she couldn't quite make out. Each time she glanced at the handsome teenager's photo now saved on her smartphone, her mind had traveled to Norway, where she was born and raised for a while. Could this guy be Norwegian or something? Malin shrugged. She'd find out.

The family friend there she came to call 'uncle' would always lead her to the woods, where she'd play with his dog. "You can play out here anytime you want," he'd tell her. "Since your mom won't allow you to have a pet in the house."

She wouldn't dare share such memories with her mother. The woman was already so fragile and working so hard to make a new life for them now.

Oh well, she thought. *Back to my big moment meeting my handsome date tomorrow.* Even his name was enough to entice Malin. He sounded like a movie star. "Bo," Lucinda had told her. "Bo Du Feu."

ACKNOWLEDGEMENTS

I'd like to start by thanking my dear family, friends and colleagues who've had to put up with my sleep-deprived self, due to the absolute call I felt to pour this sequel out in one year; in contrast to the multiple years I'd had in wrapping up its predecessor, 'The Catalyst'. Regardless of the shorter time, I truly feel every part of it has continued to be authentic with regards to things I've gone through or experienced around me. Hopefully, it can inspire others to write and always live their most authentic lives.

Both in my fiction writing as well as in my poetry, I often touch on concepts of duality and cross-cultural fusions. 'The Penance' has certainly been a pleasure for me to write, where I really dug down into the struggles with identity all of these characters deal with in various forms and with different levels of severity. I find myself often relaying morally ambiguous and gray characters- leaving it up to the reader to decide whether or not they can understand where they're coming from. Therein lies the beauty of reading novels, in my humble opinion, aside from entertainment; to be able to relate to a character with whom we may not otherwise have much in common, ask ourselves what we would do in their situation, and/or really think about what we can take away from the story long after we've finished it.

I hope you, dear reader, will agree, and continue to follow me on this cathartic path as I look forward now to wrapping up this story- tying up all remaining mysteries (with additional intrigues, of course) for the last one in the series, *The Nestlings*.

'The Catalyst' was always supposed to be a stand-alone book, and if it hadn't been for encouraging readers and fellow-writers I ended up collaborating with- I would never have thought to re-release it with a trilogy in mind. I'm so grateful- the more I wrote, the more I realized these characters bursting out of my soul and onto the keyboard weren't finished just yet.

Finally, I'd like to express my continued hopes and prayers for innocents paying 'penance' with absolutely no crimes committed, starting, of course, with my daughter's dear father and my supportive husband, Kemal. May 'penance' turn into 'salvation' and liberty for everyone in need of this most basic human right.

XOXO

Selin Senol-Akin

ABOUT THE AUTHOR

SELIN SENOL-AKIN is a political scientist and adjunct language instructor, aside from her creative writing and featured spoken/published poetry.

The Catalyst, which reached the online new release chart at #1 during the pandemic, is now being re-released as a trilogy: with *The Penance*, and *The Nestlings* to follow, respectively.

Her acclaimed #1 release poetic collections, *Write Out Your Drops* and *Set Free Your Flow* (half poetry/half coming-of-age memoir) will also soon be followed by a third book, *Earth Up Your Roots:* all a part of the multi-modal *'Elemental'* collection.

She lives in New York with her young daughter and family.

Visit selinsenolakin.com for updates

Collaborations including the author:

'Versos Estivales' (2019)
'Flash' (2020)
'The Media High School Journal of Academics & Fiction' (2021)
'Write Out Your Drops'- audiobook version (2021)

*The Catalyst is also available in audiobook format (2021)

Milton Keynes UK
Ingram Content Group UK Ltd.
UKHW040955110624
443871UK00002B/3/J